THE FOURTH WALL

THE FOURTH WALL

Beth Saulnier

This title first published in Great Britain 2005 by
SEVERN HOUSE PUBLISHERS LTD of
9–15 High Street, Sutton, Surrey SM1 1DF,
by arrangement with Warner Books, Inc.
This first hardcover edition published in the USA 2005 by
SEVERN HOUSE PUBLISHERS INC of
595 Madison Avenue, New York, N.Y. 10022.

British Library Cataloguing in Publication Data

Saulnier, Beth
    The fourth wall. - (An Alex Bernier mystery)
    1.   Bernier, Alex (Fictitious character) - Fiction
    2.   Women journalists - New York (State) - Fiction
    3.   Investigative reporting - Fiction
    4.   Murder - Investigation - Fiction
    5.   Detective and mystery stories
    I.   Title
    813.5'4 [F]

    ISBN 0-7278-6197-2

Printed and bound in Great Britain by
MPG Books Ltd., Bodmin, Cornwall.

Dedicated to:

Bob Burns

and

the Starlight Stage Company
for letting a kid do what she loved most

With many thanks to:

Miss C. A. Carlson
for her excellent homicidal instincts

Bill Malloy
editor extraordinaire

Jimmy Vines
a true gentleman with a name out of *Guys & Dolls*

Paul Cody
for getting me started

&

my friends and family who know how things work:
Brad Herzog (baseball), Matthew Hammond and
Betty Saulnier (law), Paul Smith (photography),
Amy Griffin (theatre), Mark Saulnier, Ph.D. (chemistry),
and Mark Anbinder (my iMac)

Prologue

THEY SAY ALL THE WORLD'S A STAGE, AND ALL THE MEN AND women merely players—and people have been lying to me so much lately, I'm starting to believe it. I'm not just talking about your normal, everyday, "that dress looks great on you" kind of lies. I'm talking about the whoppers: "Yes, you can trust me." "It's all in your head." "Nobody's going to get hurt, I promise."

And then there's my favorite: "I didn't kill her."

Good liars know that the trick is to stay as close to the truth as possible. Amateurs get into trouble, because they try to weave elaborate stories and wind up tripping over the threads. But keep it simple, only fib about one thing at a time, and it's much less likely you'll get caught. Or at least it takes a whole lot longer for someone to catch up with you.

That's what happened to me this fall. A couple of people I thought I knew pretty well turned out to be total strangers—ugly strangers too. As liars go, I'd have to call them above average; if I were their homeroom teacher I'd give them a B-plus, with an A for effort. They had the whole town fooled, though, and not just the ones who wanted to be. If somebody hadn't had the bad taste to commit murder, nobody would have been any the wiser.

The things that people lie about and the things they kill for are pretty much the same, when you think about it—and I've been thinking about it a lot lately. As a cop friend of mine once told me, you've got your seven deadly sins and that's pretty much it. People lie for greed, lust, pride, and so on (I tend to lie for sloth myself), and those are the same reasons they kill.

It may seem odd that I've done a study of this, but I haven't had much choice. I didn't go looking for it—not at first, anyway—but in retrospect it feels like the whole nasty mess went looking for me. And since it found me, and turned what might have been a perfectly pleasant couple of months into an enormous drag, I might as well pass on the few tidbits of wisdom I picked up along the way.

First off, if there's one thing that successful liars and murderers have in common, it's self-discipline. You have to make a plan and you have to stick to it. No embellishments, no second-guessing, no returning to the scene of the crime. Second, you have to decide that you don't give a damn if you get caught; tension over the consequences will just make you sloppy. And third and probably most important, you have to believe your own story. Because if you don't, nobody else will.

Okay, I know those are wild generalities. Every lie is its own little universe, and no two murders are alike. But what I've been learning lately is that there's a depressing consistency to it all. Regardless of the means, the end is always the same. Lies mean that somebody gets betrayed. And murder, at the risk of putting too fine a point on it, means that somebody gets *dead*.

This fall, that somebody was a nineteen-year-old girl. She was born normal enough, but by the time she died she was something spectacular: the sort of person you could call a goddess and still not exaggerate too much. That made her demise way more than just another sad story here in Gabriel. Although most folks are pretty embarrassed about it now, the truth is that it was a local obsession. This is a college town, and its residents are supposed to be preoccupied with more rarefied things—art, philosophy, liberal politics, the rising price of goat cheese. Forget it. There was only one thing that anybody here talked about from Christmas to Easter, and that was the death of a teenager that none of them had ever even met.

So why did they go so crazy? It wasn't just the normal freak-out over having someone die young, thereby reminding the rest of us that we're all on a one-way trip to the obit page. No, this was the sort of collective mourning that only happens when the corpse in question is really gorgeous. Add wealth, and a touch of mystery, and it adds up to hysteria—the kind that sells a lot of copies of *People* magazine with Princess Di on the cover.

The woman whose body was found in December wasn't quite that famous, but she was on her way. She wasn't exactly rich either, but I think fortune would have followed fame. She was beautiful, though; of that there can be no doubt. I've seen photographs, and although they were black and white I've colorized them in my imagination: chestnut hair, green cat eyes, a ruby mouth that was always French-kissing the air. She had cheekbones so sleek and sharp you could open a bottle on them. Her bosom was full but not *too* full. Her waist was tiny and her legs were impossibly long, like the ones on the Barbie dolls my mom wouldn't let me play with because of the body image thing. And when she smiled, the whole package came together and just blew you away.

But it wasn't just her looks that made people so insane when she first disappeared. It was also the idea that she was on the brink of something big, and to a mere mortal all that wasted potential was really galling. She seemed fundamentally happy, at least on the outside, so there was no rationalizing that death might have been preferable. And then there was the fact that she was in love, and someone loved her back, which made the loss seem not only senseless but downright cruel.

In short, she had the kind of life a person would kill for. And the ironic thing is, someone did.

1

Her name was Ashley Sinclair. If it sounds fake, that's because it is; her real name was Dolores Strunk. My Spanish isn't very good, but even I know that "Dolores" means "pain," which hardly makes for a promising start. Not that changing it did her much good. Becoming Ashley, after all, didn't stop Dolores from dying at nineteen.

But back in October, before her body was found smack in the center of downtown Gabriel, no one was in the mood to think about anything that depressing. It had been an astoundingly hot fall, nearly eighty degrees every day, and nobody was ready to admit it wasn't summer anymore. The municipal pool had been kept open an extra month by order of the mayor, a card-carrying socialist who knows the will of the masses when he sees it. Even the engineering grinds up at Benson University weren't taking school too seriously, and over at Bessler College—an academically flaccid place to begin with—the powers-that-be were threatening to cancel the whole semester if the kids didn't stop sunbathing and come to class. And down in the city of Gabriel, the body politic was preoccupied with precisely two things: global warming and homegrown tomatoes.

You wouldn't think the local paper could get much

mileage out of those topics, but you'd be wrong; there was a picture of either a scruffy-bearded master gardener or a pointy-headed meteorologist staring out of the *Gabriel Monitor* just about every morning. And unfortunately for me, a fair number of those stories had my byline on them.

The reason for all the weather coverage was simple: there was nothing else to write about. After a summer that was voted "Worst Ever" in the annual *Monitor* readers poll—not because of the rain so much as the escapades of the city's own serial killer, now retired—the fall was shaping up to be positively moribund. And although I wouldn't have admitted it in public, that was fine by me.

It did, however, mean that our daily editorial staff meetings were the journalistic equivalent of raw tofu: dull and extremely tasteless. There are few things more dangerous than a bored reporter, and the stories we tossed around the city editor's office just to stay awake weren't the sort of thing you'd want in a family paper. The most wholesome among them—and one that actually ended up in print—was a feature story on the She-Wolf Sweat Lodge by my friend Jake Madison, the paper's science writer. Apparently, spending three hours in a steaming hot tent with eleven naked women wasn't quite as tasty as it sounded; by the time he got back he was soaking wet, pink as a radish, and demanding combat pay.

"You've got no idea what those chicks do in there," he was still saying three days later. "I mean, they've got this huge . . ."

"Christ, I *know*," I said. "How many times you gonna tell it?"

"Come on, Bernier. This is my manhood we're talking about." He leaned back against the wall, making the Truman-era radiator we were sitting on tilt forward and groan. "I'm never gonna be the same."

"There's a tragedy."

"They called me *phallocentric*. Can you believe that shit?"

"Shocking."

"Yeah, and they were the ones with this huge wooden—"

"Would the two of you please shut up?" This from Bill, our esteemed city editor. "I mean it, Madison. If you don't quit bitching about that place, I swear I'm sending you back. You wanted it, you got it."

"But nobody told me they'd—"

"Don't piss me off." Bill jammed a chopstick into his lo mein, offering vague threats of impalement. "I'm this close to giving you another feature on the Rainbow Peace Camp. Come on, people. Whatcha got for me?"

There were five of us crammed into Bill's cubicle for yet another excruciating edit meeting. This time, though, the mood was less than jovial; we were under orders from the managing editor to come up with something interesting *or else*. As usual, Bill was leaning back in an ancient swivel chair with his feet propped up on a stack of press releases. Marshall, the business reporter, had snagged the only other chair in the office; Lillian, who's covered schools for one paper or another since my mother was in first grade, had rolled her ergonomic throne over from her desk and was perched in the doorway in the hopes of a quick exit. Having arrived last, Mad and I got stuck on the radiator, which, despite the heat, was presently blowing rusty air up our bottoms.

"So what you got for me?" Bill said again. We stared at the carpet en masse. "Come on, gimme a break. Marshall?"

"I'm workin' on a thing 'bout that new store on the Green," he said in his Dixie drawl. "Little biz profile."

"Economic growth. Great. Publisher'll eat it up. What store is it again?"

"You don't wanna know."

"Not another damn aromatherapy place—" Marshall joined us in the carpet-staring. "Jesus, what's this one called?"

"Er . . . 'Centered Scents.' "

"Spike it. Oh, Christ, who am I kidding? It'll probably end up on page one. Gimme a sidebar on the Gabriel aromatherapy boom. Come to think of it, it's probably time to do the damn F.P. again."

Marshall looked like he wanted to fall on Bill's chopstick. The F.P. (or as it's known in the newsroom, the "F.U.") stands for Finger on the Pulse, a regular feature instigated by our publisher last spring to impress the ladies at the Rotary Club. It consists of a map of each storefront in downtown Gabriel, color-coded according to what kind of business it has, plus a forty-inch story on the state of the local economy. The last time they had to put it together, Marshall and the graphic artist made a pact to jump in the gorge if it ever ran again.

"Don't know why I didn't think of it before," Bill was saying. "F.P. it is. Feel free to get the hell out of here and start working on it." Marshall got up to leave, and before I could make a move Mad beat me to the empty chair. "Lillian?"

"Well . . . It's Girl Scout cookie time again." She had the good grace to look mortified. "I thought, um, perhaps I might trot out the 'pint-sized entrepreneur' angle."

He opened his mouth to object, then closed it again. "Fine. Find the brat who broke the record last year and follow her around."

"That was my general intention."

"Give the photo request to Wendell. He loves that kiddie crap. Okay, be gone. Madison?"

"Nanofab guys up at Benson are making itty-bitty computer chips."

"You did that last week."

"Yeah, well, now they're even smaller."

"Next."

"Plant sci builds a better broccoli. No?" He unrolled a tube of press releases from the Benson news service. "How about rice breeding? Here's something . . . 'millet, the wonder grain.' Oh, and the pomology guys are releasing a new apple."

Bill dropped his feet to the floor and just managed to catch his head in his hands before it hit the desk. Then he made a sort of groaning noise. "Oh, Christ, package 'em and get out of here." Mad had almost made good his escape when Bill opened an eye. "Wait. They name the apple yet?"

Mad looked at him warily. "What difference does it make?"

"Grab a shooter and do a walk-and-talk."

"On what?"

"On what people think they should call the goddamn apple."

"No *way*."

"It's called a sidebar."

"You gotta be—"

"The walk-and-talk or the peace camp. Up to you."

Mad bolted, leaving me alone without even bothering to look sorry about it. I decided it was time to stage a diversion. "So when are we getting a new cop reporter, anyway?"

Bill's head fell back into his hands, harder than you'd think would be good for him. "Damned if I know."

Our last cop reporter, a sweet Midwestern kid who'd fled at the first sign of homicide, had been gone since early last summer. So far, all attempts to replace him had flopped—

and the cop beat was rotating among Marshall, Mad, and myself. "What's the deal?"

"Never mind."

"Come on."

"Don't worry about it. We'll get somebody sooner or later."

"Curiosity is the hallmark of my profession."

He snorted, which didn't sound like a compliment. "How about giving me something to run in the goddamn newspaper?"

"You mean, like, tomorrow?" I was in danger of being throttled. "Okay, um . . ." I shuffled through my own meager stack of press releases. "Women's group up at Benson is having a pumpkin-carving contest. 'Great heroines of feminism.' "

"And?"

"You know, you gotta carve a pumpkin that looks like Betty Friedan."

"That's not hard. When's it happening?"

"Next week."

Again with the awful groaning noise. "You're not helping me."

"Well . . . there's supposed to be another rally to save the Starlight Theatre."

He perked up, but cautiously. "Next week?"

"This afternoon."

"Cover it." I didn't move. "What's the problem?"

"Do you remember how many people showed up to their *last* rally?"

"Fifty?"

"Try two."

"Alex, you're killing me here."

"Hey, it's not my fault the whole town's on Prozac." He looked as though he could use some himself. "Okay, how about something on the new exhibit at Historic Gabriel?" I waggled a piece of paper at him. "It's called, um, 'Tunneling into the Past: Nineteenth-Century Manhole Covers as Objects of . . .' "

"Skip it. Next?"

"Well, City Hall's putting in a new voice-mail system. You know, 'Punch one for the mayor, punch two to register as domestic partners, punch three to—' "

"Enough. Just go to the goddamn rally."

"But . . ."

"Spin it as a roundup of landmark buildings downtown. Maybe get one of those preservationist loons to rank them in order of historical importance."

"That sucks."

"Might as well do a sidebar on the manhole covers while you're at it. Not that I'm going to be around here tomorrow anyway."

"Huh?"

"When the boss hears what page one looks like, she's gonna fire my ass. Maybe everybody else's too."

With that, he invited me to get the hell out of his office and went back to taking his aggressions out on his lo mein. I wandered around the newsroom looking for sympathy, but everybody had phones stuck to their ears. That left me no choice but to actually do some work, so I called the historical society to get a few comments on the goddamn manhole exhibit, which I'd been half hoping would turn out to be a practical joke; no such luck. I wrote it up—including a quote about how the objects in question weren't just sewer covers but also "place-conscious historic signifiers"—and decided I'd earned my lunch. I dragged Mad away from his story on transgenic broccoli long enough for a couple of pitas on the Gabriel Green, the city's much-loved (and entirely paved) pedestrian mall.

"What time's this protest of yours?" Mad was saying through a mouthful of hummus.

I swiped at the tahini dripping down his chin. "They ought to be parading around any second now."

"Then I'm outta here."

"Come on, keep me company. There's probably going to be all of five of them anyway."

"What kind of loser gets all hepped up over some rotting old building?"

I took another bite of my falafel. "Bored professors' wives, mostly. One of them's married to the head of chemistry."

"Sissy Dillingham?"

"You got it."

"Man, she's a piece of work."

"Didn't you have your manly way with her one time?"

He shoved me with a tahini-covered hand, smearing the stuff all over the sleeve of my leather jacket. "Piss off, Bernier. I did *not* bang the woman. What I said was she grabbed my ass at the chem department Christmas party. I never said I took her up on it. Jesus, I've never been *that* drunk. Give me some credit."

"You don't even *have* an ass anyway. There's nothing there to grab."

"Yeah, well, she was so crocked on Sambuca she didn't notice. Lucky for me, she probably doesn't even remember it."

"Actually, she asks after you every damn time I see her."

"And she's going to be at this thing?"

"Probably."

He shot up so fast his paper plate went spinning across the Green like a Frisbee. "I am *definitely* out of here."

"I thought you wanted fro-yo. I'm buying."

"Raincheck," he said, and hustled his nonexistent butt toward the paper.

I went into Schultz's Deli and got a chocolate-and-vanilla twist cone from their newly installed frozen yogurt machine; since I talked them into buying it I feel a moral duty to partake at least once a day. I licked my way out of the store and returned to perch on the edge of the Green's fountain, which has been turned off ever since an environmentalist shackled himself to it during a mid-eighties drought.

The so-called Save Our Starlight rally was scheduled for one o'clock. It was already five after, and nobody had shown up. There was still no action by the time I polished off my wafer cone, so I fished the press release out of my backpack just to make sure I hadn't gotten the day wrong or something. But there it was, complete with yet another obnoxious acronym from the Gabriel protest set. The headline screamed "S.O.S.!!!!!!" in two-hundred-point type; underneath, it said, "Rally to Save Our Starlight, one P.M. Wednesday, the Gabriel Green." Right place, right time, no protesters.

I stuck around for another fifteen minutes; obviously, this rally had lured even fewer people than the last one—two fewer, to be exact. I was on my way back to the newsroom when it occurred to me that, given Bill's frame of mind, returning empty-handed was probably not a good idea. I muttered some nasty words loud enough for an aromatherapy-shopping matron to tell me to watch my language, then dug out the press release again. There were two contact names at the top of it: Cynthia (a.k.a. Sissy) Dillingham, who lived up in the posh professorial enclave of Benson Heights; and Barry Marsh, a retired banking type who served as head of the Gabriel Arts Coalition. Marsh and his arts group had been dragged into the Starlight thing by his wife, a former ballerina who ran a perennially failing dance school and just happened to be Sissy Dillingham's best friend.

I decided to drop by his office, just so I'd have something

to defend myself with when Bill read me the riot act. Despite the fancy name, the Arts Coalition is headquartered in all of two rooms on the fifth floor of the Walden County Savings Bank building, where Marsh used to work. Since the bank is in the center of the Green, I was practically standing in front of it anyway.

Walden County Savings is housed on the first two floors of a six-story granite building with offices above. The elevator is constantly out of order, so I hoofed it up four flights of stairs, then walked down a narrow hall past a string of doors with names of lawyers and accountants stenciled on milky glass; Perry Mason would feel right at home. The lights were on inside the Arts Coalition office, and since "PLEASE COME IN" was painted right on the door I didn't bother to knock.

The girl at the battered reception desk didn't look old enough to have tackled the SAT—whip-thin, slumped shoulders, firmly in the ugly-duckling phase. She was wearing headphones, and I could hear someone screaming his sincere admiration for Satan from ten feet away. When she finally noticed me standing there, she ripped off the headphones and shoved them into an empty box of Kleenex on her desk. "Good afternoon," she said, in a voice that sounded like she'd been rehearsing it. "May I help you?"

"I'm Alex Bernier from the *Monitor*. I was looking for Barry Marsh."

"Oh." She picked up a pencil and started chewing on it. "Okay."

"Is he in?"

"Um, I think so."

"You think so?"

She stopped chewing long enough to jab the pencil toward the coat rack. "Well, his jacket's there."

"So can I see him?"

She glanced at the closed door of Marsh's inner office. Her secretarial training was clearly being stretched to the limit. "Um, I guess."

She didn't seem inclined to move, so I went over and rapped on his door. No answer. "You sure he's in there?"

"Yeah, I think so. He was on the phone to somebody a while ago."

She got up and did the knocking routine herself, and when there was still no answer she tried the knob. She must have expected it to be locked, because she yanked so hard the door flew all the way open, hit the wall, and nearly slammed shut again. It didn't close all the way, though— which was really too bad, because what was on the other side of it was pretty disgusting.

Barry Marsh was sitting at his desk; or more accurately, he was pitched across it. His head was lying to one side on the shiny mahogany surface, one eye wide open and staring right at us. It looked like he was drooling, but it was hard to tell because his tongue was so bloated it took up most of his mouth. *Yuck.* His right arm was folded under him, and the left was splayed across the desk, hand hanging limply over the edge. He must have dropped the phone, because it was on the carpet, off the hook and making a honking sound.

"Holy shit," the girl said. She took a step forward, which I definitely considered to be the wrong direction. "You think he's dead?" I started to open my mouth to say something, then shut it on the grounds that I might yak any second. I took a step back. She took another step forward. "Should we, like, call somebody?" She sounded way more intrigued than freaked out, which didn't make me feel like a grown-up. "911 maybe?"

"Um, good idea." I tried to back up farther, then realized I'd encountered the wall. Humiliating.

"You're not s'posed to touch anything, ya know."

"Wouldn't dream of it," I said, wondering which episode of *America's Most Wanted* was serving as her point of reference.

I followed her out, and after she called the ambulance I dialed Bill's number. He picked up on the first ring. "Do *not* tell me your story fell through," he said before I could get a word in.

"Yeah, well, the protest didn't happen."

"Son of a—"

"But I've got something for you." I was trying to sound all cool and callous, in the interest of retrieving some dignity in the eyes of the Tabloid Princess. "Something runnable."

"You better."

"Um . . . how'd you like a dead guy on page one?"

I don't want to say that Bill actually shouted anything like "Yippee!" But since journalists are supposed to report what really happened, I guess I have to admit that he sure as hell did.

2

WORD SPREAD AROUND THE BUILDING IN A MATTER OF MIN-
utes, mostly because Marsh's secretary went up and down
the halls telling everybody. Folks don't drop dead in their
offices all that often around here, and pretty soon the hallway was clogged with panty-hosed women trying to look
grave. The EMTs got there almost immediately, two burly
young guys in red windbreakers with Sand's Ambulance
printed on the back. The ambulance service is owned by the
same family that runs Sand's Funeral Home (the two are
housed in adjacent buildings, which always struck me as a
bit tacky), and people often wonder if they drive a little
slower when money's tight. This time, though, they were
pretty much guaranteed repeat business.

The EMTs came rushing through the outer office, winded
from running up the stairs; apparently, the secretary hadn't
bothered to mention that there was no hurry. It took them all
of two seconds to figure out the guest of honor had already
checked out. Then the shorter one said something into a
walkie-talkie—probably telling the casket salesman it was
time to dust off the merchandise—and the two of them
picked up their gear and repaired to the hall for some girl-
watching.

I was perched in the corner of the outer office when the police came in. At first there were only two uniforms, whose investigative procedure consisted of standing in the transom between the two rooms and staring at the body. They had their backs to me, but when they turned around I caught the phrase "bum ticker," and one of them complaining that his wife wouldn't let him eat bacon anymore. I have often heard the Gabriel police force compared en masse to Gomer Pyle, and at the moment they weren't doing anything to contradict it.

Then I heard a woman's voice demanding to know what was going on, and Marsh's wife came flying through the door in a blur of Burberry plaid. The two uniforms tried to object, but they were no match for her; she blew right by them, saw the horror show that used to be her husband, and proceeded to scream her head off. She was still yelling his name—and shaking him like she thought he might actually wake up if she did it hard enough—when two suits showed up: a detective and the police chief himself.

The detective sprinted over to her, pulling her away from the body and into the other room. She tried to get free of him and back to her husband—her agility was pretty impressive for a gal of advancing years—but he held on until she calmed down. He sat her at the secretary's desk and reached for the Kleenex, only to discover that the box contained nothing but a knockoff Walkman. He seemed torn between baby-sitting the wife and checking out the body, but Chief Hill came over then, dragging a chair from the other side of the desk to sit beside her. It was obvious from the way he put his arm around her that they already knew each other—no surprise since they traveled in the same Gabriel civic circles. Thus liberated, the detective stalked over to the uniforms.

"You guys ever heard of securing a crime scene?"

"Crime scene?" the bacon martyr replied. "The guy keeled over of a heart attack. So what?"

"Oh, so you're an M.E. now? When did you go to med school?"

"Come on, it's obvious," the other one said. "Look at him. He was yapping on the phone, and he just—"

"Dropped dead so fast he never even got out of his chair?"

"It happens."

"Pretty damn rarely. And what about whoever he was talking to? Don't you think they might have wondered what the hell happened? Maybe called somebody?"

"He was probably calling for help when he croaked."

"Could be. But until you know it was natural causes, rule is you treat it like it's not. Remember?"

"Christ, Cody. You'd think homicide if he got a goddamn splinter." He chuckled at his own joke, and his bacon-loving buddy patted him on the back. "That what it was like down in the Big Apple?"

"I'm from *Boston*, you moron." Cody looked like he wanted to wipe the smirks off their faces, but he got a handle on himself. "You better hope you're right about the vic. Now go clear the hallway. M.E.'s on his way." He muttered something under his breath as he watched them saunter out of the office. Then he finally noticed me. "What are you doing here?" he said, striding over to stand not six inches away. He was a big guy, and he had me cornered.

"Just lurking."

"Lurking in my crime scene?"

"Lurking *near* your crime scene."

He stepped even closer. "I could yank your press pass for this."

"Is that so?"

"Or I could have you hauled out of here in handcuffs."

I leaned forward to whisper in his ear. "And what are you going to do to me then?"

He cracked a nearly invisible smile, and I got a little thrill in the pit of my stomach. "Probably the same thing I did to you last night."

"Then I definitely confess."

At this point, it might be prudent to mention that Detective Brian Cody is—for lack of a better word—my boyfriend. And so caught up was I in our witty banter that I was actually on the point of kissing him square on the mouth when I remembered that we were in the company of (a) the chief of police, (b) a grieving widow, and (c) a drooling corpse. I poked him in the stomach instead. "Where'd you take off to this morning?"

He looked around to see if anybody was listening, then leaned in to me again. "Running off your pesto. Went to the lake and back. I dropped the dogs at your place after, but you were already gone."

"This is getting frighteningly domestic."

"You'll make some good man a nice little wife someday."

"Oh, the horror."

"So what are you doing here, anyway? One of those two geniuses let you in?"

"Actually, I let *them* in."

"What?"

"I came up to do an interview with Marsh. Secretary opened his door and there he was."

Cody is an enlightened guy, but he's never been big on me and corpses. "You okay?"

"You gonna catch me if I faint?"

His smile got noticeably wider. "Don't I always?"

I pictured myself collapsing into his arms in the lobby of the Gabriel cop shop—which, believe it or not, is how we met. "You're one for one so far."

"It's my highly trained reflexes."

"How's Marsh's wife doing?" I peered around the solid hunk that is Cody to see her still weeping into the chief's hankie. "Looks pretty broken up, huh?"

"She really lost it for a while there. I guess she was supposed to meet him for coffee. Walked in and found the crowd."

"So you think he had a heart attack?"

"You asking as a reporter or my best girl?"

"*There's* an issue we haven't dealt with in a couple minutes. Okay, I'm asking as a reporter."

"The cause of death will not be determined until the Walden County coroner has conducted a postmortem."

"Wow, that was good. They teach you that stuff in cop school?"

"Actually, yes."

"And how about if I'm asking as your best girl?"

"I haven't had a chance to look around, but I'd say the poor slob probably died of a heart attack."

"So why did you ream out those uniforms?"

"Because sooner or later they're going to run across some poor slob who *didn't* die of a heart attack, and they're going to screw it up bad."

In walked the coroner, a part-time pathology professor at the Benson med school who actually seems to enjoy getting rousted out of bed at four in the morning to go look at dead people. Cody told me he had to go deal with the body, and he'd just ushered me out into the hall when something struck him. "You know, Alex, you should probably make a statement."

"Huh? Why?"

"You found the guy."

"Who probably died of a heart attack."

"Yeah, but the wife moved the body all over the place, and I'd just as soon dot the i's and cross the t's."

"I wasn't the only one who saw it. There's—"

"Those two jokers, plus the secretary. I'd rather have you go on the record, thanks just the same."

"I know there's a compliment in there somewhere. Look, I have to get back to the paper. This story's gotta be page one."

"Even if it's natural causes?"

"It's still a news obit. Marsh was a solid citizen, big charity type. Used to be president of Walden County Savings. Ran for council a couple years ago. Even if he died at home in bed we'd probably put him above the fold. Croaking in his office with Goth Girl outside the door makes it even bigger."

He gave a low whistle. "Man, and I thought cops were cold-blooded."

"So listen, I really have to get back to the newsroom. Can I do this statement thing after work?"

"You want to come by the station?"

"I want you to come by my bedroom with a notebook and a big Hershey bar."

"I'd love to. Unfortunately, the department frowns on cops taking statements from their girlfriends."

"In that case," I said, "it'll have to be just you and me and the Hershey bar."

Back at the *Monitor*, the mood was embarrassingly jovial. Our managing editor, a woman who can break a whole stack of boards with her head if she wants to, was actually doing a little dance around her office. Bill looked happier than I'd seen him in weeks. And the new intern, a Jerry Springer wanna-be who'd been moping around all semester at the lack of scandal, was positively bouncing off the walls with glee.

"Christ, look at 'em," Mad said as I walked up the newsroom stairs. "All this over some old guy who dies banging his secretary."

"Where'd you get that?"

"Marshall."

"You should know better than to believe what you hear from a reporter."

"He said Bill said you said so."

"Huh?" It took me a second to follow his chain of evidence. "I did *not*. What I said was his secretary was sitting *outside*. Jeeze, no wonder he was so psyched."

"What was it like up there, anyway?"

"Mob scene. Office girls clutching their Kleenex."

"Sweet. You get a good look at the dead guy?"

"Way too good."

"And?"

"And what? He was dead as a mackerel."

"And that's all I'm getting?"

"Christ, I thought you grew out of this crap."

"I'm developmentally challenged."

"You got that right." I plopped down at my desk, which is diagonal to Mad's in the block of four cityside reporters. "Okay, he was kind of lying across his desk. Like he tried to stand up and just sort of collapsed on top of it. Only reason he didn't fall on the ground was that his butt landed back in his chair. His face was all purply and his tongue was hanging way out." I demonstrated for him. "Big bulgy eyes. You satisfied?"

"Yep."

"Good." I started riffling through the enormous lump of papers on my desk, looking for a list of the Arts Coalition's board of directors so I could figure out who to call for comment. I knew I'd seen it recently, but given my complete lack of organizational skills, I wasn't sure where.

"You know, Bernier, you're sure taking this well."

"I am?"

"An hour ago you were eyeballing a corpse, and now you're all calm. What gives?"

I stopped moving papers around and looked up. "For the record, I nearly hurled. But, you know, the guy just *croaked*."

"So?"

"So it's not the same thing." He gave no sign of getting it. "You gotta be kidding me. Do you really think that after all that's gone down around here, I'm gonna faint over seeing some guy kicked off of a heart attack?"

"Oh." He seemed fundamentally unsatisfied. I went back to my excavation. "They sure he died of a heart attack?"

"Officially it's they don't know pending autopsy. Cody said he thought so, though. But he hadn't looked at the vic yet."

"Jesus, Alex. You're even starting to *talk* like a cop."

"Sorry. I guess I've been hanging around Cody too damn much."

"Nah, he's cool." For Mad, this was roughly the equivalent of offering to give the bride away. "He giving you the inside track on this one?"

"No way. You know the drill. No mixing business with pleasure."

"He pours his guts out to you in the sack, and you conveniently forget it the next morning."

"Something like that. But it's never anything big anyway."

"And what are you gonna do when it is?"

"What are you now, my social worker? Why don't you worry about your own love life?"

That shut him up. For the past few months, Mad has been dating my housemate Emma, a radiology resident at the Benson vet school. Emma is British—kind of a cross between James Herriot and the two ladies from *Absolutely Fabulous*, if you can picture it. Anyway, their romance has broken Mad's record for relationship longevity by several orders of magnitude. Recently, she's been taking him to task for being "too clingy"—quite a hoot for those of us who've been watching him love 'em and leave 'em for the better part of four years.

Mad went back to his mutant broccoli piece, and I started getting together a rundown of who I was going to call for the Marsh story. A news obit is just like a profile, only backward; you interview everybody *but* the guy you're writing about. You basically tell the person's life story, drawn mostly from clips in the newspaper's library, and get a bunch of quotes about what a saint he was. If it's somebody who's been in the public eye a lot (and Marsh was) you get to have a little more fun with it, though you usually catch hell later. For instance, when a former Benson president shuffled off last winter at the ripe old age of a hundred and two, I did a piece on his whole career—including the fact that he'd been booted out when it came to light that he'd once ghostwritten a scholarly article *in favor* of school segregation. I got hate mail for weeks, both from ultra-loyal Bensonians who thought we were dredging up the past for no good reason, and from readers who just thought it was a sin to speak ill of the dead. I believe one of them is praying for my soul at this very moment.

Marsh didn't have any civic skeletons in his closet, at least as far as I knew. But since his death was the closest thing to news we'd had in weeks, it was going to get way more play than it deserved—and that meant I'd have to dig up enough stuff to fill thirty column inches plus a sidebar or two. I finally found the Arts Coalition list, in the last place I would have thought: my filing cabinet. Marsh had been the director of the agency, but the chairman of its board was a retired Benson theater professor. I called his house, and the answering machine said he was in London for the month. *So if you'd like to burglarize me*, I thought, *now would be a lovely time.*

I went down the list in search of the vice chair, who turned out to be none other than Sissy Dillingham. I figured she had her hands full with the Widow Marsh, so I decided to leave a message on her machine to call me if she had the chance; you wouldn't believe how huffy people can get if you don't ask them for a comment about the dearly departed.

Imagine my surprise when she answered on the third ring.

"Hi, Mrs. Dillingham," I said. "This is Alex Bernier from the *Monitor*. I'm sorry to disturb you at a time like this, but I was wondering if I could talk to you for a story I'm doing on Mr. Marsh."

"Why would you be doing a story on Barry?"

Uh-oh. "Er . . . you haven't heard?"

"Heard what?"

"About Mr. Marsh."

"What about him?" She was getting annoyed. "Miss Bernier, I'm right in the middle of something. We have a protest for Save Our Starlight scheduled in a few minutes. I'm just on my way out the—"

"I thought that was at one."

"No, it's at three. Where did you get that idea?"

"It was in the press release." We were getting way off track. "I went to the Green, but nobody showed up."

She gave an exasperated growl, sounding way less lady-like than usual. "Those imbeciles . . ." She cleared her throat and gathered her manners. "Someone must have made a typographical error in the press release. It's actually at three. I hope we'll see you there?"

"Er, well, about Mr. Marsh . . ."

"Yes, what is it?"

"He's, um . . . He passed away earlier today."

I heard her gasp—really melodramatically, like she'd just spotted the mummy in an old horror movie. *"What?"*

"He had . . . Well, I think maybe he had a heart attack." I wanted to sink into the mustard-yellow carpet. "I thought you'd know about it. I thought maybe Mrs. Marsh would have called you by now."

"Right," she spat out. Even from the one word, I could hear she'd dropped both her guard and her patrician accent. "I'm the last one she'd call. Oh, God, Barry . . ." She started sobbing, and I heard a clunk as she put the phone down. I could catch fragments of what she was babbling, which mostly consisted of "I can't believe it . . . I can't believe it . . ." I had no idea what to do, so I just sat there with the receiver plastered to my ear.

"Um, Mrs. Dillingham?" I said after a while. "Are you still there? Hello?"

The crying got louder, then stopped. It wasn't that she'd calmed down; she'd hung up on me. But before she did, I could have sworn I heard her say something like this: "I can't believe . . . she finally killed him."

3

You may have noticed that Barry Marsh is not a nineteen-year-old girl. There's no denying it; neither is his name Dolores Strunk. Marsh died weeks before anybody had even heard of Dolores, and since time was crawling by slowly that fall, it seemed even longer. By the end of October, Barry Marsh had been buried and mourned and mostly forgotten. He did have a seat dedicated to him at the local summer-stock theater, though; it had a bronze plaque screwed onto the back, and a mediocre view of the stage.

The official cause of death was a heart attack. That was the unofficial one, too. But there was something else, something that never wound up in the paper despite the pleas and lamentations of one very ambitious intern. Marsh had died of a heart attack, but he hadn't quite died of natural causes. His bum ticker, as the cop had so eloquently put it, had conked out courtesy of a dose of *sildenafil citrate*; believers in better living through chemistry might recognize it as Viagra.

We knew this because the intern, a Benson senior from Long Island whose name I could never seem to remember, had somehow managed to get a copy of the autopsy report. He'd come blazing into the newsroom, crowing about how he'd snagged the scoop of the century, only to have his wings clipped by the managing editor—a champion wing-clipper if there ever was one.

"Listen to me, you brat," Marilyn was saying at top volume. They were in her office, but since the door was open and she was yelling, the conversation was pretty much open to the public. "This is a newspaper, not the goddamn *National Enquirer*. Why are we gonna print that the geezer was on Viagra?"

"Because it's *great*," he said, sounding thoroughly unintimidated. "City father drops dead trying to get his jollies off. Don't you think it'd make—"

"It's not news. It's dirt. Someday you'll learn the difference."

"I thought journalists were supposed to report the truth."

"Would you listen to this kid? We reported that he died of a heart attack, which *is* the truth. *Why* he had the heart attack is none of anybody's business."

"What if he had a heart attack while, you know, jogging or something? You'd report that, right?"

"You may not've figured this out yet, Brad, but jogging and fucking aren't the same thing."

"But . . ."

"Marsh's sex life crosses the line. Get it?"

There was a pause, and I could hear Marilyn playing with one of her martial-arts toys. I was hoping she'd decapitate him. "Hey," Brad said finally, "maybe the widow would want to do it out of the goodness of her heart. You know, warn others about the dangers of . . ."

"That's pathetic."

"But . . ."

"Pathetic, but promising. Always try to make the source

see what's in it for him. Brad my boy, there may be hope for
you yet."

"So can I give it a try?"

"No."

"But why?"

"Use your head. Guy's popping Viagra in the middle of
the day. Do you really think he was getting doped up for his
wife?"

I can't say that the details of Barry Marsh's sex life had
ever crossed my mind before. In fact, Marsh was one of
those white, preppy, middle-aged guys who you couldn't
picture having sex under any circumstances—not even if he
was dropping acid while reading the *Kama Sutra* in a
whorehouse.

But there we were on a Wednesday night before Halloween, ensconced in the window seat of our favorite bar on
the Green, contemplating Marsh's adventures in the saddle.
Representatives of just about every other news organization
were getting crocked all around us: a reporter and anchor
from the local TV station; the editor of the weekly *Gabriel
Advocate*; a couple of radio guys; a trio of flacks from the
Benson news service. If anybody wants to erase the local
media in one fell swoop, I'd strongly suggest blowing up the
Citizen Kane around ten any night of the week.

We were in a temperate mood, drinking-wise. Mad and
O'Shaunessey (the *Monitor*'s sports editor and the loudest
man alive) were only on their second pitcher of Molson, and
I was still nursing my first Tanqueray and tonic. My rela-
tionship with Cody was in danger of turning me into Mother
Teresa.

"So riddle me this," I was saying. "Why does a sixty-
something married guy quaff Viagra in the middle of the
day? And in the office, no less?"

Mad poured himself another drink. "Because he's phalli-cally challenged."

"You just can't resist using your new word, can you?" I said. "So what do you think? He's gotta be stepping out, right?"

"Clearly, he's drilling the secretary," O'Shaunessey of-fered, whacking his mug on the table for emphasis. "Clearly."

"The secretary was barely out of braces."

The guys exchanged a look that said I was from another planet. It fell to O'Shaunessey to translate. "Fine thing."

"She was a work-study kid from the alternative high school. And not a whole lot to look at, frankly."

"So," Mad said, "he had another piece on the side."

"That's the thing. His wife said they had a date for cof-fee. He was supposed to meet her at Café Whatever, but—"

"Flag on the play," O'Shaunessey interjected. "Don't you think they're way overboard with the slacker thing?"

"Yeah, well, the coffee's good. Anyway, when hubby didn't show she figured he forgot. Went up to his office looking for him, and there he was. Dead like doornail."

"How old was he again?" O'Shaunessey asked.

"Sixty-two. So here's the question. Did he take the Via-gra figuring he'd have some afternoon delight with the wife? Or did he really forget he was supposed to meet her, and schedule some extracurricular activities with his lady friend?"

"Or here's another question," Mad said. "Who gives a rat's ass?"

"Oh, come on. Play nice. What else have we got to talk about? Besides, I'm kind of fascinated by the whole thing. I never thought of Marsh as much of a swordsman, and now here he is expiring in the name of love. Kind of a hoot, don't you think?"

"You're such a bitch," Mad said with a smile, waggling

the empty pitcher in the direction of the bar. "So why did he kick off, anyway? Isn't that stuff supposed to be safe?"

"Yeah, well, I guess some guys just can't take the heat."

"Did Marsh have a heart condition?"

"Not that I know of."

"You're not supposed to take it if you're on nitro," O'Shaunessey offered. We both stared at him. "At least," he mumbled into his mug, "I think I read that someplace."

Mad seemed about to say something, then changed his mind. I played with the limes in my drink. "So," Mad said after a minute, "did Marsh take nitro or didn't he?"

"Like I said, not that I know of."

"And the question on the table is . . . ?"

"The wife or the girlfriend."

"Gotta be the girlfriend," Mad said. "I mean, Belinda Marsh is in damn fine shape for a chick her age. But you've gotta be crazy about what you're getting at home to go out of your way to pack it for the office."

"What?"

"You've gotta be really juiced up about the home cooking to . . ."

"Oh, for God's sake, would you just say it in English?"

"It takes a major libido to want to diddle the wife at home *and* at the office. And you said Marsh wasn't that kind of dude."

"Not that I could tell. He failed the cleavage test, anyway."

"The what?"

"One of the fringe benefits of wearing a thirty-four double-D bra. If a guy doesn't check out the merchandise, he's either gay or over the hill. Trust me."

"Maybe he just doesn't dig the big . . ."

"Doesn't matter. It's ingrained in your DNA. Believe me on this one."

"So how did I do?"

"You parked your eyes on them like a plane on a runway. Both of you." It was hard to tell which of them was more relieved. "So your best male opinion is that he wasn't playing on the home team?"

Mad leaned back and put his feet up on the chair across from him. "Correct."

"Couldn't he and the wife have, you know, rekindled the old flame?" The bartender came over with a new pitcher. "And besides, he was supposed to be having coffee with her. Do you really think he'd forget about it and make a date on the side?"

"Maybe the guy was an amateur in the adultery department. Or maybe his memory was going. We already know things were slipping south of the border, huh?" He looked to O'Shaunessey for appreciation, and got it.

"So who do you think it was?"

"Man, Bernier, you're obsessed. Aren't you getting enough yourself? Where is Supercop, anyway?"

"He took his mom out to dinner."

"What a kind and noble . . ."

"Are you going to play name-the-chippy or aren't you?"

"I don't even know these people."

"Sure you do. You know the prime suspect."

"Which is?"

"Sissy Dillingham."

He choked on his Molson. "You gotta be kidding me."

"You should've heard how she reacted when I told her he was dead. She was just south of hysterical. I say she was in love with him."

"In love with her best friend's husband?"

"Come on, you know that whole town-gown crowd is worse than Peyton Place. Somebody told me they still have key parties."

"No *way*. How come I never get invited?"

"And besides, they weren't even friends anymore. Sissy blurted it out when I dropped the bomb about Marsh. Maybe that was why they split—'cause Sissy fell for Barry."

The onomatopoeia was too much for them. "Sissy and Barry up in a tree, K-I-S-S-I-N-G," O'Shaunessey chanted, then Mad joined him. "First comes love, then comes . . ."

"You are *so* infantile."

"Not infantile," Mad said. "Just sober."

Whether or not Sissy Dillingham had been in love with Barry Marsh, his death definitely seemed to shake her up. Until then, it was pretty obvious (to me at least) that the Save Our Starlight thing was just another charity hobby for her, to be sandwiched between an AIDS walk and the Junior League ski-and-skate sale. But after Marsh died, she threw herself into it with a fanatical devotion usually reserved for blowing up buses. She started organizing meetings, holding protests, even swearing she'd chain herself to the wrecking ball if that's what it came to.

You may be wondering just what the Starlight Theatre is, and why anybody thought it was worth saving. Since I've spent the last few months of my life writing about the damn thing, I might as well fill you in. The Starlight is an old vaudeville house located just off the Green; when it was built in 1917, people called it the most beautiful theater outside New York City. In its heyday, the Starlight saw its share of big names: Erich von Stroheim, Katharine Cornell, George M. Cohan, Helen Hayes, Orson Welles, the Ballet Russe. It had a grand marble staircase, shiny brass railings, terrazzo floors, crystal chandeliers imported from Austria. It seated more than eighteen hundred people in the orchestra and two balconies—and there were four others like it in downtown Gabriel.

But just like my generation saw video kill the radio star, an earlier one saw film kill the stage. In 1950, the Starlight was converted into a movie theater; eventually somebody had the bright idea of turning each balcony into its own screening room, which was sort of like using the Mona Lisa as a tablecloth. By 1970, it was showing porno. Five years later, it was closed.

Then something amazing happened. In the early eighties, a nonprofit group got together to revive the place. They bought it out of foreclosure, drummed up millions in preservation grants from the federal government, and declared that the Starlight was going to be the centerpiece of a revitalized downtown. Practically the whole city volunteered to help, from schoolkids to frat boys to Army reservists. They ripped out the godforsaken movie screens, painted and plastered for more than a year, and got the theater put on the National Register. The Governor of New York christened the place himself, snipping the red ribbon and sitting through a high school production of *Waiting for Godot*, which was probably above and beyond the call of duty.

It closed less than a year later. Apparently, the powers that be at the Gabriel Performing Arts and Cultural Alliance never stopped to think that a creaky old building big enough to fit nearly two thousand people costs a hell of a lot to heat in the winter. Or that it was impossible to book acts that might actually draw that big a crowd when they can play Syracuse or Binghamton, which are actually somewhere near a major highway. Or that the roof needed to be replaced. And so on, and so on—until the Starlight shut its doors for good.

By the time I moved to Gabriel, the Starlight was a glorified ruin. The leaky roof had collapsed in places. Then the sprinklers broke, and it rained all over the red velvet seats that the Tri-Delt sorority girls had so lovingly restored. Pigeons set up housekeeping, so that anyone who ventured inside had to wear a mask or catch some awful avian virus. The plaster started to disintegrate, big chunks of it falling from the ceiling like gilded hail. Outside, most of the bulbs in the marquee had been broken by rock-wielding teenagers. The title of its final show—a Christmas production of *Amahl and the Night Visitors*—was still up there, the letters disappearing one by one until it just said MA, like it was crying for its mother.

The first time I had to write about the Starlight was when the fire chief stood up in the middle of a city council meeting I was covering and demanded that it be torn down. He was waving news clippings about how another abandoned theater in Elmira or Utica or somewhere had just burned down in a spectacular blaze, taking seven firemen with it. He swore up and down that none of his people were going to risk their lives to save the place, and that if it caught on fire the whole department was "goddamn well going to sit on the sidewalk and roast marshmallows and watch it burn," which is what I quoted him as saying in the paper the next day. He was not pleased.

Within weeks, council was in the process of removing the theater's historic designation, the first step in turning the building into a parking lot. That was when Belinda Marsh and Sissy Dillingham formed Save Our Starlight. They promised the mayor they could raise half a million dollars by the end of the year, and came up with all of twenty-three thousand. They proceeded to beg for reprieve after reprieve, missing every deadline the city set and occasionally bursting into tears in the council chambers. In a city chock-full of effete volunteer groups, S.O.S. was shaping up to be the lamest of them all.

Gabriel's city council consists of eight Democrats, one Independent, and a Green; it's presided over by a mayor whose political leanings are somewhere to the left of Stalin. I mention this by way of emphasizing that they weren't a particularly tough crowd; there wasn't a development maven among them. They were all into historic preservation and organic gardening and literacy programs for jail inmates. The idea of tearing down the Starlight was just about killing them—the debate ran into six-hour meetings, the most agonized I've ever covered—but none of them could figure out how to save it.

By the time Cody took me to the Adirondacks for my twenty-seventh birthday at the end of September, the council members had finally come to the end of their collective rope. The fire chief was making noises about filing some sort of public-safety lawsuit, and a civic group had formed to get rid of the Starlight on the grounds that it was an eyesore, and dangerous to boot. Council was just about to demolish it— the vote was just days away—when Barry Marsh died.

And since Gabriel prides itself on being a touchy-feely sort of place, Marsh's death gave the Starlight an automatic stay of execution. There was no way anyone on council was going to vote to tear down the theater when Marsh's body wasn't even cold. The building had been empty for a couple of decades, the thinking went, so what difference did another few weeks make?

But in that next month, Sissy Dillingham went into hyperdrive. She recruited a passel of high-profile arts types to wax eloquent on the future of the Starlight, and for a while people almost believed it. You couldn't turn on cable access TV without running across Sissy and her troops talking about how the theater was going to bring the downtown arts scene back to life (and they didn't much appreciate it when one of my stories pointed out that their predecessors had said exactly the same thing).

Through all of this, one person was conspicuously

absent. Lindy Marsh, the former ballerina who'd dragged her husband into the Starlight mess in the first place, never attended a single meeting. She never came out against it, at least not in public. But there were plenty of rumors, and the most popular among them was this: If Sissy Dillingham wanted to save the Starlight, then Lindy Marsh was willing to rip out the bricks with her fingernails.

4

THE WEEKEND BEFORE HALLOWEEN BROUGHT A NASTY COLD snap that finally killed all the tomato plants and seemed to settle everybody into a properly sober mood for a Gabriel fall. Most of the populace was just as glad; this is a skeptical, glass-is-half-empty sort of town most of the time, and all the waiting for the meteorological shoe to drop was driving us crazy with dread. Besides, the folks at the Chamber of Commerce were starting to complain that the warm nights were going to mean no decent foliage for the autumn tourist season, which was already half over anyway.

For a newspaper, holidays of all descriptions are both comforting and deeply nauseating. Comforting, because you know you're going to have some tried-and-true stories to fill up the budget—like, say, the Dickensian moppet who gives all her toys to the poor at Christmas, or the Miss Lonelyhearts who spreads joy on Valentine's Day by sending handmade cards to each and every nursing home patient in the county. Why journalists find holidays nauseating requires no further explanation.

In Gabriel, Halloween means that articles on the following topics must be duly reported, written, edited, published, and used to train incontinent puppies throughout Walden

County: (a) the annual elementary school costume parade; (b) the protest by Parents for Christ over the satanic implications of the annual elementary school costume parade; (c) the Wiccan Pride Breakfast; (d) the protest by Gabrielites for Christ over the satanic *and* lesbian implications of the Wiccan Pride Breakfast; and (e) the kickoff of the Junior League winter coat drive, which has nothing whatsoever to do with Halloween but is always held on October 31 any way.

This year, though, our cauldron runneth over: In addition to the mid-October feminist-carving contest, some enterprising students up at Benson caused much head-scratching by impaling a pumpkin on the spire atop the university's trademark library bell tower. How they did it was a genuine mystery; the roof is scary-steep, and the only access is through a locked hatch, twenty feet below the peak and, according to all reports, untouched by the perpetrators. The Benson Pumpkin, as it eventually came to be known to wire editors around the country, was the primary topic of local gossip—at least until Ashley Sinclair/Dolores Strunk made her appearance, and kept the spirit of the macabre alive well into the new year.

In addition to writing most of the aforementioned stories, I churned out a grand total of thirteen pieces on Save Our Starlight—not a lucky number for either one of us. The coverage included a piece about a Halloween-themed protest for which the activists dressed up as characters from shows performed at the theater in its heyday. This required me to troop over to the Starlight in the freezing cold and watch Adele Giordano-Bronstein, recently jettisoned wife of a prominent materials science professor, parade around dressed like the Duchess of Malfi. Madeline Hoover—a Gabriel alderwoman, community theater buff, and preservationist zealot—wore a diaphanous (and, considering her ample girth, voluminous) evening gown and ghostly white facepaint; she was Elvira from *Blithe Spirit*. Sissy Dillingham, who apparently still thought of herself as an ingenue, came as Cecily Cardew from *The Importance of Being Earnest*. Roger Nash, a Benson theater professor and one of exactly two men who showed up, got decked out in full naval regalia as Sir Joseph Porter from *H.M.S. Pinafore*, and kept singing "I Am the Monarch of the Sea" until Sissy Dillingham hit him with her parasol.

Interestingly enough, Lindy Marsh was also present and accounted for—whether to stifle the rumors or just to confuse everyone, I couldn't tell you. Her choice of costume sent some tongues a-wagging, however; she came as Lady Macbeth.

I was starting to like her.

Mad has a theory about the sexual competition of human females being about half a step beyond the tiger cage at the local zoo, and the scene at the Save Our Starlight protest didn't do much to prove him wrong. Lindy Marsh and Sissy Dillingham marched around with two dozen or so others in a scraggly oval, carrying signs and smiling for the hypothermic cameraman from Nine News. They managed to position themselves as far apart as possible, which, due to some basic laws of geometry, meant that they were directly opposite each other at all times. A casual voyeur might have missed it, but if you were watching them closely (and I was), you could catch them glancing at each other every few minutes. Once in a while they'd do it at the same second and their eyes would lock, and they'd exchange the kind of look my dog Shakespeare gives the canine interlopers who wander into the yard. Narrowed eyes, clenched jaw, subtle baring of teeth. At one point, I could have sworn I even heard them growl at each other.

Inevitably, the urge to speechify came upon the group.

There seemed to be a general flash of panic about which one of the lady carnivores was going to get to do the honors, but Sissy Dillingham hustled to the podium before it could go too far. She proceeded to give a rousing speech on the glorious future of the Starlight—and do it in a fake British accent so appalling it would have made my roommate Emma pelt her with Wheatabix, or maybe just strangle her with her bare hands. She even went so far as to end it with a rousing chorus of *Hurr-AH! Hurr-AH!* Lindy Marsh may have taken the trouble to get dressed up as a Scottish psychopath, but I didn't catch her cheering.

It was pretty obvious what the Save Our Starlight crowd was up to. City council convenes the first and third Wednesdays of the month; the first meeting is just informational, the second is for voting. Through the usual political tap dancing, S.O.S. would try to sell council on its new plan to resurrect the theater in time for the November information meeting. Meanwhile, they'd whip the local arts community into a frenzy. The hope, in other words, was that the public outcry—plus whatever financing scheme they'd managed to concoct, plus any lingering pathos over the late lamented Barry Marsh—would add up to enough smoke and mirrors to keep the ax from falling when council voted at the end of the month.

For the most part, it seemed to be working. At least now, the average Gabrielite was actually thinking about the Starlight on a regular basis. Every day after the protest-cum-costume-party, a different quotation appeared in three-foot-high letters on a banner draped from the Starlight's marquee. It got to be a local curiosity; people would go out of their way to see what the protesters had come up with, which was probably the point. *"Virtue preserved from fell destruction's blast! (Pericles)"* was the first one; the second was *"Cry woe, destruction, ruin, and decay! (Richard II)."* By the time the third one went up—*"And pale destruction meets thee in the face! (Henry VI, Part I)"*—I was convinced that it wasn't so much the work of a theater scholar as somebody with the complete works of Shakespeare on CD-ROM.

As it turned out, two could play at that game; after about a week, somebody ripped down one of the signs and replaced it with a banner that said *"Welcome destruction, death, and massacre! (Richard III)."* Underneath it was a big "A" inside a circle—the universal sign for anarchy. In Gabriel, even the local graffiti artist has a PhD.

Halloween finally came and went, bringing an end to the journalistic torpor. As usual, I hosted the annual newsroom monster mash; also as usual, Mad and O'Shaunessey refused to wear costumes, showing up with two cases of Rolling Rock and claiming to be dressed as traveling liquor salesmen.

"Great party, Bernier," Mad was saying, shouting to be heard over the dulcet tones of five dozen drunk people. "You sure know how to throw 'em."

"Steve was Mister Decoration," I said with a glance at the fake spiderwebs draped from every conceivable crevice. "I guess he went a little nuts."

Steve, a nocturnal migration specialist who works at the Benson ornithology lab, is our third roommate. There used to be two more, but the fourth dropped out of vet school last spring—right after the fifth was murdered. Splitting the rent three ways instead of five was just about bankrupting us, but nobody seemed to have the heart to admit that neither one of them was coming back.

". . . listening to me?"

"Huh?" I shook the cobwebs from my head, figuratively and literally. "What'd you say?"

"I said are you even listening to me?"

"Sorry. I kind of started thinking about Marci and C.A."

"Not a good idea maybe."

"Yeah."

"Well, um, it really is a great party."

He was right. The Rolling Stones's *Tattoo You*, always an essential ingredient to a good bash, was blaring at top volume. There was a crowd boogying shoulder-to-shoulder in the living room, where we'd pushed the furniture against the walls to make a dance floor. The food (eight kinds of cheese, a bucket of guacamole, and a gigantic pumpkin filled with fruit salad for the health conscious) seemed to be disappearing nicely. People were even playing Steve's dopey games, like the lobster pot he'd filled with water and three boxes of Trojans; it was on a table with a sign that said "BOBBING FOR CONDOMS."

Almost everyone had shown up in costume, some of them pretty elaborate. At the end of the night, Marilyn was supposed to stop necking with her husband long enough to give out the prizes. Steve had even dressed my dog Shakespeare in a Superman cape and Cody's dog Zeke in a Batman outfit, though they'd promptly torn them off each other and started ripping them to bits. I'd borrowed one of Cody's old sets of military fatigues and come as G.I. Jane, although the uniform was so big for me I basically looked like an idiot. (My friends from boarding school have yet to get over the fact that a peacenik like me is going out with, of all things, a former Navy SEAL.)

Cody, for his part, was dressed as some Boston Red Sock I'd never heard of, and the sight of his extremely attractive buns in a pair of baseball pants was making me slightly light-headed; then again, it may have been the sangria I'd been swilling all night. Either way, I had to admit that the mutual attraction hadn't slacked off one damn bit since the first day he kissed me in the kitchen, prompting me to drag him up to my bedroom and abandon a perfectly good omelet.

"Hey, baby," he said, wrapping his arms around me from behind and resting his chin on the top of my head. "Got any Guinness left?"

" 'Got any Guinness left, *sir.*' "

He gave a mock salute. "Sorry, Lieutenant."

"I'll let it go this time, soldier."

"Thirst makes me forget the chain of command."

"Good thing I hid your beer in the vegetable drawer."

"Brilliant woman." He gave my shoulders a quick little rub, pecked me on the cheek, and went off toward the kitchen. I felt in danger of an actual swoon.

For the record, I still haven't gotten used to dating someone who calls me "baby" on a regular basis—I'm a little worried that *Ms.* magazine is going to revoke my subscription—but from Cody it's so ridiculously sweet I've never gotten around to asking him to stop. Besides, when somebody practically gets himself killed trying to save you from a homicidal maniac, it seems to me he can call you anything he damn well wants.

"Christ, Bernier," Mad said when Cody was gone, "you got it bad."

"I do not."

"You should see yourself right now. You look like a goddamn advertisement for lust."

"I'm just drunk is all."

"Yeah, well, *in vino veritas* and everything."

"Oh, shut up."

"Why don't you two just get a room?"

"Mad, this is my house. I *have* a room."

"Right. Hey, you seen Emma anywhere?"

"So that's why you're picking on me."

"So have you seen her?"

I looked around. Emma is pretty tall, but I couldn't see her over any of the other heads. "She was around here a while ago. Did you two have a fight or something?"

"Nah. I mean, nothing big."

He was frowning into the dregs of his beer, and I realized I'd never seen him look at an alcoholic beverage quite so glumly. "What happened?" He didn't answer. "Come on, what is it? Did you try to book her up for the next five nights again or something?"

He scowled at his drink some more. "What's wrong with wanting to *see* the woman, anyway?" he said after a while. "Don't you chicks, you know, dig that kind of thing?"

It's hard to describe just how astonishingly weird it was to hear Mad complain that a woman wouldn't commit; the fact that we were surrounded by four radio reporters dressed as the Teenage Mutant Ninja Turtles made it only marginally more surreal. I figured now was not the time for levity. "You know, she's got a crazy schedule up at the vet school. She works three times as hard as you and me. Maybe she's just swamped. She probably needs some time to herself."

"You think?"

"Why don't you just ask her?"

"I . . . um . . . I tried. She says I talk about . . . relationship stuff too much."

"*You?*" I was trying very hard not to spit sangria all over his blue oxford. The temptation of cheap laughs was getting to be too much. "Don't go telling me *I'm* the one who's got it bad," I said, and considered it restraint.

I was plenty relieved when Cody came back; Mad would chop off his arm before he'd talk about his heartache in front of another guy. Furthermore, he was carrying two bottles of Guinness, which had to have a positive effect on Mad's mood.

"So what do you make of this?" I asked Cody, sloshing

my glass toward the macarena that, most lamentably, was forming in the middle of my living room. "You think it's really different from a cop thing?"

He gave me a smile that said *you have no idea*. "Cops tend to get loaded and talk about the job all night."

"Which is pretty much what's going on in this room."

"Yeah, but it's a different kind of job."

"Makes for a different kind of mood?"

"I'll say."

"Less testosterone. More . . ."

"Big words."

I laughed and kissed him on the lips. Out of the corner of my eye, I caught Mad sticking his tongue out at me over his beer bottle. "Would you two do me a favor and have a goddamn argument once in a while?" he said. "Oh, I forgot. You have nothing to fight about, because you have *absolutely nothing in common*."

It was one of the bitchiest things he'd ever said to me in public, and for a second I thought Cody might get pissed. Luckily, though, he decided just to clink bottles with him and say, "Secret to a perfect relationship."

Mad let out a defeated groan and proceeded to change the subject. "So, Bernier, you let Cody in on the Barry Marsh action?"

Cody raised his eyebrows at me. There I was, caught red-handed with my baser impulses. "It's kind of a betting pool we've got going in the newsroom," I said, "about, um, who he was popping the Viagra for."

"Jesus *Christ*. You guys are even worse than cops. So who's the favorite?"

"Guess."

"I'd say definitely not the wife."

"Although," Mad offered, "she's not a bad-looking older lady."

Cody had the good sense not to express an opinion.

"You're right," I said. "At this point, Lindy Marsh is a twenty-to-one long shot."

He took off his Red Sox cap, scratched at his apricot-colored hair, and put it back on again. "Cynthia Dillingham, right?"

I whacked him on the arm. "How'd you know?"

"I'm a highly trained policeman. Plus, when the chief asked Mrs. Marsh if she wanted him to call Mrs. Dillingham for her, she said, and I quote, 'I don't want that lying bitch anywhere near me.' "

"No way."

"She was upset. Lost control of herself."

"When was this?"

"Day he died."

"So you think he had the hots for Sissy?"

The subject of Sissy Dillingham's sex appeal was enough to make Mad stop sucking on his beer and speak up. "If he did, the guy was out of his gourd."

"Mad isn't Sissy's biggest fan," I said. "She doesn't get the hint. Keeps sniffing around. Poor Mad is scared to go within a mile of the chem department."

"Creating a hostile work environment, huh?" I stared at Cody. "Department sensitivity training. Want me to show you the difference between a good touch and a bad touch?"

"Later."

Mad reached between us to get some beer nuts off an end table. "So is your money on Sissy or what?"

"What're the odds?" Cody asked.

"Two to one."

"Way too short. And I'd bet against her anyway."

"Really?" I said. "So who?"

"I don't know many of the players, so I couldn't say.

Case turned out to be open-and-shut. I didn't really get into the personalities."

"Death by orgasm," I said. "What a way to go."

"Truth is, I doubt he had time to get his jollies off. But I'll tell you this much. Whoever it was, he must've wanted her pretty bad."

"How come?"

"Case is closed, so I guess it's no big deal." Cody drained his beer, put the bottle on the end table, and grabbed a handful of peanuts for himself. "We talked to his doctor. Marsh went to him for Viagra, but the doc wouldn't give it to him because of his heart condition. So Marsh goes and gets it over the Internet."

"How'd you know?"

"We found the bottle in his desk and tracked it down to an on-line drugstore in Kentucky. Charged it on his credit card and had it sent right to his office. Wife didn't even know he was on the juice. Pretty stupid."

"Not being a little sneakier?"

"Popping some drug your doctor said might kill you."

"Well, I guess the impotence thing wasn't working for him."

The two of them exchanged some inscrutably manly look, then took an intense interest in their beer nuts.

"You know," Mad said finally, "I think I'm going to go look around for Emma."

The party finally wound down around two. Mad, never having found his date, eventually put his tail between his legs and walked home alone. Cody helped me clean up for a while, and we repaired to my bedroom for the best part of any Halloween party: costume removal.

"You know," he was saying as he unbuttoned my olive-green shirt and found something black and lacy underneath, "I think I had this exact fantasy in boot camp."

"Really?" I was trying to sound all sexy and sly. "Want me to leave the hat on?"

"Um, actually, yeah."

He leaned in to kiss me, and the bills of our caps knocked into each other; so much for my smooth moves. I threw his Red Sox hat onto a chair and pulled his baseball shirt over his head. His skin was white and freckly like a little boy's, but the muscles underneath made up for a lot. "Who are you supposed to be again?"

"Bernie Carbo."

"Who's he?"

"On the Sox from '74 to '78. Hit a three-run homer in game six of the '75 series against the Reds."

"They win?"

"The game. Not the series."

"So why are you so high on him?"

"He had his moment of glory. Not everybody does."

"So," I said after some more removing of garments, "I take it this means you think you're gonna score tonight?"

"Baby," he said, "I was kind of hoping for a triple."

5

SISSY DILLINGHAM LIVED IN THE SORT OF HOUSE PEOPLE LIKE
to call a "showplace." Unfortunately, it wasn't a show I particularly wanted to see. It was located on a big corner lot in
the Heights, Gabriel's priciest neighborhood. Some of the
houses up there are rather modest—let's face it, even Bev-
erly Hills has its version of the slums—but there are plenty
of long, wide streets lined with one mansion after another.
Not one of them dates from before the twenties, but their
owners go to great lengths to make them seem ancient. It all
comes off as fake, though, because the designs are from
wildly different periods—as if Tara had been built next door
to Cinderella's house and across the street from Dracula's
castle.

Chez Dillingham, in fact, would have done quite well as
Scarlett O'Hara's summer place. It had enormous white
columns out front, and topiary shaped like pineapples, and a
couple of springer spaniels running around inside an invisible fence. Indoors, it was decorated within an inch of its life,
stuffed to the proverbial gills with elegant frippery. I know
because I got the grand tour, which took almost an hour.

I'd been summoned to the house because Sissy and her
cohorts were dying to tell me about their plans to save the

Starlight; the *Town & Country* bit was an unexpected bonus. As we went from room to room, I got kind of desperate to find a flaw—a crooked picture, some dust on the chandeliers, a misaligned tie-back, *anything*—but I couldn't find so much as a slipcover out of place. Frankly, it all struck me as kind of . . . sad. Maybe it's just the sour grapes of someone who still transports her earthly belongings from rental to rental in garbage bags. But it seemed to me that by all that's holy, no human female should have so much time on her hands that she feels compelled to coordinate her valances with her napkin rings.

The walls were painted in warm-but-muted shades, and every single room had either stenciling or a paper border. The kitchen had one of those zillion-dollar Sub Zero refrigerators and an actual restaurant-quality Vulcan stove, which (okay, I admit it) made me mad with desire. The dish soap by the sink was in a tall crystal decanter instead of a plastic bottle, and inside the glass-doored cupboards I saw the gilded edges of what looked like service for fifty.

If you were thinking things got more modest up in the boudoir, think again. The master bedroom was too girlie even for me, with lace and ribbons and cabbage roses all over the place; how Sissy's husband got a decent night's sleep in there was beyond me. And as for the children's rooms, well . . . you had to see them to believe them.

The daughter's looked like somebody had ripped Fantasyland out of Disney World and plopped it down in Benson Heights. There was a mural of a medieval landscape along one wall, with a bas relief of a castle tower sticking out of it. The bed had layer upon layer of gauzy material swooping down from the canopy, and one of those conical Guinevere hats at each corner. The boy's had the same sort of wretched excess, except the theme was Major League Baseball— complete with stadium mural and bats where the bedposts ought to be. The clock was shaped like a scoreboard, with the home team perpetually winning 7–0.

Once we'd dutifully ooh-ed and ah-ed, we settled in the living room around a big platter of dainty snackables. Present and accounted for were: Sissy, Madeline Hoover, Adele Giordano-Bronstein, Ivy Bator, Bunny Roberts, and Charmaine Donaldson-Merke. I'd never actually met the last three before, and since they looked and sounded so much alike I had to resort to the old reporter's trick of recording their quotes according to what color shirts they were wearing (Ivy was BLU, Bunny was PNK, Charmaine was WHT) and matching the names up later.

Sissy started the meeting off with a little pep talk about how they'd all done a ton of charitable work before, but that this project was "absolutely, without question, the most important thing any of us will ever be involved in." (I had a feeling the AIDS Walk people would disagree with her.) Then she went around the room and had each one of them say why she thought the theater should be saved, and when they were done she said something about how she hoped my story would include "each individual perspective."

The meeting went on like that for a while, Sissy and her chorus singing the same old song while I took notes and ate far too many cherry tomatoes stuffed with blue cheese and pignoli. Finally it came to the point where they expected me to ask some questions, and since I'd spent the afternoon as a glorified (albeit well-fed) stenographer, I was damned if I was going to lob a softball.

"Actually, Mrs. Dillingham, there's something I've been wondering about," I said. "Save Our Starlight's been around for, what, a year? Why are you so . . . passionate about it all of a sudden?"

I hadn't meant to send her around the bend, but apparently I did a pretty good job of it. The color rushed into her face faster than you'd think the laws of physics would allow; she looked like somebody had stapled one of the miniature tomatoes to each cheek. She started to answer, then stopped and started again three separate times before she made it all the way through the sentence—and even then it was slow going. "The, um, the . . . The Starlight is . . . Things are different now. The theater is . . . It's being threatened as never before."

"But it's been heading in this direction for years, hasn't it?"

"Perhaps. Well, yes, I suppose it has. But none of us . . . We never . . . No one ever thought it would come to this."

"You mean you never thought the city'd actually sell it?"

"That's right."

"But I don't understand. If Mr. Marsh hadn't died, the sale would have happened three months ago. Wouldn't it?"

She didn't answer, just sat there with her mouth agape. I could tell from the sour looks around the coffee table that they wanted to toss me out on my ear. Adele Giordano-Bronstein seemed about to say something to that effect when Sissy finally spoke up.

"Barry Marsh was *thoroughly* dedicated to saving this theater." She seemed like she was about to bawl, but she kept talking. All of a sudden, I felt like three different kinds of fink. "And now that he's no longer with us, we all feel a . . . special duty to keep his dream alive. Can you understand that?"

"Um, sure . . ."

"And one thing that Barry . . . that Mr. Marsh understood very well was that public opinion is essential. Unless the people of Gabriel rally around the cause, the theater will . . ." She clearly didn't want to think about the what-ifs. "We simply have to have public opinion on our side, that's all. We simply have to."

Adele saw her opening, and jumped in. "Please, Alex, you have to help us," she said, leaning forward to touch me on the knee. "I don't think you understand how much of this is in your hands."

"What?"

"You have the power to make this happen. You can help us get people excited, raise their consciousness, focus their energy . . ."

She sounded like she was running a goddamn Scientology seminar. "No offense, Mrs. Bronstein, but that's really not my role."

"But it could be. This Wednesday's council meeting is *so* important to us. Surely if you wrote an article emphasizing that the theater would be an essental part of—"

"Look, I'm really not allowed to take sides here."

"But this is a community *service*." She seemed to like the sound of that, so she said it again. "Saving the theater is a community service. Don't you think so?"

"Well, there's sort of a difference of opinion about that at the moment."

"I'm sure I don't know what you mean."

"The fire chief thinks it's a safety hazard, for one."

"But not if it's restored," Madeline offered. "He just doesn't want it to stay abandoned. Well, neither do we."

"I'm sorry, but I don't really get what you think I should do."

Adele leaned forward again, and I got a noseful of Giorgio along with her zeal. "Can't you just . . . accentuate the positive? Point out all the potential benefits to the community?"

"Don't you think the paper has given your side a fair shake?"

"It's not that," Adele said with a grim little smile. "It's just that with the developer having so much pull, we . . ."

"Pull with whom?"

"Well, he does advertise his rental properties in the paper every single day. Surely that has to have some influence on . . ."

"It does *not*."

Bunny Roberts put down the raspberry linzer cookie she'd been nibbling on and arched a well-plucked eyebrow at me. "Are you seriously telling us that your stories are wholly unaffected by Kurtis Osmond's"—she cast about for the right word, then pounced on it—"*contribution* to your advertising revenue?"

"Look, I have no idea who advertises what, and frankly I couldn't care less."

"Well," Bunny said in a tone that made it abundantly clear she thought I was full of it, "I'm sure we're all very relieved to hear that."

"Listen, I don't mean to be rude, but I gotta tell you that whenever you cover something like this, everybody always thinks the other side got the better end of things. I'm sure if you asked Mr. Osmond, he'd think the paper has been giving S.O.S. way too much play. In my experience, that means we're being fair."

I don't know what they thought of my little speech, because right after it came out of my mouth the front door flew open and in walked Sissy Dillingham's kids. They must have been close together in age—twins maybe—because they both looked on the cusp of adolescence. They had matching European-style bookbags and beleaguered expressions, and although their mother said something bright like "Hello, darlings," they blew right by her and into the kitchen without so much as a glance. I was starting to see why she poured her heart and soul into the wainscoting.

The meeting broke up a few minutes later, which wasn't soon enough for me. I fled through Sissy's "mud room," out the side door, and into my crappy-but-faithful Renault before any of them could try to talk me into writing their press releases for them. As I drove down her back driveway (what she'd called the "everyday entrance") I tried to picture myself living there, and couldn't. It wasn't a question of money; my parents aren't exactly on the dole. It was more like, well, *suffocation*. There was something about Sissy Dillingham's house that seemed more stage set than home, and more—yes, that was it—way more dead than alive.

The first thing I did when I got back to the paper was pick up the phone and call Kurtis Osmond.

This, of course, was the prototypical journalist's reaction to Sissy and her cohorts trying to convince me to join up and take the pledge. *Try to influence me, will you! Well just watch while I go interview the other guy!*

Truth was, though, if the paper had been biased it'd been in favor of the Starlight-savers. It probably wasn't surprising that the prevailing sentiment had crept into our news pages; after all, Osmond is Gabriel's most-hated landlord—a man who, I've been told, likes to get dressed up in his Italian suits and ride along with the sheriff on eviction runs.

So in the name of journalistic integrity (the fact that I'd get to stick it to the S.O.S. folks was just a fringe benefit, I swear), I set up an interview with Osmond. I'd gotten his side of the story in dribs and drabs, but if I was going to do a piece for Wednesday morning's paper—an advance on the council meeting that night—I figured I'd better talk to him in person.

Osmond is notorious for being the college-town version of a slumlord. He buys one-family houses near Benson and Bessler, carves them up into as many apartments as the law allows, and rents them out to students—whereupon they devolve into unsightly wrecks with ratty couches on the porches, and the property values go *plop*. Then, of course, he gets to buy the adjacent houses for a song, and . . . well, you get the idea.

In addition to the academic flophouses, Osmond owns a couple of ultra-fancy apartment buildings that take advantage of the fact that a lot of foreign students have both money to burn and parents who think Gabriel is located just north of Harlem. And as if that weren't enough, he also holds the leases on half the stores on the Green—the astronomical rents being a major reason why the average business survives less than two years. The general consensus is that if Kurtis Osmond weren't so obsessed with making a quick buck, the downtown economy would be in a hell of a lot better shape, a working-class family could afford a decent apartment, and there would be an end to war and world hunger.

Nobody likes him.

He is, I must admit, one smooth character; if he weren't such a creep I might think of him as an Attractive Older Man. He has icy blue eyes, and a wide mouth with lots of white teeth in it, and (this is kind of icky) longish salt-and-pepper hair that he slicks back over his head. His camel-hair coat always looks immaculate, even during the spring mud festival, and his business cards look like they cost a pretty penny. And no; as far as I know, he isn't related to Donny and Marie.

His secretary was less than enthusiastic when I told her I was from the *Monitor*, which was no big shock; when we come a-knocking, it usually means somebody is suing him. It took me a while to convince her I wasn't doing an exposé on his latest mass eviction, but once I got the point across she said he'd see me in half an hour.

Osmond's office is smack in the center of the Green—right across the street from the building where Barry Marsh met his final reward, as a matter of fact. He has big glass windows that look down on the slacking masses, and a gigantic air conditioner that rains bucketloads of condensation in the summer, which is probably the closest some of them ever get to a bath.

The first thing he did when I walked into his lair was offer me a shot of espresso, which he made using individual slugs of Italian grounds he loaded into the machine. It was, predictably enough, damn tasty; when you're charging $750 a month for a one-bedroom, you can afford really good coffee. The second thing he did was tell me how much he admired my movie column. This was either evidence of his excellent taste, or another method for weaseling into my good graces.

"I'm thrilled to bits your paper is finally taking an interest in my little project," he said once he'd plied me with caffeine and anisette biscotti. "But I gotta ask . . . What's the catch?"

"Catch?"

"Your city editor—what's his name?"

"Bill Densmore."

"Right. The man's never made a secret of the fact he thinks I'm a no-goodnik. Am I wrong?"

"Mr. Osmond, I . . ."

"Am I wrong?"

Oh, what the hell. "Mr. Osmond, if there's anybody in this town who *doesn't* think you're a no-goodnik, it's news to me."

He smiled, and although it was probably an optical illusion, I could swear his teeth got bigger. "Ah. So you're a pistol."

"Excuse me?"

"You didn't just come here to kiss my ass."

"What gave you that impression?"

"People generally come here for one of two reasons. They either break my balls, or they kiss my ass. My secretary informed me that you weren't here to break my balls, so I figured you must be here to kiss my ass."

"And why exactly would I do that?"

"Who knows? Everybody wants something."

"So you want to know why I'm here?"

"Baby," he said, with none of Cody's niceness, "I'm all ears."

"Could you do me the favor of not calling me 'baby'?"

"Whoa, you *are* a pistol."

I was on the point of asking him what precisely that meant, but I decided to skip it. "I'm doing a story for Wednesday's paper, an advance on the city council meeting. I already talked to the Save Our Starlight people, so I thought I'd come over here and . . ."

"And pay me lip service."

"And get your side of the story. For the record."

"For the record"—he tossed back his espresso and smacked his lips—"I intend to tear down that ugly son of a bitch of a building, and put up some damn pretty little condos. You might want to rent one of them. I'll give you a deal even."

"Thanks, but I'm not the condo type."

"And just what type is that?"

"I like houses."

"You married?"

"No."

"Kids?"

"No. What the—"

"Then what do you want a house for?"

"My dog prefers it."

"Ah, too bad. All my buildings are no pets."

"So I've heard."

"So what was it you wanted from me again?"

"Your plans for the Starlight property."

"Right. We're gonna tear that fucker down."

"And . . . ?"

"And build forty gorgeous little units. Balconies, laundry, goddamn Internet access. Penthouse is gonna be mine."

"Well, can you at least understand why some people in town are upset about you wanting to tear it down?"

He snorted, not a pleasant sound. "Story of my life. No matter what you do, there's always naysayers."

"But, well, isn't this one a little different? I mean, the Starlight is a historic landmark . . ."

Again with the snorting. "So you *did* come here to break my balls."

"You know, for a man who dresses pretty well, you sure talk like a lowlife."

That cracked him up. "And this offends a Vassar broad such as yourself?"

"How did you . . . ?"

"I do my research. I'm not some dumb hump who just fell off the concrete mixer."

"Nobody said you were."

"Yeah, well, they better not."

"So . . . what are you going to do if S.O.S. comes up with enough money to get the city to—"

"Never gonna happen."

"How can you be so sure?"

"When you've been in this game as long as I have, you learn a few things. Those preservation types make a lotta noise, but when push comes to shove they never get the lettuce."

"The what?"

"The lettuce. The green. The *money*."

"Oh. So you're not worried?"

"Let's just say I'm not losing sleep over it. We done here?"

"Um, I guess so." I got up to go.

"Hey, you and me should go out some time."

"Are you serious?"

"Yeah, you're a pistol."

"Yeah, and my boyfriend carries one."

The teeth got even bigger. "Right, you're with that big-city cop. I heard that."

"So long, Mr. Osmond."

"Call me Kurt. I insist. Hey," he said as I was about to walk out the door, "you know what that Dorothy Parker said about you Vassar broads?"

Jesus Christ. In this town, even the slumlords read The New Yorker.

"Come on, don't be a killjoy. Do you know?"

"Yeah, but it's a misquote. She really said it about the girls at the Yale Pr—"

" 'If every Vassar girl were laid end to end,' " I heard him say as I escaped down the hall, " 'I wouldn't be surprised.' "

6

IF YOU EVER DOUBT THE ADAGE THAT "ALL POLITICS IS LOCAL,"
check out the Gabriel city council some Wednesday night.
Its twice-monthly meetings, held in the council chambers on
the third floor of City Hall, are a civic addiction—and a
spectacle roughly akin to pro wrestling. They've been
broadcast on the government-access channel for the past
couple of years, and I know of a half-dozen bars (including,
of course, the Citizen Kane) where they monitor the action
on wide-screen TV, and sell more liquor than they do during
Monday Night Football.

The meetings, which can last anywhere from three to five
hours, are often exasperating, occasionally vicious, and *always* behind schedule; what they never are is dull. Even
when the topic at hand is the maintenance of municipal
storm drains, there's always someone with their knickers in
a twist. Maybe it's an environmental angle, or labor rights,
or a town-gown thing—everybody on council has his political pet peeve. By all that's holy, this should get pretty damn
tiresome. But there's something exciting about the sheer
predictability of it all. It's preordained, for example, that Joe
Kingman (a Benson law professor, Democratic councilman,
and perennial thorn in the establishment's derriere) is going

to turn everything into a debate about social justice. But how, one wonders beforehand, is he going to apply it to a vote on repainting school crosswalks?

Council, in other words, is quite a hoot even when it's business as usual. When there's anything remotely interesting going on, the atmosphere is positively festive. And during the Save Our Starlight episode, it was a goddamn Vegas floor show, complete with (literal) dancing girls and a (figurative) effort to pull a rabbit out of a hat.

That first Wednesday in November, it was also a mob scene. I'd never seen so many people packed into the council chambers, not even during the screaming fights of the now-fabled youth curfew debate a year or so before. All the S.O.S. hoopla had drawn upward of two hundred people— so many, in fact, that for the first time in living memory the fire chief invoked the posted occupancy limit of a hundred and sixty-eight, and several dozen Starlight fans were reduced to watching the action on cable.

The room was veritably sizzling with anticipation. All week, Sissy Dillingham and her cohorts had been hinting that they had some sort of ace in the hole, a surefire scheme to save the theater. They hadn't told the mayor what it was, and they sure as hell hadn't told me. So there we all were, on the edge of our orange plastic seats (courtesy of the same sort of seventies-era redecoration that had made everything in the *Monitor* newsroom a lovely shade of mustard) and looking at a two-hour wait before the issue even came up for discussion.

Luckily, though, one of the more practical types on council suggested they switch the Starlight to the top of the agenda, and the rumble of glee that ran through the crowd let the rest of the aldermen know that they'd better agree to it or else. Madeline Hoover, who'd served on the board of Historic Gabriel for years but had to resign her seat when she was elected to council, made a motion to reopen discussion of the Starlight sale. Joe Kingman seconded it, and Mayor Martin Anbinder—who runs the meetings under what's technically a "common council" system—invited Sissy Dillingham to come to the podium.

She just stood there a while as the room fell silent, shuffling her index cards and savoring the moment. That gave everyone in the room the chance to admire her outfit, which was plenty expensive. She wore an indigo wool dress, cut demurely below the knee; simple but classy. Around her shoulders was a bloodred pashmina shawl that definitely cost more than my car, held together by a brooch shaped like comedy-and-tragedy masks. It was gold with diamonds in the eyes, and the size of a baked potato. Her bag matched her shoes, which is something that's never happened to me personally. I was willing to bet that if she felt compelled to strip naked, her panties would be the same color as her bra. Wow.

"You may wonder why we should save the Starlight Theatre," she began, sounding stiff and way more nervous than I would have thought. "The Starlight Theatre belongs to all of us. It is a vital part of Gabriel's artistic heritage. For nearly a century, actors, dancers, and musicians have entertained people under its roof. It is, um . . ." She'd accidentally skipped an index card, and had to pause until she found the right one. "It is vital to Gabriel's economic health. Imagine the crowds that will flock to witness the glory of a restored Starlight Theatre. Imagine the benefit this will have on the local economy . . ."

It was an astoundingly bad speech, one that had been written and rewritten until all the heart had been scraped out of it with a soup spoon. What's worse, Sissy—of all people—seemed to be cracking under the pressure. I hadn't heard such lame public speaking since Marilyn made me volunteer as a judge for the Gabriel High Forensics Jam.

I looked around the rectangular table that serves as the council's press gallery, and caught the eye of the bearded guy who's been covering government for the weekly *Gabriel Advocate* since the dawn of time. He crossed his eyes and bit his tongue for a millisecond, and I had to clap my hand over my mouth to stop from laughing out loud. I wrinkled my nose back at him, my angry rabbit impression. In the corner, two radio reporters started playing Hangman.

". . . will promote cultural unity, bringing together both young and old," Sissy was saying when I started listening again. "Lovers of the performing arts will come from miles around to see the golden age of vaudeville restored to its former glory. But we do not only have dreams for restoring this beautiful theater. We also have definite plans for how to do so. I have here in my hand a list . . ."

She waved a piece of paper, blissfully unaware of the McCarthy reference. I caught a few snickers as other people got the joke; even Mayor Marty, who's witnessed plenty of freak shows during his five years in office, seemed in danger of busting a corpuscle.

". . . A list of no fewer than seven local performing arts groups who have pledged to perform each and every one of their performances at the Starlight Theatre. These include the Mohawk Chamber Orchestra, the Benson Savoyards, the Pennywhistle Players, and the annual Gabriel High School talent show."

That made my ears perk up. Conspicuously absent was the one organization that had rallied behind the Starlight early on: the Gabriel Ballet, whose annual production of *The Nutcracker* might actually get some butts in the seats—but whose board chair was none other than Lindy Marsh. Interesting.

"In conclusion," Sissy Dillingham said in a voice faltering from the emotion of it all, "the Starlight Theatre is vital to the future of this community. It is the heart and soul of Gabriel, New York. We must not allow this precious resource to be destroyed."

She sat down, inspiring a rather stupefied silence. The same question was on every face in the room: *Was that it?* By my count, her speech had included three separate uses of the word "vital," and exactly nothing useful in saving the Starlight. If she thought a commitment by the Pennywhistle Players (a children's theater troupe that makes all its sets, props, and costumes out of *objets trouvés*) was going to do the job, she was in for a blind date with the wrecking ball.

Then the quiet was broken by a squeal. Sissy shot to her feet and ran back to the podium, face as red as her six-million-dollar shawl. "Ooooh! I forgot the most important part!" Her elegant diction was gone, and her composure, which had been precarious to begin with, was shot to hell. She cleared her throat and tried to get it back, frisking herself for the index cards before realizing she'd shoved them into her purse and left it by her chair. She retrieved them, cleared her throat again, and started reading. "In conclusion, the Starlight Theatre is vital to . . ." She caught herself and skipped to the next card. "But just like George Bailey in *It's a Wonderful Life*, the Starlight has a guardian angel this holiday season. An anonymous donor has pledged two hundred fifty thousand dollars to insure that this vital link to our artistic heritage will be preserved for future generations."

That sent a hundred and forty pairs of hands to clapping—my rough estimate after subtracting the elected officials, the press, and the few Starlight opponents who'd dared to show their faces. The mayor banged his gavel, which always seemed to make him feel like he was actually in charge of something. Then there was some organizational shuffling from the peanut gallery, and the next thing we knew a chorus of children dressed in Save Our Starlight T-shirts was lined up next to the podium. They opened their little mouths and sang to the tune of the most cloying song in the history of musical theater: "Tomorrow," from *Annie*.

I wrote down the chorus, because it was my damn job.

"The Starlight, the Starlight,
We all love the Starlight.
Please don't take our dream away."

I glanced around the press table again. The radio guys were still playing Hangman, and the word they were working on was "VOMIT." They did, however, pause long enough to note the counter numbers on their tape recorders; three guesses what was going to hit the airwaves at eleven.

The mayor thanked the kids, gritted his teeth, and opened the issue up for public comment. A groan rippled through the room when he announced that each speaker would be limited to one minute—although said groan stopped well short of the press corps. A line started forming behind the podium; within seconds it stretched to the back of the chamber and started snaking along the walls, mercifully blocking the hideous allegorical mural (entitled *Our Gabriel*) that was the legacy of some bloody-minded teacher at the alternative high school.

I caught Mayor Marty reaching for the Pepto-Bismol tablets he keeps in his jacket pocket. He caught me catching him, gave me a good-natured wink, and popped two pink pills into his mouth.

Predictably, the first few speakers tested the waters of the mayor's sixty-second decree—and found that he was dead serious. What followed was a reasonably well-behaved and overwhelmingly repetitive series of pleas to save the theater, delivered by everyone you'd expect. There were representatives of all the arts groups Sissy had mentioned, plus a few more; historic preservationists from both town and gown; civic boosters, one of whom used the word "dandy" even more times than Sissy had used "vital." The usual public-comment suspects—the ones who say something at every meeting, regardless of the topic, and always sound like they've forgotten to take their medication—were also present and accounted for, looking a little dazed by the size of their audience.

Exactly two people spoke against waiting any longer to demolish the theater. One was the fire chief, and the other was Kurtis Osmond.

When it was over—a good forty-five minutes and twenty-three Hangman games later—the mayor closed the comment period and opened it up for council discussion. Madeline Hoover spoke passionately about how too many upstate cities had demolished their history in the name of progress, and Joe Kingman was just getting on a tear about how the developer was both a union buster *and* an oppressor of the common man when Mayor Marty shut him up before he said something actionable on the public record.

It went on like that for another hour, until they finally ran out of things to say. Then Alderman Jerry Abbott—who always lets everyone else put their cards on the table before he says a word—leaned back in his chair and spoke as though he were delivering news from the mountaintop.

"What I want to know," he said in a slow baritone, "is just who the heck this anonymous donor is."

All eyes turned to Sissy Dillingham, who stood up and gaped at him. "But he's . . . *annonymous.*"

Abbott, who teaches history at Bessler College—and, like the rest of the faculty over at Benson's idiot stepcousin, has something of a Napoleon complex about it—gave her a look that said she was the biggest loser he'd ever clapped his eyes on.

"But . . ." she stammered, clutching her pricey purse in front of her like it was made of Kevlar. "That means he doesn't want anyone to know who he is."

"We all know what 'anonymous' means," Abbott said. "But at this point, council is not inclined to play games."

"Games . . . ?"

"Frankly," he said, "I have to tell you that I don't entirely believe that this person exists."

That did it. A collective hiss spread through the Save Our Starlight contingent, and Sissy Dillingham's righteous indignation kicked in with a vengeance. "How *dare* you?" she spat at him. "Are you calling me a *liar*?"

"Well, no . . ." he began. "But you have to admit that—"

"Admit *what*? That you people are content to sit here and let a beautiful old building disappear because you're too *incompetent* to do anything about it?"

"Now just wait a minute . . ." he stammered. The mood over at the press table was improving rapidly. Abbott is a real pill most of the time—judgmental, self-righteous, an all-around insufferable jerk—and seeing him at a loss for words was quite the early Christmas present.

"I will have you know," Sissy Dillingham was saying, "that this anonymous benefactor is *a very important person* in the international arts community." Her words were clipped, precise, with sharp edges on every side. I wondered if we were seeing what it was like to be some poor shoe salesman who had to tell her he was out of the Ferragamos she wanted. "He is someone who *cares* about the future of local theater. And although he prefers to keep his name out of this because he is a very *humble* person despite all of his accomplishments, he has told me that if council requires him to step forward, he will do so."

"Well then," Abbott said, trying very hard to sound as if he'd just won the argument, "who is it?"

Sissy paused for a moment, and when she opened her mouth she sounded very much like Alistair Cooke. It wasn't her, of course; it was a man sitting in the back row who had really good projection. And what he said, in a voice even more imperious than hers, was this:

"It is I!"

I'm not kidding.

Whoever he was, he'd been delivered directly from Central Casting—though for what production, I couldn't exactly say. The man who emerged from the back row was a character the likes of which the Gabriel council chamber had never seen. And it's seen a lot.

He didn't walk, he wheeled. Or rather, he *was* wheeled, in an old-fashioned chair with a high woven back pushed by one of the S.O.S. minions. The guy sitting in it was at least eighty years old—and that was assuming he hadn't had a face lift, which I got the feeling he had from the stretchy look his skin had in all the wrong places. He wore a black evening jacket with a burgundy silk scarf and matching pocket square; atop his head was a little oriental cap like you see millionaires wear in old movies. The whole outfit was immaculate except for the black wool blanket across his knees, which had an oval of white fur exactly where a cat would go.

He had his handler put him dead center in front of the council table, so he was directly across from the mayor. The volunteer from the cable-access station scrambled to reposition the video camera that had been focused on the podium, and the man just sat there until the red tally light went on.

When he spoke, his accent wasn't quite British, but not American either. The only word I can think of to describe it is *theatrical*.

"Good evening," he said, stretching out the last word to three syllables. *Ee-ven-ing.* "No doubt, many of you already know me." I looked to my pals in the press and got blank stares all around. A couple of the councilmen were nodding, though, and the mayor looked like he'd just acquired a really bad toothache. "But for those who don't"—he made this sound like the worst sort of bad fortune—"please allow me to introduce myself. My name is Robert Renssellaer. I am an actor." He pronounced it "act-*or*," making it sound slightly superior to *brain surge-on*. "No doubt you remember me from . . ."

He launched into a list of movies I'd never heard of. It wasn't until hours later—after the aldermen had finally agreed to postpone the Starlight vote until December, to give S.O.S. the chance to raise the rest of the half million— I finally figured out why the name Robert Renssellaer was vaguely familiar.

A couple of weeks before, when Cody and I were spending a rare night apart and I couldn't sleep, I'd caught part of a dreadful old flick on cable. It was three in the morning, and my only other choices were a monster truck rally and an infomercial for spray-on hair. So, in an insomniacal haze, I'd watched a grainy black-and-white print of *Fluffy, My Pal* on some channel that (as far as I was concerned) was devoted entirely to films nobody ever picks up at the video store.

I don't remember much about the movie, except for these three things: it had something to do with a beautiful blond boy and his spunky Pomeranian; it starred someone named Robbie Renssellaer Jr.; and although the kid got top billing, the dog was by far the better actor.

7

By Thanksgiving, Sissy Dillingham and her Starlight-
savers were going whole-hog. They held bake sales, where
volunteers hawked (admittedly quite tasty) sugar cookies
shaped like little theaters. They inundated the editorial pages
of both the *Monitor* and the *Advocate* with letters and opinion pieces. They held so many rallies, you couldn't swing a
dead cat around your head without hitting someone with an
S.O.S. sign. And on one eternally memorable Friday afternoon, the entire Gabriel Belly Dancing Cooperative clogged
traffic on State Street with an interpretive work entitled
"The Starlight Forever."

On Thanksgiving itself, when I was working as holiday
reporter, S.O.S. staged a benefit feast at the Greater Gabriel
Girls' Club. I had to cover it as part of the *Monitor*'s annual
Turkey-Tofu Day Roundup—which is how I wound up sam-
pling stuffed Hubbard squash with Sissy, who was dressed
for a date with Miles Standish. I'd expected the event to
draw the usual S.O.S. characters and pretty much no one
else, but the place was packed to the gills. Even Lindy
Marsh was there, sitting as far from Sissy as possible but apparently having an okay time with the head choreographer

from the Ballet Guild. The woman was really starting to confuse me.

Tickets to the feast were thirty dollars a person, and according to Sissy they'd fed nearly five hundred. Conservatively, that meant they'd netted over ten thousand dollars. Maybe the S.O.S. folks might actually pull it off, I thought; the theater might not be rubble by Christmas Eve after all.

I made my escape from the girls' club by three, filed my story, did the usual round of cop calls to make sure I wasn't missing any good mayhem, and fled down the back stairs to my Renault. Then I remembered I'd left the flowers for Cody's mom in the newsroom refrigerator, so I fled back up again. It was a little after four when I showed up on her doorstep, half an hour late and madly brushing dog hair off my pea coat.

He answered the door, which gave me the chance to sputter my apologies in relative privacy. "It's no big deal," he said as he plucked off my coat. "Her son's a cop. She's used to it by now."

The entire Cody clan was spread out in the living room, and I felt like I'd stumbled into a meeting of the Irish Tourist Board. There were exactly two people present who didn't have red hair, and I was one of them. There was his older sister Margaret, her husband Josh (mercifully a brunet), and their three carrot-topped moppets. Cody's younger sister Deirdre was sitting on the floor, doing a Cookie Monster puzzle with a little girl who resembled a Hibernian Botticelli. And Deirdre's new fiancé, a fellow countryman who looked so much like Cody they might have been brothers, was hanging one of Margaret's little boys upside-down by his ankles.

I went into the kitchen to give Cody's mom the flowers and see if I could help her with dinner, which of course she wouldn't let me do, so I told her how great everything smelled and escaped back to the living room.

I've been dating Cody for over four months, and his mom has never been anything but super nice to me. But there's something about her that makes me a tad uncomfortable, and it took me about two seconds after I met her to realize what it is.

The woman is a domestic paragon. I have never seen a molecule of dirt in her house. Her food is prepared to utter perfection, her clothes are immaculately pressed, and her whole demeanor is something of the benevolent goddess.

I'm not quite sure how to relate to her.

Cody says his mother likes me just fine, though. Apparently she's filed me under "career girl," decided she'll never understand me, and left it at that. That I eat all the food on my plate and ask for seconds doesn't hurt either. Also, I have the benefit of not being Cody's ex-wife, a woman his mother hated on sight—and who, after playing the devoted spouse for a year or so, dumped him for his lieutenant.

Unsurprisingly, dinner was fantastic. Mary Cody doesn't believe in scrimping on butter and cream—not something I'm used to, having a mother who orders her toast dry, and who once trained for (and ran) the Boston Marathon on a dare. Everybody tried to feed me turkey at least once, not out of antivegetarian malice but because they'd looked at my plate and assumed I'd already finished mine. For dessert, there were three kinds of pie—pumpkin, apple, and chocolate-pecan—and the general consensus was that you were breaking tradition if you didn't have at least a piece of each.

The Codys are an unusual family: they actually enjoy spending time together. After dinner we all sat around the living room, sipping Baileys and playing charades and singing along with Deirdre on the piano. The kids started getting less angelic as the night wore on, and finally Margaret and her husband picked them up and hustled them off to bed. The grown-ups came back down in their pajamas half an hour later, and Deirdre made a happy little chirping sound and went in search of hers. Within minutes there were Codys draped in front of the fireplace in their nightclothes, sipping hot cocoa and making faces and giggling at each other.

Not one of them was espousing a political philosophy that inspired a brawl and the tossing of cranberry sauce. No one was complaining that the National Organization for Women had gone so soft it might as well be the Future Homemakers of America. Nobody used the word "cretin," not even once.

This was a strange holiday indeed. Either the Codys were the happiest family in the world, or Rod Serling was about to walk in and make a speech.

"How late do you think this is going to go?" I whispered to my date.

He smiled, looking as blissful as I'd ever seen him with his clothes on. "I'd say all night."

"Too bad you didn't bring your pj's."

"Mom keeps a pair here for me."

"Yikes. I think this may be my cue to exit."

"You don't have to, you know."

"I better go home and let the dogs out." I was taking care of Emma's standard poodle ("Tipsy") while she was spending the holiday in Philadelphia, in addition to the canine lovebirds Shakespeare and Zeke. "Besides, I have to deliver their care package from your mom. Yummy turkey parts."

"You don't mind?"

"Course not. Have fun with everybody. But if you end up singing 'When Irish Eyes Are Smiling,' please don't tell me about it later."

"I, um, thought I might spend the night."

"I kind of hoped you didn't plan on driving home in your jammies."

He gave me a weirdly assessing look. It was an expression I hadn't seen since we were first getting to know each other, sizing each other up across the cop-reporter frontier. "You really don't mind?"

"Christ, Cody, why would I?" He didn't answer, but I had a guess. "It's a Lucy thing, huh?"

"Ancient history."

"Apparently not."

"Well . . . she always found the family thing kind of threatening. Like she didn't want to compete."

"Then it's a damn good thing I'm such a saint. A normal woman would try to tear you away from the sisters you never get to see."

"I'm not kidding."

"Yeah, well, I am." I kissed him on the cheek, which I hoped was demure enough to pass muster with his mom. "Now go put on your pj's before I change my mind and decide to have a tantrum."

And with that, I went home to share my bed with twelve paws and three tails.

The next day, when most of civilization was anticipating the Messiah's birth by jockeying for parking places at the mall, I was stuck in a meeting with Bill, Marilyn, and our much-despised publisher, Chester. The topic, lamentably, was our coverage of the Starlight Theatre—specifically, that we didn't have enough of it. He had to be out of his tree.

"We are a community newspaper," he was saying, "and this is a prime community issue. The *Monitor* has a duty to cover it."

"We *have* covered it," Marilyn said, with a look that

managed to hide the fact that everybody knew he didn't actually read the paper. "There've been, what, twenty stories in the past six weeks?"

"Well, be that as it may, the *community* feels that it's not enough. I had lunch with Cynthia Dillingham just yesterday, and . . ." *Jesus, what an idiot. She takes him out for a goddamn Cobb salad, and he lets her dictate how we cover the story. The newsroom basketball team isn't nicknamed the Chester Detesters for nothing.* ". . . devoted to the story fulltime."

"*What?*" I had a feeling I'd missed something big and unpleasant.

"I said, I want you to work on the story full-time. Make it your top priority."

What did he think this was? Abscam? "Well, er, what kind of coverage did you have in mind?"

"Put together a three-day package." He was getting on a roll, like he does at least once a year when he decides it's time to play newspaper. If he put on his fedora, I was going to kill him. "We'll run it three consecutive Fridays. The first day will be all about the history of the theater. The second about the current debate. The third . . ." *Let me guess. The plans for the future.* ". . . will be about the plans for the future. We'll set up a reader reaction line and run it on the editorial page. We should have one of those photo question-and-answers every day, coordinated to go with the stories. Alex should ask the questions, not an intern. That way they'll know we care."

That we *what?* "Okay," I said, and got up to leave before it got any worse. He didn't seem to notice, so I sat back down.

"And we should have some sort of contest. Hmm . . . Starlight historical trivia. That's it. Run it on the first day to kick off the series. Advertising will coordinate the prizes.

We should make sure and ask businesses whose ad contracts are running out. Have circulation promote it with rack cards."

Marilyn had a feral look in her eyes. "That it?"

"Alex should do a profile on the theater's new benefactor. Robert . . ."

"Robert Renssellaer," I mumbled, and promptly started praying for my own death.

"He's expecting your call."

Marilyn gave me a look that promised a large gin and tonic later. "And which day did you want that to run?" she said, so angelically it was downright scary.

"Oh, I'll leave that up to your good judgment. And Bill's." Bill grunted, which was the first noise he'd been called upon to make. Lucky him. "Perhaps it might fit with the historical pieces," Chester went on. "Did you know his acting career actually began at the Starlight? Isn't that interesting?"

Know it? The man had handed out copies of his résumé and flapper-era head shot at the council meeting—a dead giveaway that he'd never intended to be an anonymous anything.

"It will be a *perfect* way to bring the history of the theater alive for our readers. Mrs. Dillingham promised he'd supply some old photos for us to use." I pictured bales of black-and-whites being delivered to the loading dock by forklift. "And we should make sure that families feel included," Chester was saying. "There should be something here for the children . . ."

It went on like that for a while, a guy who'd never written a news story in his life telling me whom to interview, and how. Finally, his secretary came in to say he was going to be late for a lunch date with one of his Rotarian buddies.

He was still preening in the mirror of his tiny executive john when the three of us escaped back upstairs to the newsroom.

"I swear that man was put on earth to make me atone for some goddamn thing," Marilyn said when we got to her office. "Alex, be a good girl and go get something for my head. And a big Diet Coke." She handed me a ten-dollar bill. "You might as well buy yourself lunch with the change." I was halfway down the stairs when she shouted at me to come back. "Get Bill a carton of those disgusting noodles of his," she said, and shoved another ten at me.

"And a ginseng tea," he yelled from her office couch.

"And a ginseng tea. I'll take a ham sandwich from Schultz's. Don't forget the extra mustard. Chips too. Salt and vinegar if they've got them. Oh, and tell that kraut bastard not to forget my pickle this time."

"I'll say it verbatim. Anything else?"

"If you're going to Schultz's, you might as well get me some rice pudding," Bill said, not bothering to lift his head. "But not if they put raisins in it today. Then I'll have tapioca. Hold the whipped cream. But cinnamon."

"You got it." At this rate, there was going to be about a buck fifty left for me.

"Get back here as soon as you can," Marilyn said. "We've got our work cut out for us."

"Yeah?"

"*Somebody*'s got to figure out how to make this whole thing not completely suck."

"Oh," I said, "then I think you better give me another ten."

"What for?"

"Breakfast."

8

ROBERT RENSSELLAER, FORMER CHILD STAR OF STAGE AND screen, lived just where you'd want him to: in a creepy old mansion in Benson Heights. The place had turrets and spires, little leaded windows, and an overgrown garden that made it feel like an untended cemetery. My subject had refused to be interviewed before five P.M., and when I arrived I got the feeling it had a lot to do with atmosphere. There were no bright lights on outside, just a huge pair of iron sconces framing the doorway, and when I got out of my car I nearly broke my ankle on what turned out to be a marble toad.

I rang the bell and waited for the door to be opened by Lurch from *The Addams Family*. It wasn't opened at all. I rang again, and was eventually faced with a beleaguered-looking young woman in a nurse's uniform.

"Are you from the *Monitor*?" I nodded. "Thank *God*. He's been driving me crazy all day. 'Move this, dust that, clean off my smoking jacket.' Do I look like a maid to you? Well do I?"

"Um, no . . ."

"You can hang your coat up over there," she said, pointing to a shadowy corner that hid a wrought-iron rack. She promptly sprinted to it herself and put on a tan wool jacket. "I'm going home. He's all yours."

"But where . . ."

"Shrine at the end of the hall," she said, and left.

I scuttled down the passageway—frankly, there wasn't much more light indoors than out—and girded myself for whatever Buddhist prayer room lay beyond. The door was slightly ajar, and when I knocked it drifted open.

"You may enter," he said.

Once I got a look inside, I wasn't sure I wanted to.

The room was overstuffed, with chairs and sofas and tables packed in together; it felt more like a furniture store than a living room. A fireplace took up most of one wall, a big stone thing you could pitch a tent in. The entire room was lit with candles, creating a mood so overblown and creepy you expected to see Liberace and Vincent Price arm-wrestling on the settee.

But that wasn't what made the room so unpleasant. No, that honor went to the artwork that obscured most of the velvet wallpaper.

The subject of all of it was . . . Robert Renssellaer. Every single one. No joke.

There was a formal portrait over the fireplace that depicted him at sixteen or seventeen, standing in front of what must have been a stage curtain. He had his arms crossed, and a spotlight shone on him from above—or maybe it was supposed to be the holy rays of heaven, I don't know.

There were a dozen gigantic movie posters, way bigger than anything you'd see at the multiplex—the kind they used to put outside theaters back when they actually played one film at a time. One said "ROBBIE RENSSELLAER JR. *IS* LITTLE LORD FAUNTLEROY" over a painting of a boy in a blue velvet suitcoat and short pants. Another said "ROBBIE RENSSELLAER JR. STARRING IN . . . THE

GEE-WHIZ GANG!" This one actually had some other kids in it, but Robbie's head was painted bigger than theirs by a factor of four. The Fluffy series was well represented, and I learned that in addition to *Fluffy, My Pal* it included *Fluffy, My Hero, Fluffy & Friends, Oh, Fluffy!*, and *Go, Fluffy, Go!* All five of those depicted Robbie with his arm around an orange furball, both of them staring beyond the artist to some point above the horizon. But while the dog stayed forever young, Robbie aged incrementally from (I guessed) nine to seventeen. By the last one, Fluffy looked in imminent danger of being crushed under Robbie's armpit.

There were a few prizes on the wall, including a nomination for Best Youth Performance from some antique version of the People's Choice Awards; and a plaque for Most Promising Juvenile from the Upstate Theatre Critics Guild, 1924.

"Won't you come in?" he said from the general direction of the unlit fireplace. "Please, do have a seat."

I couldn't see exactly where he was sitting, so I tried to zero in on his voice as I wended my way through the lacquered obstacle course, hoping not to knock over any of the candles and burn the damn house down. ("*MONITOR* REPORTER INCINERATES ELDERLY EGOMANIAC.")

He was perched in a big wingback chair, its worn upholstery the same shade of burgundy as the wallpaper, the carpet, and his smoking jacket. He was wearing the same little cap he'd had on at the council meeting and another silk scarf, canary yellow this time. He had the black wool blanket over his legs, and the suspected cat was out cold on his lap. There was no wheelchair in sight, and since the nurse had already taken off I figured he only used it for outings. Either that, or I was expected to carry him up to the john later.

He offered me a drink, not verbally so much as with a

grand theatrical gesture toward a bottle-covered credenza nearby. "I would enjoy another glass of port, if you would be so kind," he said, and when I realized he was drinking ten-year-old Burmeister I poured one for myself. Yum.

"I trust you have received the material from Mrs. Dillingham," he said when I sat down in a matching wingback across from him. The chairs were huge, and since I'm short (and he was shriveled), we looked like Alice after she bit the mushroom.

"Um, yes I have. Thank you for sending it." I'd been wrong about the forklift, but just barely.

"Of course, that was simply preliminary information for your records."

"Oh, right. Of course."

"I anticipated that you would require a lengthy interview, so I have cleared my schedule for the rest of the evening."

Again with the *ee-ven-ing*. Oh, criminy.

After you've been a reporter for fifteen minutes, you realize there are pretty much two kinds of people in the world: the ones who don't want to talk to you, and the ones who won't shut up. In some ways, the former are easier to deal with than the latter. There are all sorts of ways to get a person to open up against his will. But getting someone to tell you only what you need to know—without reciting his entire life story like it was the plot of *Dr. Zhivago*— is a whole different kind of headache.

I decided to resort to what you might call the Busy Journalist Dodge. Simple, but effective.

"That's so kind of you," I said, hoping I was doing a better acting job than he had in the first Fluffy movie, "but I'm afraid I have another assignment at seven. I'm sure we'll have plenty of time to cover everything." Actually, what I had was a pizza date with Cody, but there was no way I was going to cancel it so I could spend the next six hours of my life with this guy.

"But Sissy made canapés!"

I tried not to laugh, but it was hard since this was just about the silliest sentence I'd ever heard. *I'm sorry, General. I can't go to the front. Sissy made canapés!*

". . . in the oven as we speak. Perhaps you could retrieve them."

"Huh?"

He made yet another grand gesture, this time toward the door I'd come in. Not being able to think of an appropriate response, I got up and wandered down the hall until I could smell something cheesy. Maybe the ee-ven-ing was looking up. Sure enough, I followed my nose to an industrial-sized kitchen with a pair of industrial-sized ovens, the top one containing a cookie sheet full of mini quiches.

I turned the oven off, wondered if such things ever happened to Woodward and Bernstein, and rooted around for a dish to put the food on and a spatula to do it with.

When I had the quiches loaded onto a blue Wedgwood platter, I cracked one open and prayed there wasn't anything meatish inside; I didn't feel like explaining the basic tenets of vegetarianism to an old guy in a smoking jacket. Luckily, there was nothing but egg and onion, with a liberal coating of cheddar on top. I sampled one, and the crust veritably melted on my tongue. Sissy Dillingham wasn't known as the Martha Stewart of faculty wives for nothing.

I was about to go back to the shrine when I remembered something my mom had told me about behaving like a civilized human being, so I found two little glass plates, a pair of what were probably sugar tongs, and some lacy paper napkins. I brought the lot back to Renssellaer, who licked his lips and loaded eight of the quiches onto his plate one by one.

Once I'd settled back into my gigantic chair and con-

sumed a couple of quiches, I pulled out my notebook. Renssellaer eyed it suspiciously.

"Where is your tape recorder?"

"I don't usually use one."

"Then how do you propose to conduct an interview?"

"I take notes."

It was obviously not the right answer. I recalled how ab-
surdly pleased he'd been in front of the goddamn cable-
access camera at the council meeting, and wondered if the
guy just had a fetish for being recorded. If so, I was ruining
his good time.

He didn't say anything more about it, though. He just
gave me a petulant look and took out his aggressions on his
quiches—which, as far as I could tell, hadn't done a thing to
deserve it.

I'll spare you the gory details of the next two hours; suffice it to say that it was more of a monologue than an interview. Worse, it made me twenty minutes late to meet Cody
for dinner. As it turned out, though, he'd only just beaten me
there; I nearly barreled into him as he was taking off his
overcoat in the vestibule.

Albertini's is Gabriel's best-kept secret, food-wise. It's
several miles out of town, cash only, and as dimly lit as
Robert Renssellaer's living room. It is, therefore, the locale
of choice for shady deals, extramarital assignations, and
(rumor has it) relocated federal witnesses. For a while, it
was also the favored rendezvous spot for a certain cop and
journalist who were trying to keep a low profile, before they
figured out everybody was on to them anyway.

The restaurant is fancier than your average pizza joint, but
there's a comforting laissez-faire attitude about the place.
Nobody cares what you order, or the identity of your dining
companion, or whom you might be planning to kill later

on—just so long as you pay the bill, leave a nice tip, and clean up your messes. The place is never more than half full, but it doesn't seem to have any cash-flow problems, judging from the excessive number of busboys and the fancy cashews on the bar. As we sat down, the phrase *laundered mob money* flitted across my brain, and not for the first time.

"Leave the gun," Cody whispered. "Take the cannoli."

"You know, the maître d' is going to hear you say that one of these nights."

"It's okay. I'm armed."

I reached across the table to pat his shoulder holster. "You get to shoot anybody today, honey?"

"Nah. You?"

I shook my head. "Wanted to, though."

"Oh, yeah, how was your interview with Roddy Mc-Dowall?"

"Robbie Rensselaer. Junior."

"So what's his story?"

"Let's have high-level pizza negotiations first. What do you want?"

"Sausage and onion, like always. What do you want?"

"Mushroom and pineapple. Like always."

"This relationship is doomed."

"Not as long as they'll keep making it half and half."

We ordered the pizza and a big salad to split, plus a beer for Cody and a glass of Chianti for me. I was afraid the quiches had filled me up too much for tiramisù, but I was willing to give it a try later.

"So what was up with your interview?" Cody asked, distracting me long enough to snag the last olive from the complimentary relish tray. "Sounds like he likes to hear himself talk."

"I'd say he told me his life story, except that two hours only got me through the first quarter of it."

"Wasn't he some big movie star or something?"

"Child actor back in the thirties. You really want to hear this?"

"Baby, I spent the whole day with a guy who makes fake credit cards. I guarantee you this is more interesting."

"You know, it kind of *is* interesting. Maybe if he didn't try to tell me about every damn line he ever said, I might not have wanted to strangle him so much."

"How did a guy like that ever end up in Gabriel?"

"Grew up here. His dad was mayor back in the twenties—Robert Renssellaer Senior. I guess there's a bust of him in City Hall, not that I ever noticed it."

"The chief says he's quite a pain in the rear. The son, I mean."

"Oh, yeah?"

"His security system false alarms every other week. Chief thinks the guy sets it off himself when he gets lonely."

"It's a pretty big house for an old guy and his cat."

"He tell you how he got into the movies?"

"Cody, the man told me *everything*. Apparently he started getting cast in community theater productions when he was, like, six. Then the traveling companies used him when they needed a munchkin and didn't bring their own. I guess it was hard to find a kid who could go on tour for months, and anyway some local talent helped sell tickets. So Robbie was in a couple of minor shows at the Starlight, and eventually he got his big break in a production of *The Quinn Affair*. Last out-of-town tryout before the Broadway run, which won every award in the book. Plus, it was directed by Austin Cusack."

"Good Irish name."

"You've never heard of him?" He shook his head. "I bet your mom has. Pretty big stage director, then a huge Hollywood type for like twenty years. Won three Oscars. You've really never heard of him?"

"You're the film critic. I just put people in jail."

"I only know all this because Renssellaer told me twenty times. Anyway, he was in this production of *The Quinn Affair* with Priscilla Morton . . ."

"Now *her* I've heard of."

"Right. So Cusack thinks the kid's a genius and gets some big Hollywood producer to come up from New York to see the show. He loves him, signs him to a studio contract, and the rest is history. Little Robbie makes thirty movies, and retires to his hometown to spend the rest of his life in a multimillion-dollar mausoleum."

"He said that?"

"Well, that last part was me."

"Why did he quit making movies, anyway?"

"He said he wanted to devote himself to charitable works. Like Nixon resigned to concentrate on his golf game."

"You gonna eat those croutons?"

"They're all yours."

He munched on them for a while. "So what happened? Robbie couldn't hack it as a grown-up?"

"Well, he was pretty awful in the movie I saw on TV. But he made me sit through part of *The Tower Princes* on video, and he was okay in that. I think he was an incredibly cute kid, which was probably a major part of the job description. Most child stars back then weren't what you'd call method actors—performing seals is more like it. Once he wasn't so cute anymore, he was out of a job. Even happened to Shirley Temple. Still happens to a lot of them."

"Kind of sad, don't you think?"

"Nah. More like Bernie Carbo."

"How do you figure?"

"He had his moment of glory," I said. "Not a lot of people do."

9

THE NEXT DAY, I FINALLY GOT A LOOK INSIDE THE STARLIGHT Theatre. My first reaction had nothing to do with the glory days of vaudeville; it was that I was never going to eat eggs again as long as I live.

This may seem strange, until you realize that the theater was the pigeons' version of Flanders Field—there were corpses everywhere. Plus (and for some reason I found this infinitely more disgusting) you couldn't walk six inches without stepping on eggshells. They crunched under the soles of my Bean boots and stuck to the outsides, so as I tramped around the place with my flashlight and notebook I dragged two crusty white rings of pigeon ova along with me. So much for my lifelong love affair with the Egg McMuffin.

There were three of us inside the theater, working on a story set to run on the second day of my Starlight package. Melissa was taking pictures with a pair of bulky lights, and the deputy building commissioner was there to make sure we didn't break our necks—or take off the surgical masks we were wearing to protect us from whatever diseases might be lurking in a passel of decomposed birds. His presence was more about staving off bad P.R. than avoiding litigation; we'd already signed a document holding the city harmless from lawsuits over everything from emotional distress to flesh-eating bacteria.

Just getting inside the place had taken two weeks of negotiations between Marilyn and the fire chief. He'd been dead-set against the idea—until she hinted, without actually saying it, that people might be more disposed toward tearing the building down if they knew what a pit it was in there. The S.O.S. people, meanwhile, had been thrilled; they figured if only people knew how beautiful it was, they'd rally to save it.

From where I was standing—ankle-deep in dead birds— I was willing to put my money on the fire chief.

The field trip had been my not-so-brilliant contribution toward making the series, as Marilyn had put it, "not totally suck." Our general consensus was that if there was enough genuine reportage, it might offset Chester's idiotic gimmicks. So there I was, my story deadline just hours away, dying to take a shower and wondering if you can get mad cow disease from rotting pigeon parts.

Melissa, meanwhile, was busy making a big deal over how heavy her camera equipment was. Never mind that I'd seen her haul it up and down the gorge trail on more than one occasion; she was enjoying the gentlemanly aid of the deputy building commissioner, a thirty-something guy named Drew who looked very much like he should be branding cattle in Montana. That left me to wander the theater on my own, if I wanted to see anything beyond what Melissa was shooting—which, at the moment, was the lobby.

Originally, the Starlight's front entrance had consisted of three double doors: a big one in the center and two smaller ones on each side. Now the middle and right doors were boarded up, and the leftmost was sealed with a chain and padlock, which Drew had unfastened on our way in.

The lobby itself was enormous, its three interior walls lined by Moorish arches leading into other small rooms. That design, Madeline Hoover had told me during one of her quasi-orgasmic architecture lectures, had been one of the Starlight's defining elements. In other small-town theaters, the amenities had been squished in together to save money; here, everything had its own luxurious little enclave. There was a coat room, perennially staffed by gals with gorgeous gams; a gentlemen's smoking room and a ladies' lounge, each with a circular couch upholstered in green velvet; a concession stand that sold petits fours and candied nuts in fancy paper cones; two S-shaped bars, inlaid with cut glass and illuminated from below, which reportedly served all manner of delights, even (for the right customers) during Prohibition.

In its heyday, intermission at the Starlight had been a phenomenon unto itself—a forty-minute social whirl that was the main reason a lot of people came to the theater in the first place. A pianist in evening dress played a Steinway grand in the center of the lobby, where people who hadn't the least interest in Eugene O'Neill could linger to see and be seen. They'd come from as far away as Buffalo and Rochester to prance about in their finery and pick up a little culture; legend had it that F. Scott Fitzgerald once parked himself on the grand staircase and watched the action for three nights running.

Now the place looked like the last reel of a disaster movie. There was junk all over the floor—popcorn cartons and bird carcasses and rusty folding chairs and other stuff I didn't even want to think about. I picked up a piece of paper from the thousands moldering on the terrazzo, and it turned out to be letterhead for the long-departed Gabriel Performing Arts and Cultural Alliance. The initials were spelled out in elaborate curlicues on top, surrounded by icons of musical notes, ballet shoes, and the omnipresent comedy-and-tragedy masks. Even damp and yellowed it looked expensive, and I wondered whether the stationery had been an act of faith or just a waste of money.

I headed up the central staircase, which, again according to Madeline Hoover, had been built with the same ratio of height to depth as the Spanish Steps. At the top of the landing, the stairs split off to either side, and since my flashlight hit fewer pigeon corpses on the right, that's the way I went.

At the top of the stairs, the wall curved around to the left, following the shape of the auditorium behind it. There were three doors leading down into the seats on the right side of the house, and another at the end of the hall that had "STAIRS TO BOXES XI TO XX—TICKET-HOLDERS ONLY" stenciled in flaking gold letters. I went back to the main staircase and up another flight to the first balcony, shining the flashlight on each step to avoid treading on any more dead birds than absolutely necessary.

The second landing was a mess, obviously the site of somebody's Saturday night hijinks. There were a pair of beer balls, smashed and covered with so much dust the perpetrators were probably mortgage-paying grown-ups by now. Hundreds of singed copies of the program for *Amahl and the Night Visitors* were stacked in a pile, as though someone had tried to start a campfire and thought better of it—a damn good thing, since the fire chief had said that one stray spark would make the place go up like a garment factory.

As on the floor below, the second landing led to doors along the curved wall. There were two on each side, feeding into the first balcony. I decided to go up to the top floor—this time the left staircase seemed slightly less appalling—and found exactly the same arrangement, but with one door on each side.

It hadn't been much of a climb, but the face mask had me all sweaty and the too-big hardhat was making my head itch. I paused a second to get my act together, and when I stopped walking and crunching eggshells the silence of the place was astounding. I just stood there for a while, shining my flashlight through the arched doorway and seeing nothing but space. It was incredible how quiet the place was, built so solidly that none of the traffic noise of a Gabriel weekday could begin to creep in.

At the mall multiplex, you could hear the action-movie explosions from three screens over. I was beginning to think the place might be worth saving after all.

What I saw next clinched the deal. I'd taken a few steps down into the top balcony, and suddenly the room was lit up by a blinding white light. It took a minute for my eyes to adjust—and for me to realize that Melissa and her hunky Sherpa had set up her equipment somewhere in the orchestra seats. But once I got my bearings, I just stood there with my mouth agape and my tongue plastered to the inside of my surgical mask.

The Starlight was amazing. It was huge, for one thing— the balcony I was standing on hovered over an even larger one, with the orchestra seating spread out a hundred feet below. There were little details everywhere, way too much to take in at once. Cherub faces and swirling ribbons decorated the walls at intervals, and the wooden arm of each seat was its own carved work of art. The chandeliers were dingy and missing pieces, but they were gorgeous—one tier of glass rising out of the next like a crystal fountain. Around the stage, the proscenium arch was decorated with intricate coats of arms symbolizing . . . I didn't know what; I made a note to ask Madeline Hoover about it later. On the ceiling, tiny bulbs formed celestial constellations. Madeline—who had lived through the theater's previous restoration and failure—had told me that when the house lights were dimmed, it felt as though you were outside under a cloudless night sky.

I know reporters are supposed to stay objective and all that, but in my youth, I was a real drama rat. I actually went off to Vassar planning to major in acting, only to be scared stupid and flee to the newspaper. And there I was, alone in the moldering second balcony of the most beautiful theater I'd ever laid my eyes on—graffiti and dead birds and all. For the first time, I understood what Sissy Dillingham and her cronies were so upset about. If this place got demolished, it was going to be a goddamn crime against humanity.

"You guys down there?" I yelled, and got a rather blood-curdling scream in response.

"Jesus Christ, you scared the *crap* out of me," Melissa shrieked. "Where the hell are you?"

I walked to the end of the balcony and leaned over in the direction of the stage, where Melissa's voice was coming from. "I'm up here. In the top balcony."

"Jeepers. I was worried the ghosts got you or something."

"Ghosts? What ghosts?"

"Huh? You gotta yell louder. I can barely hear you down here."

"Really? I can hear you fine. This place has great acoustics."

"What?"

I raised my voice a few notches. "I said this place has great acoustics."

"Oh. Yeah."

"But I guess it's only supposed to go in one direction, huh? I can hear you, but you can't hear me."

"What?"

"Never mind," I shouted back at her through my mask. "What the hell do you mean 'the ghosts'?"

"This place has to have some, don't you think? Maybe some old character actor *died* during his last performance," she said, staggering around and feigning a heart attack at center stage. "Or maybe somebody got killed during a wild west show." She cocked her hands up like six-shooters and went *bang bang bang*. I was afraid she was about to keel over and land on a pile of dead pigeons.

"Would you be careful down there? There's an orchestra pit right in front of you, you know. And there's a ton of crap all over the place."

"What?"

"I said watch out for the damn orchestra pit. Where's Drew, anyway?"

"Getting the rest of my stuff from the lobby."

"Love blooms among the pigeon guano."

"What?"

"Nothing. You gotta get a shot from up here. The view is fantastic."

"Good idea. I'll hit that next. Are you done?"

"Pretty much. I'm just going to check out another couple things."

"What?"

"I said I'm pretty much done. I'll meet you back down-stairs."

"*What?*"

This was getting old fast. "I'm almost done," I yelled. "I said I'll meet you."

"Okay, I'll see you back there," she said, and I heard her camera shutter clicking as though she were standing next to me. Wow.

I went back down to the lobby, waving to Drew as he started carting Melissa's equipment up the stairs. I checked out the various alcoves, trying to picture what it must have looked like when F. Scott himself (if it was true) had soaked up the scene. It wasn't easy, since the place reeked of various bodily fluids, and umpteen generations of rodents had taken up residence in the circular couches.

The bars, however, had been made of sterner stuff. They were rusty about the edges and dirty all over, but the inlaid glass and elegant lines were pretty much intact. I tried to picture what the glitterati might have ordered—Manhattans, maybe, or Cosmopolitans; I don't know much about the history of mixed drinks. Either way, I gave them credit for getting wittier (rather than just drunker) with every libation. I found the coat-check room, its revolving rack still bolted to the ceiling and a couple of jackets hanging from it. They were hardly vintage, though, unless you think of the eighties as a historical era; one was a hideous gray vinyl thing with "MEMBERS ONLY" sewn onto the sleeve, and the other had mold all over it.

I walked down a hall off the lobby and found a door marked "PRIVATE," which looked promising. It turned out to be a cramped office equipped with a Commodore 64 computer, its monitor bashed in and the brick still sitting in it. The room was filled with filing cabinets, their drawers open and the contents thrown around higgledy-piggledy. Clearly, Gabriel's juvenile delinquents had spent many joyous hours in here before the city finally sealed the place up.

I found another door a few feet down the hall, also labeled "PRIVATE." At first I thought it was locked, but I gave it a shove and barely stopped myself from plunging down a flight of stairs. I followed them down, and they curved twice before spilling into another hallway. At the far end of it was yet another set of stairs, with the word "STAGE" painted on the brick wall and an upward-aiming arrow underneath. All the doors on the hall were open, and when I shined my flashlight into the room nearest the stage stairs I saw a blinding light and a woman staring right back at me. Naturally, I screamed my little head off—before I realized I was looking at myself in a mirror. Then I felt like the village idiot.

It was a dressing room, a smallish space with chairs and clothing racks and a long, bulb-lined mirror along one wall. There was another room just like it across the hall, and when I looked at the doors I saw they were labeled "LADIES" and "GENTS." Down the hall from those were two smaller dressing rooms opposite each other, each with a gold star on the door. There was nothing particularly luxurious about either one, though; they had the same ratty feel as the rest of the hall, which looked like ship's steerage compared to the splendor upstairs. The actors, after all, were the hired help.

I peeked in the final door near the staircase I'd come down, and found an enormous boiler and other janitorial-looking things inside. This brought to mind all those Freddy Krueger movies I'd watched during my misspent youth, and all of a sudden I was scared silly.

What the hell are you doing? said one side of my brain to the other. *You're wandering around the basement of an abandoned building alone with a cheap-ass flashlight. Melissa distinctly mentioned the word "ghosts." Are you out of your tiny little mind?*

I tried to shake it off, but I'm basically a scaredy-cat at heart; once ghosts and killer janitors entered my head, I had a hard time getting them out. Naturally, my flashlight picked that moment to turn a shade yellower and dim a little, so I decided to get the hell out of there. I ran up to the top of the stairs, caught my breath so as not to make a complete ass of myself in front of Melissa and Drew, and called their names.

No answer.

I went into the lobby and up the main staircase, yelling for them with what was, admittedly, mounting hysteria. Still nothing.

I tried the first balcony, then the second. I went back down to the lobby and into the various alcoves, with no luck. A suspicion tried to sneak into my cranium, but since it was very, very bad, I decided to ignore it. I went back into the orchestra, just in case we'd crossed paths somehow, but they were nowhere in sight.

I went to the door and tried it. It didn't even budge. Then I realized I was opening the wrong one—the left one coming in would be the right one going out—so I breathed a big sigh of relief and went to the other door.

It wouldn't open either. It gave a little, rattled against the chain, but it was locked. From the outside.

Son of a bitch.

I'm not sure how I figured it out so fast—call it terror-inspired clarity. But since I knew there was no way they'd lock me in on purpose, I realized right then and there what must have happened.

Melissa couldn't hear me from the balcony. Melissa thought I was done. Melissa said she'd see me back there— *which meant the newsroom.*

I was locked inside the Starlight Theatre. I was trapped in an abandoned building, with no food or water, with dead birds all over the place and avian viruses and ghosts and eggshells and broken glass and Freddy Krueger on his way up from the boiler room as we speak.

Calm down. Cody says never panic. Cody says most people die not because they have to but because they freak out and do something stupid and get themselves killed. Calm down. Come on, you can do it. Think about something nice. Think about what you're going to get him for Christmas, or some damn thing.

I thought about dog-print ties and Calvin Klein boxer briefs and the five boxes of Girl Scout cookies I'd been hoarding for his stocking. I thought about the matching red-

and-green checked bandannas I was going to buy for Zeke and Shakespeare. I thought about a new pair of Timberland waterproof hiking boots, size eleven medium.

And then, because I'm my own worst enemy, I thought about the last time I'd ever seen a man named Adam—dead on a bridge, his body broken and his face gone. I thought about finding my roommate murdered on a wooded trail, and the terror on a teenage girl's face as she stared out at me through the bars of a metal cage.

They weren't crazy fantasies, which made it worse. It was all real. No use saying nothing bad can happen. It can, and it has, and it will.

That's when I started screaming for real. I ripped off the stupid mask, pounded on the door, and yelled for help at the top of my lungs. I knew that the theater was set way back from the road, and that it was built like a goddamn fortress, but I did it anyway. I yelled myself hoarse, and I started crying, and I yelled some more.

Then my flashlight went out.

10

I'M NOT SURE HOW LONG I STOOD THERE IN THE DARK, SINCE my watch isn't the kind you can read if you're stuck all alone with no flashlight in a goddamn abandoned theater in the middle of upstate New York.

Calm down, I told myself again. *You've been in way worse situations than this. When you don't show up in the newsroom, Melissa will figure out what happened and they'll come and let you out. And then you can kill her.*

That made me feel a little better. I used my trusty Bean boots to scrape all the crap off a square yard of the floor, so at least I'd have a relatively hygienic place to wait it out. I sat down and leaned against the door, poised to hear if anyone came near the entrance, and tried to calculate how long it might be before I got rescued. Melissa would go back to the newsroom, start developing her film, and wonder why she hadn't seen me. An hour, tops. Right?

Or maybe she'd have lunch with Mr. Burly Building Commissioner, flirt with him for a while, go on an assignment, develop some film, get called out to shoot a car crash, print the pictures, go to dinner, have a roll in the hay with her new boyfriend, and not spare me another thought until the next morning, when it was time to gloat.

In my present frame of mind, the second version seemed infinitely more likely. Oh, crap.

I sat there for a while, cursing myself for not bothering to check the batteries in my flashlight; no wonder I'd never made it past the Brownies. I shook it again, which did no good whatsoever. Then I tried opening it up and swapping the positions of the two batteries and—miracle of miracles —it actually gave off a little light. Hallelujah.

I thought about looking around for another exit, maybe the stage door, but scrapped the idea immediately. After all the vandalism, the city had made sure the theater was sealed up tight—and anyway, I was terrified of having my flashlight give out when I was deep in the guts of the theater. Plus, what would happen if somebody came to let me out and I wasn't at the entrance? Would they just figure they'd made a mistake and lock me in again?

And come to think of it, how did I get myself into this mess in the first place?

I spent a little more time cursing at Melissa, contemplating how I was going to separate her cute little head from the rest of her body. Was it really that she couldn't hear me? Or was she so bloody intent on flirting with Luke Duke that she wasn't paying any attention? How could she be such a goddamn flake?

Or maybe she couldn't. What if she hadn't blown me off? What if she was still in here somewhere, and I just hadn't found her? What if something awful had happened to her? What if some big psycho had killed her and Drew, chopped off their heads and hung them from the chandeliers?

Like I said, I have an overactive imagination. I had to stop myself from getting up and running around like a maniac, the very sort of panic Cody had warned me about. I took a deep breath and tried to calculate my assets, which seemed like the sort of thing he might do. I had a notebook, two pens, a hardhat, a face mask, and a really cheap flashlight. My backpack—complete with granola bars, bottled water, Spyderco penknife, and (most lamentably of all) the cell phone my parents had just given me for my birthday—was under my desk in the newsroom, where it did me no good whatsoever.

I surveyed my assets again and didn't come up with any sort of explosive device I might have missed. I racked my noodle for something ingenious, but all I could think of was to write "HELP! I AM LOCKED INSIDE THE STARLIGHT THEATRE—NOON DEC. 7—PLEASE CALL POLICE—THIS IS NOT A JOKE" in big letters on a piece of notebook paper. Then I did it three more times, tore the pages out, shoved them through the crack between the double doors, and hoped that the wind would take them someplace useful. Then I felt pretty foolish.

Spirits flagging, I decided to try singing; I remembered seeing Tom and Becky do this in an old Tom Sawyer movie, when they were lost in a cave and they wanted to distract themselves from the fact that their candles were running out and Injun Joe was trying to kill them. I went through most of the Duran Duran oeuvre and was just starting on Gordon Lightfoot when my flashlight finally conked out for good.

This was not progress.

I spent more time sitting there in the dark, making little atheist pacts with the universe about how I was going to be a much, much better person if only someone would come and *let me the hell out of here*. Apparently the universe had something better to do, because it didn't seem to help. I tried to think if I'd seen any candles or matches anyplace—maybe up by the ersatz bonfire?—but then I remembered what the fire chief had said, and decided it would be too risky; spending the night here was better than burning to death while the Gabriel fire department toasted marshmallows over my corpse.

That inspired some more banging and kicking and yelling for help. Still nothing.

I slumped back down to my little square on the floor, pretty damn thirsty and wondering where my next Snapple was coming from. I started fantasizing about what I was going to do when I got out—a long list that started with eating a big falafel pita and ended with burning the clothes I was wearing.

And then, to my complete and utter delight, I heard someone fumbling with the chain outside. The door opened before I could move, so I went flopping backward onto the concrete walkway and my head landed on somebody's feet. I heard a scream, and when I looked up I had a view clear up a pair of stockinged legs to a slip and some very conservative white undies. Another scream, a backward leap that took some of my hair with it, and I was gazing up into the horrified face of Madeline Hoover.

"Thank God," I said.

"Eek! Eek! Eek!" she said.

I scrambled to my feet and, overcome by an excess of gratitude, grabbed her around her matronly middle. "Thank you, thank you, thank you," I babbled. "You saved my *life*."

"Alex? What in heaven's name are you still doing here?"

"I got locked in," I said, stamping my Bean-booted feet to shake off the eggshells.

"My *word*." This from Adele Giordano-Bronstein, who was standing next to her. "For how long?"

"I don't know. Three or four hours maybe." I looked at my watch. "Oh. I guess it was only, like, forty-five minutes. It sure seemed like longer . . ."

"You poor thing." Adele came forward as though to pat

me on the shoulder, sniffed the air in my general vicinity, and stepped back. "But whatever happened?"

"Melissa and Drew—the photographer and the guy from the building office—they must have thought I was already out when they locked up."

"That's *terrible*." Madeline clucked like a disappointed schoolmarm. "I'm going to make sure the building commissioner hears about this."

"Oh, no, please don't. I don't want him to get in trouble. It was really my fault. It was a huge misunderstanding. I'm just glad to get the hell out of there."

"Well," she said, giving me a sour look for using the H-word, "thank goodness we happened to come along."

"Yeah, no kidding. What are you doing here, anyway?"

She sighed, and segued from clucking to more of a *tsk-tsk*. "Originally, I was just going to make sure the door was good and locked after your visit. But then Adele thought we might go in and look around . . ."

"Don't you need, you know, a hard hat and a mask and everything?"

"Oh, we're all prepared. Got our Wellies right here." She waved at a matched set of public-radio totebags, each with a pair of red rubber boots sticking out. "I know I'm not really dressed properly," she said with a glance down at her skirt and hose, "but who knows how much longer we'll have . . ."

"What do you mean?"

Adele got a freaked-out expression on her face and shot Madeline a look that said *shut-up*. Madeline, for her part, seemed on the verge of a genuine dither. "Oh, I really can't talk about it." She fumbled with the chain, dropped the padlock, picked it up, and snapped it shut.

"Weren't you going in?"

"Yes, of course . . ." More fumbling. She went to undo

the padlock, then realized she'd put the key back in her purse. She dug it out, and when she looked up again there were tears in her big moony eyes.

"Are you all right?"

"Oh, yes, I'm fine." She swiped at her eyes. "It's just that we've worked so hard, and now everything's so *awful*."

"Come on, Maddy," Adele said, grabbing her elbow. "Let's go inside, shall we?"

I took a few steps after them. "What's going on?"

Madeline waved me off. "I can't, I just can't . . . If only you hadn't done that story . . ."

"What story? Did something happen about the theater?"

"I'm sorry, Alex. I'm really not at liberty to say. I shouldn't even have told Adele, but I just . . . Oh, sometimes I *hate* this council business."

That was all I could get out of her. She put down her bag and leaned against the building as she swapped the heels for the boots, and Adele did the same. Then they each pulled out a flashlight and hard hat, and disappeared into the theater.

I thought about going after them, but shelved the idea after two seconds. Yes, the curiosity was killing me—but nowhere near enough to make me go back in there.

I went to the paper instead, getting all manner of weird looks as I walked across the Green. When I got up to the newsroom, I was greeted by Mad pinching his big Nordic nose and saying something like "Jesus, Bernier, you *stink*." I went into the ladies' john to look in the mirror, and wished I hadn't.

My face was filthy, and I had the worst hat-hair you can possibly imagine. There were pigeon feathers sticking to my dad's old suede coat, and the backside of my jeans looked like a goddamn science experiment. I went looking for Melissa—I figured she deserved to have to smell me—and found out she'd gone to lunch with, quote, "some guy from the building department."

I went home, and was promptly assaulted by Shakespeare, Zeke, and Tipsy, who'd decided I smelled like prey. I threw my clothes in the washer (the urge to immolate them had passed), put my coat in a garbage bag for immediate transport to the cleaners, and spent half an hour in the shower with a scrubby brush. Thus exfoliated, I got dressed and shared a frozen Stouffer's macaroni and cheese with my tormentors. Then I went back to work.

I loitered in Bill's doorway until he was off the phone, a rare occurrence that requires the patience of a birdwatcher. "Something's up," I said, and flopped down in the chair in front of his desk.

"A Starlight something?"

"Tithe," I said, sticking my hand out for a chunk of his Cadbury Dairy Milk bar. He obliged. "Yeah, it's a Starlight something."

"It better be. You've been gone half the damn day."

"Yeah, well, not by choice." He raised an eyebrow. "Never mind. Long story."

"So what's up?"

"I think the Starlight deal's going south. I ran into Madeline Hoover and Adele Bronstein on the way out of the theater, and they were a mess. Wouldn't tell me what was up exactly, but it isn't good."

"Well, what *did* they say?"

"That the theater might not be around much longer, that all their hard work had been for shit, and . . . How did Madeline put it? If only I hadn't written that story."

"What story?"

"That's when she clammed up."

"Too bad. Did you squeeze her?"

"Yeah, I squeezed her," I fibbed. "She said she couldn't

talk about it because she was on council. At least, I think
that's what she meant."

"So what story was she talking about?"

"I've been thinking about it for the past hour. It's gotta be
something from the first day of the package."

"Because . . . ?"

"I don't know, it's just a hunch. She seemed really . . .
traumatized. Like she just got whopped with some bad
news. My Friday package was the most recent thing."

He plucked a paper from the stack by his desk, nailing
Friday's on the first try and barely jostling the ones above it.
Truly, the man's a magician. "Hmm . . . What have we here?
Mainbar on the history of the theater. Sidebar on the architect. Bulleted list of major plays and performers. Starlight
timeline, going back to 1917. Profile of Robbie what's-his-
name. Walk-and-squawk on the common man's Starlight
memories. Bunch of old pics. Lame-ass trivia contest.
Roundup of the other theaters they used to have downtown,
now all kaputski. So what's the problem?"

He waved the paper at me. Stripped across the top of each
page was the package's title: "STARLIGHT . . . STAR
BRIGHT?" Chester's idea. The opener ran across the cen-
terfold of the A section—it's called a "double-truck," in case
you care—and the longer stories jumped to the following
pages.

"Damned if I know," I said. "There's nothing controver-
sial in there—nothing everybody didn't already know, anyway. It's just the same old stuff about how the theater shut
down, and the cultural alliance or whatever it's called tried
to save it, and it flopped and they blew all that federal
money. I mean, it's not exactly flattering, but it's nothing
new."

"So what is?"

I sucked on another piece of Dairy Milk and thought

about it for a minute. "There's nothing. That was the historical part, remember? All the current stuff is running tomorrow. There was nothing in last Friday that hadn't run ten times already." I was about to snag some more chocolate when I noticed the towheaded moppet staring out at me in black and white. "Wait. Of course there was. Robert Renssellaer."

"The rich guy?"

"The big benefactor. That's got to be it. He's the only new thing in there."

"And?"

"And so maybe he's backing out."

"Why the hell would he do that?"

"Beats me. Maybe all he wanted was some attention, get his name in the papers, and he's got zero intention of forking over the two hundred and fifty thousand clams."

"Would he really screw them over that bad?"

"I don't know. He seemed like a pretty big fruitcake to me."

"So make some phone calls. If you're right, we gotta rework the whole goddamn package for tomorrow."

He threw the rest of his candy bar at me for inspiration, and I hightailed it to my desk. I tried calling Renssellaer but there was no answer, not even a machine. Then, figuring I'd given him a fair shake, I started working the phones in earnest.

I called someone at the county clerk's office, a sixty-something gal my friend Gordon had hooked me up with during his brief stint as the *Monitor*'s cop reporter. For a box of good cookies and the chance to run her mouth off, she'll dish all manner of dirt on anybody who's ever registered a deed. I chatted with her for a while, promised her some Walker's shortbread, and rang off. Then I tried a guy I know at the Walden County Savings Bank, a morally upright type who'd never dream of revealing some old lady's account balance—but, being a red diaper baby at heart, has been known to gossip when large sums of money are involved.

Those two helped me out some, but they didn't connect the dots. I tried a dozen more sources (including Madeline Hoover, who held her tongue even though she sounded like she was cracking up), but to no avail.

Then I dialed Joe Kingman's office at the Benson law school. I'd been saving him as a last resort—not because I thought he wouldn't talk, but because this was one marker I didn't feel entirely comfortable calling in.

Last summer, I'd helped save the life of his seventeen-year-old daughter. Without melodrama, and with what I suspected was complete sincerity, he and his wife had told me they would do anything I asked them to do as long as they lived. *You ever need to know anything we know, call us. We'll tell you. You ever need a ride back from Chicago or Denver or someplace, we'll come and pick you up. Anything. Just ask. We owe you. Do you understand? We owe you everything.*

That's what they'd said. And here I was, taking advantage of it for the sake of some idiotic scoop in the next day's paper; at least I had the good grace to feel bad about it. But when I put the question to Joe Kingman, he sounded immensely relieved—like he'd been waiting months for the chance to do me a favor.

So I asked, and he answered. He wasn't actually on the committee in charge of the Starlight sale, but he always had his ear to the ground and he knew what was going on. He told me everything I needed to know, anonymously but on the record, and before I got off the phone he even invited me and Cody over for dinner.

But there was something else I didn't know, as I sat there dialing and scribbling and scarfing the dregs of Bill's candy bar. Yes, Kingman had spilled his guts because I'd saved his daughter's life. But telling me what he knew didn't turn out to be such a favor after all. As a matter of fact, I'm pretty sure it got somebody killed.

11

HE DIDN'T HAVE THE MONEY. THE WHOLE EXPLANATION IS more complicated, but that's the long and the short of it. Robert Renssellaer Junior lived like a crazy millionaire, but the truth was that he was "overextended." This, as far as I could tell from a whole afternoon of interviews, was a polite word for "flat-broke."

The guy was in debt up to his saggy eyeballs. He'd made a ton of money, he'd spent a ton of money, and now he lived on a measly nine hundred bucks a month from investment income. That he even had that much wasn't due to his own foresight, but because some banker back in the fifties had the good sense to bully him into setting up a blind trust. He didn't even pay for his own perennially martyred nurse; she came courtesy of a middle-aged nephew in Philly, who'd decided that hiring her was a hell of a lot easier than dealing with Uncle Robbie's phone calls every hour on the hour.

Nobody else knew any of this, of course. Renssellaer might not have lit up the screen in *Go Fluffy, Go!*, but he was enough of an actor to make everyone think he was still rolling in dough. He talked a good game, describing trips to Cannes as though they'd happened last summer, not forty years ago. He wore expensive clothes, and nobody noticed that they were ancient because he was too; it was just his style. No one knew that his house actually belonged to the nephew, who'd bailed him out when he couldn't cover the mortgage—not so much out of the kindness of his heart but because he was planning to fix it up and triple his investment the minute his uncle stopped breathing. Except for the occasional Arts Coalition dinner, the former child star spent most of his evenings alone. He lived on grilled cheese, if the nurse was around to make it for him, and microwaved cream of mushroom soup if she wasn't. No wonder he was so excited when Sissy made canapés.

The jig was up when the president of Gabriel Savings—Barry Marsh's successor, in fact—saw my profile. He wasn't the type of guy to watch council on cable access, but he read the *Monitor* cover to cover with his bran flakes every morning. As it turned out, he was also the guy who'd denied Renssellaer a second mortgage a few years back; he knew damn well that the man didn't have a quarter for the parking meter, much less a quarter of a million to bail out the Starlight. He'd called Renssellaer and asked him what the hell was going on, only to have him babble about how he was going to get the money from "some powerful friends in Hollywood." Then he hung up on him, which pissed off the banker enough to turn around and nark on him to the mayor. End of deal.

The Hollywood line must have been working for Renssellaer, because he used it on me when I showed up on his doorstep. He seemed genuinely upset, really in a tizzy, and he kept repeating the same thing over and over. All he needed was time, he said. He thought he'd have until the council vote to come up with it—thought no one would have to know about his "temporary insolvency." He was sure he could have gotten the money, he said, because there were plenty of people out in Hollywood who'd never want the Starlight torn down.

"Oh dear, oh dear," he muttered as the nurse shut the door in my face, "if *only* you hadn't written that story."

"That story" was nothing compared to the one that ran in the *Monitor* the next day. It was the new mainbar to the package on the Starlight's modern-day woes, and it detailed how the theater's guardian angel had turned out to be a big fat fake. It quoted a quasi-hysterical Sissy Dillingham as saying she hadn't felt this betrayed since she found out there was no Easter Bunny. A marginally calmer Madeline Hoover said she had no idea what was going to happen now but she knew "something would just have to work out," while the recently re-Catholicized Adele Giordano-Bronstein pulled out her rosary and started praying.

Renssellaer's little stunt left the S.O.S. coffers back in the low five figures, nowhere near the half million that council had asked for. Sissy and her generals tried to rally their troops, but being jerked around like that seemed to have taken the fight out of everybody. There were a couple of marches, poorly attended. The Starlight cookies were duly baked and sold, but nobody seemed to notice the shape anymore; they were only in it for the butter and sugar.

At council's discussion meeting the first week in December, the mood was downright grim. Sissy and Adele went up to the mike during the public comment period and pleaded with them to postpone the vote; they even burst into tears in stereo, but this time it didn't do any good. Madeline Hoover made a motion to give them another month, and Joe Kingman seconded it—not because he thought S.O.S. could get its act together, but just to spit in the eye of the capitalist pig who wanted to buy the place, tear it down, and build apartments too expensive for average working folk.

But when the time came to vote on whether to delay any

longer, the tally was six to four against. Madeline had to excuse herself from the council table to go cry in the ladies' room, and Adele ran after her, her rosary in one hand and a large pink hankie in the other. Sissy Dillingham, by contrast, seemed to take a that-which-does-not-kill-me-makes-me-stronger kind of attitude. She stiffened her spine, straightened her shoulders, and walked out of the chamber like a debutante at a deportment lesson.

The final installment of my Starlight package ran two days later. It was supposed to be the part devoted to the theater's future, and since we'd advertised it that way I had no choice but to churn it out. Problem was, nobody except Sissy Dillingham and a handful of other people thought the place even *had* a future. Still, we had to be fair about it, so I did a piece summing up S.O.S.'s plans for the Starlight on the off chance that it somehow escaped the gas chamber. I talked about how they were going to restore the glass-topped bars and circular couches to their former glory, how the Benson Savoyards and the goddamn high school talent club were all hepped up to do performances there. Frankly, it felt like putting lipstick on a corpse.

Marilyn had decided that the only way we could avoid looking like a bunch of dimwits was to give equal weight to both possible outcomes: restored theater or luxury flophouse. Therefore, I did another interview with Kurtis Osmond, who brought his architect along—both to give some comments on the new building and to deliver a computer-generated elevation of it they'd done on three hours' notice. The S.O.S. people had also promised a rendering of what the restored building would look like among the modern storefronts, but on Thursday Sissy had called to tell me it wasn't coming; once the news about Renssellaer came out, the Benson architecture professor who'd volunteered to do it turned around and bailed on them. Therefore, the drawing of a spanking new apartment building—complete with glass-enclosed entryway, individual balconies, and fancy potted shrubbery—ran opposite a picture of the theater in its present state. It didn't seem like a good omen.

With less than two weeks until the council vote, the letters to the editor were still running ten-to-one in favor of saving the building. The problem was, nobody knew how to do it. A lot of them were outraged that council was even contemplating such a thing—ignoring the inconvenient fact that the city had been wrangling with the issue for the better part of a decade. Jerry Abbott wrote an opinion piece to that effect, and Madeline Hoover responded with an opposing version that ran two days later. The next thing you knew, the two of them were taking their dog-and-pony show on the road, going head-to-head on drive-time radio and getting into verbal catfights on cable access. Mad (who has a few years on me) said the two of them reminded him of an old *Saturday Night Live* sketch—the "Point-Counterpoint" one where Jane Curtin would give a speech on some issue and Dan Aykroyd would just look at her and say, "Jane, you're an ignorant slut."

The Friday after the package ended, the *Monitor* finally came out with an editorial on the Starlight. Benjamin, the edit page editor, had called me into his office the day before and grilled me on the whole thing, chomping on his unlit pipe as I told him everything I knew about the place. The man is quite a weirdo, even within the context of the psycho ward that is the *Monitor* newsroom. He wears red suspenders every single day, puts references to classical mythology in every damn thing he writes, and has a name right out of a Dickens novel: Benjamin Boodle. He originally came to the paper as features editor, with the understanding that he'd take over edit when the lady who'd been in charge of it since the Kennedy administration finally retired. Well, she never did—and poor Benjamin waited ten long years until she expired, twenty minutes after filing her last column.

I'm not sure what influenced his editorial more—my manic monologue about how we were all going straight to hell if the place was demolished, or the fact that he reads *Opera News* like other guys read *Juggs*. Either way, he came up with a rather stirring piece about how the Starlight was a precious commodity, and that if it was torn down part of the city's soul was going to disappear along with it. He showed it to me before he sent it down to Chester for approval, grinning like a little kid and babbling about the production of *Lucia di Lammermoor* he'd seen in Cooperstown last summer.

The next time I ran into him, he was fuming. Chester had decided the editorial was, quote, "too much," and made him tone it down.

"That cretin doesn't give a tinker's *damn* about good writing," he said, making me a little homesick with his choice of insult. "All he cares about is not going out on a limb. That, and making sure Kurtis-bloody-Osmond keeps advertising his rental properties. I haven't been so angry since he made me write that blasted serial killer column. Do you remember that?" The editorial, a four-square condemnation of serial murder as a career choice, had earned me heaps of humiliation from my fellow journalists. "I'm *not* rewriting this. I'm *not*," he said, and retreated to his office to do just that.

Late Friday morning, after a considerably more wishy-washy version of the column had landed on doorsteps throughout Walden County, the fax machine spit out a press release from Sissy Dillingham. She was calling a press conference for noon Monday, to be held in front of the theater. "It is ABSOLUTELY URGENT that ALL local media attend," the release said, giving no clue what it was about beyond an opportunity for every reporter in town to freeze his butt off. Since my editors like to know what they're in for, I gave her a call.

"Oh, no, I *can't* tell you," she said. "It's a surprise."

"Yeah, well, can you at least give me a hint?"

"But then it won't be a surprise."

"Listen, Mrs. Dillingham, I gotta tell you the truth," I lied. "We've been covering the Starlight a lot lately. I'm not sure my editor's going to let me go if I can't at least give him an idea of what it's about."

"But all the other reporters are going to be there . . ."

"For sure?"

"I . . . I certainly assume they will."

"Well, you never know what else is going to come up on Monday . . ." I let the threat hang there for a while. "I'd hate to miss something important, but it's really up to my editors . . ."

There was a long pause, so long I thought she might have hung up on me. "Off the record," she said finally. "Can I trust you to keep a secret?"

"Sure," I said, trying hard to sound convincing.

"Well . . ." Her voice lowered to a whisper. "I'm going to make an announcement."

"About . . . ?"

"About the theater."

"What about the theater?"

"I suppose it couldn't hurt to give you a little hint." I waited for her to start hinting. It took a while. "It's something *wonderful*," she said, "something that's going to change everything."

"Change it how?"

She gave a girlish little giggle. "Let's just say I wouldn't plan on renting an apartment in the Starlight Arms anytime soon."

"What happened? Did someone else come up with the money?"

"Oh, that's all I can say for now. Will you come to the press conference?" She sounded anxious, like she was inviting me to donate an organ or something. "Do you promise to come?"

"Sure."

"Oh *good*. I guarantee, your editors won't be disappointed."

My editors, frankly, were as sick of the Starlight story as I was. But I didn't share this fact with her, just got off the phone and started trying to figure out what my weekend stories were going to be. It was my turn to work Saturday and Sunday, which meant I not only had to cover cop duty but also turn out two features for the Monday paper. Since it was nearly Christmas, there was no way I was going to get out of doing at least one holiday thing; as it turned out, I got stuck with two.

One was a profile of the Gabriel cop who'd been dressing up as the Toys for Tots Santa for the past twenty years. On Saturday afternoon, I was wandering around the empty newsroom, eating a bagel and thinking about starting the other story—a feature on a family whose house had a gigantic homemade crèche with so many blinking lights it looked like Baby Jesus lived at Caesar's Palace—when the scanner on the cop reporter's desk started squawking. I didn't recognize the dispatcher's voice; whoever she was, she was having a bad case of the first-day jitters.

Emergency control to Gabriel monitors. Report of a . . . um . . . a one-car MVA with injuries on um . . . Larkspur Drive. No street number given. GPD and . . . and . . . an

*EMT unit are requested to respond. Sand's Ambulance is en
route to the scene.*

I debated whether or not to call a photographer, then realized Melissa was on duty; what better way to get back at
her for the Starlight fiasco than dragging her away from her
Saturday to shoot a banged-up Volvo? I was halfway to the
two-way radio when I remembered the *Monitor* had actually
entered the twenty-first century, and all the photographers
were carrying cell phones. I found her number on the call
list, dialed, and let it ring a good ten times. I was just about
to hang up when she answered.

"Hello?"

"Hey, where are you?"

"Brunching."

"Who with?"

"Um, just a friend."

"Yeah, I wonder who *that* is. You two gonna bury somebody alive this time?"

"Come on, Alex, it was an *accident*."

"Funny you should mention that, because it just so happens that . . ."

"Oh, no *way*."

"Yep."

"You don't have to sound so goddamn happy." She
groaned, a scarier sound than you'd think could come out of
a girl her size. "Okay, what is it?"

"One-car MVA."

"That's it?"

"With injuries."

"Wonderful. Where?"

"Larkspur Drive."

"Where the hell is that?"

"Pick me up out back and I'll show you."

I grabbed a notebook and my backpack—which, after my

Starlight interment, I'd become extremely attached to. I went down to the parking lot to wait for Melissa, who showed up five minutes later with a fried egg sandwich in her hand and a sour look on her face. She followed my directions up the hill, crossing the gorge and winding her way through the outskirts of the Benson campus toward the Heights. The roads are all curvy and confusing up there— people joke that they made them that way to keep out the downtown riffraff, which is probably true—so we came upon the accident scene almost before we knew it. There were two police cruisers there, along with an ambulance and an EMT unit from the Heights outpost of the Gabriel fire department.

Funny thing, though: there was no car.

Melissa backed up her Toyota so it wasn't so close to the scene; rescue workers don't appreciate being crowded by the press. She got out her camera gear, and we walked around the corner toward the flashing lights. It was just starting to snow, big thick flakes that filtered the blue and red and made it all look kind of . . . Christmasy.

"What do you think is up?" she whispered, handing me her camera so she could dig a pair of thin leather gloves out of her pocket.

"Beats me."

"Where's the car accident?"

I shrugged. "Maybe the dispatcher got it wrong. Sounded like she was pretty green. Anyway, they don't seem to be in much of a hurry over there."

"Well, there's *something* going on."

We stayed on the opposite side of the street from where the action was, but once we got past the big EMT unit we had a better view. There were three cops that I could see— no, four; one was leaning over near a squad car, the back of his heavy uniform jacket dusted with snow.

"What's he doing?" Melissa asked.

"I can't tell." So far the cops had been too preoccupied to notice us, but I had a feeling that as soon as they did we were going to get the boot. "You know, I was just up in this neighborhood for a . . ."

"Oh, my God. He's throwing up."

"What?"

"He's yakking. Must be a rookie."

"No he's not. I know that guy. He's Santa Claus."

"Huh?"

"I'm supposed to interview him tomorrow. He's the Toys for Tots guy. He's been on the force for like twenty years."

Melissa aimed her camera toward the crowd and started fiddling with the lens. "Come on, move out of the way . . . That's a good boy . . ." She shifted from side to side trying to get a view, and then gasped. "Holy *shit*."

"What is it?" She lowered the camera, and her face was so white it was almost funny. "Come on, what's up?"

"You don't want to know."

"Of course I do." She shook her head. For a minute I thought she was going to join Kris Kringle in some Yuletide vomiting. "Come on, let me see." I reached for the camera, and she pulled it away. I grabbed for it again, and without another word she gave it to me.

I lifted it and squinted one eye shut. At first all I could see were the blurry backs of uniforms and shapes of trees silhouetted against the sky. I moved the camera around until I found where Melissa had been aiming, and the thing that had made a veteran cop toss his cookies jumped into perfect focus.

It was a body. Or, rather, it was an approximation of a body. The form that lay on the grass by the side of the road was so distorted, so broken and battered, it was hard to think of it as human. There was blood everywhere, all around the corpse and underneath it—so that it looked, perversely enough, like someone had rolled out the proverbial red carpet. The arms and legs were twisted at weird angles, and though I couldn't really tell—or maybe I just didn't want to know—I had a feeling that pieces of them may actually be missing.

The face was the worst part of all. Not because it wasn't recognizable, but because it was. The mouth was stretched unnaturally wide and there was blood where the hair should have been, but I'd seen that face often enough that I knew whose remains were staring back at me through the telephoto lens. The snow was falling on the body, and it must have still been warm, because it melted almost instantly. The sight of it made me flash back to a story Cody had told me about a hooker whose mutilated body he'd found in the Combat Zone one winter, the snowflakes falling from the sky and landing where her face used to be.

I handed the camera back. When Melissa saw my face, hers lost its I-told-you-so expression.

"Christ, Alex, are you okay? Maybe we better get out of here."

"We gotta call Bill. Tell him this is page one for Monday."

"Sure, it's a fatal." She was getting her composure back and, in the tradition of journalists everywhere, was trying to cheer herself up by sounding extra callous. "If it bleeds, it leads, right?"

"Yeah, well, that's not the only reason."

"What do you mean?"

"The victim . . . It isn't just anybody." I shook my head to get the image out of my brain. "It's Sissy Dillingham."

12

IT'S A RUNNING JOKE AMONG THE GABRIEL NEWS MEDIA THAT
all the really interesting crime happens over the weekend,
when the TV station is closed. Nine News is something of a
joke to begin with, since it puts out all of two and a half
hours of original programming per week—a half-hour
weekday show that's the bane of local insomniacs, as it pre-
mieres at six P.M. and proceeds to repeat every hour on the
hour, all night long.

Gabriel is one of the smallest markets in the country to
have a TV station in the first place; the only reason it's there
at all is that it was required under the city's contract with the
cable company. Anyway, the reporters there are paid even
worse than we are, if you can believe it. They're notoriously
short-staffed, so there's no way they can spare somebody to
work Saturday and Sunday. If they ever do cover something
on a weekend, it's because the anchor (my friend Maggie,
who, incidentally, just turned thirty and launched into what
she calls a "major-league husband-hunt") hauls out a camera and shoots it on her own time.

The death of Sissy Dillingham was no different. After the
news hit the scanner—once the new dispatcher finally figured out the difference between a one-car MVA and a hit-

and-run—there was a clutch of reporters and photographers camped at the curve of Larkspur Drive, but nary a TV camera to be seen.

As it turned out, I'd been right about us getting the boot; as soon as the cops noticed us, they told us to back off or else. Then they started stringing crime-scene tape around trees and mailboxes and utility poles, closing off both ends of the street for a hundred yards in each direction.

Eventually, the exiled reporters were joined by a rather pissed-off couple who lived in the charming little Greek Revival mansion next door and weren't being allowed into their own driveway. They didn't bother to argue with the cop, just flipped open a StarTac and made a call. Ten minutes later the cop came back, lifted the tape high enough to accommodate their Jaguar, and let them through.

Barely a minute later he came back and did the same thing, only this time it was for the chief's official car. As it glided past us around the corner we got a glimpse of the passenger seat, which was occupied by none other than Brian Cody. We locked eyes for a second, him in the cop car and me in the press pool, and the looks on both our faces said *here we go again.*

"Wonder who's gonna get the inside track on *this* one," one of my radio colleagues said, earning himself an elbow in the gut.

"Piss off."

"No kidding," offered the other one—a woman who I thought might have been a bit more charitable to one of her own kind. "Nothing like being in bed with the cops for real, huh?"

I employed my other elbow. "Would you two cut it out? Everybody knows damn well he doesn't tell me anything about—"

"Yeah, right," said the first one, a talk-radio reporter who (at least according to his ex-girlfriend) keeps a police scanner in his bathroom. "I've definitely got to get up close and personal with that new lady cop. Might be kind of a turn-on to date a chick who could kill you if she felt like it . . ."

It went on like that for a while, until finally the chief came over and everybody shut up. He looked cold, a little surly, and way more beleaguered than you'd think after spending all of ten minutes at the scene. Then again, Sissy Dillingham's body was enough to ruin anyone's good mood.

"Okay, this is all you're getting," he said. "Hit-and-run. One victim. Female. No names until we notify the family. Now go away."

"Do you suspect foul—" the second radio reporter began, only to be interrupted by yours truly.

"When's the next, uh, briefing?"

"Ten A.M. tomorrow at the station. That's not going to mess up anybody's deadline, now is it?" And with that, he turned around and stalked back toward the corpse.

"Why did you do that?" The girl turned on me, her cheeks flaming more from anger than the cold. "That was *incredibly* rude."

"Take it easy," said the guy from the weekly paper. "She just saved your ass. You ever cover the chief before?" She shook her head. "Yeah, well, when he says 'This is all you're getting,' he means it. It's nonnegotiable."

"Are you serious?"

"Yeah, trust me," I said. "Trying to drag anything else out of him just pisses him off. It's even been known to get a girl kicked off a crime scene. You just gotta live to fight another day."

"Where's the fun in that?" She sighed, packed up her tape recorder, and scuttled away with the rest of us.

The snow was falling harder as Melissa and I drove back

down the hill, passing the coroner's car and a few more cruisers on their way up to the scene. The wipers on her old Corolla were no match for the weather, and by the time we pulled into the *Monitor* lot she was hunched over the steering wheel and trying to see through a hole roughly the size and shape of a Nerf football. She went straight to the darkroom to process the film, and when it was ready to print she asked me to come in and keep her company. I stood there under the creepy red light while she slid the negative into the enlarger and exposed the paper, then dropped the print into a tray of developing fluid. We watched as the white sheet started to tinge with gray, then solidified into a mangled mess that, a matter of hours ago, had been Sissy Dillingham.

"Jesus Christ," I said. "I didn't know you shot any of those."

"Me neither. I guess I did it without even thinking. There's three frames, all pretty much identical."

"They're never gonna let you run this, you know."

"No shit." She picked up the print with a pair of rubber-coated tongs and dunked it into the foul-smelling stop bath for a couple of seconds, then dropped it into the fixer.

"Would you if you could?"

She shook her head. "No way," she said. "Not even me. No fucking way." She dropped the print into a tub at the bottom of the sink and slid over to print another shot.

"You know, I was just over at her house a couple of weeks ago for an interview."

"So that's how you knew who the corpse was."

"No, I actually recognized her face—what was left of it, anyway. You want to hear something weird? It never even occurred to me it was the same house. It's on this huge corner lot and she had me come in another entrance, so I didn't even recognize the place. Can you imagine living like that?"

"In my dreams. So what was she like?"

"Kind of an odd duck. Really overbearing and shrill, but she was always working her butt off over some cause or other, which I guess is better than shopping all day long. Plus, she always seemed so miserable you sort of felt sorry for her despite yourself."

"I think you just described my mother."

I pointed at the print in the sink. "Can I pick this up?"

"Sure."

I plucked it from the little fountain of running water. The print felt cold and sticky, like leftover pasta. "What a way to go, huh?"

"You said it. What do you think happened up there?"

"Cops said hit-and-run."

"You think they'll catch the guy?"

I moved out of the way so she could drop the new print into the developer. "I hope so," I said. "Christ, he must have been going pretty goddamn fast to mess her up this bad."

We waited as the second image took shape, and the blank sheet became a wide shot of the road, the cars, and the cops clustered near the body. "And we think *our* jobs suck," she said. "How'd you like to deal with this shit for a living?"

"Huh?" I was concentrating on the picture. Something about it was bothering me, and it wasn't just that there was a mangled corpse at the edge of the frame.

"They've gotta let me run that one. I mean, you can barely even see the body, right?"

"Check this out," I said. "What's wrong with this picture?"

She dropped it into the fixer and took a closer look. "I

know, the composition's not great. I was trying to shoot fast before they kicked us out of there." She put her hands together to make a frame, and started peering at the print from different angles. "Maybe if I crop it a little off the right . . ."

"I'm not talking about it like a goddamn work of art. I mean, what's wrong with this *scene*?"

She dropped her hands to her hips and looked at it again. "I don't know. Do you see something?"

"It's what I *don't* see that's bugging me."

"Which is?"

"Skid marks."

I killed an hour banging out my piece on the star-spangled manger, then went home to feed the dogs. As I figured, Cody had dropped Zeke off with a note asking if I'd mind watching him overnight. I walked all three of them, which is quite an adventure since only Zeke knows what the word "heel" means. Then I drove back to the paper, made a quick pit stop at Schultz's Deli, and walked over to the cop shop.

"Hey, Joey." I said to the uniform perched behind a rather unwelcoming two inches of bulletproof glass. "Is Cody around?"

"Depends. You friend or foe today?"

I held up two paper bags. "Dinner."

He punched a button and picked up the phone. "Hey, Detective, there's a pain-in-the-ass reporter down here waving a coupla sandwiches around." He winked at me. "You want I should lock her up for you? Okay. You got it." He hung up. "He said to throw away the key."

"No problem. There's plenty of single guys over at the fire department."

He pushed a button, and a screaming buzzer informed me that the door was unlocked. I made my way up the stairs to what the local press (which is as overeducated as everyone else around here) refers to as the "sanctum sanctorum." As far as I knew, I was the only reporter who'd ever been up there.

I walked into a room filled with desks, computers, and grim-looking people who stopped talking the minute they saw me. Cody got up, threw an arm around my shoulders, and steered me down the hall to a break room that was only slightly larger than Shakespeare's dog bed.

"You're a lifesaver," he said, flopping down in a chair. He rolled his head from side to side, like his neck hurt. "What'd you bring me?"

"Roast beef on rye. Lettuce, onions, cheddar, Russian. Two pickles. Sourdough pretzels and a root beer. Oh, and a rice pudding."

"I think I love you." I let that one pass, since not talking about such things had, so far, been the key to romantic bliss. "You really carried a dead cow around for me?"

"I made them double-wrap it."

He leaned across the rickety little table and pecked me on the lips, then tore into the bag. "I'm *starved*. What'd you get yourself?"

"Swiss cheese orgy with mustard. The usual."

We sat there eating, Cody devouring his sandwich and me taking dainty little nibbles. Actually, I'm lying. I finished even faster than he did, but a lady doesn't like to admit it.

"You coming home tonight?" I asked when we'd moved on to the pudding course.

"Yeah. Not much to do here at this point."

"You get a hold of the husband?"

"How did you . . . ?"

"I got a pretty damn good look at her, Cody."

"I'm sorry to hear that."

"Yeah, well, so am I."

"And you weren't tempted to run with it?"

"Tempted, sure. But since there's no Sunday paper, it's a moot point. Chief'll release the name tomorrow, and I'll get it in Monday morning. Radio's gonna scoop me by a whole day either way. At least it's not two."

"You knew her, didn't you?"

"Course I did. Save Our Starlight thing's been my major assignment for the past two months. I spoke to the woman, like, three times a day."

"You want to tell me what she was like?"

"That's kind of what I came up here to talk to you about." He got a wary look on his face, one that I hadn't seen in months and definitely hadn't missed. "Don't worry," I said. "I didn't come up here trying to bribe you with pickles."

He cracked a smile, which went a long way toward allowing me to resume normal breathing. "It's a Class-E felony, you know."

"Then it's a good thing I'm the one offering information."

"You serious?"

"Unfortunately. It might be nothing, but I thought you should hear about it."

"Something about Cynthia Dillingham?"

"Something she said to me yesterday. As in the day before she got killed." He put down his pudding cup. I definitely had his full attention. "She'd called a press conference for Monday. You knew that, right?" He nodded. "So I called her up and asked her what it was about. She said she couldn't tell me, she wanted it to be a surprise. But I kind of threatened not to show up—you know, I've been covering this thing like forever, and I wanted to know if it was gonna be the same old song and dance S.O.S. has been doing for months. Kind of makes me feel like a rat at the moment. Anyway, the most she would say was that she had some big news that was going to change everything."

"Meaning . . . ?"

"Meaning they'd figured out a way to save the theater."

"Think about it, Alex. It might be important. What did she say exactly?"

I contemplated it for a while, taking the opportunity to dispatch more pudding. "She said that she wouldn't count on moving into the Starlight Arms anytime soon," I said. "That's the complex Kurtis Osmond wants to build once they tear down the theater. They're supposed to vote on the sale this Wednesday."

"Could that be reason enough for someone to want her dead?"

"Who knows? I mean, yeah, Osmond wants to get his mitts on the property, so there's got to be a fair amount of dough involved. He's been building all these ultra-lush buildings up on the hill, and from what I hear he's always been looking for someplace to put one downtown. The Starlight is sitting on prime real estate, right off the Green, and the lot is pretty huge. That's another reason some people on council wouldn't mind tearing it down—all that land just sitting there without paying any property taxes. It's a big deal, 'cause so much of the city is tax exempt."

"You mean Benson?"

"Yeah, and Bessler too, but Benson's a whole lot bigger. Property taxes are front-page news around here, you know. It's a major town-gown thing, trying to get Benson to pick up its share of the tab for fire and cops and stuff. Pretty exciting, huh?"

"But would it be enough to kill somebody over?"

"Jesus, I don't know. Maybe if it was true. But frankly, I didn't even believe her."

"Mrs. Dillingham? Why not?"

"Because she already pulled the same thing with Robert Renssellaer—making some big announcement and then having it turn out to be a dud. I mean, I'm not saying that she didn't *think* she had something earth-shattering. I just don't think it would have amounted to much, that's all."

"Who else knew about it?"

"I have no idea. Seemed like she wasn't going to let the press in on it until Monday. Probably the rest of the S.O.S. people knew what was up, though."

"Who did you tell?"

I stared at him. "What difference does it make?"

"Probably nothing. I'm just wondering."

"Bill. Marilyn. Melissa. Oh, and Mad, but I don't think he was really listening."

"You want to tell me everything you know about Cynthia Dillingham?"

"Do I have to do it here? This plastic chair is making my butt numb."

"Nah. I can meet you at your place in an hour or so. Notebook and a big Hershey bar, right?"

"Those are my usual terms."

He crammed the empty wrappers into the bags, then stood up and tossed them into the garbage. "Thanks again for dinner."

"My pleasure."

The door was closed, so he felt no compunction about grabbing me and kissing me for a while. Then I spent some time wiping lipstick off his freckles.

He was about to open the door, but I stopped him. "Hey, Cody, can I ask you something?"

"Seems only fair."

"You guys really treating this like an accident?"

"What do you think?"

"I think not."

"Smart woman."

"So am I correct in assuming that I'm not the only one who noticed there were no skid marks in the middle of Larkspur Drive?"

"Meaning . . . ?"

"Meaning you know damn well what. That whoever hit Sissy Dillingham didn't even try to stop."

"Some accidents happen that way."

"Yeah, if the driver never even sees the person. I covered one like that a couple of years ago. Happened at night, really foggy. This happened at, what, one in the afternoon? Before it was even snowing?"

He gave me one of his patented looks, green-eyed and assessing. "You know, Alex, you'd have made a damn good cop."

"So you've mentioned."

"You don't believe me?"

"No, I believe you," I said, kissing him one more time before he opened the door. "Just please, promise you'll never say it in front of my editor."

13

CHIEF HILL'S TEN A.M. PRESS CONFERENCE WAS REMARKABLE for only one thing: It told me absolutely nothing I didn't already know. To the other reporters nursing their Sunday morning hangovers, the revelation that the victim was Sissy Dillingham was big news. But for me, the most interesting thing about the briefing was how the cops had decided to play it. Chief Hill, looking very fatherly and official, stood in front of the Nine News camera (there was Maggie, working off the clock again) and appealed to the driver to turn himself in. He made the usual pitch about sparing the family any more pain—and, incidentally, sparing the perpetrator an even longer stint in the slammer once he got caught.

It was a good speech, aimed toward the two great human motivators: guilt and fear. Last summer, when a serial killer was leaving bodies in the chief's backyard, he'd essentially handed the investigation over to Cody, who was from the big city and knew how to cope with abject evil. But a hit-and-run is the sort of thing that's supposed to happen around here—it's not nice, but it's part of the natural order—and the chief knew how to play it. He came off as regretful, concerned, determined to see justice done. On the off-chance that Sissy's death really had been an accident, whoever mowed her down might actually come forward. But either way, it was a smart move; it let them run a murder investigation on the sly, while the killer figured he was off the hook. And maybe, just maybe, he'd get sloppy.

The press conference lasted less than half an hour, a lot of it consisting of side-stepped questions about witnesses and physical evidence. I hoofed it back to the newsroom afterward, making extra sure to look both ways before I crossed the road; having seen what a car could do to the human body. I was eyeing every kid-stuffed minivan like it was a Saturday Night Special.

Bill and Marilyn were waiting for me in her office, drinking coffee and slathering butter and jam on a pile of croissants. Bill tossed me one, and since nobody else was around Marilyn let me tap her private cappuccino machine.

"So what you got?" she asked once I'd been sufficiently caffeinated.

"Right now, they're treating her death as an accident. Nobody at the cop shop will say any different."

"Not even your boyfriend?" I gave her an insubordinate look. "Okay, I know, that's hitting it past the foul pole. Forget I asked. So they're treating it like an accident. If that's the official position, then we run with it. It's a first-day story anyway. Long as nobody else's got anything we don't . . ."

"They don't."

"Then we do the tragic hit-and-run angle, and let the rest of it speak for itself. The scene, how banged-up she was . . ."

I thought about what I'd seen lying on the shoulder of Larkspur Drive. "Banged-up" seemed an awfully polite way of putting it. "The chief said she died of 'severe trauma.' Truth is the woman looked like she'd been through a mulcher."

"I saw the pics."

"We running them?"

"The long shot. Period."

"Even Melissa didn't think you'd run a close-up of the corpse."

"So what can you file for tomorrow?"

"Mainbar on the hit-and-run and the investigation. Obit on Sissy. Sidebar on where all this leaves the Starlight."

"Which is?"

"I talked to Mayor Marty last night. He said as far as he knows, the vote's still on for Wednesday."

"You gotta be shitting me."

"Yeah, I know it sounds pretty harsh. But you gotta remember this whole thing happened once before already. They delayed it when Barry Marsh keeled over of a heart attack because they thought it was the decent thing to do. All it got them was three more months of arguing about it, and they ended up exactly the same place they started."

"That's the word on the street?"

"So far. But the only person I've been able to track down is Jerry Abbott, and he's at the extreme end of things. A couple of people are out of town until tonight, and everybody else is probably off doing Christmas stuff. Hopefully I'll get some callbacks later."

"When can you file?"

"On the hit-and-run, in an hour. I've already got a ton of stuff on Sissy, so assuming I can track down a couple of people for comment I should be able to file it by three. The Starlight thing may take a little longer."

"Fine. When you finish the mainbar, make sure your notes are legible for once."

"What difference does it make?"

She looked at me like I was exceedingly dense. "Because you're handing the story over to Madison."

"How come?"

"Isn't your friend Brian Cody the lead detective on the case?"

"Oh. Yeah."

"The door swings both ways, Alex. You don't want to take advantage of your personal life, and I don't want one of my reporters in a screaming conflict of interest."

"I know. You're right. I should have thought of it sooner."

"Good girl. By the way, if your boyfriend happens to say anything interesting in his sleep, feel free to write it down."

"Am I still covering the Starlight thing?"

"At this point, I can't see why not. If I stuck Madison with it he'd probably quit on me anyway. Speaking of which, have you seen today's *Times*?"

"Not yet. Why?"

"Check out the front of the Metro section. You might find it amusing."

"Hey, what about the husband?" Bill asked, finally interrupting his croissant-munching to say something.

"You mean Mark Dillingham? What about him?"

"Who the hell is he?"

"Head of chemistry up at Benson."

"So what's his story?"

"I don't know. I never met him. He never showed up at any of the S.O.S. stuff, which I always thought was kind of weird."

"What does Madison have to say about him?"

"I never asked."

"Well, ask."

"What for?"

"Call it a hunch," he said. "But I know this much. If there's anybody in the world who'd be inclined to run me over with the car, it'd be my wife."

I spent the rest of the afternoon working on my stories, and when I was done I was in need of three things: a drink, a newspaper, and the dirt on Mark Dillingham. Luckily, all were available at one convenient location. I walked the hundred and thirty-two steps to the dilapidated pit Mad calls home, and found him lounging in front of the TV in his boxer shorts.

"I assume the bar is open?"

"You assume correctly."

"What might be on tap for this evening?"

"An amusing little Cabernet Sauvignon."

"In an amusing little cardboard box?"

He waggled his wine-filled salsa jar at me. "Hey, this stuff isn't bad."

"If Emma ever finds out you drink wine out of a carton, she'll dump you like a stinky kipper."

"Yeah, well, what she don't know won't hurt me. Besides, she's somewhere over the Atlantic right now. Are you drinking or aren't you?"

"I'm drinking."

He siphoned me some wine into a mostly clean jar, refilled his own, and we settled on his lumpy couch. "So I hear you got quite an eyeful up in the Heights yesterday."

"Who told?"

"Melissa. She was out at the Citizen last night with some guy."

"Solid-looking fellow, sandy blond hair, sounds like he escaped from a Clint Eastwood movie?"

"That's him."

"I figured as much. What'd she tell you?"

"That you peeped through her camera and saw Sissy Dillingham in pieces on the ground."

"That pretty much covers it, yeah."

"What's the scoop?"

"I'm glad you asked, since it's going to be your headache from now on."

He rolled his eyes and took a big gulp of wine. "Jesus, we've got to get ourselves a goddamn cop reporter. What the hell is taking so long?"

"My guess is Chester's trying to save some dough. He probably needs to balance the budget or his father-in-law's going to disown him again."

"Marilyn would never let him get away with screwing her out of a cop reporter. Would she?"

"Up 'til this, the beat's been pretty quiet. Maybe now she'll call him on it. You saying you don't want to cover the Dillingham thing?"

"Bernier, I'm a goddamn science writer. That means I write about *science*, not some lame-ass car accident."

"It might not be so lame after all. Didn't Melissa tell you about the skid marks?" I filled him in on what little I knew about the story so far, and it made him marginally less annoyed about getting stuck with it. "Okay, so what can you tell me about Mark Dillingham?"

"First let me get a refill. You?" I handed him my jar, and he commuted to the kitchen.

"Why don't you just bring the box in here and leave it on the coffee table?"

He stopped in the doorway on his way back, giving me the same boy-are-you-dense look I'd just gotten from Marilyn. "Because," he said, "that would mean I drink too much."

"Oh. Right. My mistake."

"Okay, so Mark Dillingham." He sat down and stretched his legs the length of the couch, despite the fact that this meant dropping them across my lap. "He's a very smart man."

"You don't say."

"He's what, maybe . . . mid to late fifties. Did his undergrad at Chicago, got a PhD in orgo from Dartmouth."

"Orgo?"

"Organic chemistry, you dumb little Frog."

"I also majored in Spanish, you know."

"Nice to be so well rounded. Anyhoo, Dillingham came here as a post-doc and never left. Been head of the department for the past, I'd say, five years."

"So what's he like?"

"Pretty much your normal science type."

"Define."

"Loves research, hates teaching. Considers himself God's gift to his field. Thinks students are a big pain in the ass, which they are."

"So why'd he want to be chairman of the department?"

"It's a big deal, prestige-wise. Plus, they bought out part of his teaching load."

"What's his research on?"

"He synthesizes a class of drugs called indolocarbazoles. They're really just indole alkaloids, which is what he did his doctoral work on at Dartmouth—made a new Ellipticine analog which they're now using to treat cancer. Anyhow, his latest research is specifically involved with the synthesis of fluorine containing indolocarbazoles. They're drugs that target an enzyme called topoisomerase I, which gets used for DNA synthesis during cell division. So they're basically a new set of cancer drugs—mostly for colon cancer, I think."

"I am so incredibly sorry I asked."

"Liberal-arts loser."

"Riddle me this. What was up with Dr. and Mrs. Dillingham?"

"You mean besides the wife trying to grab my ass at the department Christmas party?"

"Again?"

"No, I mean last time. I didn't see her there this year."

"Interesting."

"Come to think of it, you hardly ever saw them together. He's basically married to his lab. Nights, weekends—anytime I need to talk to him for some story, he's always there." A wicked look crossed his face and parked there. "You know, I bet you ten bucks he's there right now."

"Mad, his wife got *killed* yesterday. And he's got *kids*."

He picked up the phone. "I'll give you three-to-one odds."

"This is beneath even us."

"You in or you out?"

"Oh, hell, I'm in. Wait. What are you going to say to him if he actually answers?"

"You want me to ask him if he ran over his wife with the Lexus?"

"No, I do not. Just put the phone down."

But he'd already dialed, and was grinning like an idiot as he held up the receiver so we both could hear. It rang three times, and a voice said . . . *Mark Dillingham*. Then Mad hung up.

"Pay up."

I forked over the ten bucks. "I don't believe it. He must be trying to take his mind off his grief or something."

"Bernier, I bet you dollars to daiquiris the man barely even noticed he *had* a wife."

"Which is how she ends up getting soused and hitting on the local media."

"That, and incredibly good taste."

"The lonely faculty wife. What a cliché."

"Hey, don't knock my hobbies."

"You know, back when Barry Marsh died I definitely got the feeling she was into him. I had a sneaking suspicion that maybe this whole Save Our Starlight thing was—I don't know—something she had to do because it was all she had left of him."

"You chicks can get so damned emotional."

"Emma's out of town one day, and you're already back to the caveman routine." He banged on his chest and did a mediocre interpretation of a Tarzan yell, which I ignored. "The question is, were the two of them really involved? Or did she just have a fatal attraction for him?"

He seemed rather let down that I hadn't taken the bait, but after another long swill he answered me. "Sounds like she was taking things pretty far overboard if it was all in her head, don't you think? What do you know about the guy?"

"Barry Marsh? Not much. Actually, less than that. I mean, I never would have pegged him as much of a Romeo, and it turned out he wanted to get it on so bad it killed him. I guess I'll have to ask around."

"You really think somebody killed Sissy on purpose?"

"I don't know. I mean, I hope not. But you'd have to be the worst driver on the planet to do it by accident, right? The speed limit's thirty on every street in the Heights, and it was broad daylight. No snow, no nothing."

"They know what she was doing in the middle of the road?"

"Getting the mail. The boxes are all on one side of the road up there, which was across the street from her house. Apparently she died clutching a copy of *Saveur*."

"Huh?"

"Fancy food magazine. That's all you've got on Mark Dillingham?"

"There's not much to get. Like I said, he's totally crocked on his work. I've never even heard about him taking a trip that wasn't to a conference."

"Can you think of any reason he'd want his wife dead?"

"Are you serious?"

"Bill says the only person who'd run him over is Betsy."

"He's got that right."

"What if Sissy really was running around behind his back, whether it was with Barry Marsh or someone else? Would he get mad enough to . . ."

"Trust me, Mark Dillingham isn't the type. I can't imagine him getting excited about anything you couldn't put under an electron microscope."

"Makes you wonder why he bothered to get himself a wife in the first place."

"I ask myself the same question about every married guy I know."

"Well, if it wasn't personal, it's got to have something to do with the theater."

"What makes you say that?"

"Because as far as I know, that was all she did lately— host dinner parties and agitate over the Starlight. And like I told you, she swore she was going to drop some big bombshell on Monday, something that was going to screw up the sale to Kurtis Osmond."

"Yeah, but you also said you didn't buy it."

"But what if she was actually on to something? Maybe there really was some millionaire who was going to bail them out. Or even if she was full of it, maybe just the threat of it was enough to get her killed."

"Is this deal really worth that much money? Enough to kill somebody over?"

"Building's supposed to be condos. Forty of them. Local real estate type just told me they'd probably start at a hundred grand a pop. You do the math."

"Yowza. I'd kill for half that."

"Oh, hey, I almost forgot. Do you have today's *Times*?"

"It's in the trash."

"Are you ever going to learn how to recycle?"

"I know how. I just don't bother."

I went to the kitchen and started digging for the paper

among the orange rinds and empty beer cans. "Did you catch something interesting on the front of Metro? Marilyn said there was."

"Screw New York," he said happily. "I see a dateline in the five boroughs, I skip over it as fast as I can."

"They put the Upstate stuff in there too, you know." I finally found the section, which Mad had (quite literally) used to wrap fish—specifically the can of sardines he'd had for lunch. "Ugh. This thing smells gross." I carried it back into the living room and smoothed it out on the coffee table. " 'Schoolteachers protest crappy pay.' Okay, that's not it. 'Mob connection in waste hauling industry.' Whew. Stop the presses. 'Why all other cities suck and we don't.' "

"You made that last one up."

"Yeah, you caught me." I moved to the bottom of the page. "*Holy shit.*"

"What?"

"That *asshole.*"

"Who are you . . ."

"Look at this." I shoved the paper toward him. Stripped across the bottom was the headline, "COMEDY AND TRAGEDY IN EFFORT TO SAVE HISTORIC GABRIEL THEATER."

"So the *Times* finally noticed there's a whole big state north of Westchester. Good for them."

"Look at the byline."

"Ooh. Gordon strikes again."

"So what does it say?"

He picked up the paper and stretched out on the couch again. "Hmm . . . Same-old same-old. Sissy Dillingham, Starlight memories, God's gift to local history, yadda-yadda. Pretty decent overview, though. Guy does his homework."

"He get any good quotes?"

"Not bad."

"I can't believe he was up here covering this and he didn't even *call* me."

"That's just Gordon. No use getting all huffy over it."

Gordon Band had been the *Monitor*'s cop reporter during a fifteen-second hiatus from the *Times*. The three of us had broken the biggest story of our careers together, and the son of a bitch still didn't know how to use the goddamn telephone.

"But don't you think he should have at least . . ."

"He's a guy."

"That's your universal excuse for everything."

"Hey, whatever works."

I snatched the paper back and waved it at him. "Well, this layout is probably punishment enough."

"What do you mean? It's on the goddamn front of Metro."

"That's true," I said. "But nothing pisses Gordon off like being stuck below the fold."

14

THERE ARE SIX BILLION PEOPLE IN THE WORLD, AND ON ANY given day you can be fairly certain that most of them aren't going to call you. The coach of the U.S. Olympic figure skating team, for instance, is unlikely to pick up the phone and recruit me on the strength of that double axel I almost landed in the sixth grade. The Chief Justice of the Supreme Court is probably not going to invite me to join up and make it an even ten—nor, for that matter, is Harrison Ford going to ask me to marry him and brighten up his golden years.

There were, in other words, plenty of people less likely to call me than Lindy Marsh. But when she invited me to her house for lunch, I still just about keeled over from the shock.

So there I was, eating a big slice of onion tart at her kitchen table. I'd already polished off a Caesar salad, hold the anchovies; she'd barely touched her food but was more than doing justice to a bottle of Gewürztraminer.

We'd been through all the pleasantries, from the weather to the abject beauty of her seventy-dollar MacKenzie-Childs salad bowls. Finally she pushed back her plate as though it nauseated her, took another slug of what appeared to be very good wine, and said this:

"My husband was a son of a bitch."

"Excuse me?"

"My husband was a son of a bitch." Her voice got louder, more screechy. I was glad the windows were closed. "Barry Marsh was a son of a bitch. *A son of a bitch.* What do you think of that?"

"Are you, like, telling me this for publication or something?"

"Do whatever you want with it."

"To be honest, I, um . . . I still don't really understand why you asked me over here."

"I'm not drunk, you know. I don't get drunk."

"I didn't think you were."

Actually, I thought she was fully three-quarters in the bag, but I decided to be polite. She didn't answer, just swirled her wine around her glass. I'd never seen Lindy Marsh be anything but composed—except, of course, for the day her husband died—and I was starting to wonder if her body had been taken over by some PMS-ing alien.

"Listen, Mrs. Marsh, are you upset about something? I mean, something other than . . ."

"Than the fact that my husband was a son of a bitch?"

"Other than that, yeah."

"You must think I'm a *pathetic* creature."

"No I don't."

"*I* do. Twenty-six years of marriage to . . ." I was laying odds she was going to say a *son of a bitch*, but she surprised me yet again. ". . . someone you adore, or whom you *think* you adore. But he was never really there at all. Was he?"

She looked like she expected me to answer, but I had no idea if she wanted a yes or a no. "Is there something you wanted to tell me? Maybe if . . . you know, if you get it off your chest it might make you feel better."

It took her a long time to answer, and when she finally did her voice sounded small, tight, and far away.

"Sissy . . ." *Oh, here we go.* "Sissy was my . . . my best friend. Oh, God, poor Sissy . . ."

Poor Sissy?

Her eyes were starting to fill up, and she fumbled for a flowery paper napkin so she could blow her nose. When she came up for air, she seemed a little calmer.

"I suppose I should . . . begin at the beginning. Can I get you anything else? Are you sure you wouldn't like a glass of wine?"

"Ice tea's fine for me."

She gave me a refill from a painted glass pitcher, then settled back into her chair and sat there for a minute before she started talking again. "I know you must be confused about why I asked you to come. I'll . . . I'll get to that. But at the moment I think I should begin at the beginning." She looked like she wanted permission, so I sort of nodded at her. It seemed to do the trick. "I met Barry in London. Did you know that? No? I was spending a year abroad studying dance, he was getting a master's at the School of Economics. Sometimes when I look back on it I like to tell myself that I was drawn to him because he was so . . . appropriate. So much the sort of young man my parents assumed I'd bring home one day. But the truth is that I fell in love with him. I would have given up anything to be with him. Did, in fact. When his term was over I left the academy to follow him back to the States."

"And then you got married?"

"Then we got married. He started work for a bank in New York, and things were . . . lovely. We had a subscription to the ballet, and I met the most interesting people. Barry worked all the time, of course, but we had *fun* too. But then his company . . . they bought out a bank with a number of upstate branches, and Barry was promoted and transferred to Rochester. Then Buffalo, then Syracuse, then Binghamton—always moving up for him, moving down for me. Have you ever *been* to Binghamton? Well have you?"

"Um, they have a really nice minor-league baseball park . . ."

It didn't seem to impress her. "There were quite a lot of consolidations in the 1980s. Barry became the person the bank sent out after a takeover to get things under control, whip them into the company line. He was very good at it. People liked him. He could lead with the carrot instead of the stick, because he always made everyone want to please him. It made things go much more . . . smoothly.

"We came to Gabriel ten years ago last September. The bank recruited Barry to be president, and he thought it would be a nice place to retire. Gabriel was better, of course—smaller than where we were used to but much more hospitable. I'd never lived in a college town before, but I found I was the happiest I'd been since we left New York, at least in terms of where we were living. People here appreciate culture, don't they? I'd wanted to open a ballet school in Syracuse, but I could never find just the right location, and Barry said there were too many of them there already. But I found the perfect spot here right away. You've been to the school, haven't you?"

"I did the *Nutcracker* story two years in a row."

"Oh, of course. Did you know our Clara is studying with the A.B.T.? Kimmie Vanneman. She's going to be a *great* talent."

"I think it was in the paper."

"The school has been . . . Well, I suppose it's been my life. Barry and I wanted to have children, but I had four miscarriages and neither one of us wanted to adopt. But now I have my girls. Have you ever read *The Prime of Miss Jean*

Brodie? She said, 'Give me a girl at an impressionable age, and she is mine for life.' It's true, you know."

I gave her another vague nod, which again seemed to be all the validation she was looking for.

"That was how I met Sissy, when she brought her daughter Adriana in for lessons. She was only six or seven years old, and not very . . . promising. But there's not a little girl in the world who doesn't adore the ballet, now is there?"

I decided not to mention that around age eight, in the brief lull between quitting swimming lessons and bailing on the Brownies, I'd thrown my baby-pink tutu out a second-story window.

"Of course," I said. "Everybody loves ballet."

"It's so *true*. And once Adriana graduated into Intermediate Beginners, she really blossomed. Sissy helped out with costumes and hair, that sort of thing, and we got to be friends. Best friends, in fact." She paused again, this time to take a gulp of Gewürztraminer. "I'm not going to say I didn't eventually . . . That I didn't suspect what was going on. There were signs. But I never thought . . . I didn't think that even Barry would be so cruel as to . . . With Sissy . . ."

"She and your husband were having an affair."

Her mouth curved into a creepy little smile. " 'Womanizer' is a rather outdated term, don't you think?"

"It's not exactly politically correct."

"But Barry wasn't what you'd call a liberated man. And he wasn't what you'd call faithful, either. Even when we were engaged, he was seeing another girl in the corps de ballet. Then there were, oh, all sorts of women—executive secretaries, wives of golf partners, department store clerks, stewardesses. He liked them skinny, boyish-looking, no matter how old they were. Once he . . . After she was older, of course, but once he even . . . One of my Claras."

"Jesus Christ. How come you stayed with him?"

"Do you want to hear something ridiculous? I still loved him. The more he ran away from me, the more he hurt me and humiliated me, the more I wanted him to love me like he used to. Like I *thought* he used to . . ."

"Didn't you ever call him on it?"

She shook her head. "When your husband comes home with lipstick on his collar fifty nights in a row, you can't exactly confront him about it on the fifty-first, now can you?"

"That's crazy."

"I take it you've never been married."

"Me? Oh, God no."

"I don't recommend it. I'm convinced marriage isn't a natural state for men, and if it's no good for men then it can't possibly be any good for women, now can it?"

"I'm not sure I understand."

"Once a man thinks he owns you, any sense of respect, of desire . . . it doesn't last."

"That's pretty pessimistic."

"How old are you?"

"Twenty-seven."

"Yes, well, let's see what you think twenty years from now." *Yikes.* "I spent quite a number of years pretending I didn't see what Barry was doing. And when I couldn't ignore it, I blamed the women. I certainly blamed Sissy. I *hated* her. Then she . . . died, and hating her didn't seem so simple anymore. It didn't seem so . . . pure. I found myself thinking about *why* I hated her. Betraying our friendship was part of it, of course. That's only natural. But the truth is that I hated her most of all for making me see things clearly."

"Clearly how?"

"Here was a good woman, a kind woman, a *friend* of mine, and she fell for Barry's charms just the same. Her husband barely gave her the time of day, and whatever Barry was offering her must have seemed so . . . She wanted it so much that she was even willing to break my heart."

"Listen, Mrs. Marsh, I'm sorry, but I don't really understand why you're telling me all this."

"I know you've been confused about where I stand on the Starlight Theatre issue. Well, so have I. I worked for a long time to save that building, but it was also the thing that brought Sissy and Barry together, and for that reason I wanted it gone. But I want you to know that as of now, I'm supporting S.O.S. again. It's probably too late, but it's important to me that there be no more confusion on that point."

"Fair enough."

She gave me a mildly disappointed look. "Please don't humor me, Alex. You can't possibly believe that's the only reason I asked you over here."

"It's not?"

"No, it's not. I want you to do something for me."

"Do what?"

"How well do you know the Gabriel Police Department?"

"As well as any reporter, I guess."

"I was under the impression you had a rather intimate connection."

"You mean Detective Cody."

"That's right."

"If you already knew, why did you ask?"

"Don't be so ingenuous. We both know that reporters are very fond of asking questions they already know the answers to."

"So what's your point?"

"As you may know, I'm an acquaintance of Chief Hill and his wife. I wouldn't go so far as to call us friends, but he was very kind when Barry died. Still, at the moment I'm in a rather . . . unfortunate position with the Gabriel police. I'm afraid I've earned a reputation for being somewhat . . . hysterical since Barry died, and Sissy . . . Well, nothing I say is taken seriously. I have tried to bring certain . . . evidence to their attention, and it hasn't done a bit of good."

"Bring evidence to whom?"

"To the chief. To your Detective Cody. To Sergeant Kirkland, who's the highest-ranking woman in the department. None of them want to listen."

"Cody's usually pretty reasonable."

"It's only natural that you'd defend him, but you're forgetting one thing. When it comes to Sissy, he considers me a suspect. Everyone knows she was seeing my husband. Everyone knows I knew. Who had more of a reason to want her dead?"

"What about her husband?"

"Mark? He probably hasn't even noticed she's gone."

"And you want me to . . . what? Try and talk Cody into taking you seriously?"

"Not exactly. To begin with, I just wanted to know where you stand."

"Cody and I try to keep our work lives separate from the rest of our relationship." She seemed amused, and not in a good way. "Okay, so it's not easy. But that's the idea."

"Who do you think killed her?"

"Maybe it really was an accident."

"I've already asked you not to humor me."

"Sorry."

"Do you think I killed her?"

"I have no idea."

"At least now you're being honest. Let me tell you something. I didn't kill her. But I want to know who did."

"So do the cops."

"We have that in common, at least. But I'm convinced they're looking in the wrong direction."

"What do you mean?"

"They're looking at me, for one. And at Mark, since whenever a woman is murdered the odds are that it's her husband who did it. They're going through their finances, trying to find a reason he'd profit from her death, looking for evidence he was having an affair of his own. When they're not slinging mud at one or the other of us, they're concentrating on something to do with Save Our Starlight. And I can tell you right now, there's nothing there."

"How can you be so sure?"

"Because although I should be the last one to admit it, S.O.S. was a lost cause to begin with. If you seriously think Sissy Dillingham was a threat to the sale of that building, you're mistaken. I'm sure she'd be flattered to know you think it, but that doesn't make it any less absurd."

"If not the theater, then what?"

"Barry."

"*What?*"

"There's one thing I'll say for him. Barry was a very *monogamous* adulterer. He always strayed with one woman at a time, and only one woman. From what I could tell he always had the next candidate lined up before he moved on, but he was never involved with more than one of them at once."

"And you want me to . . . what?"

"I want you to find out who killed Sissy."

"Listen, Mrs. Marsh, I'm a reporter, not a cop. And because of the conflict of interest thing with Cody, I'm not even covering the Dillingham story anymore. Jake Madison is."

"And I know very well the two of you are thick as thieves."

"What do you—"

"I read the newspaper, Alex. I watch television now and

then. I know what happened to you last year, when your friend Adam Ellroy was murdered."

"What does that have to do with—"

"I know what you did last summer, when those poor girls were being killed. The police didn't stop it on their own."

"What's your point?"

"Don't feel the need to be rude. I'm giving you a compliment. I'm telling you that you come to this with certain . . . unique qualifications."

"Which are . . . ?"

"You know Gabriel. You knew Sissy, a great deal better than any policeman did. And you also know that tire tracks or no tire tracks, finding out who killed her is not a matter of physical evidence. It's a matter of the heart."

"Nobody knows that for sure."

"I do."

"But wait a minute. What you're saying doesn't make sense. By the time Sissy was killed, Mr. Marsh had been dead for weeks already."

"Yes, but that doesn't change the fact that he must have left someone for her, don't you see?"

"And you seriously think that whoever he dumped to be with Sissy was still mad enough to kill her? Even though Mr. Marsh was already dead?"

"I'm certain of it."

"I don't know. I mean, that's hardly your typical crime of passion. Wouldn't that be awfully . . . cold?"

That unsettling smile spread across her face again. "You may be too young to understand this yet," she said, "but that's just the right temperature for revenge."

15

THE DEATH KNELL FOR THE STARLIGHT THEATRE CAME THE day before Christmas Eve, in the middle of a blinding snowstorm that started exactly fifteen minutes too late to cancel the meeting. Like all executions, it happened a whole lot faster than you'd think, considering all the melodrama that had led up to it. The issue came up on the agenda, Jerry Abbott moved that they approve the sale of the building to Kurtis Osmond, and somebody seconded it. Then they opened discussion on the issue, and since this is Gabriel, everybody immediately bent over backward to be fair to the less fortunate.

Council gave Save Our Starlight the chance to say something, anything, before the ax fell. That dubious task went to Adele Giordano-Bronstein, as Roger Nash was too upset to come to the meeting, and Sissy Dillingham was occupying several drawers in the Gabriel city morgue. She spoke less than five minutes, a sad little speech that amounted to throwing herself on the mercy of the court. No, they hadn't been able to raise more than sixty thousand dollars in private funds. Yes, their guardian angel had let them down. No, they hadn't been able to get any grants from the government; the theater's previous restoration and failure, which had flushed a lot of federal dollars down the commode, had made it all but impossible.

She had no excuses, and no answers either. All she knew was that the Starlight was worth saving, and though they hadn't been able to do it she was sure someone else could. She told them that saving the theater might be the most important thing they did in their council careers. She told them future generations of Gabrielites would thank them for it. She told them she'd said a Novena on the subject, and she was pretty sure *God* wanted the theater to stay standing. She told them—and okay, this was the lowest blow of all—that they should do it for poor, shredded Sissy Dillingham.

Then she sat down.

"I think we've spent enough time debating this issue," said Mayor Marty, inspiring both the aldermen and the press to stare at him in mild shock. The man usually presides over council with the benign neglect of a lunchroom monitor, but for once he was actually taking charge.

"This has been going on for far too long," he said. "The city of Gabriel has been dealing with this issue, one way or t'other, for the past fifteen years. Now, I don't know about you people, but I'm ready to be done with it. Either let's decide we're going to throw the resources of this city behind saving the Starlight, if somebody can tell me how to do it in a reasonably cost-effective manner, or let's tear the damn thing down before it kills somebody. Now I'm going to ask for a straw vote. Any objections?"

Madeline Hoover opened her mouth, but she didn't say anything. Everybody else stared down at the council table, looking oddly chastened, like they were getting a lecture from their coach for bad sportsmanship.

"Good. Now before I take the vote, I'm going to say two things, 'cause I'm the mayor and I can. The first is that I'd be thrilled to bits to see this theater reopened, but after all these years I'm at a loss for how anybody's going to do it. The second is that abandoned properties are one of the worst things a city can have. I know a lot of you think I'm somewhere to the left of Lenin, and maybe I am, but I know that much.

"We all have our ideals, and frankly I think mine are better than anybody's. But sometimes we have to be practical, because that's what they elected us for. Now, unofficially, who would vote to scrub the deal with Mr. Osmond and try and figure out how to save the place?" Five hands went up, then down. "Okay, who would vote to consummate the sale right here and now, so Mr. Osmond can tear the thing down and build himself some expensive real estate?" Up went the other five hands.

Mayor Marty shook his head and gave a sigh that seemed to go deep down to the soles of his Birkenstocks. "That's what I was afraid of. Nobody's undecided?" They all shook their heads. "Then I guess it's up to me. If nobody objects, I'm calling the formal vote. All those in favor of the sale?" The same five hands went up again. "All those against?" Ditto.

"Then as per council rules, I have to cast the tie-breaking vote. But before I do, I want to say that I'm damn sorry it's come to this. We're a smart town, smarter than most, and we should've been able to save the place. But there's way too much water under the bridge at this point, and as mayor I can't let the building sit there disintegrating any longer. It's a hazard, it's an eyesore, and it's a waste of potential tax revenue. So I vote in favor of the sale. It's a damn shame." A collective moan arose from the handful of S.O.S. people present, and he whacked his gavel as though for catharsis. "Now let's move on to the next agenda item," he said. "And let's try not to muck it up as badly as the last one, shall we?"

That was it. The end of the Starlight came not with a bang but with a really pathetic whimper. On her way out of the meeting, Adele Bronstein said something about suing and asking for an injunction, but nothing ever came of it. Kurtis Osmond had all of his demolition permits polished and ready for filing; the only thing standing in his way was a niggling little thing called Christmas.

I spent the holiday back home in the Berkshires with my parents, Shakespeare, Tipsy, and a pair of unexpected guests: Detective Brian Cody and his faithful dog Zeke. He'd been planning to drive his mom to Boston to spend Christmas and most of the week after it with the rest of the clan, but now he had the Sissy Dillingham case hanging over his head, and he couldn't leave town for that long. Having worked Thanksgiving, I was liberated for both Christmas and New Year's—a tactic I'd used every year I'd been working at the paper, and which no one else had seemed to catch on to yet.

We threw the three dogs and two bags of presents into the back of my Renault hatchback around two on Christmas Eve, and I spent most of the four-and-a-half-hour drive trying to prepare Cody for the existential frenzy that is my parents. He was relieved, however, to learn that their conservatism was political rather than social; in other words, we weren't going to have to sleep in separate rooms. "Oh, don't worry, they're going to love you," I said. "My dad lives for the whole law-and-order thing. Did I tell you the two of them actually support the death penalty?"

I waited for some moral outrage, and didn't get it. "You know, Alex, the truth is that it has its . . ."

"Oh, right, sorry, we've had this argument five times already."

"And you always win it by taking your clothes off."

"Not so practical when I'm driving."

"You really think your folks will like me?"

"Well, my mom's a lawyer, so she'll probably ply you with turkey until you're all full and helpless, then pick your brain for ways to get her clients off the hook. My dad will just try to talk you into giving him shooting lessons."

"With my service revolver? You know I can't . . ."

"Oh, don't worry, he's got plenty of his own."

"Your dad keeps guns? Are you serious?"

"Unfortunately. He studies the Civil War, so he got into it that way, then he just kind of got hooked on it. He says it has something to do with the sociology of weaponry, but frankly I think he just likes to shoot at stuff. At first my mom wouldn't let him keep them in the house, but then she got death threats over some case and she had him bring a couple home for protection. Don't worry, it's all licensed and everything. From what I hear my mom's a damn good shot."

"Man, Alex, where did you come from?"

"My parents have been asking themselves the same question ever since I could talk."

"Your dad ever get you out on the range?"

"He's been trying for years, but I always tell him it offends my lefty sensibilities."

"Am I really giving him shooting lessons?"

"Do you mind?"

"Course not. I was more wondering if *you* mind."

"Nah, you guys can have male bonding. Mom and I'll hit the after-Christmas sales. Besides, he's already reserved time at the range for all of Saturday morning. What's so funny?"

"No wonder you thought my family was so . . ."

"Norman Rockwellesque?"

"Not the word I was going to use, but yeah."

"You think *this* is weird," I said. "Wait until you've survived the dinner conversation."

We got back to town Sunday afternoon, after a three-day visit during which both of us, and all three of the dogs, were severely overfed. Shots were fired, presents exchanged, and stockings duly hung—including two I'd embroidered with *Zeke* and *Cody*. (The latter raised some eyebrows, but if I ever called him by his first name he'd probably think I was about to dump him.) The fateful parent-boyfriend introduction had gone well; too well, in fact, because at the end of it they proposed cutting me loose and adopting him instead.

I dropped Cody at the station so he could get filled in on anything he'd missed over the past seventy-two hours, and I went home to unload the dogs and my Christmas loot. I was just trying on my new red cashmere sweater set when the phone rang.

"Good, you're back," Bill said. "I need you to get over to the Starlight, pronto."

"What's up?"

"Ever heard of the expression 'chaining yourself to the wrecking ball'?"

"Yeah."

"Well, they are."

"You mean they're already demolishing the place? On a Sunday? Right after Christmas?"

"Apparently, Osmond had the whole thing ready to go as soon as the sale went through. Didn't want to give anybody the chance to change their mind."

"Or sue."

"It's quite a scene down there. Melissa's shooting it as we speak, so go cover it."

"I'm off today."

"Very funny."

"Am I at least getting a couple of bucks for overtime?"

"Since when are you so particular?"

"Since I saw my last credit card bill."

"We'll talk."

I hauled the rest of the presents into the house, made sure the dogs were fed and watered, and drove to the paper. Then I walked across the Green to the theater, and found out it was a good thing I hadn't tried to drive straight there. The whole street in front of it was blocked off, and there were a couple of pieces of majorly heavy equipment being run—or rather, occupied—by several equally heavy young men. I say occupied, because they weren't actually doing much beyond drinking coffee and looking bored. Clearly, they were getting paid whether they knocked something down or not.

There were at least a dozen uniformed cops swarming around, but I didn't see any other reporters; every media outlet in town was on a skeleton crew for the holiday weekend. I made my way to the front of the theater, and found it wasn't there anymore. There was just a gaping hole where the doors used to be, and a clear shot into what was left of the lobby. The only thing blocking the view was the line of protesters strung across the front, holding hands like paper dolls. It was freezing out, and they were bundled in so many layers of winter clothes they resembled nothing so much as a human chain of Michelin men.

"How long they been out here?" I asked one of the cops.

"Middle of the day yesterday."

"When did they start tearing it down?"

"First thing Saturday morning. Then these loony birds came running down here, and they've been stalled ever since."

So they'd actually spent the night out there; it was

amazing nobody'd frozen to death. I walked closer, and the bulky forms turned out to be a bunch of people I knew. There were ten of them, including Lindy Marsh, Madeline Hoover, Roger Nash, and Adele Giordano-Bronstein. I did some interviews, and got just the sort of quotes you'd expect—all about how they were going to stay put as long as it took, and that if Kurtis Osmond wanted to rip the building down he was going to have to get through them first. Adele won the award for Most Melodramatic Sound Bite: "Within fifty years each and every one of us will be in heaven with our Lord," she said. "But, God willing, the Starlight will still be standing. And before I'll allow one more brick to be torn down, I for one will freeze to death right here on this spot."

As it turned out, they had a system going. Every couple of hours one of them would drop out of the line, go warm up, get some food, hit the bathroom, and come back to relieve somebody else. Very clever.

I was still interviewing them when Mayor Marty showed up and tried to talk them into packing it in. "Look," he was saying, "nobody likes a good protest more than I do. But come on, this is pointless. They've already demolished the front wall, and who knows if the building's even structurally sound anymore. You people could get yourselves killed standing there." When that didn't work, he tried another approach. "I hate to say it, but as of Wednesday this is private property. It belongs to Kurtis Osmond, and he says if I can't talk you into leaving of your own accord, he's going to have you all arrested."

Nobody budged.

"Okay, I respect your convictions. Everybody knows I've spent a fair amount of time in the back of a paddy wagon myself. I'll tell the chief to make sure they use the plastic handcuffs."

"Wait," Madeline Hoover said as Mayor Marty was walking away. "If we leave quietly, will Mr. Osmond stop the demolition long enough for us to remove some historical artifacts? Architectural elements, that type of thing?"

The chief went over to the Mercedes where Osmond was busy seething. I thought it would be over in a couple of minutes, but the mayor stood leaning over the driver's window for a good long time.

"That man is an ass," he said when he got back. "But he's seen the wisdom in cooperation. He says his men will help you take whatever you want out of the building for the next thirty-six hours. That gives you until Tuesday morning. I'd take it."

"We want it in writing."

"I figured as much," the mayor said, taking a sheet of paper out of his jacket pocket and holding it in front of her nose. Madeline read it and, thus satisfied, finally resigned her link in the daisy chain. That inspired her comrades to do the same, and before I knew it the only thing between the Starlight and the wrecking ball was me. I decided to move.

As promised, the demolition halted until Tuesday morning. Then it started up again and went on for a solid week, ninety-some-odd years of theater history getting knocked down and carted away. Madeline Hoover and an army of volunteers from the historical society had, at least, managed to save a tractor-trailer's worth of stuff, from lighting fixtures to floor tiles to every single one of the carved seat arms. I know, because I did a story on it.

By the following Tuesday, most of the Starlight had been consigned to the theater of memory. The upper floors had been flattened, and some sort of enormous backhoe had moved in to scoop out what was left of the basement. I was standing at the edge of the rubble, wearing a hardhat and working on one last story on the building's demise, when the big yellow machine suddenly went silent. Two of the men emerged from the ruins a minute later, red-faced and breathing hard.

"Do you have a phone with you?" one of them asked. I nodded. "I think you better call the cops."

"About what?" I pictured one of the S.O.S. protesters flinging herself under the backhoe in a last-ditch effort to save . . . I didn't know what.

"You're not gonna believe what we found down there."

"What is it?"

"A body," the second one said. "And it looks like it's been down there a pretty goddamn long time."

"You mean you found a *corpse* down there?"

"More like a skeleton."

"Are you serious?"

"No, this is our idea of a pretty fucking funny joke," said the first demolition guy. They were both pissed at me, irrationally so, and I got the feeling they were actually more pissed at themselves for getting so rattled.

"You don't believe us, go take a look for yourself," his partner said.

"Yeah," the other one said. "Why don't you check it out, if you think we're so full of shit."

"Wait, I . . ."

But I was already talking to their backs. The two of them were stomping toward the theater, workboots clomping on shards of brick and tile. I followed them, because I didn't know what else to do. They half slid down a ramp of dirt that had been dug to access the foundation, and tried not to break my neck as I shuffled after them. The ground leveled out, and I suddenly realized where I was standing: the Starlight dressing rooms, or what was left of them.

I followed the two men down what used to be the hallway, though there were only bits and pieces of the walls left.
It was the final stage of the demolition process, and there
was barely enough of the building left to be recognizable; it
reminded me of old pictures of London during the Blitz. The
two workers turned right, and I followed them into what
would have been a room, if a backhoe hadn't just taken out
the far wall.

"See for yourself," the first guy said, and they both stood
back to let me pass.

I went up to the wall and perched on tiptoes to see over
the rubble. "I don't see . . ."

"All the way on the left," one of them said from behind
me.

I looked, and there she was.

I say "she," because although the person inside had been
reduced to a smirking skeleton, there was still a gold locket
around her neck. There were also the remains of a skirt and
blouse, and a dainty little watch around her left wrist, and on
her feet were a pair of brown leather pumps.

She looked like she was waiting for something. I know
it's silly, but that was the first thing I thought. The way her
body had come to rest against the stack of dirt and bricks—
half reclining, one arm outstretched—gave the rather absurd illusion that she was about to stand up, would get to
her feet and go about her business just as soon as the time
was right.

The whole image was peaceful somehow, not the chamber of horrors you might expect. Maybe that was because it
was so out of context: a bright winter day, burly men in
hardhats, me in my new cashmere beret. In the background
were the sounds of post-Christmas shoppers returning the
presents they'd just unwrapped, trading teapots and slipper

socks and aromatherapy pillows for something they actually wanted.

And there, in the shelter of what remained of the Starlight Theatre, was the body of a woman who'd been waiting to be found ever since . . . Since when? Since someone had put her there, and crossed his fingers, and hoped like hell the rest of the world would forget.

I stared at her, not because I wanted to but because for some reason I couldn't make myself look away. Then, after I'd been standing immobile for so long even the construction workers started to worry, I finally snapped out of it and pulled out my cell phone. I called the station and asked for Cody—not so much because it was his job to deal with death but because, well, I felt like I needed him.

And that was how I first came face-to-face with the remains of a dead girl. She had once been very, very beautiful. She was only nineteen years old. And her name, as you may already have guessed, was Ashley Sinclair.

16

THE TABLOIDS CALLED IT "THE MYSTERY OF THE WOMAN IN
the Wall." Pretty melodramatic, I know—kind of Nancy
Drew meets *Tales from the Crypt*. You wouldn't think that
trash TV (or, for that matter, even the city papers) would
care much about one dead girl dug up in the middle of upstate New York, but I guess the romance of it got to them.
There was the idea of this abandoned theater, which had
seen so much glamour only to be reduced to a pit full of rubble; there was the fact that the girl had been sitting there un-
noticed for the better part of a century. Put them together,
and you got something surreal: a place where once upon a
time people had sipped cocktails and laughed at their own
jokes and clapped at curtain calls—and all the while, a
woman was decomposing in the dark, alone.

Whether it was that sort of psychological complexity
that grabbed the headlines—or just a really slow news
cycle—is probably one for the media scholars. Either way,
it turned out to be a lucky thing the story got so much play.
Once my first piece hit the AP wire, news about the body in
the wall ricocheted around the country until it finally
landed on the TV screen of someone who actually knew
something about it. He was a professor of theater history at

NYU, and when he saw the ninety-second piece on CNN he picked up the phone and called the *Times*. He was transferred to the reporter covering the story, and the next day the identity of the dead girl was revealed under the byline of . . . Gordon Band.

This, by the way, made me mad enough to spit.

The girl's name wasn't a sure thing, of course; at that point, it was really just an overeducated guess. But the mere suggestion of it was enough to unleash an orgy of lurid curiosity, and nowhere was the party more festive than right here in Gabriel. Plumbers, journalists, chartered accountants, effete intellectuals—we were all obsessed by it, to the exclusion of all else. It didn't help that the discovery of the body came smack on the heels of the Sissy Dillingham murder, which already had the town in a state of mild hysteria. And poor Sissy, whose corpse was considerably fresher and whose assailant was presumably still breathing, got shunted below the fold, both literally and figuratively.

"Come on, Bernier," said Mad, who was as caught up in it as anyone else. "Be a good sport and read me the story out loud."

"Oh, for Christ's sake, I've already read it twice."

We were in our usual window seat at the Citizen, where Mad had come for his regular after-work libation, and I'd come to drown my sorrows in a couple of Harvey Wallbangers.

"Don't be such a sore loser."

"I'm not a sore loser."

"You are so."

"Hey, why would I be a sore loser? Just because some egghead calls up Gordon and spills his guts and the next thing you know he's scooping me in my own backyard—which, by the way, is a place he doesn't even give a damn about, like you're a total goddamn loser if you don't live in the 212 area code . . ."

"Oh, yeah, you're taking it real well."

I stuck my tongue out at him and dispatched my second Harvey Wallbanger. With all the orange juice and licorice liqueur, the vodka was going down dangerously smooth. "Okay, just to prove there's no hard feelings, I'll read the damn thing again." I picked up the paper. " 'BODY FOUND IN GABRIEL THEATER MAY BE LONG-LOST STAR-LET,' by Gordon Band."

"And this time, try it without the bitchy comments about how lame the writing is."

"Man, you are *no* fun today. And it *is* lame, but okay." I cleared my throat for dramatic effect. " 'BODY FOUND IN GABRIEL THEATER MAY BE LONG-LOST STAR-LET,' By Gordon Band. Dateline, Gabriel. 'The body of an unidentified woman discovered during demolition of a historic vaudeville house in this bucolic upstate college town . . .' Man, why do they always have to call us that?"

"Spare me."

"Fine. '. . . discovered during demolition of a historic vaudeville house in this nowhere-hayseed-upstate college town may be that of an actress who disappeared without a trace in 1926, said a professor at New York University. According to Chadwick H. Sweet, 57, a professor of theater history at NYU, the discovery of the corpse inside a base-ment wall of the now-defunct Starlight Theatre may end a decades-long mystery about the fate of Ashley Sinclair, a 19-year-old starlet who vanished in the midst of a theatrical tour.' "

"What are you stopping for?"

"I need another drink." I waved my empty glass at the bartender, who brought me a refill and, to spare himself the inevitable, a second pitcher for Mad. "Okay, where was I?

'Miss Sinclair, a former child actress who made her Broadway debut at age 11, was familiar to national audiences for her leading role in the successful silent film *Heavens to Betsy*. Her disappearance, during production of a play at the Starlight, sparked a national fascination that Professor Sweet compares to the death of Elvis A. Presley.' Do I really have to read the quotes?"

"Don't be such a pain in the ass."

"Oh, *fine*. '"At the time, the search for Ashley Sinclair was a distinct sociological phenomenon," Professor Sweet said. "People became obsessed with finding her. You might call it a mild case of mass hysteria. She was supposedly sighted in a theater in Pittsburgh, a drugstore in Omaha, even hitching a ride along a roadside near Miami. In many ways, this phenomenon presaged . . ."' "

"All right, all right, you can skip that part. I get enough of that crap right here at home."

"Don't you want to hear about . . . hmm . . . 'the role of early electronic media in American cultural dialogue'?"

"No."

"Okay . . . 'Modern constructs of the cult of celebrity,' yadda-yadda . . . Here we go. 'According to Gabriel Police Chief Wilfred G. Hill, 52 . . .' Hey, did you know he was that old? I really didn't think he was a day over forty-five. Anyway, according to the chief, '. . . a forensic examination is now being conducted by the Walden County pathologist in the hope of definitely establishing the identity of the victim. Police are also attempting to trace the three pieces of jewelry found on the body: a gold locket, a wristwatch, and a sapphire ring. Police will not comment on whether the locket resembles a necklace Miss Sinclair wore in a publicity photo for the Broadway production of *Mothers & Daughters*.' " I fanned the paper in his direction. "Can you believe they got a hold of this picture so fast?"

"They're the goddamn *New York Times*."

"True."

"So what do you think?"

"About what?"

"About what police will not comment on."

"The necklace?"

"You saw the body. It look like the same thing to you?"

"I couldn't swear to it, but yeah."

"Man, what a babe." He snatched the paper for a proper ogle. "You know, Bernier, I'm not usually one to go all sloppy, but I gotta tell you . . ." His voice trailed off with what I could swear was wistfulness. Between this and the Emma thing, I was starting to wonder if he was going to join the Promise Keepers.

"You gotta tell me what?"

"This may be the most beautiful woman I've ever seen in my whole miserable life."

"You might not want to let that slip to your girlfriend."

"I'm serious. I mean, maybe she'd turn you off the minute she opened her mouth, like most chicks. But you know . . . I just can't picture it. She seems too . . . real. Like an angel."

"Real like an angel?" I stared at him, then his beer mug. It was still mostly full. "Are you taking estrogen or something?"

"Come on, Bernier. I'm not going all gay on you. There's just something about this woman."

I took the paper back. "I know. She's got . . . I don't know. *It*."

"I'll say." Again with the wistful gazing. "Say, what did she look like when you . . ."

"When I saw her?"

"Yeah."

"She looked thinner. Much, much thinner."

"Since when are you such a bitch?"

I sighed and tipped back in my chair. "Oh, hell, I guess I'm just jealous."

"Why?"

" 'Cause I don't have *it*."

"Yeah, well, not many people do."

"If you want the truth, it was just incredibly sad. I couldn't stop looking at her. All I could think of was whether, you know, she was still alive when she got locked in there."

"What did the cops say?"

"Nothing yet."

"I thought they weren't being as close-lipped about this one."

"They're not. Seems to me they're treating it more like a curiosity than a homicide. What's the point, when you think about it? The case is seventy-something years old. It's not as if whoever did it is still walking around. But even though they're not being as anal as usual, they're still not releasing anything until they're sure. I mean, you can't really blame them. Practically every TV news show in the country is breathing down their necks, not to mention a bunch of papers and the wire guys. Oh, and us."

"What does Cody make of all this?"

"Kid in a goddamn candy store."

"You serious? How come?"

"I'm not really even sure. My guess is maybe, like, how often do you get to see murder as an intellectual exercise?"

"I don't get it."

"Neither do I. I'm just telling you impressions. I think it's a fascinating case with zero pressure—call it the opposite of the Sissy Dillingham mess. It's not as though whoever murdered Ashley Sinclair is out there somewhere, and the cops have to stop him before he kills somebody else. It's not even like Cody has to worry about seeing justice done, because there's never going to be any. Whoever killed her probably went to his grave without ever spending a day in the slammer. He got away with murder, right?"

"Right."

"So that part of it's a moot point. There's no witnesses, no forensic evidence beyond the body. Probably the only person still alive who was even around there back then is jerky old Robert Renssellaer, and he was all of, like, six."

"So?"

"So it's a perfect mystery."

"You mean a hopeless case."

"I'm not sure Cody sees much of a distinction."

He eyed the upside-down photo again and shook his head. "It's a damn heinous thought, isn't it? The idea that somebody might have buried her alive . . ."

"Hard to think of anything worse."

"What a goddamn waste," he said. And then, with a total disregard for the full pitcher on the table, he ordered himself two shots of tequila.

After Gordon's piece came out, the Ashley Sinclair story inhaled my working life like the Starlight thing had a couple of weeks before. The vox populi was hollering for more-more-more, and Chester was determined that the *Monitor* was going to give it to them, by God—whether it killed me or not. He even made noises about taking me off my regular beat—having someone else cover City Hall, which has been my baby these four years—but Marilyn managed to talk him out of it before I opened my big mouth and put myself on the fast track to unemployment.

It wasn't that I didn't want to cover the Ashley story. But at that point, I hadn't really gotten into it—which, by the way, made me quite the weirdo here in Gabriel. Within days of her photo appearing in the *Times*, people were practically swapping Ashley Sinclair trading cards. Her nasty demise and melodramatic disinterment were the major (or, more accurately, the only) topics of conversation at Café Whatever, Schultz's Deli, the Citizen Kane, and just about everyplace else.

Was it just because she was so beautiful? One Benson psychology professor thought so, laying out her arguments in a rather scathing letter to the editor she'd dashed off after overhearing an unidentified dean call Ashley "a bodacious Betty with baby-porn lips." Most of the students were out of town for winter break, but there were enough members of the Feminist Alliance on e-mail to produce an opinion piece about how much it sucked to realize a woman's worth was still all about her looks. "Poor Ashley Sinclair was hidden inside the walls of the Starlight Theatre in 1926, and in many ways society's valuation of women has been just as frozen in time," they wrote. "But isn't it about time someone asked, 'Who was she? What were her thoughts, her hopes, her dreams, her political beliefs? Did she strive to transcend the limitations of her era? Was she as beautiful on the inside as she was on the outside?' As long as Ashley Sinclair remains nothing more than a face in a glossy photograph, American women will forever be as trapped within the constructs of a male-defined world."

Bad prose—but good questions. I hated to admit it, but for once those crop-haired bra-burners got me thinking. Who was Ashley Sinclair, anyway? Where did she come from, and what really happened to her? How did she go from child star to Broadway actress to bricked-up corpse? Who killed her? And how could anyone solve a murder that was more than seventy years old?

Such was the romantic banter between Cody and me as we wandered into Albertini's on New Year's Eve. I'd forgone hosting my annual bacchanalian bash for the sake of

relationship maintenance: an early dinner and a quick
drink with the gang at the Citizen before repairing to my
house to ring in the new year in the company of three dogs
in funny hats. Call me a loser, but it sounded like a good
time to me.

"So what's your next move, story-wise?" Cody was saying. "How do you report on something that happened during
the Coolidge administration?"

"The what?"

"President between Harding and Hoover."

"No wonder my dad fell in love with you."

"I think it was mostly 'cause I helped him figure out
which way to point his new Ruger Redhawk." I gave him
another clueless look. "It's a forty-four caliber revolver, part
of his James Bond collection. Gardner-era, not Fleming. Really pretty gun."

"You two are a match made in heaven."

"He's a nice guy. Not a great shot, but he practices like
crazy."

"He says if he and Mom ever had a duel, she'd kill him."

"Baby, I think *you* could probably kill him. So what do
you think?"

"I don't really want to kill him. Not anymore, anyway."

"I mean about the story."

"I was going to ask you the same question. How do you
investigate a crime that happened way before you were even
born?"

"Essentially the same way I'd do if it were now, only the
job's a lot harder. Try and dig up everything I can about who
she was, who she knew, who her enemies might have been.
See if anybody had anything to gain from her death."

"Sounds like exactly what I'm in for. Monday, I'm going
to start digging around at the Benson archives and Historic
Gabriel. They've got a lot of stuff on the old theater scene in

town. Did you know there used to be a movie studio here around the turn of the century? They used to make all sorts of silent films, cowboys and Indians in the gorges, that kind of thing."

"Really? What happened to it?"

"They figured out that if they moved to L.A. they could shoot more than five months a year." I poured him another glass of Chianti. "So, you gonna let me in on what you guys know so far? Or do I have to wait until the press conference like everybody else?"

"And why would I do that?"

"Because even the chief isn't treating this like a regular case. Because if you do crack it, which is next door to impossible, the killer's still gonna be some guy who died forty years ago. Oh, and because I look unusually cute in this dress." I dipped a bread stick in olive oil, tried to munch on it seductively, and got laughed at for my trouble.

"Enough with the womanly wiles."

"Was I being that obvious?"

"I'm trained to notice these things."

I leaned across the table and fed him the rest of my bread stick. "So you've said."

"All right, Mata Hari. Here's the scoop. First off, we opened up Ashley Sinclair's locket, and the photo inside was—drumroll, please—of her parents."

"Rats."

"Sorry to disappoint you. Now for the interesting stuff. You want to hear about the cause of death?"

"Hell yes."

"She didn't get buried alive. She got hit over the head, but good. Hell of a lot better way to go, if you ask me."

"Creepy to say, but I agree with you. How do you know, anyway?"

"Her skull was fractured. Badly."

"Could it have been an accident? Maybe some scenery fell on her or something."

"I suppose it's possible. But even if it were, someone put her inside that wall on purpose. Smacks of malice aforethought, don't you think?"

"Or at least after."

"Right. Either somebody planned on killing her and hiding the body, or he did it on the spur of the moment and was desperate to conceal the evidence."

"I wonder why."

"Why he killed her?"

"That, and why he hid her away instead of just letting her be found. I mean, do you think there might have been some reason why it was important to have her disappear?"

He ate all the blue cheese off the top of his salad before answering. "You know, that's a good point. I hadn't really thought of it, beyond the obvious."

"The obvious?"

"If there's no body, there's no murder investigation. It's just a missing person's case, and probably not a very high-priority one at that."

"How come?"

"I'm just speculating. But frankly, if somebody from a traveling acting troupe disappeared in the here and now, odds are the cops wouldn't take it that seriously. They'd just think she . . ."

"Flaked out."

"Right. I'd imagine that went double back in the twenties. You probably know a whole lot more about this than I do, but weren't they kind of suspect back then? The women especially?"

"Somewhere between gypsy and hooker, most likely. I think that was changing by the twenties, but when it comes to the local cops, you're probably right. I just started reading up on it. You want me to let you know what I find out?"

"Sure."

"Does this mean I get to be deputized? Can I have a toy badge and everything?"

"We're all out," he said with a grin. "But if you're a very good girl, I'll let you play with mine."

At Albertini's, there's no such thing as a quick dinner. The restaurant prides itself on its European style, meaning the check never comes until you ask for it. You can loiter all night if you want to—and if some city inspector tried to enforce the municipal no-smoking ordinance, he'd probably find himself sleeping with the fishes.

I mention this by way of explaining why Cody and I were still sitting there three hours later, drinking cappuccino and eating pistachio-encrusted cannoli and chatting about homicide. We were just about to contemplate removing our overstuffed carcasses to the Citizen when I saw a familiar face over in the corner. It wasn't smiling.

"Oh, hell, what's *he* doing here?"

Cody craned his neck. "Who is it?"

"Gordon Band."

"The guy from the *Times*? I thought he was a friend of yours."

"It's complicated."

"Ex-boyfriend?"

"Oh *God* no."

"Then what's the problem?"

"Call it a hyperactive sense of competition."

"Yours or his?"

"His. *Definitely* his." He gave me a highly unflattering look, and I kicked him under the table. "Okay, both of ours. But he started it."

"You want to invite him over?"

"I thought we were just about to leave."

"Come on, Alex. The poor guy's all alone on New Year's Eve."

"Jesus, do you have to be so decent all the time? Okay, you're guilting me. I'll take pity on him."

I'd never actually seen anyone table-hop at Albertini's, so it was with some trepidation that I ventured across the darkened dining room. I got to Gordon's corner without anyone gunning me down, but when he looked up from his menu his face screwed itself into an even bigger scowl.

"Alex?"

"Happy New Year to you too. And by the way, what the hell are you doing here?"

"Having dinner, what do you think?"

"Why here?"

"Everyplace else was booked."

"I mean what are you doing up in Gabriel? And on New Year's Eve, no less?"

"It's snowing."

"So?"

He looked at me like I was exceedingly dim.

"So I'm trapped."

"But it's hardly even flurrying out there."

"You'd have to be crazy to drive in this stuff."

I was about to call him a big wimp when I remembered I was supposed to be making nice. "Nifty scoop you had on the Ashley Sinclair thing, huh?"

"Thanks."

"You still covering it?"

"More or less."

"What does that mean?"

"I, um, I finally got my own beat."

"So why do you look like you're telling me you finally

got a frontal lobotomy?" He didn't answer. "What did they give you? Staten Island or something? You poor baby . . ."

"Don't even joke."

"What's the problem? You've been dying to get back on a beat ever since you popped your editor in the snout, right?" He pretended to concentrate on his menu. "Come on, Gordon, it can't be that bad. What is it, Queens? You know, I hear there's four other boroughs down there besides Manhattan, and they're all perfectly—"

"Oh, Christ, would you cut it out? They made me their new upstate reporter, okay?"

"*Upstate*? You're their *upstate* reporter? You gotta be kidding me." I made a big show of collapsing into a chair with laughter, which probably didn't satisfy anybody's definition of making nice.

"They're in some big goddamn push to up their in-state circulation, so they want somebody to concentrate on . . . Would you please stop laughing?"

"Are you seriously covering everything north of Westchester?"

"North of Westchester and west of Albany. They've already got a capital bureau there."

"But don't they know you hate it up here?"

"*Everybody* knows I hate it up here. But after the story you and Mad and I broke last year, and then the serial killer thing . . ."

"But you busted your butt on those."

"Exactly. The upstate beat is what those bastards consider a reward for faithful service."

I indulged in more uncharitable chuckling. It didn't enhance his mood. "Come on, Gordon, you gotta see the humor."

"Oh, believe me, I've spent plenty of time savoring the sweet fucking irony of it all."

He downed the rest of his beer, and I took the opportunity to get a good long look at him. He was even more rumpled than usual, with his hair standing up on one side (the man likes to scratch his head a lot) and the wrong end of his little flowery tie sticking out from under the front. The circles under his eyes were pretty standard for Gordon, but I didn't think I'd ever seen him quite so exhausted. And this is a guy who manages to combine "depressed" with "high-strung" on a daily basis.

"So where are you living?" I was just trying to make small talk, but it flopped. He didn't answer. "Christ, don't tell me they're making you work out of Elmira or something—"

"Are you insane? I'm still on the Upper West Side."

"But don't you have to live up—"

"Officially, yes. But I'd rather chop off my testicles."

"You know, I think they serve that here with a lovely Milanese sauce."

"Hardy-har-har."

"So if you're still living in the city . . ."

"I commute up and down a lot, when the weather's fit for a human being. Otherwise I crash in motels, or else—" He cut himself off, and I got the feeling he'd said way more than he'd meant to.

"Or else what?"

"Never mind."

"What do you do, sleep in your car or something?" He got a tad crimson around the gills. "Gordon, you have a tiny little Honda. It's not even a hatchback."

"I sold that when I moved back to the city."

"So now what are you driving?"

"Never mind."

"Whatcha got? A Winnebago?"

"Oh, screw you. It's a Volkswagen van, okay? Now will you let me order my dinner in peace?"

I got a handle on myself, if barely. "You want to come over and sit with us? It's New Year's Eve and everything . . ."

"Sit with you and who?"

"Brian Cody."

"The cop?"

"The very one."

"Isn't he the guy on the Ashley Sinclair case?" He stood up so fast, he nearly tipped over his chair.

"Don't even think about pumping him."

"From what I hear, you've been doing plenty of that yourself."

"Are you going to be nice?"

"Are *you*?"

"I will if you will."

"Is your boyfriend carrying his gun?"

"I think so," I lied.

"In that case," he said, "I'll be a perfect gentleman."

17

THE MONDAY AFTER NEW YEAR'S MARKED THE OFFICIAL postholiday return to reality. No more orgiastic shopping sprees in the name of Jesus, no more eating like you were on the way to the vomitorium, and (in my particular case) no more rationalizing that baked Brie is a fat-free food.

It also marked the beginning of my dubious career as the *Monitor*'s girl-on-the-spot for all things Ashley. Never mind that we still knew next to nothing about her; Chester was already starting to fantasize about another three-day package—specifically, all the awards it was going to win, and how it was finally going to make his father-in-law take him seriously as a journalist. He meant it too.

I kicked off this new phase of my life by attending Chief Hill's press conference, where I jockeyed for space among the TV cameras for the pleasure of writing down everything Cody had already told me, and trying to look surprised while I was doing it. That dispensed with, I banged out my story for the next day's paper; it ran under a Chester-mandated headline ("ASHLEY DIED OF VICIOUS HEAD WOUND, SAY COPS") that had tongues wagging about our imminent merger with the *New York Post*.

After a lunch of Frau Schultz's vegetarian pea soup, I felt

sufficiently braced to hoof it through the snow to Historic
Gabriel. The historical society is housed in an old brick
mansion halfway up the same hill that Bessler College is on.
Its driveway rises from the road at what I'd swear is a forty-
five-degree angle; the one time I tried to take my Renault up
there during the winter, I just about bobsledded back down
to the Green.

By the time I got up there I was an icky combination of
cold and sweaty, a sensation that always reminds me of
many miserable hours spent chasing a hockey puck at
boarding school. Lucky for me, the head of Historic Gabriel
is a firm believer in bribing her clientele; she serves free
lemonade in the summer, hot cocoa in the winter, and sweets
all year 'round. I got there just as the door was being unlocked—it's only open to the public on weekday afternoons,
which is probably why no one ever goes—so I had the place
to myself and, more importantly, no competition for the
walnut brownies. Thus revived, I asked my hostess to point
me in the general direction of old theater memorabilia.

You're probably picturing the head of the historical society as a fussy schoolmarm type, or maybe a quasi-obsessed
matron like Madeline Hoover. Fat chance. Angela Giordano
is one tough cookie, a black woman adopted by an Italian
family that proceeded to expel her when she came out as a
lesbian during her valedictorian's speech at Gabriel High.
She eventually put herself through Benson with degrees in
political science and women's studies and knocked off a
master's in record time, then shelved plans to move away
when she fell madly in love with an ornamental horticulture
professor named Rachel Goldstein. (Their twenty-year romance has produced two Goldstein-Giordanos, two Gior-
dano-Goldsteins, and the most spectacular garden in town.)
She's been a major fixture on the local activist scene for as
long as anybody can remember, on topics from domestic

partnership to breast cancer awareness to an antidieting thing she calls "size acceptance." The latter was the subject of her latest book, *A Fat Chick Gives You the Finger*, last fall, she even convinced Mayor Marty to declare a citywide Size Acceptance Day, which I celebrated by skipping my usual fifteen-mile bike ride and eating most of a box of Little Debbie's Nutty Bars.

Angela has been running Historic Gabriel for nearly ten years; like most of her fellow townspeople, she's underpaid, overqualified, and damn glad to have a job that lets her stay in this zip code. She spent the first five trying to straighten the place out after fifty years of sloppy management, and the second five chronicling the contributions of two centuries' worth of Walden County women—who, if you ask her, have been screwed out of their due by two centuries' worth of Walden County men.

I like her. A lot.

"Where is everybody, anyway?" I asked through yet another brownie. "I figured this place'd be besieged."

"Besieged by whom?"

"Other reporters. Haven't they been storming the castle over the Ashley thing?"

"I've gotten a few phone calls, all of them from people expecting me to do their work for them."

"Nobody's come in? Not even the tabloid TV guys?"

"Now what would make you think a television reporter would be bothered with the likes of us?" She gestured past the manhole-cover exhibit to the open door of the documents room—a dingy, overstuffed maze which (unlike Angela) satisfied every musty stereotype you could think of. I got her point. "Someone from the *Times* did leave a message, but I gather he was too busy with his other stories to come in during the week. He wanted to know if I'd let him in on Saturday."

"And are you?"

"Of course not. It's shabbos. Which, judging from his surname, he should damn well have known."

"Did you tell him that?"

"Of course."

"And what did he say?"

"That there was no fanatic like a convert."

"And then he asked you to do it on Sunday, right?"

"I take it you know this character."

"You take it right. Are you gonna do it?"

She nodded and sighed, both at the same time. I was willing to bet she could pat her head and rub her tummy to boot. "The sign says we're also open by appointment, and he made an appointment," she said. "There goes my baking day."

"You know, these brownies are *amazing*."

"Have another one. And don't go telling me you're on a diet. I assume you're still determined to exercise yourself into the hospital?"

"Don't go trying to sell me on that size acceptance stuff. I'm way too shallow."

"Pity." She stood up, and I followed her into the archives. "All right, the theatrical history of Gabriel. Whatever we've got, it's all in there."

"Where do I start?"

"There are individual files on all five downtown theaters—the Starlight, the Mohawk, the Palace, the Orpheum, and the Grand Gabriel. Do you know what Benson students used to call them back in the day?" I shook my head. "They were nicknamed according to how far they were from campus. The Starlight was the closest, so they called it the Near-Near. The Mohawk was the Near-Far, the Palace was the Far-Near, and the Grand was the Far-Far. Get it? Oh, and the Orpheum was the Armpit."

"Why?"

"Apparently, it smelled like one."

I got out my notebook, on the trail of some story color. "Would you mind running over that again?" She did, and I kicked myself for not knowing about the Near-Near thing while I was writing all those Starlight stories. Might have made a good headline: " 'NEAR-NEAR' NEARS DE-STRUCTION."

"I'm not sure how interested you are in this, but all that Near-Far business was also a handy way for the fraternity boys to torture their newbies. The pledges had to know what was playing at all five theaters off the top of their heads—had to recite the show times on command or else get paddled on the bum with an oar, or some such nonsense. But I suppose that would be in the fraternity files . . ."

"Have you looked through any of this stuff since the Ashley Sinclair thing broke?"

She shook her head. "I wanted to, but I've been up to my ears in grant proposals. Frankly, I think the last person to touch these things was you, when you were working on . . . No, wait. It was Sissy Dillingham, poor thing."

That got my attention. "Sissy? What was she looking for?"

"A miracle, I expect."

"Huh?"

"It was after the episode with that elderly actor . . . What was his name? Robbie someone . . . Dreadful old coot, from what I saw on access. At any rate, she came charging in here saying she wasn't going to leave until she found something impressive enough to save the Starlight. Ridiculous, I know. But I could tell there was no talking her out of it, so I just let her have the run of the place."

"For how long?"

"Hmm . . . I'm not certain. Maybe two, three days?"

"Straight?"

"Practically so."

"Did she find anything?"

"I can't imagine that she did, but I couldn't say for sure. She was gone when I got here in the morning. Left a mighty mess, too, though it's bitchy of me to say it after what happened to her. Do you think the police will ever catch who ran her over?"

I was about to say I had no idea, but then I figured I should display some girlfriendly loyalty. "I'm sure they will."

"You know something?"

"I wish. I'm not even covering it. Jake Madison is."

"Now *there's* a throwback for you."

"He'd probably consider it a compliment."

"Did you spend a lot of time with the Save Our Starlight bunch?"

"A whole hell of a lot, yeah."

"Can I ask you something?"

"Sure."

"How's my sister?"

"Your . . . You mean Adele? Oh, *right*. I totally forgot you two were related."

"Apparently, so has she."

"Don't you ever . . ."

"Not since I came out. When Mom and Dad were alive it was because they made her swear she'd stay away lest I turn her into a dyke. Now it's because she thinks I'm going to hell."

"Jesus Christ."

"Exactly."

"You mean your parents never let up about you . . ."

"Not an inch. You'd think if they were open-minded enough to adopt a little black girl back in the fifties they'd cope, right? Well, no such luck."

"And Adele went along?"

"She was the center of their universe, the natural kid they never thought they could have. Made it a hell of a lot easier to give me the boot, if you ask me." She shook her head. "Why the fuck am I telling you all this?"

"Don't worry about it."

"Anyway, how's she doing?"

"Okay, I guess. She was really into the S.O.S. thing along with everybody else. It was kind of this little club they had—a meeting at a different person's house every week, punch and cookies, that kind of thing. Word is they're going to try to save the old armory next."

"But she seems all right?"

"Why? Are you worried about her?"

"I tried to get in touch with her after Artie left, but she wouldn't talk to me. I'm just glad she's got friends."

"They're definitely pretty thick—her and Madeline and Sissy . . . I mean, before Sissy got . . ."

"You know, I rather got to like Sissy, believe it or not. I'd always thought her a deeply silly woman, but she really went to the mat over the Starlight. It was a lost cause from the start, but you have to admire that kind of screw-the-consequences gusto, don't you think? Particularly when all her neighbors care about is keeping the deer off their ornamental shrubbery."

"You know, Lindy Marsh said the same thing—that it was a lost cause. Why do you think so?"

"History 101. Those who don't learn from the past are doomed to repeat it, right?"

"And?"

"And there were five big theaters in Gabriel, once upon a time. They all disappeared. The Save Our Starlight people didn't seem to understand why it happened, the reasons why the world passed them by. They managed to restore the Starlight once, and down it went. I never heard a single rational explanation as to how this time was going to be any different. Good intentions just don't cut it."

"Seems a strange thing to be coming out of your mouth."

"Well, I'm a strange chick."

"Listen, Angela, is there anything else you can remember about what Sissy was doing here? What sort of thing she was looking for, maybe?" She started to shake her head. "You said she left a big mess. Do you remember what she was into?"

She thought about it for a while. "I wish I could help you out, but the truth is she was into everything—the files on the Starlight, the artifacts in storage, real estate documents, information on the other theaters, the old Mohawk movie studio, vaudeville, touring companies. You name it, she messed it up." She clapped her hand over her mouth. "There I go again, speaking ill. Good thing Rachel isn't hearing this."

"You said she was gone when you got here in the morning. Do you remember what morning that was?"

"Let's see . . . It would have to have been a Thursday. Just a couple of days before she died, now that I think of it."

"Are you sure?"

"I'm positive. I remember saying that to Rachel when we heard about the accident, how I'd just seen her. You know how people like to sling that melodramatic bullshit—'Oh, how eerie, she was just in my office and now she's dead.' As if it somehow made you part of the—"

I never found out what she was going to say, because the office phone started ringing and Angela dashed down the hall to answer it. Left to my own devices, I looked around at the stacks of boxes and umpteen filing drawers, pondering some melodramatic bullshit of my own.

Had Sissy Dillingham actually found something here, some big bombshell she thought would save the theater? And if she had, was it really worth killing her over?

Whatever it was, I knew one thing for sure: I had no idea

how to find it. I figured I should start with the Starlight files, but those alone had thousands of documents in them: architectural plans, actors' contracts, invoices for lighting equipment, records of concession sales. I'd already started nosing through it all when I was researching the Starlight package, and the sheer volume of stuff had scared me off faster than you could say Kenneth Branagh. The proverbial needle in a haystack seemed like a cakewalk by comparison; at least you knew what the goddamn needle looked like.

I downed the last of my cocoa and decided I needed some sort of strategy. Since I was supposed to be digging up info on Ashley Sinclair, I thought I might as well concentrate on her and see if anything else jumped out at me.

Nothing did. For six straight hours, I dug through everything from old posters to coal invoices, and never found a single thing labeled "DANGER—IF YOU READ THIS YOU MAY GET SQUASHED BY A BUICK." I did, however, find Ashley Sinclair's name on a handful of old programs, which I copied and shoved in my backpack for the trek back down the hill. The rest of the boxes would have to wait until I mustered the energy to deal with them.

By the time I got to the paper it was nearly eight—and I was good and late for yet another dinner with Cody. I stopped at the newsroom to get my messages, since the *Monitor* hasn't seen fit to invest in voice mail. The pink phone slips included two from him, presumably wondering where the hell I was. I decided to drive over there and rehearse my apology on the way.

Cody had given me a key to his apartment last summer, when I had to run some errands for him while he was in the hospital. He'd never gotten around to asking for it back, and I'd never gotten around to giving it to him; eventually, and without anybody ever actually saying it, our relationship got to the point where knocking seemed downright stupid. He wound up with a key to my place through the same sort of accidental intimacy; clearly, a good shrink would have a field day.

I bounded up the stairs two at a time, which isn't easy for someone of my shrimplike stature. I was already babbling my excuses when I opened the door, but one look inside Cody's living room shut me right up.

He was on the couch, and there was a very pretty blond woman sitting next to him. Actually, "sitting next to him" isn't technically accurate; "wrapped around him like an anaconda" was more like it. As happens at least once every six months, I was speechless.

"You must be Alex," she said, unfurling herself from my boyfriend and coming over to, of all things, hug me. "I'm just *so* glad to meet you."

"Just . . ." My voice cracked, which was damn embarrassing. "Just who the hell would you be?"

"Guess." She was positively beaming.

"Are you serious?"

"Come on, go ahead. Guess."

I looked from her to Cody, who appeared to have a really bad migraine. It was contagious. "I, um . . . I think I'd rather not."

"Oh, don't be like that. Be a sport."

"Long-lost cousin?" She shook her head, and her smile widened even farther into her dimply cheeks. I wondered if a second set of teeth were going to come shooting out and bite my face off, like the monster in *Alien*. "Old buddy from the SEALs?"

She found that particularly jolly. "You're so *silly*. Try again."

"You know, I'm really not enjoying this."

"I'm Lucy Cody, of course," she said finally. "I'm his wife."

18

Ex-WIFE. *Ex*-WIFE. *Ex*." THIS FROM CODY, WHO FAIRLY LEAPT off the couch to stand between the two of us. He told me later that, based on my body language, he'd been worried I might actually smack her. "And you know damn well your name isn't Cody anymore. It was in the goddamn divorce, remember?"

"Brian, please don't swear," she said. "You know I don't like it."

"Yeah, well, I didn't like it when you started screwing my . . ." He got a hold of himself. "Oh, hell. I'm sorry, Alex."

"I take it dinner's off?" I said, for lack of anything else.

"I think we should all go, all three of us," Lucy said. "Wouldn't that be fun?"

We both stared at her. Then I stared at Cody. He looked miserable—and so, for that matter, did his dog. "You actually married this person?"

"I told you, I was young and stupid."

"Brian, that is *so* mean," she said. "Say you're sorry."

He squinted his eyes shut and rubbed the top of his head, like he was trying to jump-start the blood to his brain. "Lucy, please just go home. I told you, we don't have anything to talk about."

"But we *do*."

"We don't. Really, we don't."

She looked like she was about to cry. And since she had one of those waifish, blondish, helpless airs about her, I almost felt sorry for her myself. Almost.

"Brian, would you *please* just tell me where your corkscrew is?"

It wasn't what either one of us expected to come out of her mouth. Cody stopped his auto-lobotomy and looked at her. "My what?"

She plucked a bottle off the coffee table. It turned out to be white zinfandel, which didn't improve my opinion of her. "I brought some wine. I'd like to have a glass, if you don't mind." He still didn't answer. "I'll find it myself," she said, and stamped off toward the kitchen.

The door swung shut behind her, and we could hear the muffled sound of drawers opening and closing. Cody promptly walked over to the couch and sat down with a thud.

"*Brian*," I said, way more sarcastically than I should have, "would you mind telling me just what the hell is going on?"

"She showed up about an hour ago."

"What the fuck does she want?"

"Me."

"*What?*"

"Come on, Alex, could you please not look at me like that? I didn't ask her to . . ."

"So what does she want?"

"I told you. *Me*."

"How about being a little more specific?"

"She says she still loves me. Says she wants me back, she made a huge mistake, won't I give her a chance to make it all up to me, the whole nine yards."

"And?"

"And what?"

"And are you, you know, tempted?"

"I can't believe you'd even ask me that."

"The whole first love thing can be a big draw."

"Do you have to sound so goddamn cold-blooded about it?"

"Look, don't go taking this out on me."

"Yeah, well, don't go taking it out on me either."

"What do you want me to do, drag her out by the hair?"

"Be my guest."

"I can't believe you're being such a . . ."

I tried to think of something really unpleasant. Then, because all my go-rounds on the flume ride that is modern romance haven't been entirely wasted, it occurred to me that perhaps Cody didn't need two crazy women on his hands at once. "Sorry," I said. He didn't answer. I went and sat next to him on the couch. "What's taking her so long in there, anyway?"

He glanced at the kitchen door and shook his head. "She's probably looking for wine glasses. I don't have any."

"Did she really come all the way from Boston to try and get back with you?"

"Yeah."

"Any idea what brought this on?"

"She says she realized the error of her ways."

"Please tell me that's not a direct quote." He rolled his eyes at me. "So . . . what are you going to do?"

"The same thing I've been doing, I guess. Keep telling her no, and hope she gets the hint."

"Where is she staying, anyway?"

"I have no idea."

"Would she go over to your mom's?"

"Hell no. Mom hated her guts even before she dumped me."

"I did not *dump* you," said Lucy, standing in the doorway with a water glass filled to pinkish. "I told you, I made a mistake. Can't a person make a mistake once in a while?"

"Taking the wrong exit off the Pike is a mistake," Cody said. "Cheating on your husband with his own lieutenant is... Oh, hell, don't ask me what."

Her eyes got very big and blue all of a sudden, which was a neat trick. In the unlikely event we ever got chummy, I'd have to get her to teach it to me. "Brian, don't you even care about me one little bit?"

I saw his neck muscles tighten. "In case you haven't noticed, I'm seeing somebody else. And she's sitting right here, so could you please cut the theatrics and give it a rest?"

"I'm sure Alex wouldn't blame a wife for trying to put her family back together. Would you, Alex?"

I waited for Cody to say something, but apparently it was his turn to be speechless. I had a feeling I was about to be involved in my first genuine catfight. "Can you possibly be for real?"

"What is *that* supposed to mean?"

"That's supposed to mean I think you should get the hell out of here."

"I will *not*."

"You will *so*." Okay, I'm not proud of it, but it was the best I could come up with on short notice.

"Just who do you think you are?"

"I think the technical term would be his girlfriend." She looked shocked. Really, truly shocked. It kind of threw me for a loop. "You seriously thought you could just come waltzing in here and get him back, didn't you?"

"Well, I ..."

"Do you have any idea how pathetic that is?"

"That's . . . It's not . . ." Her voice was really tiny all of a sudden. "That's not very nice."

"You know, I really think you should leave now."

"But . . . but where am I supposed to stay?"

"Where did you think you were going to stay, for Christ's sake?"

"With my husband, of course."

That was enough to snap Cody out of whatever coma he was in. He shot to his feet and turned on her. "You don't *have* a husband. We are not married anymore, and your name is not Lucy Cody. I only asked for two things in the divorce, remember? I wanted Zeke, and I wanted my name back. I didn't want you running all over Boston with it, screwing anything with a shield. And even if I weren't in love with somebody else, there's no goddamn way in the goddamn world I'd ever take you back. Got it? Now please, do us both a favor and get out of my life."

Yikes. I'd never seen Cody that pissed off before—at least not at anyone without a felony record. Lucy took it surprisingly well, though; better than I would have, at any rate.

"I can see I've come at a bad time," she said with a brave little smile. "I'll come back when you're more in the mood to talk." And before he could get another word in, she walked out the door—head held high and wine still in hand. Zeke, for one, looked deeply relieved.

I locked the door behind her. "I think she just stole your glass."

"She can keep it."

"Jesus Christ. What a drama queen."

"That just about sums it up."

"You okay?"

"Yeah. No . . . Just give me a minute to calm down."

"Come sit on the couch with me."

He did. "I am incredibly sorry you had to see that."

"Don't sweat it."

"I think you just saw my wretched underbelly."

"Yeah, well, I think you just saw mine too. Oh, and by the way, if you ever talk to me like you just talked to her, I'll kick your ass."

"Duly noted."

"What are you going to do if she comes around again?"

"Am I supposed to have a plan?"

I didn't have an answer for him. "Man, how did you ever . . ."

"What?"

"Forget it."

"You want to know how I ever fell for her, don't you?"

"Forget it. It's not a fair question, which I realized two seconds after I opened my big mouth."

"It's okay. I'd be wondering the same thing if the shoe were on the other foot."

"Cody, if you ever met the Dungeons & Dragons-obsessed nerd I dated in college—and who, by the way, dumped me for a girl who also enjoyed sleeping with ladies—I'd die of shame. Don't worry about it."

"Yeah, well, maybe I need you to know." He gave a huge sigh and flopped onto the couch. When he finally spoke I wished he hadn't. "Well, first off, she was really beautiful. Long blond hair, amazing blue eyes, gorgeous body . . ."

"Do I really have to hear this?"

"Sorry. I know it makes me sound shallow. And let's face it, I was a nineteen-year-old guy, so I was plenty shallow to begin with. But I think the thing that really got me was how . . . vulnerable she always seemed to be. She was this tiny little thing, and it was like she really needed me to protect her. I don't know. I guess it made me feel like a man or something. Turned out she had the same kind of relationship with her dad and her brothers—all cops, by the way. Which, as you know, is how I wound up in the family business."

"Like you said, you were young and stupid."

"That pretty much covers it. Not about the job, just about everything else."

"Was she always like . . . this?"

"A . . . What did you call her?"

"Drama queen."

"Toward the end, pretty much."

"Jesus. If I ever start acting like that, feel free to kick *my* ass."

"Duly noted again."

We didn't talk for a while, just sat there and listened to the traffic noise. After ten minutes or so, I decided maybe I should do something nurturing. "Hey, are you hungry at all?"

"Starving."

"Should we go out? Or barricade ourselves in here in case she's waiting on the front stoop?"

"I really am sorry about all this. I'm sure you weren't planning on spending your Monday night watching me yell at my ex-wife."

"Actually, I think I yelled at her more than you did."

He sat up and brushed some hair behind my ear, the quintessential intimate gesture. "You know, Alex, I meant what I said before."

"About being sorry? It's really okay . . ."

"No, what I said to Lucy about being in love with somebody else." My stomach did a little flip-flop. "I know we never talk about this stuff. Maybe we should, maybe we shouldn't. But I do love you, you know."

I swallowed hard enough for us both to hear it. Humiliating. "The last time a guy said that to me, it didn't end well."

"And the last time I said that to a woman, it didn't end well either. As you just saw in living color."

"Cody, I . . ."

"You don't have to."

"Oh, hell, yes I do. I can't let you sit here pouring out your guts all by yourself. You know damn well I love you back."

"Yeah, I know."

"Really?"

"You told me. Last summer, when you thought I was about to die and you could get away with it."

"Oh. Right. Kind of rude of you to live and . . ."

"I'll try to go quietly next time," he said, and leaned across to kiss me. And I'll be damned if there wasn't something more in it this time, the L-word having been swapped. Go figure.

"So what are we going to do about dinner? All I've eaten all day is a bowl of soup and six brownies."

"Well . . . would I be a total male chauvinist pig if I asked you to make something while I lie here on the couch and feel sorry for myself?"

"You might."

"I gotta tell you, Alex. Between Cynthia Dillingham and Lucy *Anderson*"— he shouted the word in the direction of the closed door—"I'm pretty beat."

I repaired to the kitchen to do my Edith Bunker impression, even going so far as to bring him a Guinness. When the food was ready I got him to move the ten feet from the couch to the table, which seemed to take all his energy—odd for a man who's been known to swim across Mohawk Lake for fun.

"Don't take this the wrong way, but you look like hell."

"I'm exhausted."

"She's an exhausting woman."

"Thanks for feeding me."

"It's your food."

"Yeah, well, I usually don't make it taste this good. What are we eating, anyway?"

"Just your basic canned tomato and garlic thing. I tossed in a couple of boullion cubes and some dried basil. Oh, and olives. The bread was in the freezer."

"It's good."

"I work well under battlefield conditions."

"This is probably way out of line," he said after he'd put away a fair amount of spaghetti, "but can I ask you for some advice? About Lucy?"

"Are you insane? I mean . . . Sure, I guess."

"What the hell do I do?"

"Don't you think she'll get the hint sooner or later?"

"It's the later I'm worried about. I was lying here, trying to figure out what's bothering me so much, and it finally hit me. As long as I've known Lucy, I've never seen her *not* get something she wanted. It could be little stuff, like where we'd go on vacation, or something big—like me quitting the service to join the force. And all those guys she was with after me, the ones I told you about, they were all married men. But once she decided she wanted them, she just kept at it. And yeah, I know they're just as responsible as she was. All I'm saying is, I've never known her to take no for an answer."

"And you think . . . what? That if she keeps it up you'll eventually give in?"

"Christ no. She could beg me seven ways from Sunday and I'd never even think about getting back with her. I just don't think she's going to give up too easily."

"You could always arrest her for stalking."

"Don't tempt me."

"Seriously, what do you think she's going to do?"

"I don't even want to think about it."

"Okay, you asked me for advice. And I know this is going to sound awful. But since you pretty much make her out to be a big baby, all I can think of is to treat her like one. Deal with her in a way she can understand."

"Like how."

"Like . . . Well, kind of like training a puppy."

"You want me to bribe her with hot dogs?"

"I was thinking more along the lines of delivering a consistent message. Keep telling her no, and make sure she doesn't get rewarded for bad behavior. Like if what she really wants is to spend time with you, don't let her."

"Makes sense."

"You know, it would help if you could figure out what's behind all this."

"Huh?"

"You're a cop. What's her motive?"

"I told you, she says she realized she made a big mistake."

"Yeah, but what made her realize it? Why did she all of a sudden decide to stop sleeping her way to the top of the Boston P.D. and come after you?"

"It's not just because I'm irresistible?"

"No offense, but she did leave you in the first place, thank God. But what made her want you back after, what, almost three years?"

"I have no idea."

"Maybe she got dumped by the deputy commissioner or something."

"Oh, hell, I don't know. Let's just change the subject,

okay? I'd sooner talk about something pleasant, like homicide."

"You mean Sissy Dillingham?"

"I could use your help, actually."

"Oh my God, I can't believe I forgot to tell you. I spent the afternoon at Historic Gabriel, right? And the director tells me that the week she died, Sissy hunkered down in their archives for like three days. Said she wasn't leaving until she found some way to save the theater."

"And?"

"And she left on Thursday. Friday, she announced the press conference, like I told you. The next day she was dead."

"Did the historical society say what she'd found?"

"That's the problem. They have no idea. Apparently, Sissy dug through anything and everything on local theater history. Angela—that's the director—she said there was no way of knowing what particular thing she was into on Thursday. I spent six hours there, and I hardly made a dent. I sure didn't find anything that might have saved the Starlight."

"Maybe she took it with her, whatever it was."

"You know, you're probably right. Sissy was pretty obsessed with the theater. If she actually found something that might have made a difference, I'm willing to bet she'd keep her hands on it. Can you search her house?"

"We already have."

"You got a search warrant and everything?"

"You don't need one for the victim's place."

"Oh. Did you find anything?"

"Lots of stuff related to the theater—whole filing cabinets of it—but nothing like what you're talking about."

"Does it really matter what it was? I mean, if you're looking at the theater as the most likely motive for running her

over, isn't it enough to know that whatever it was, Sissy
thought it would be a deal-breaker?"

"Probably, but not necessarily."

"I don't get it."

"Look at it this way. *How* could it have been a deal-
breaker? That might be the key to the whole thing."

I thought about it for as long as it took to eat a slab of
garlic bread. "Well, if we follow the example of what happened with Robbie Renssellaer, she might have found
something that would discredit somebody involved in the
sale."

"That's what I've been thinking. And once we know what
it was, we know who had the most to lose."

"What about what I told you about Lindy Marsh? She really seems to think this is all about revenge over Barry."

Cody shook his head. "Don't remind me. She's been bad-
gering the chief about it ever since it happened. Kirkland
too."

"And you don't buy it?"

"I'm not saying it's out of the question, but as far as I'm
concerned it's way at the bottom of the pile. Not that I'm
surprised that she *wants* to believe it."

"How do you mean?"

"Human nature. She stuck with her husband for what,
thirty years? She's gotta make herself feel like he was really
worth it, despite everything he put her through—like he was
such a great catch he was worth killing over. Plus, all his
cheating . . . It made her life miserable, so to her it's this
nine-hundred-pound gorilla. She can't stand the idea that to
the outside world, it doesn't matter that much. Trust me,
Alex. I know what I'm talking about."

"I know you do."

"I guess the bottom line is that to her, having her husband

be the motive for the Dillingham murder is kind of, well . . . comforting."

"That's sick."

"She's a very unhappy lady."

"No kidding. Hey, have you talked to Kurtis Osmond yet? Seems to me *he'd* be the number-one suspect."

"Oh, we've talked to him."

"I take it he was less than cooperative."

"He and his lawyers were very generous with their time. And not much else."

"He have an alibi?"

Cody laughed. "The best one possible."

"Meaning?"

"He was at a chamber of commerce thing with the chief. Hill was actually standing right next to him when he got called to the scene."

"Not that a guy like that'd get his hands dirty in the first place. In his line of work, I'm sure he's met a lovely assortment of gentlemen in the construction trades."

"I know I've told you this a hundred times, but you'd really . . ."

". . . make a good cop. Thanks, but I think it's too late for a career change. I better stick to the reporting game."

"Speaking of which, did you get the release about tomorrow's press conference?"

"I must have missed it when I blew through the newsroom. What's the deal?"

"Another fact from the autopsy report. Something the M.E. missed the first time around, but then he went back to the scene, and—"

"Back to the scene? I don't get it."

"He thought he found something, and he wanted to be sure."

"Sure of what?"

"When he examined the body again, he found a bone fragment he hadn't noticed before. It made him go back to the scene and take a closer look. Sure enough, he found the rest of the skeleton right there in the wall. I don't know how the crime-scene people missed it, except that there were dead rats and birds all over the place, and they weren't looking for it. I sure as hell wasn't."

"Looking for what?"

"Another skeleton."

"What?"

"Another *human* skeleton."

"I don't get it."

"Whoever murdered her also killed her unborn baby. Ashley Sinclair was three months pregnant."

19

WHEN I GOT TO WORK THE NEXT MORNING, I DECIDED IT
was time to get organized. Since such things don't come naturally, I wasn't sure how to start; an onion bagel with green-
olive cream cheese seemed as good an idea as any, and a big
hazelnut coffee struck me as a reasonable follow-up.

Eventually I got out a reporter's notebook and, emulating
the greats of my profession, wrote stuff down.

TO DO:
1) Get rid of Cody's ex-wife.
— Poison? Hit man? Throttle? Run over w/ car à la
   Sissy?

I admired it for a while, amusing myself to no end. Then,
because I've seen way too many movies where the innocent
guy goes to jail on circumstantial evidence only to rot there
for thirty years before some plucky law student gets him out,
I tore it up into little bits and tossed it into three separate re-
cycling bins.

Then I started over. It was a lot less fun.

TO DO:

1) Ashley Sinclair story.
— Check *Monitor* morgue (other papers back then?)
— *NYT* on microfilm @ Benson
— Interview NYU prof. (screw Gordon)
— Call Equity. Stage name?
— 20s theater mags. "Backstage," etc.
— Make appt. w/ Roger Nash
— Who's the father? Gossip columns, etc.
— Robbie Renssellaer = last resort

2) Sissy Dillingham / Starlight
— What did she find @ hist. soc.?
— Who knew?
— Who has $$ stake in apt. building?
— Any other reason to kill her?
  • Personal?
  • Enemies?
  • B. Marsh affair?
  • Jealous husband (hers)?
  •   "   wife (his)?
  • Is Lindy on the level?
  • Where was she? Alibi?

I stared down at the page for a while and waited for inspiration to strike. It didn't, so I drew little doodles in the margins, feeling increasingly dopey.

Why would someone kill Sissy Dillingham? She could be plenty annoying, but that hardly seemed like a good enough reason. Lindy Marsh was convinced it was something personal. But the fact that she'd been killed within hours of finding something that would stop the sale of the theater—or at least she thought it would—couldn't be a co-incidence. Could it?

What else was brewing in that insular little town-gown world of hers? Was her husband really as unplugged as Mad and Lindy thought? And would somebody really want to kill her just because she'd been involved with Barry?

The idea didn't make any more sense to me than it did to Cody. Would some woman scorned really bother to off her when Marsh was already six feet under? Like I told Lindy, that would take someone with a serious taste for vengeance. I mean, if you were going to commit the proverbial crime of passion, you'd have to do it in the heat of the moment, right? You'd knock her off to get her out of the way—sort of like me fantasizing about beheading Cody's ex with a chainsaw. You'd either do that, or you'd . . .

You'd kill them both.

Holy shit.

I stared down at Barry Marsh's name, which I'd triple-underlined during my doodling frenzy.

Was it possible? Could Sissy's death really have nothing to do with the Starlight? And was there any way on earth that Barry Marsh's death wasn't an accident?

Poisoning somebody with Viagra. It sounded absurd. Besides, Cody had said that Marsh ordered the drug himself over the Internet. But maybe he had second thoughts about taking it. What if somebody found out the drug might kill him, then slipped it to him with malice aforethought? Wouldn't that also explain why he died in the middle of the day—and in the office, no less? Lindy said he was a world-class adulterer, but would even he have blown off their coffee date to get laid on the fifth floor of Walden County Savings?

And speaking of Lindy . . . Hadn't Sissy blurted out that she'd "finally" killed him? Could Lindy have found out he ordered the drug and gotten so pissed she killed him with it? And then . . . what? Finished up her revenge a few months later when she ran Sissy over with the car—then invited me to lunch so she could pretend to cry about it? Now *that* would take a—

"So how goes it with Ashley?"

I looked up to see Marilyn, who wasn't smiling.

"Ashley . . . ?"

"Ashley *Sinclair*. Jesus, do I really have to remind you? How's the goddamn story going?"

"Which story?"

"Alex, I swear, if you're screwing around with—"

"I'm working on it. I really am. See?" I held up my note-book with the list of sources to check out. "I just meant, which story in particular?"

"Whichever one inspired Chester to do *this*." She brandished a sheet of paper from behind her back. It said: "ALEX ON ASHLEY—Benier tells the whole Sinclair story—*THE MONITOR*, Saturday."

"Please tell me that's not a rack card."

"One of five hundred, hot off the presses."

"You've got to be kidding me."

"Are you telling me you didn't know?"

"Of course not. What do you think I am, nuts? I've barely even started to—"

"Well, Chester's blown the entire quarterly promo budget on this."

"On five hundred rack cards for the vending boxes?"

"On that, and an ad running on Nine News, and a full-pager in the *Monitor* every day for the rest of week. Oh, and apparently he's rented the side of a bus."

"*No.*"

"Yes."

I snatched the card out of her hands. "He spelled my name wrong."

She glanced at it. "So he did."

"Oh, hell. Did you know 'Benier' sounds just like the French word for doughnut?"

"Yeah, well, you've got bigger things to worry about."

"Meaning?"

"Meaning where the hell's my story?"

"I told you, I just started . . ."

"You've got 'til Thursday."

"But that's, like, forty-eight hours from now."

"More like fifty-six. I'll be nice and let you file at the end of the day."

"But how am I supposed to—"

"Are you a daily news reporter, or do you work for a goddamn bimonthly magazine all of a sudden?"

"Give me a break. Ashley Sinclair has been dead for, what, eighty years? It's not exactly like covering a common council meaning, you know."

"Jesus Christ, don't whine."

"But . . ."

"You know, some reporters would be flattered their editor has so much confidence in them. So start typing."

"At least give me Mad."

She thought about it for a minute. "He's swamped. But I tell you what. You can have Intern Brad."

"No thanks."

"Suit yourself."

"I *really* need Mad."

"I said . . ."

"I bet the *Times* is giving Gordon plenty of resources, and not some woman-hating intern, either."

She narrowed her eyes at me, then shrugged. "Fine. Take Madison."

"Thank you."

"Oh, and in case I haven't made myself clear, this had better be the best story of your life, or we're all screwed."

I decided it was time for Mad to share my joy. I checked the sign-out sheet on the newsroom secretary's desk, but all he'd written was "Madison—on campus—noonish." Foiled again.

I scuttled back to my desk and perused my to do list, which was looking increasingly lame. Still, the first idea— checking the old *Monitors*—seemed like a halfway decent place to start. I grabbed my new Maglite flashlight out of my backpack and headed down to the morgue.

If anybody needs someplace to shoot a medieval epic, the paper's basement would make a nifty dungeon. It's creepy in every way you can think of: dark and dank, with lots of big stacks of things for some psycho to hide behind. What's worse, the door's so old and rusty that nine out of ten new hires lock themselves in the first time they go down there— which is probably going to earn the paper a whopping emotional-distress suit one of these days.

I flipped the light switch at the top of the stairs, and a few fluorescent bulbs sputtered to life, if barely. That gave me a chance to try out the Maglite, which had been a Christmas present from Cody in honor of my Starlight adventure. The thing is enormous, and so powerful (we're talking four D-batteries) that you can pick out a squirrel at fifty yards. It looks just like something a cop would carry, except that it's metallic red. In the context of our relationship, it was actually kind of romantic.

The *Monitor* keeps more recent clips upstairs in the library, but the old ones are downstairs, organized according to subject. Once upon a time, the newspaper took the filing thing pretty seriously; there was somebody whose full-time job it was to keep all the old stories in order. But, as the legend goes, the last official librarian retired in the late eighties—the same week as a particularly horrifying hike in the price of newsprint. Chester's predecessor balanced the budget by freezing the position, and the archive system has been a disaster ever since.

Lucky for me, though, whoever'd been in charge of the library during the Ashley era was downright obsessive. It took me a while to find the right filing cabinets, but once I did I was buried in paper. There were folders marked "ARTS—PERFORMING—LOCAL" and "THEATRES (LIVE)—NEWS"; and "THEATRE REVIEWS"; and "ACTING TROUPES (TRAVELING)". I looked under "S" for "Sinclair" and ran across a file on the Starlight; this was news to me, since I'd assumed the active one upstairs was the only one around. I went backward through the "S" section, and there it was: a folder labeled "SINCLAIR, ASHLEY." It was gray around the edges and it smelled funny, but I kissed it anyway.

Then I got the hell out of there.

Safely upstairs with another big coffee, I set the other three inches' worth of clips aside and went straight for the Ashley folder. Newspaper stories are supposed to be filed according to date, with the most recent on top. Most of the ones upstairs are all jumbled from being manhandled by lazy reporters like yours truly. This one was in perfect order, though, and I had a feeling it hadn't been touched since the long-ago librarian had filed the last clip—marked April 8, 1931.

It was pretty dreadful.

By LETITIA HARWOOD
Special to The Monitor

She was beautiful. She was talented.
One day, she might have been a star. But

five years ago today, Miss Ashley Sinclair vanished without a trace.

In the intervening years, some of her theatrical colleagues have gone on to great success or faded into obscurity. The Gabriel Police Department has considered her case inactive for more than three years. But for the family of Miss Sinclair, née Miss Dolores Strunk of Hoboken, New Jersey, the sorrow is as fresh as it was the day they learned their beloved daughter was missing.

"I still can't believe it. I keep hoping that someday our little Dolly will just walk through the front door. I can't give up hope that someday she will come home to us," said her mother, Mrs. Reginald Strunk, her voice choked with tears.

Anyone who follows the theater—indeed, anyone who reads the newspaper or listens to the radio—will recall the disappearance of Miss Sinclair, a most promising young actress who made her debut on the Great White Way at the tender age of 11. At 19, she was poised for stardom in Austin Cusack's famed production of *The Quinn Affair*, only to disappear just days before opening night. Time and again, the hopes of Mrs. Strunk have been raised by alleged sightings of her daughter, only to be dashed again when those sightings proved mistaken or cruelly false.

"It is so difficult," said Mrs. Strunk, who lost her husband to a heart ailment just two years after her daughter's disappearance. "If anyone has any information on where my daughter might be, of what became of her, I would beg them to come forward."

Will there ever be an end to this mother's suffering? The authorities are not optimistic. Although Chief of Police Arthur Dobbler will not entirely rule out a happy resolution to the case, my sources in the Department report that the prospects are, at best, grim.

I shuffled to the next story, hoping like hell it hadn't been written by Letitia Harwood. It had. It was dated April 8, 1927, and it was essentially the same thing all over again— but pegged to the first anniversary of Ashley's disappearance, rather than the fifth. I was just gathering the courage to look at the rest of the file when Mad walked in, and I had the pleasure of informing him that he was my slave for the next two days.

"No way, Bernier. I'm working on this big story on transgenic corn, and . . ."

"I thought it was broccoli."

"Ancient history. Now there are these two researchers up at Benson who're ready to rip each other's guts out over whether or not this genetically engineered shit can kill the . . ." I held up the rack card. "What the fuck is that?"

"Help me."

"Does that mean *this* Saturday?"

"Marilyn wants me to file in two days."

"Shouldn't be a problem. Should it?"

"Mad, do you have any idea how long it's going to take to go through all this . . ."

"Easy does it, Bernier. How much have you got so far?"

"Not too damn much."

"Hey, look, they spelled your name wrong."

"You don't say." I handed him a stack of file folders. "How about you go through those, I'll go through these, and we regroup in an hour? Then somebody's gotta go up to the Benson library to look up the *Times* on microfilm. Oh, and we've gotta grab a phone interview with that guy from N.Y.U. who ID'ed Ashley to Gordon. Why don't you call him? You're better with those egghead types than I am. I was going to try and hunt down Roger Nash for the local theater-historian angle . . ."

"The what?"

"Oh, and I was going to call Equity to try and get her real name. No, wait—I don't need to. It's right here." I showed him the first clip from the file. "Dolores Strunk. Doesn't exactly roll off the tongue, does it? Anyway, I thought maybe we could try and see if any of her family is still around anyplace."

He scanned the story and handed it back. "Jesus, who wrote this crap?"

"Somebody named Letitia Harwood. I guess she was the *Monitor*'s resident sob sister back then. You know, a lady reporter who gets people to spill their guts so she can write some treacly—"

"I know what a sob sister is, for Christ's sake. It just makes me want to yak."

"Sounds like she made up the quotes to boot. 'I can't give up hope that someday she will come home to us.' Nobody really talks like that."

"So what do you want me to do again?"

I told him. "I have to go cover this press conference in"—
I looked at my watch—"half an hour. Get a load of this.
They're breaking the fact that Ashley was pregnant when
she died."

"How did you find . . . Ah. Nice to be in bed with—"

"Oh shut up. Speaking of which, you are not going to believe who just slithered into town." I filled him in on the
Lucy situation.

"Man, what a mess. Poor guy."

"Poor *guy*? What about poor Alex? My boyfriend's ex-
wife is swearing up and down she's going to get him back
no matter what, and the woman doesn't know how to take
no for an answer. Don't I get any goddamn sympathy?"

"Poor Alex."

"Thank you. Anyway, enough about my little crisis.
Where were we with the Ashley thing? Oh, right. If she was
pregnant, she must have been seeing somebody. So who was
it?"

"You think you can get that for the story?"

"We could try. I thought we could at least get a jump on
the competition, maybe look up some old gossip columns.
You in the mood for some wild speculation?"

"Aren't I always?"

"My hero."

"Sounds like a lot of work, though. I assume you're providing all my meals for the next two days."

"Deal."

"Hey, what if something breaks with Sissy Dillingham
between now and Thursday? Am I still supposed to be covering that too?"

"Actually, I kind of wanted to bounce something off you.
What do you think," I asked, "of murder by Viagra?"

20

THE NEXT THREE DAYS SET A RATHER UNAPPETIZING RECORD: it was the longest Cody and I had gone without speaking since we started dating. It wasn't that we were avoiding each other or anything, just that we kept crossing signals. I'd leave a message at the station, he'd call me back when I was out on an interview; he'd talk to my answering machine, I'd turn around and get a busy signal at his apartment. I'd try his cell phone, and find it was either busy or he was out of range. I was so crazed with the Ashley story, I might not have even noticed the sudden lack of intimacy—except that I was fairly sure that wherever he was, Lucy was right there, turning up the volume on her womanly wiles.

For the most part, though, I was too damn busy to think about it. Tuesday night found me and Mad huddled in a booth in the back of the Citizen Kane, surrounded by stacks of papers, a gaggle of reporters' notebooks, a bowl of beer nuts, a lowball glass filled with olives, and a pitcher of martinis big enough to lubricate the Rat Pack. Being a regular has its advantages.

"So what do we know?" I asked Mad, who was dropping a quartet of olives into his glass. "Where are we so far?"

"Well for one thing, we know there aren't nearly enough underage chicks in this bar anymore."

"Mack said he heard there was gonna be a crackdown. Couple of joints up on the hill got busted by undercover juveniles."

"Christ, haven't the cops got anything better to do?"

"I think it's the state liquor authority."

"Bastards."

"Let's get back to the point, okay? What do we know about Ashley Sinclair so far?"

"You want her life story?"

"Please."

He gulped down half a martini, then started shuffling papers. "Okay. Born January 19, 1907, Hoboken, New Jersey. Mother Agnes is a housewife. Dad Reginald teaches high school math. They have three sons, and little Dolly comes along late in the game. She's a total dish from day one. People stop them on the street to say how gorgeous she is. Everybody says she oughta be in pictures." He paused to finish his olives and pour another drink. "Okay, when she's eight or nine they start taking her into the city to get her into vaudeville, and guess what—she's pretty damn good. Starts playing lots of cute little-girl parts. Makes her Broadway debut at eleven in"—He checked his notes—"something called *The Wages of Virtue*. Remind me to give *that* one a miss. Does a bunch more plays and a couple of musical revues, then lands the lead in a silent movie called *Heavens to Betsy*. Becomes a minor celebrity. Manages to survive the awkward-teenager phase. Gets cast in some big-deal play called *The Quinn Affair*, comes to Gabriel to start the out-of-town tryouts, and—"

"Hold on a second. What was that play called again?"

"*The Wages of Virtue.*"

"Not that one. The other one."

"*The Quinn Affair.*"

"You know, that sounds familiar . . ." I riffled through a few notebooks until I found the right interview. "I *knew* it."

"What?"

"That was the play goddamn Robert Renssellaer was in. The one that gave him his big break."

"So?"

"Maybe he knows more about this than he's been letting on."

"I thought you said he was, like, six years old back then."

"Oh. Right. Actually it was seven."

"Couldn't he be lying about his age?"

"Nah, I looked up his birth certificate when I did that big profile on him. Thought I might use it for color or something. But doesn't it seem like one hell of a coincidence? Robbie Renssellaer, our resident prima-donna-pain-in-the-ass, gets his big break in the same play Ashley Sinclair is doing when she vanishes?"

"I guess it's kind of wacky. But why does it matter?"

"I have no idea. Maybe it doesn't. It just seems weird is all."

"Great. What do we have that's runnable?"

"Let's go over what we got from the interviews. How about that guy from N.Y.U.?"

"Professor Chadwick Sweet. Now *there's* a fourteen-karat pain in the butt."

"What'd he say?"

"Well, first off, he wanted to make sure I knew about every piece of academic crap he ever churned out. Then he held forth on the decline and fall of modern theater for the better part of an hour."

"Nice to think Gordon may have suffered a little. Did he give you anything that wasn't already in the *Times*?"

"Nothing worth printing."

"Wonderful. Okay, Roger Nash. He was kind of helpful, actually. I got the feeling he was pretty pissed at himself for not thinking of the Ashley Sinclair thing before Sweet did. Got scooped on his own turf, much like yours truly."

"Hey, he give you anything on Sissy Dillingham?"

I shook my head. "Said he had no idea what she might have found."

"You believe him?"

"Seemed like he was on the level. He sounded totally surprised to hear Sissy might have actually had something. So did the rest of the S.O.S. bunch, for that matter."

"You talked to all of them?"

"Most of them. They all said Sissy was being tight-lipped about the whole thing, which was damn unusual for her."

"So what did Nash have to say about Ashley?"

"I brought him some theater programs I copied over at the historical society, and he gave me the skinny on a few of the characters. Christ, you know, I should have made the Robbie Renssellaer connection right then. I can't believe I didn't. This Lucy thing must be killing brain cells . . ." I dug out the program for *The Quinn Affair*. "Wait a sec. He's not even on here."

"What part was he supposed to be playing?"

"Um . . . I guess it'd have to be 'Jonah, Evelyn's young son.' Seems like the only kid in it. But here it says it was being played by somebody named Richie Edgar."

"Maybe Renssellaer had to fill in for him or something. You don't think he was just plain lying about it, do you?"

"Honestly, I wouldn't put it past him to pad his résumé. But then again, Nash made it sound like this was a pretty famous play. The director was a really big deal—went out to Hollywood and won a bunch of Oscars. I can't believe even Robbie'd think he could lie about something like that and get away with it."

"Okay, so let's assume for the time being that he wound up playing the part after all. What difference does it make?"

"I don't know. I guess it doesn't. I'm just confused."

"So to get back to your buddy Nash . . ."

"Right. He told me lots of stuff about what it was like to be in a traveling theater company back then. Gave me some good color. Like, apparently there was this big ego thing attached to how well you could pack your trunk. I guess a sloppy trunk made you a big loser."

"Fascinating. So how was our friend Ashley at the trunk-packing biz?"

"He had no idea."

"Did he give you anything useful?"

"Well, he knew a lot about some of the actors. Like, there was this guy named—"

"Aren't we supposed to be concentrating on the girl?"

"How are we supposed to figure out who killed her if we don't know who the other characters are?"

He pulled the pitcher across the table. "I'm cutting you off."

"What for?"

"Alex, we have a day and a half to write the definitive profile of some chick who died seventy-five years ago. I think you better focus."

"I *am* focusing. But while we're covering the story, what's the harm in keeping our eyes open for who might have done it? I mean, wouldn't that be the scoop of the century?"

"Call me nuts, but aren't the cops supposed to figure out who killed who?"

"Come on, Mad. Think about it. For once we've got a totally level playing field. The crime happened ages ago, so the forensics don't matter a damn. We're probably in a much better position to solve this one than the cops are."

"How do you figure that?"

"Because it's not about catching the bad guy so much as piecing the story together. Which is what we do, right?"

"I guess." He started to push the pitcher back my way, then stopped. "Wait a minute. This wouldn't have anything to do with your boyfriend's ex-wife, now would it?"

"Meaning what?"

"Are you thinking that if you solve this little mystery, it'll give you a lock on cop boy?"

"You're an asshole, you know."

"I know. But I'm not a liar. If you want to figure this thing out for yourself, go for it. If you want to do it to screw Gordon to the wall, I'm your man. But if this is some cock-eyed way to impress Cody, I think you're out of your tree."

"Oh, for Christ's sake. It never even occurred to me. You're the one who brought it up."

"I thought it needed saying."

"Good for you. Now can we talk about the story?"

"Sure."

"So like I was saying, Nash told me a bunch of stuff about the acting company. It was called the Genesius Players—named after the patron saint of actors, apparently. They were a pretty tight-knit group, did some big radio plays together, kind of like Orson Welles and the Mercury. Austin Cusack was the head honcho. Used to be an actor himself, then got into writing and directing. The leading man was his best buddy from high school, a guy named Brandon Bartlett. Total hunk. Married awhile, but like every other guy in the world he turned out to be gay. Got outed and blew his brains out."

"Who outed him?"

"His ex-wife."

"*That's* gotta hurt."

"Ashley joined up when she was, like sixteen. Her best friend was a girl named Priscilla Morton."

"The movie star?"

"Yeah, but way before she hit it big. And get this. After Ashley disappeared, Morton was the one who got her part in *The Quinn Affair*."

"So?"

"So you ever see *All About Eve*?"

"If there's no shooting at helicopters in it, then no."

"You heathen. Anyway, in *All About Eve*, there's this seemingly sweet young thing who spends the whole movie engineering her big break. She gets rid of the leading lady so she can go on instead."

"She kills her?"

"Well, no . . ."

"And Priscilla Morton was in it?"

"No, that's not the point. All I'm saying is, maybe we've got a suspect. I mean, so far she's the only one who obviously had something to gain."

"Did they suspect her at the time?"

"Not from anything I saw in the clip files. But remember, back then, they didn't even know for sure Ashley was dead. They spent months assuming she'd just flaked off somewhere. And even if the cops did think it was a murder case, which they didn't, I seriously doubt they'd look at some pretty teenage girl as the doer."

"You really think she killed her best friend to get ahead?"

"She didn't just get ahead. She got it *all*. She married Austin Cusack—who, by the way, the gossip columns had linked to Ashley more than once. She moved to Hollywood, and spent the next twenty years as the reigning movie goddess. Not bad, huh?"

"She still alive?"

"Died in the late eighties. Hadn't really been out in pub-

lic for twenty years, though. Kind of turned into a Brigitte
Bardot type—lived alone in a big mansion with about a hundred cats."

"What happened to the director?"

"Died in the fifties or sixties, I think. Drank his liver all
to hell."

Mad raised his glass. "Then here's to Mr. Cusack."

"You're sick."

"Hey, he sounds like my kind of guy. So you really think
Priscilla Morton whacked her best friend over the head,
bricked her up in a wall, stole her career, married her
boyfriend, and lived happily ever after?"

"Hmm . . . It does sound kind of far-fetched when you
put it like that."

"How else you want me to put it?"

"Well, she probably couldn't have done it alone."

"What are you thinking? Pushy stage mother?"

"Okay, so it sounds idiotic. I'm open to alternate theories
of the crime, believe me."

"What else do we know about the victim?"

"Well, for one thing, she was definitely in the family
way."

"Right. How pregnant was she?"

"About three months, which from what I hear means
you're about to start showing it, if you haven't already."

"So Ashley's dirty little secret was about to be out of the
bag."

"Zig-zactly."

"And if it was Mr. Cusack's problem, maybe he wasn't
exactly hot to step up to the plate."

"Huh?"

"Maybe he didn't want to marry her."

"Oh. Yeah, that was my other bright idea. The only other
one, as a matter of fact."

"Maybe he thought marrying her would ruin his career."

"Hard to see how. I mean, being a director isn't like being a matinee idol. You don't have to stay all single and hunky. And besides, marrying Priscilla Morton didn't hurt him. Probably helped him, actually. They were quite the Hollywood power couple in their day. Hey, wait—maybe it's *An American Tragedy*."

"I'll say."

"The Theodore Dreiser story, you dope. The one they made into that Montgomery Clift movie—*A Place in the Sun*. The boy falls in love with the girl of his dreams, but he's stuck with the girl next door 'cause he knocked her up. Shelley Winters."

"Shelley Winters?"

"She played the murder victim. Monty drowns her so he can have Elizabeth Taylor. I think he winds up on death row or something. Anyway, it won six Oscars."

"You are just a fountain of movie lore today."

"I guess I've got it on the brain."

"So now you think . . . what? Cusack killed her so he could be with Priscilla?"

"Could've."

"Great. Any other earth-shattering insights?"

"Would you be nice?"

"Come on, we're getting nowhere."

"Be good, or I won't tell you what Emma told me."

That got him. "What? Come on, Bernier, don't be such a . . ."

"She said she missed you while she was gone."

"Really? How much?"

"Some."

"What did she say *exactly*?"

"You know, you're really starting to resemble an eighth-grade girl. Okay, okay. I think what she said was 'I missed that wanker more than I bloody well thought,' or something else inscrutably British. Either way it was a compliment."

"What do you think it means?"

"That you're not in imminent danger of having her dump your ass."

"Cool."

"Will you be nice to me now?"

"Sure."

"Then let us continue. As it turns out, it wasn't the first time Ashley was in Gabriel. This was a pretty big theater town once upon a time, and Nash knew of two other shows she'd been in that played here."

"So you think she might have been offed by somebody local?"

"It's possible. At least, it's more possible than if she'd never been here before."

"Right. So who?"

"I have no idea. Maybe somebody who saw her in a play and really flipped for her or something."

"Like a stalker?"

"Could be."

"Christ, Bernier, you're starting to give me a headache."

"Sorry. I just . . . ."

"Look, if you're really gonna go this route, at least think about it logically. Don't forget what happened to the girl." I stared at him. "Come on, what happened to her?"

"She got whacked over the head and bricked up in a wall."

"Exactly. So whoever did it had to have access to the goddamn wall, right? It had to be someone who knew the ins and outs of the theater."

"Oh. Good point."

"Hey, did Cody tell you if they think she died in the theater, or if she got killed someplace else and moved?"

"I didn't ask him about it. But at this point, I think the forensics tell them zip. But think about it—there'd have to be a hell of a lot of blood from that kind of head wound, wouldn't there? Moving her would've been a damn messy proposition, unless you took the time to clean her up and wrap the body in something, and there was nothing in there with her, no towels or blankets or anything. I doubt very much they had Hefty bags back in 1926. And besides, I can't believe this thing was premeditated."

"Why not?"

"Because there are a hell of a lot of better ways to kill somebody. This way's messy, and it's unpredictable. Why not just strangle her and get it over with? No, this had to be a spur-of-the-moment thing, and it happened right there at the theater."

"You sound pretty damn sure of yourself."

"I'm not. It's just that this totally seems like a crime of opportunity, and the cleanup too. If whoever killed her did it, say, in her hotel room, why not just toss the body into the nearest furnace? Why not weigh it down and throw it in the lake? Why the hell would you take the trouble to bring it to the Starlight and brick it up in the wall? It was two days before opening night of a big play, so the place had to be crawling with people around the clock. I'd bet my boots somebody killed her in the heat of the moment, shoved her in the wall, bricked her up, and tried like hell to forget about it."

"What was the deal with the wall, anyway? Were they doing construction or something?"

"I actually know the answer to that. Nash used to teach a course on the actor's rights movement—the rise of Equity and all. From what he told me, things could get pretty ugly, especially on the road. You'd stay in these dumpy hotels, have to make your own costumes, get stiffed for your pay if a performance got canceled. He said Equity went on strike over it a while before. Anyway, another big thing was dressing rooms—they'd be way too cramped and either freezing cold or boiling hot. Most places just blew it off, but I guess the Starlight actually gave a damn about attracting top talent. They did some excavating down in the basement and expanded the dressing rooms, not that it turned out to be any great shakes. Must have been a real pit before."

"And this was going on when Ashley disappeared?"

"Right."

"Interesting."

"So to answer your question, people who knew what was up with the construction would be the acting company, the theater staff, and every brick mason in town."

"Okay, there's who had opportunity. What about motive?"

"The pregnancy's the obvious one. Then there's the whole career competition thing. or it could be something else entirely."

"Such as?"

"Such as how the hell do I know? Maybe she stiffed the wrong bootlegger. It was Prohibition, wasn't it?"

"Yep. From 1919 to 1933." I raised an eyebrow at him. "Hey, you gotta know thine enemy. You want to hear about the Volstead Act?"

"No."

"But there goes the access issue again. You really think Capone and his boys were hanging out in the Starlight basement?"

"You know, I heard the bar at the theater was nowhere close to dry. Maybe she stumbled into something she shouldn't have."

"Tough to think how. Everybody was running rum back then. Nobody gave a damn but Elliot Ness."

"But wasn't there big money involved?"

"Probably."

I slouched down and put my feet up on the seat across from me. "My head hurts."

"Welcome to the club."

"Okay, enough with the theorizing. What have we got that we can print?"

"You really are all over the place tonight."

"Have pity."

"All right . . . I had Intern Brad look up those old *Times* stories for you . . ."

"I don't want that little weasel anywhere near this thing."

"Come on, Brad's my boy. And you don't have the luxury of being pissy anyway."

"Fine. What did he come up with?" He handed over an inch-thick stack of paper. "You look through these yet?"

"Some of it. There's more than just the *Times* there. He found lots of stuff in other papers—the *Sun* and the *Herald*, I think. Anyhoo, most of what's in there from before she disappeared is either reviews or gossip columns, which you can deal with. There's a hell of a lot from afterward, though. Looks like she got more coverage than O.J."

"Any speculation back then about what might have happened to her?"

"In the *Times*? No way. They were even squarer then than they are now. The tabs did do a little navel-gazing about the state of modern society. Half the time they made Ashley out to be the victim, half the time she was some artsy weirdo who skipped town. A couple places did big profiles of her, which we can crib from."

"Excellent. What about her three brothers?"

"They've gotta be dead by now."

"Right, but maybe they've got kids and grandkids—

somebody who could wax eloquent about what Aunt Dolly's disappearance did to the family."

"You shameless little vulture you."

"Come on, we've gotta have an eensy bit of primary reportage in this thing, or we're screwed."

"I got news for you," Mad said. "We're screwed anyway."

21

We FILED THE STORY AT QUARTER AFTER SIX ON THURSDAY night. It was fifteen minutes late, but Marilyn decided to overlook this point. She did, however, spend the next hour telling us how much it sucked. The thing was chock-full of facts, she said, but it never gave you a sense of just who the hell Ashley Sinclair was. "What made her tick?" she said, leaning back in her chair and whirling her beloved numchucks. "What did she sound like, move like, *think* like? What made her so goddamn special? I don't get a sense of any of it—not even close. You've got three thousand fucking words here, and it reads like an entry in the goddamn Encyclopedia Britannica."

She went on like that for a while, her raving and me wondering just how much my mom was going to sue the paper for if Marilyn actually killed me. We told her we'd done the best we could under the circumstances. She told us we had fourteen hours to fix it, or else. Then she went to her tae kwon do class.

"So what do we do now?" Mad was saying. "I mean, Christ, I know it's not the goddamn Pentagon Papers, but it can't be *that* bad."

"Marilyn seems to disagree."

"Yeah, well, what do you think?"

"I think there's a lot of interesting stuff in there. But I can see why she'd think it's kind of . . . flat."

"What the fuck are we supposed to do about it? 'What does she think like? What does she move like?' How the hell do we know? The last time this chick saw the light of day, my grandpappy was shoplifting Lucky Strikes."

"I thought he was a missionary."

"That was later. So what the hell are we going to do?"

"We could move to Canada."

"I mean tonight."

"So do I."

"Very funny. Okay, let's go over all the paperwork again. Maybe there's something in all those files we missed the first three times around. There's got to be some color in those old police reports, the interviews the cops did when she disappeared . . ."

"We already put that stuff in, remember? Apparently it didn't do us any good."

"Oh crap. Look, we gotta walk away from this for an hour or so. Let's go grab a drink and some food."

"Hold on a sec. Just let me make one phone call. It's a long shot, but at this point . . ."

I dialed what used to be my number and got my ex-roommate's domestic partner, a rather cute (and extremely hairy) German guy named Helmut.

"Lexie *liebling*, when are you coming over for brunch? We haven't seen you since, what, the Oktoberfest party? Didn't you have a good time?"

"Oh, sure I did. It was a blast. Except for, um, the beer part . . ."

"So what can I do for you? I'm afraid Dirk is still at the office. He should be home by ten, though."

"Isn't he still in school?"

"He's doing an internship at the Law Guardian."

"Sounds like Dirk." My darling ex-roomie is a third-year law student and certified bleeding-heart liberal whose parents are (a) totally comfortable with his sexuality and (b) utterly terrified that he's going to set a record for the lowest salary ever earned by a juris doctor. "Actually, I was calling to talk to you anyway."

"What about?"

"You still speaking to that guy who runs the B.C.A.?"

"Sure. Why wouldn't I?"

"Dirk said he wasn't exactly throwing rice at your commitment ceremony."

"True. But he got over it quickly enough. What do you want him for?"

"Story I'm doing. I've been trying to track him down, but he never answers his voice mail. E-mail either."

"Typical."

"Look, I'm desperate. Do you have any idea where I could get him now?"

"You mean *right* now?"

"Right this minute, or I'm in a world full of hurting."

"Hmm . . . What time is it?"

"Seven-thirty."

"We used to go to a Thursday night poetry slam at one of the coffeehouses—*quite* the meat market. I think he still goes."

"Which one?"

"I'm not telling until you promise to come over for brunch on Sunday. Dirkie misses you. I'll even make eggs Benedict. "

"Without . . ."

"Without the nasty bacon. "

"Deal."

"And bring that boy of yours along."

"I'll try. Things are a little funky at the moment."

"And have him wear a pair of those tight football trousers."

"I can't promise anything."

"Okay, be difficult," he sighed. "Benji's probably over at Café Whatever, wearing his latest broken heart on his shoulder."

"I think you mean his sleeve."

"*Ach*, whatever."

"Can I drop your name?"

"Sure."

"You're a doll."

"Tell me something I don't know. How's Steve, by the way?"

"Still counting the wee birdies."

"Is there a man in his life?"

"Why, are you getting nostalgic?"

"Oh *please*. Dirk met someone at Lambda he wanted to set him up with."

"You know," I said, "someday, I really hope I get to live with a man you *haven't* slept with."

It would probably have been easier just to go over to the café, but frankly I was in no mood for it. The scene over there is hipper-than-thou any night of the week, and the idea of trying to find Benji amid the pierced and tattooed masses screaming their innermost angst made me want to chew my own foot off. I called instead.

Whoever answered the phone was in no hurry to do me any favors; it took a good ten minutes for Benji to manifest himself. I explained what I wanted over the din of what sounded very much like a number of cats being strangled all at once. He said he could get to it in a couple of weeks; I told him I needed to see him right away. He was just about to tell me to go to hell when I mentioned that I'd gotten his name from Helmut, at which point he was putty in my hands. He promised to meet me in half an hour.

"Come on, get that hideous coat of yours," I told Mad. "We're going up to Benson."

"What for?"

"To see somebody."

"Who?"

"The woman of the hour."

"Come on, we don't have time to screw around. Who is it?"

"A certain sweet young thing, who . . ."

"You're pissing me off."

"Would you let me have some fun for once? Christ, what do you think? We're finally going to get a look at Ashley Sinclair."

There she was, in black and white. The image was grainy and uneven, flickering against a yellowed screen in the basement of the theater arts building, but somehow it only made her seem more . . . What? I tried out a number of words, and none of them did her justice. Unreal. Gorgeous. Goddesslike. Okay, that last one wasn't even a word. But I was positively tongue-tied. And as for Mad: he was downright catatonic.

I'd been hoping for this ever since it occurred to me that maybe, just maybe, the Benson Cinema Archive might have a copy of Ashley Sinclair's one and only movie. I'd tried calling and e-mailing the guy who ran the place, but he never got back to me. Then I'd finally figured out why his name sounded so familiar, (how many Benji Moskowitzes could there be in one zip code?) and voilà—success through emotional blackmail. Very satisfying.

The movie itself, in case you're wondering, is about a farm girl named Betsy who prays for a miracle to keep her family from starving when a drought kills all their crops. The next morning, a stranger shows up on their doorstep and promptly keels over. They can't afford to take her in and feed her, but since they're honest country folk they do it anyway. And guess what: the girl turns out to be an actual angel. Eventually, after she's laid hands on the family thresher and brought rain through the divine power of her tears (I'm not kidding), she falls ill and—suffering from Ali McGraw disease long before it was fashionable—becomes more and more attractive until she finally croaks.

Heavens to Betsy was supposed to be shown with live piano music; watching it in total silence was downright surreal. So was seeing Ashley up there on the screen, not frozen in a promo still but alive and moving and doing what she loved best, which was acting. When I first heard about the movie, I'd assumed that Ashley played the title role. I was wrong. She played the angel, which was damn good casting, if you ask me. Marilyn had wanted to know what she was like, and at least in the context of this silent penny dreadful the answer was, well, *angelic*. She had enormous eyes, hair that flowed to the middle of her back, slender white arms that swayed gently as she walked. (Benji said that most people assumed this symbolized her wings, but according to the director it was an agrarian allegory representing waving fields of wheat.) I knew from my research that she'd studied ballet, and it had definitely paid off; she was astonishingly graceful, with bucketloads of poise and a dancer's command of her body.

In French, you describe someone who's comfortable with himself by saying he "feels good in his own skin," and the main thing I took away from watching Ashley Sinclair was that she was a weird contradiction of that. She seemed physically comfortable in her own skin, but there was something in her eyes that said she wasn't entirely comfortable with *herself.* Yes, I know she was acting. All I'm telling you is my intuition, which was this: although Ashley Sinclair was beautiful and glamorous and strong, lurking right beneath the surface was a scared little girl named Dolly Strunk.

When the movie was over and she'd disappeared from under the tattered quilt, I was actually crying; even Mad was sniffling a little. Okay, so the special effects were so crude that when she vanished the whole room shifted to the right about a foot, but it didn't make a damn bit of difference. Even at sixteen, Ashley Sinclair had what it takes to be a movie star: a magnetic presence that turns you on, forces you to keep watching, makes you feel like you've lost something when she leaves the screen.

It was a while later, when I was back at my computer pounding out another draft, that something struck me. Yes, the movie was an old fashioned melodrama, formal and formulaic. But in an odd sort of way, I'd just gotten a glimpse into what had happened in the basement of the Starlight Theatre all those years ago. Like whoever had murdered Ashley Sinclair, I'd just watched her die.

22

By the time we filed the second draft of the story Friday morning, I still hadn't spoken to Cody. It was starting to get to me.

Years of chasing emotionally unavailable men have trained me to wait by the phone with the patience of a veritable Buddha, but Cody had always been Mister Present-and-Accounted-For. Now we were crossing signals right and left, and although he got credit for having an intimate relationship with my answering machine, the fact that we hadn't actually talked to each other was driving me up the wall. I started having all these paranoid fantasies about Lucy showing up in his bedroom with a negligée and a feather duster and a bottle of goddamn white zinfandel, and Cody not being able to resist the pull of those dorm room memories. That much having been established, it only made sense that he'd be avoiding me. He had to be calling my machine when he knew I wouldn't be there (classic passive-aggressive behavior) because he didn't want to lie, but he didn't have the heart to tell me the truth.

I tried to restore a modicum of sanity by reminding myself that I hadn't been able to reach him either. This only served to make me wonder how he could be out of the office so much in the middle of not one but two murder investigations. As far as I was concerned, the only logical explanation was that he was boffing his ex-wife in the nearest no-tell motel. It was only a matter of time until he got back together with her; then he'd decamp to Boston, breaking his mother's heart. What's more, Zeke and Shakespeare would never see each other again. How could a grown man—an officer of the law, no less—be so mean to a couple of poor defenseless dogs, anyway? And didn't the unfaithful rat even care about his mother? Well did he?

Okay, so I know I was something less than rational. All I can say in my own defense is that I was starting to crack under the pressure—of writing the Ashley Sinclair story, of trying to figure out what Sissy Dillingham did to get herself killed, of wondering what really happened to Barry Marsh, and (the topper of all of them) worrying that the best boyfriend I've ever had was going to dump me for his lousy cheating ex-wife.

And yes, I know he hadn't done a damn thing to make me think he wanted to; he had, in fact, thrown her out of his apartment still clutching her wineglass. But like I said, I have what they call an overactive imagination—and at that point it was on mescaline. From where I was sitting, I figured I had exactly two things in my favor: in the end, all the stress seemed to help the Sinclair piece rather than hurt it; and so far, Cody had no idea I was going postal.

The story itself ran about thirty-five hundred words, once we'd cut a bunch of extraneous facts we'd only thrown in because we had them, which is hardly the definition of quality reportage. It ran above the fold, with one of those gigantic headlines usually reserved for major wars. Mad deserved a joint byline, but by order of Chester he didn't get one; the jerk had sold the "Alex on Ashley" angle, and he wasn't going to let anything get in the way of his alliteration.

Instead, all Mad got was a little tagline at the end: *"Monitor staff reporter Jake Madison contributed to this story."* Getting him to speak to me again cost many a margarita.

It started like this:

By ALEX BERNIER
Monitor staff

A truck driver said he gave her a lift from Des Moines to Indianapolis. A doctor in Memphis swore he treated her for heat stroke. A grocer in Topeka was sure he sold her some apples and a dozen eggs. A pair of Boy Scouts claimed they'd helped her change a tire outside Boston.

They were all mistaken. When Ashley Sinclair vanished on April 8, 1926, she never left Gabriel—may never even have left the Starlight Theatre, where her body would be found three-quarters of a century later.

The fate of the 19-year-old actress was a cause célèbre that one theater historian compares to the death of Elvis, another to the disappearance of Jimmy Hoffa. Newspapers devoted front-page headlines to Sinclair sightings; radio stations interrupted their broadcasts to report the erroneous news that she had turned up in a Detroit hospital bed.

"This kind of thing shouldn't be that difficult for people today to understand," said Benson University theater professor

Roger Nash. "Nowadays, it only takes a matter of hours for the whole country to become fixated on a single event, like the Oklahoma City bombing or rescuers in Texas trying to save that little girl who fell down a well. The Ashley Sinclair phenomenon was very similar to what would become commonplace more than half a century later. The thing that's most striking about it isn't what happened, but when."

Although the Sinclair case occurred before television, talk radio, and the Internet, Nash noted that it wasn't the first of its kind. Just a year earlier, America had been riveted by the plight of Floyd Collins, a Kentucky farmer and spelunker who was trapped in a cave for two weeks, until his death from starvation. "The Floyd Collins story grabbed the national consciousness, but ultimately you could say it was just another tragedy," Nash said. "Ashley Sinclair's sudden disappearance was a genuine mystery, one that will probably never be solved."

In the six months following Sinclair's disappearance, the New York tabloids alone published more than 300 stories about her—rumors of her whereabouts, so-called "intimate profiles," interviews with her friends and family. The *Monitor* and its then-competitor, the afternoon

Gabriel Transcript, published nearly 100.
Her parents alternately pleaded with reporters to leave them alone and begged
them to keep their daughter's face in the
news in the hope it might help them find
her.

As her father told the *New York Times*
two weeks before his death in 1928: "It's
as though everyone thinks my daughter is
fair game for every kind of speculation
imaginable, but nobody really knew her at
all."

So who was Ashley Sinclair? The
question has captured the popular consciousness just as it did three-quarters
of a century ago, but with a decidedly
information-age spin.

Web sites like www.theashleymystery.
com offer photographs, a clearinghouse
for crime theories, and the inevitable
merchandising tie-ins. (One T-shirt features a close-up of the actress's eyes on
the front, with the word "WHODUNIT?"
across the back. It sells for $17.95.)

Few people who knew Ashley Sinclair—
born Dolores Strunk—are still alive. Benson Heights resident Robert Renssellaer
was 7 years old when he rehearsed *The
Quinn Affair* with her at the Starlight Theatre. He was a last-minute replacement
for a sick young actor; she played the female lead, though she would disappear

two days before opening night—to be replaced by a then-unknown named Priscilla Morton. "She was a real lady," Renssellaer said in a statement he issued when Sinclair's body was identified. "I was very young, of course, but I do recall that she took time out to play with me, to make sure I felt comfortable. Very few adult actors went out of their way to include the children, and it meant a great deal to me."

Margaret Strunk Whittaker, a retired nurse who lives in Newark, N.J., remembers finding a box of photographs of Sinclair in her grandmother's attic when she was eight or nine years old. Her parents had never told her about her aunt, who'd disappeared nearly 15 years before; Agnes Strunk's sons had convinced her to put away all reminders of her missing daughter. "I wondered who this beautiful lady was," Whittaker said. "I brought them to my grandma and said, 'Who's this? She looks just like a movie star.' My grandmother just cried and cried, and I remember it made me cry too."

The story went on for another three thousand words or so, which is damn long for the *Gabriel Monitor*. Mad and I each read it over four times before handing it off to Marilyn, who was copy-editing it personally. We filed around eleven, then went over to the Green for a celebratory falafel.

When we got back, we found out Marilyn had been

yelling for us since about two minutes after we left. Mad, being manly, fled to the men's room. I would've been more than willing to follow him in there and hide under a urinal, but I wasn't fast enough.

"Alex, get over here. *Get over here.* Where the hell's my breakout box?"

"Do you, er, like the piece?"

"Not half bad. Now where the hell's the sidebars?"

"Sidebars . . . ?"

"Don't gape at me like some goddamn intern. You seriously think Chester's gonna be happy with just a mainbar?"

"But the story's, like, huge."

"And so is, like, my mortgage. Now be a good girl and give me what I need before we both get our asses canned. You know damn well Chester wants movable parts. Where are my movable parts?"

It was the closest to flustered I'd ever seen her. It would have been quite a hoot, if I didn't think she was dead serious about us both getting fired.

"What did you have in mind?"

"You tell me."

"Um . . . we could maybe recycle the timeline from the Robbie Renssellaer thing, update it to go with Ashley . . ."

"Fine. What else?"

"A box on all the plays she was in? You know, like her theatrical résumé?"

"Boring. Not that we won't run it if we need filler. Christ, Alex, give me something sexy, will you?"

"Like what?"

"Like maybe our readers would be halfway interested in who actually *killed* the woman."

"We tried, but we—"

"A minor topic your piece hardly even *bothers* with, by the way. Let see here . . ." She scrolled through the story with vicious little finger jabs. " 'At first, the Gabriel police were reluctant to consider her disappearance a crime. The general consensus was that she was just another flighty actress who'd decamped for greener pastures—despite the fact that she'd left all of her personal belongings behind. Her boar-bristle brush was still on the makeup table in the star's dressing room; no clothing seemed to be missing from her trunk; family photographs were next to the bed in the boardinghouse suite she shared with castmate Priscilla Morton.

" 'Morton herself, a then-unknown actress who had a minor role in *The Quinn Affair* until she was tapped to replace Sinclair, urged the police to investigate. But by the time it became apparent that Ashley Sinclair wasn't coming back, the trail was cold. Efforts to find her—both by the police and the private investigators her family hired—went nowhere.

" 'It didn't help that most of the cast of characters had left Gabriel months before, scattered around the country in theatrical . . .' *There* you go."

"There I go?"

"There's your breakout box. The goddamn cast of characters. We've got art, right?"

"Yeah, I think so . . ."

"So get on it. I'll give you—" she looked at her watch, which she wears on the inside of her wrist just to be ornery—"forty-five minutes."

"You want . . . what? Little bios on everybody?"

"What are you trying to do, bore us both out of a job? I want *motives*."

"Motives?"

"Give me short bios on, say, six or eight of the people involved. The kicker is, what did they have to gain by getting rid of the girl?"

"But isn't that a little—I don't know—tawdry?"

She looked at me like I'd just suggested buggering the pope. "*Alex*. Now, come on. What is our favorite block of the news pyramid?"

I sighed and stared down at my chunky-heeled loafers. " 'Speculate wildly.' "

"Good girl. Now go sell me some papers."

I got back to my desk just as Mad was emerging from the boys' loo.

"Nice of you to back me up."

"When a man's gotta go, a man's . . ."

"Rat bastard."

"Hey, I don't see my byline anywhere."

"Oh, Christ, we can fight about that later. You gotta help me put together this sidebar."

"What sidebar?" I told him. "Now *that* sounds like fun."

"Great. I type, you free-associate."

He grabbed a cup of coffee and perched all six-foot-something of himself on the corner of my desk. "How many of these we gotta do?"

"Marilyn says six or eight."

"And how much on each?"

"Just like a couple lines, I think."

"Where do you want to start?"

"I don't know. How about Priscilla Morton?"

"Fine. 'Priscilla Morton. Sinclair's best friend and cast-mate. Possible motive: Assuming Sinclair's leading role in *The Quinn Affair* gave her her big break; she went on to become a major film star.' "

"You're frighteningly good at this."

"Next?"

"Hmm . . . Austin Cusack."

" 'Director of *The Quinn Affair*, romantically linked to Sinclair. Possible motive: The actress was three months pregnant. Did he kill her to avoid exposure?' "

I banged it into the file verbatim. "Truly, the *Post* is going to come calling any second."

"Brandon Bartlett?"

"Brandon Bartlett."

" 'Sinclair's leading man in *The Quinn Affair*. Possible motive: He'd been Austin Cusack's best friend since childhood. Did he help him get rid of Sinclair—or act alone to protect his friend?' "

"That seems a little thin."

"You got any better ideas?"

"No."

"Then type."

I did. "All right, who's next?"

"Now it's getting tricky. Hmm . . . What about those guys who kept sending her fan mail?"

"The cops looked into them once they figured out Ashley was gone for good. There was no evidence against either one of them."

"Don't be so goddamn picky. We need warm bodies here."

"Yeah, but we don't have art on them."

"Not our problem. That's why editors get the big bucks."

"Okay," I shuffled through the various mounds of paper on my desk. "Here we go. The first guy was named Jerry Taskovich. He was a train conductor from, um . . . Kansas City. Saw her in a Broadway play on a trip to New York, and got totally obsessed with her. Sent her fan mail every day for two years."

"Yowza."

"Yeah, well, apparently it wasn't quite as creepy as it sounded. All his letters were insanely respectful." I dug for another sheet of paper. "Check this out: 'My Dear Miss Sinclair. I write again to inform you of my most sincere and devoted admiration for your beauty and artistry. Please know

that if there is ever any service I might perform on your be-
half, however mean or humble, it would be my greatest
pleasure to do so.' "

"Loser."

"Yeah, well, it's better than 'Love me or I'll slit your
throat.' "

"So why were the cops even into him?"

"I guess just the sheer volume. He wrote her, like, seven
hundred times. Plus, he was in Gabriel when she disappeared."

"No shit."

"Nope. Came to town to watch her big debut in *The
Quinn Affair*."

"Interesting. Who's the other guy again?"

"Now, he's a little creepier. Name of Oscar Simsbury.
Worked as a clerk in a big law firm in New York, which
from what I can tell meant he knew just how much he could
stalk Ashley without getting arrested—not that they called it
stalking back then, or even cared about it that much. According to the chief, probably the most the cops would've
done is rough the guy up a little and tell him to leave her
alone or else. But Simsbury kept his nose clean, at least on
paper."

"What was his story?"

"Apparently, he saw her at a playhouse in New Jersey,
and he got the idea she smiled at him. Said they 'shared a
moment' or something. Totally fell for her, started proclaim-
ing his love right and left. Used to show up at the stage door
with a big old engagement ring every couple of weeks. Sent
her letters of the 'I know you really love me' variety."

"So was he in town too?"

"Not that they know of. In fact, he had tickets for the
show a couple of weeks later. But I suppose he could have

taken the train up anytime he wanted to." I typed up Taskovich and Simsbury. "How many is that so far?"

"Five."

"Good. One more and we're off the hook."

"You gotta admit, this isn't a totally useless exercise."

"It's not the speculating that bothers me. It's the putting it in print."

"How the hell come?"

"Because, by definition all but one of these people was innocent, and we're dragging them through the mud anyway."

"Yeah, well, lucky for them they're all dead already."

"Don't you think they have family?"

"Since when are you all sensitive?"

"Oh, Christ, I'm just in a bad mood. Let's get this over with before Marilyn separates our heads from the rest of our bodies."

"Who you got in mind?"

"Well, there's that lady who got all upset over *Heavens to Betsy.*"

"Huh?"

"Didn't I tell you about this?" He shook his head. "I guess I didn't really get it until I saw the movie. Apparently, there was this deranged woman who saw it and thought Ashley was a real angel."

"You gotta be kidding me."

"I wish. Started writing her letters asking her to come and cure her sick daughter. I guess she'd lost all her other kids to scarlet fever or something and it sent her around the bend. Anyway, when Ashley tried to explain to her that she was just an actress playing a part the woman got all pissed off. Wanted to know why she helped that family save their farm but wouldn't lift a finger to save a dying little girl."

"Holy guacamole."

"You said it."

"So she threatened her?"

"That's a nice way of putting it."

"So why didn't the cops zero in on her right from the beginning?"

"Because she was a sad middle-aged lady, and the whole thing seemed like it had blown over a year or so before anyway."

"What do you think?"

"Well, I'd cross her off the list except for one thing."

"What?"

"The little girl died."

"Ouch. Anybody else?"

"Not that I can think of. The last three are probably just a dead end anyway."

"Because?"

"Don't you remember what we were talking about before? Whoever killed her had to have access to the theater."

"Yeah, well, if somebody followed her around enough, maybe they could figure out a way to do it."

"Which opens up the list of suspects to everybody strong enough to whack her over the head as of April 1926."

"I see your point. Hey, what about that thing with her agent?"

"You mean her manager. She dumped him a couple of months before she died."

"We putting him in the rogues' gallery?"

"Well, I haven't found anything saying he was furious at her or anything."

"So why did she give him the boot?"

"I think she was just moving up in the world. Some big deal manager offered to represent her, and she went for it. I think it was the same agency that represented Helen Hayes, or maybe it was Katharine Cornell. I can't remember."

"This new manager get her the *Quinn Affair* gig?"

"Nah, I think it was the old one."

"That'd piss you off, wouldn't it? You get her her biggest break yet, and she gives you the shaft."

"Probably happens all the time."

"Yeah, well, this guy belongs on the list as much as anybody."

"Fine."

He dictated some copy, and I typed it in. "Hey, Alex, you really think our guy's on there?"

"You mean do I think one of these people really killed her?"

"Yeah."

"It's possible, I guess."

"Who do you like?"

"I don't know. Who do you like?"

"Priscilla Morton."

"You're joking."

"Hey, you're the one who told me about the *All About Eve* thing in the first place. Now you think it's a crock?"

"She definitely had the most to gain, I agree with you. But when you come right down to it, it's just hard to picture Priscilla Morton murdering her best friend to get ahead."

"Hey, it works for me. But then again, there's nothing I like better than a good chicks-in-prison movie. Maybe I just dig the girl-on-girl violence angle."

"Charming. Speaking of which, what's up with Emma?"

"Follows me everywhere. It's embarrassing, really."

"As she would say," I said. "I doubt that very much indeed."

Once we fluffed up the sidebar to Marilyn's satisfaction, she cut us both loose for the rest of the day—either because she was feeling charitable, or because she couldn't stand the sight of us anymore. Mad took the opportunity to spend five solid hours at the gym, while I opted to face the laundry festering in my bedroom. When I got home, I discovered yet another message from Cody on my answering machine. This time, he hadn't even bothered to call himself.

"Hello, Miss Bernier? This is Officer Bill Simon at the Gabriel Police Department. Detective Cody is tied up with a case, but he asked me to leave you a message to please meet him at Albertini's at eight o'clock. He says you only have to call back if you can't make it. I guess that's it. Okay? Bye."

Bill Simon was one of about five dozen uniformed Cody-worshipers whose names and faces I could never keep straight—and from the sound of his voice, he was about twelve years old. Still, the message made me do a happy little dance around the piles of panties and T-shirts. Clearly, this was no time to bother with cleaning. I took a bath, shaved my stumpy little legs, and set about figuring out what I was going to wear to dinner; obviously something sexy (but not too slutty) was in order. I managed to find the black velvet miniskirt I'd worn the first time Cody took me to the restaurant, and though I was probably risking hypothermia I put on a violet cashmere tank top that managed to make my bosom look even more enormous than it actually is.

I was all dressed and ready for dinner about seven hours ahead of time. Feeling like a big dope, I changed into my sweats and faced the laundry issue. Then I leashed up Shakespeare and we went tramping around the neighborhood for an hour. Steve came home at five, and spent the next half hour grilling me about who Helmut and Dirk were setting him up with, and just what the hell was a Lambda cocktail party anyway? Emma arrived around seven, and even though it was freezing out I kept her company on the back porch while she smoked a couple of Dunhills.

"Hey, Emma, can I ask you something? You were married, right?"

"Lamentably, yes."

"For how long?"

She exhaled smoke in a tight stream, like an airplane trail. "Three miserable years."

"Why was it miserable? I mean, if you don't mind my asking . . ."

"Have I ever told you why I named Tipsy Tipsy?"

"Oh, right, it was because . . ."

"Because my ex was a bloody goddamn lush who preferred life at the bottom of a gin bottle to life with me."

"Oh."

"And he was an M.D., no less. Hardly inspires confidence in the state of socialized medicine, now does it? Not that I don't enjoy a cocktail now and then, but we're talking about an order of magnitude."

"So what I was wondering was . . . If he ever came crawling back begging you to give him another chance, would you do it? If, you know, he got with the twelve-step program and said he made a big mistake and he still loved you and everything?"

"Why in heaven's name are you asking me this?"

"It's, um . . . about Cody."

"Cody's ex-wife has come sniffing around, has she?"

"With a vengeance."

"That's not good."

"No shit."

"And you're worried he might actually go back to her?"

"He says he wouldn't, but . . ."

"But you don't trust him."

"It's not a question of trust, exactly. It's more like abject paranoia."

"What's this woman like?"

"Fangs and claws."

"Goodness."

"You wouldn't believe the crap that comes out of her mouth. Everything she says is one load of melodramatic bullshit after the other."

"And you really think your Cody might prefer these . . . histrionics to his relationship with you?"

"Oh, hell, I don't know. He says he'd never even think about going back with her, but who knows?"

"Men are such unpredictable creatures."

"Yeah."

"Would you care for a fag?"

It took me a second to realize she was holding out the pack of Dunhills. I shook my head. "Cody and I made a pact to quit, remember? Course if he dumps me for Lucy, I'm planning on chain-smoking for the rest of my miserable life."

"I hope I get a chance to meet this creature."

"God forbid."

"Alex, would you mind if I played armchair psychologist for a moment?"

"Be my guest."

"Do you think that you may be . . . How to put this? Could it be that one thing that's upsetting you is that meeting this Lucy has knocked Cody off his pedestal?"

"How do you mean?"

"Well, all this time you've expressed amazement that you'd finally met such a . . . What's the expression? Such a 'stand-up guy.' Now here's Lucy, demonstrating in no uncertain terms that he's capable of rather enormous lapses in judgment. Right?"

"I guess."

"It's just a thought."

"Hey, you never answered my question. About your ex."

She eyed me over her cigarette. "Is this getting back to Jake?"

"Of course not."

"In that case, I suppose . . . If Reggie really did come crawling back, and he'd cleaned himself up and I found myself face-to-face with the med student I married, I suppose . . . The truth is I'd fall over my feet trying to get back together with him. God help us both."

I got to the restaurant a little early—hey, I couldn't help myself—and I was so psyched about actually clapping eyes on Cody again that it took me a minute to notice there were no other cars in the parking lot. I went up to the front door and sure enough there was a sign: "CLOSED FOR FAMILY EMERGENCY." *Drat.* I went back to my car to wait for Cody with the heater on.

I was just about to get into it when they got me. Don't ask me where they were hiding; I never even saw them coming. One of them grabbed me from behind and pinned my arms with one hand, which was not only painful but pretty damn embarrassing as well. It all happened so fast that I didn't even have time to scream, so the other guy couldn't have hit me to shut me up; he just hit me. He punched me across the face so hard I thought I heard my jaw snap; if I were Wile E. Coyote I would have had little birds and stars doing laps around my brain. I dimly remember hearing the one behind me say *Jesus Christ, don't fucking knock her out yet*, and then the other one started shaking me so hard my head went lolling back and forth like a Pez dispenser.

They threw me onto the hood of my car, and for one

awful second I thought I was going to be raped in the goddamn parking lot of my favorite goddamn Italian restaurant.
As it turned out, though, the only interest they had in my
body was bruising it as much as humanly possible. One of
them pulled me up off the car and punched me in the stomach so hard I doubled over and crumpled onto the slushy
ground on all fours. I wasn't wearing stockings, and I remember the shock of the cold on my hands and knees, and
that it was a welcome thing because it distracted me from
the pain for half a second. Then the other guy—or maybe it
was the same one, I'd lost track by then—kicked me in the
side, so I landed flat on my back in the snow.

I was lying there dazed, wondering just why the hell this
was happening to me, when somebody grabbed my cheeks
hard between his fingers and pulled my head up off the
ground. It hurt like hell. He squatted on the ground and
leaned down so close I could feel his breath on my face, and
for the first time I realized they were both wearing ski
masks.

"This is your only warning. You got that? You're fucking
with people you don't want to fuck with."

"Wh . . ." I tried to talk, but my mouth didn't work so
well. I tried again, and this time some sounds came out.
"Wha . . . What are you talking about?"

"Stop getting into shit that doesn't fucking concern you."

I was in serious pain and next door to hysterical, which is
probably why in the midst of getting my ass whipped by two
guys in ski masks I was inspired to say the following:
"But . . . I'm a reporter."

That's when they decided to hit me again. Several times,
in fact.

"You had enough?"

I didn't say anything, mostly because I couldn't remember how.

"We could kill you right now. Don't forget it," the other one said. "Now keep your mouth shut about the bitch who got run over by the car, or you're fucking next. You got it?" He leaned down and grabbed the front of my shirt to pull me closer, and I heard it rip. "You listening, you little bitch? Stay the hell out of it, or you're dead. It's that easy."

He let go, and my head hit the ground so hard I nearly passed out. One of them walked away, and the next thing I knew he was standing over me with a baseball bat. *Holy shit.*

He hefted it, and I braced myself for whatever it feels like to be nailed with a goddamn Louisville slugger. But then I heard a *smash*, and opened my eyes to see the guy trashing my beloved Renault. He busted every one of the windows plus the headlights and taillights, bashed the body until it looked like it'd been melted in the microwave. Then the other one took out a really angry-looking knife, and before I even had time to worry about being gutted like a trout he set about slashing all four tires. When he was done, he came and stood over me. From where I was lying, the knife looked like something out of a goddamn Sinbad movie.

"They're gonna ask you what the hell happened to you. You're going to say it was a random fucking thing, understand? *Understand?*"

I nodded, which apparently wasn't good enough for them. "I don't think this bitch understands who she's fucking around with," the guy with the bat said. The other one laughed, an ugly little sound that shocked me awake enough to get good and truly terrified. He leaned over me and ran the knife point down my body—lightly, but still hard enough to let me know it was damn sharp. He grabbed the hem of my skirt and, in one swift motion, sliced it right up the front; then he did the same to my sweater.

He stared down at me for a few nasty seconds, and was on the verge of doing God-knows-what-else to me when the other guy grabbed his knife arm and shook his head, and the two of them walked away. They'd almost disappeared into the shadows when my ski-masked Galahad stopped and turned around.

"One more thing," he said. "If you tell your cop boyfriend about this, we'll kill him too."

23

IT HURTS TO GET HIT IN THE FACE. IT HURTS A *LOT*.

I mention this because in movies you always see guys pummeling each other for hours like they don't feel a thing. I, on the other hand, found getting beaten up to be the single most painful experience of my entire life. Maybe I'm just a big wimp, but one good punch was more than enough to knock me on my ass and keep me there—and, for the record, I stayed there quite a while.

At first I figured it was only a matter of time until Cody came to meet me like he was supposed to. Then, of course, it occurred to me that he wasn't coming, had never been coming—the whole thing was a setup to begin with. Somebody rolled the dice and used Bill Simon's name, and I fell for it. Whoever it was, they'd damn well known that Albertini's was closed, and that we went there a lot, and it would be a perfect place to trap me and do whatever they wanted.

Once I got up off the ground I realized how cold I was. My whole body seemed to be numb and aching at the same time, and it struck me that I might actually freeze to death out there. I looked around for my coat, which must have been ripped off during the attack, though I couldn't remember exactly when. I finally found it in a ball on the ground, wet from the slush but better than nothing.

My keys were still in the pocket, so I brushed the glass off the driver's seat and tried to start the car. It took a second to turn over, but—miracle of miracles—it actually worked. I cranked the heat and tried to figure out what to do. In the interest of looking slinky, I'd traded my backpack for a tiny purse, which one of the men had pocketed. The good news was that all I'd lost was $32, a travel-size hairbrush, a NARS lipstick (color: Shanghai Express), and my driver's license; the bad news was that my cell phone was back home in my backpack, along with the flashlight from Cody.

But wait; he'd also given me a little blue one, specifically to put in my glove compartment. I leaned across to pull it out, and was brought up short by a wave of pain that made me worry there was something seriously wrong with my innards. I took it more slowly the second time, found the flashlight, and wondered what the hell to do next. I thought about trying to flag down a car, and tried to calculate the likelihood of getting picked up by Ted Bundy Junior. At the rate my night was going, the odds were pretty good.

Still, I didn't think I had much choice. I couldn't walk very far; frankly, I figured I'd be lucky to make it the fifty feet to the highway. The heat was flying out the windows, and sooner or later the car was going to run out of gas. For all I knew, I was bleeding internally and was going to run out of gas myself—permanently—before too long. I decided to hit the road.

It's an interesting thing, trying to get a car to stop for you in the middle of the night. On the one hand, you know damn well you'd never pull over yourself, since it's drummed into your head from childhood that picking up hitchhikers (or being one) is a very good way to find yourself bound and gagged in the back of a conversion van. But once the shoe is on the other foot—when you're hurt and bleeding and freezing your butt off on the side of the road—you realize very quickly that every driver who doesn't stop is a heartless bastard who, should a tractor-trailer hit him head-on around the next corner, is going straight to hell.

That stretch of road is pretty quiet at night, and it took a while before somebody stopped. At least two dozen cars passed me by, but finally one of them slowed down, pulled to the shoulder, and backed up the fifty yards to where I was standing. I was immensely relieved to see that it was a Subaru Forester, the universal transport of the Gabriel soccer mom. The passenger window rolled down, revealing a nicely dressed couple of about fifty. *Hallelujah.*

"Are you all right?" the woman asked. I tried to talk, but this time really couldn't. I shook my head instead, which didn't feel very good either. "Tim, help her. She looks like she's about to faint." I was dimly aware of a car door opening, and a silver-haired man racing around to help me into the backseat. "We're taking you to the hospital," the woman said, and although I wanted to say thank you, all I managed to do was get blood all over their nice leather seats.

The next couple of hours, as far as I know, consisted entirely of me trying to get some sleep despite a very annoying nurse who kept asking me my name, what year it was, what town were we in, who was the President of the United States. I recall thinking it was a piss-poor time for a civics lesson, and I eventually told her if she didn't know what year it was, maybe she belonged upstairs in the psycho ward with the rest of the mental defectives.

At some point, when I was lying on a gurney in what I

figured was the emergency room, I overheard somebody say something about doing a rape kit—probably standard procedure when they treat a woman who's had her clothes sliced off with a goddamn broadsword. I was coherent enough to tell them no, I hadn't been raped—just beaten to a pulp, thank you very much. A uniformed cop showed up a little later, asking about the "Jane Doe assault victim," and it was with some rather bleak amusement that I realized this was me. I heard someone say they'd finally gotten a name out of me, and when they told it to him he came over at a gallop.

"*Alex?*" he said, and I looked up to see Pete Donner, a sweet young guy who (like the real Bill Simon, wherever the hell *he* was) worships Cody like some sort of demigod. "I barely even recog . . ." He stifled himself, and took a deep breath. "Sweet Jesus, what happened to you?"

I opened my mouth to tell him, then remembered what was going to happen to me if I did. I gave him the edited version. "Two guys beat me up outside Albertini's restaurant. They trashed my car, and cut my clothes off . . ." I started tearing up at the memory, so it was no big surprise that he misunderstood. I knew the guy had seen some nasty shit— he was at the scene of the Sissy Dillingham murder, for one thing—but he still went a little pale.

"Were you . . . assaulted?"

"No. I mean, yes . . . I mean, not like that. Not sexually. They just beat the living shit out of me."

He looked, if it's possible, even more relieved than I was. I'm not sure how it is in big cities, but in a small town like Gabriel—where everybody knows who everybody else is dating anyway—cop girlfriends are totally in the fold. It's been pretty astonishing for me to go from despised reporter to beloved girlfriend of hero detective in a matter of weeks. Not that I'm complaining; it's damn nice to think there are a hundred guys with guns looking out for you. I'm sure Pete Donner would have busted his butt to arrest anybody who assaulted a woman and left her to freeze to death in the middle of nowhere, but the fact that I was dating a fellow cop meant that hurting me was tantamount to beating up his mother.

He tried asking me some more questions, and I was singularly unhelpful—which, considering what I'd just been through, nobody seemed to hold against me. The nurse gave me something for the pain, and the happy floating feeling that came afterward turned out to be the highlight of my whole day.

The next time I was remotely coherent, it was the following morning. I woke up in a hospital room with the sun streaming in, something that happens so rarely in a Gabriel winter that for a second I was worried I'd actually died and gone to a happier place, where no one gets Seasonal Affective Disorder. But no; there I was, stiff as lumber and aching absolutely everywhere. I shifted a little to try to get more comfortable, and it only made it worse. I tried to picture myself walking to the bathroom, which was a place I very much wanted to visit, but somehow the idea of standing up seemed way beyond me.

"You're awake." The voice came from the far corner of the room and startled me so much I actually yelped; clearly, my nerves were shot. I'd slept in my contact lenses, so my eyes were all gummy and fogged, but when I could finally focus I saw Cody's face looming over me. His eyes were bloodshot, and he looked like he hadn't slept in a week.

"Oh God, baby, I'm sorry I scared you. I've just been so . . ." He sat on the edge of the bed next to me, and when he tried to stroke my face I flinched. "Did I hurt you? *Son of a bitch.*"

He shot up and stalked out of the room, and before I could even start to figure out what to make of it, he came back in and stood in the doorway.

He was crying. It wasn't something I'd seen him do before, not even when he was in the hospital himself and no one could tell him for sure whether he was going to live or die. I knew I was the cause of it, and although I didn't ask to get roughed up I still felt like a rat for making him feel so lousy.

"Alex, I'm sorry. I don't know what's wrong with me." He rubbed the back of his neck as though his head hurt as much as mine did. "Can I come over and sit by you?"

"Of . . ." My voice sounded weak, like it belonged to somebody else. "Of course you can."

He sat in the bedside chair, one of those white plastic things that doesn't look like it could support a five-year-old, and bowed his head for a long time like he couldn't bear to look at me. At one point he seemed about to hold my hand, but stopped himself; I reached across the sheets and took his. We stayed like that for a while, and when he finally looked up at me I saw that the tears had run down his cheeks into two days' worth of reddish stubble. I tried to pull him toward me, and though I was too weak to accomplish much he got the idea. He moved up to sit on the bed again, and despite the fact that it hurt I put my arms around him. We spent a fair amount of time just holding each other and crying, which as far as I was concerned was even better than the Demerol.

"I must look awful," I said finally. He didn't contradict me.

"How do you feel?"

"Awful."

"The doctor said nothing's broken. No serious injuries either. I couldn't believe it. When I saw your car, I thought . . ."

"My car?" The thought of it made me start crying again. "How bad is . . ."

"Let's not talk about that right now, okay?"

"It's ruined, isn't it?"

"Shh . . ."

"I'm sorry." I was really sobbing now, and feeling like an idiot for it. "I know I shouldn't get so upset over a stupid . . ."

"It's okay." He squeezed my hand again. "We're having it towed into town."

"How . . . How did you see it, anyway?"

"I went out to the scene."

"You did?"

"When Donner tracked me down I came rushing over here, but the doctor said you'd be out cold until this morning at the earliest. They wouldn't even let me see you at first."

"Why not?"

"I think they thought I was going to try to wake you up and get a statement out of you. I finally convinced them I just wanted to make sure you were all right. Once I got somebody to guard your—"

"Guard me?"

"There's a uniform outside your door."

"Why?"

"In case whoever did this to you decides to try it again."

"Oh."

"Donner's partner stayed here to look after you, and he and I went out to Albertini's. I gotta tell you, Alex, your Renault scared the hell out of me. I thought if they'd worked you over like they did the car . . ."

"They used a knife and a baseball bat on it." I blew my nose. It hurt and when I made the mistake of peeking at the Kleenex I saw it had blood on it.

"But they didn't . . ."

I shook my head, another bad idea. "With me, they stuck to their fists."

It was an unfortunate thing to have said, considering how much it pissed him off. "Jesus Christ, when I get my hands on those bastards, I swear I . . ."

"Please don't yell. My head really—"

"I'm sorry. We don't have to talk about this now."

"It's all right. It's not your fault. I just feel so . . ." I cast about for the right word. "So . . . stupid."

"You didn't do anything wrong."

"Are you kidding? I fell for the oldest trick in the book. I went out there and got grabbed like some helpless idiot."

"It's not your fault."

"They beat me up, totaled my car, stole my purse, and there wasn't a damn thing I could do about it. They even . . . They even cut off my . . ."

"Shh . . . Donner told me."

"I . . . I really thought that was it. I thought I was going to die."

"Sweetheart, you don't have to talk about . . ."

"I thought they were going to drag me off someplace and rape me and kill me, you know? I couldn't believe it when they just walked off and left me there alive."

"Do you want me to get the doctor to give you something to calm you down?"

"No."

"Are you sure?"

"I'm sure. Please don't go."

"Do you really want to talk about this?"

"Yeah, I . . . I kind of feel like I need to."

"Okay." He didn't look so sure.

"Don't I have to make a statement or something?"

"It can wait."

"You always said . . . I mean, you always say it's better when a witness does it fresh."

"You're right. It is."

"I'd just as soon get it over with anyway."

He went out to the hall to talk to the uniform, and forty minutes later Pete Donner showed up with a bouquet of carnations, which he swore were from his wife.

"Do you want me to go?" Cody asked, and I said *no* so fast it was downright embarrassing. Pete asked me to tell the story all the way through, so I started with the part about getting the message on my answering machine and went on from there. When I was done he asked me a bunch of questions—Did the men's voices seem familiar at all? Had I gotten any threatening phone calls or letters? Did the attackers call me by name?—and when he was through he closed his little cop notebook, made meaningful eye contact with Cody, and left.

Cody stared at me for a while, then came over and sat next to the bed again. The silence was starting to creep me out. "What is it?"

"There's something you're not telling us."

"No there isn't."

"Alex, honey, you're forgetting I do this for a living. It's my job to know when a witness is lying."

"I'm not lying."

"No, but you're not telling the whole truth."

"I don't know what you're . . ."

"As liars go, you're not exactly at the top of the class."

"Oh."

"Come on, you can tell me. It's okay, I swear. If something happened out there you don't want anybody else to know, it'll just stay between you and me, all right? But you have to trust me with it. If we're going to nail these guys, I have to know everything."

"It's . . . It's not like that. Everything happened exactly like I told you." His eyes said he didn't buy it. "Except . . ."

"Except what?"

"Nothing. It was just something they said." I started to cry again, and he brushed the tears from my face so softly I barely even felt it.

"What did they say?"

"I can't . . ."

"Sweetheart, if they threatened you, you have to tell me. It's the only way I can protect you."

"No, it's . . ."

"Did they say they'd hurt you if you talked to the police?"

"Not me. You."

"*What?*"

"They said, 'If you tell your cop boyfriend, we'll kill him too.' "

"Tell me you'd been attacked? You gotta be . . ."

"No . . . Oh, Jesus. They said something to me. They told me why they were beating me up. It was a warning."

"What kind of warning?"

If I tell him, they might kill us both. If I don't tell him I'm a complete and total idiot. I took a deep breath. "They told me to stay away from the Sissy Dillingham story."

That brought him up short. "The Dillingham story? What about it?"

"I don't know. All they said was, 'Keep your mouth shut about the bitch who got run over by the car, or you're next.' "

"And you weren't going to tell me this?" He actually looked wounded.

"For Christ's sake, Cody, I didn't know what the hell to do. They beat the crap out of me, then told me to keep off the story—and by the way, if I tell you about it, they'll kill you too. When some guy's standing over you with a knife the size of a tennis racquet, you believe him."

"I'm sorry. I didn't mean to sound like a jerk. I'm not mad at you, honestly. I'm just glad you told me."

"So am I."

"Truth?"

"Look, all hysteria aside, I guess I knew I'd have to tell you about it. I'd have to be stupid not to. It's like when the kidnappers say 'Don't call the cops.' Only a complete asshole would actually listen to them."

"I'm glad you realize that."

"And besides, those two bastards should have known better than to pick on a reporter."

"Oh yeah? How's that?"

"They told me to keep my mouth shut," I said, "and my kind doesn't know how."

24

I LOOKED IN THE MIRROR. IT WAS A VERY BAD IDEA.

I had specifically avoided my reflection in the hospital bathroom, but once I got home I figured I had to check out the damage. The face I saw staring back at me made me want to hide at home with a paper bag over my head for the rest of my life.

I looked like some Hollywood makeup artist's idea of a bad joke. My face was practically all purple—the parts that weren't red, black, or yellow, anyway. Everything was swollen, so to add insult to (literal) injury I looked like I'd put on twenty pounds. The rest of my body was a lovely mosaic of bruises, the granddaddy of which was a whopper along my left side where I'd gotten hit with the business end of a steel-toed work boot. At least it wasn't bikini season.

Cody said all sorts of reassuring things about how it wouldn't look so bad in a few days, and it would all go away in a couple of weeks anyway. (He also said I was so cute that even the bruises couldn't mar my beauty, which put his credibility very much in question.)

By the time I got to the house Saturday afternoon, news of my adventure had made its way through the *Monitor* grapevine. To the carnations were added: a dozen roses from

Benjamin, who knows how to treat a lady; four boxes of assorted Little Debbie's snack cakes, courtesy of Melissa; a big macaroni and cheese casserole from the business reporter's wife; and a bottle of Cuervo 1800 tequila from (big surprise) Mad and O'Shaunessey. The latter came with a bag of lemons and a Post-it note that said "WE'LL BE OVER AT EIGHT."

"Your friends can be lovely when they want to be," Emma said, once she'd gotten the shrieking-at-the-sight-of-me out of the way. "They're a hell of a lot nicer than mine, at any rate."

"Come on," I said from my perch on the living-room couch. "Don't you think your vet pals would roll out the welcome wagon?"

"No offense, darling, but if I came in looking like that, they'd most likely euthanize me."

"Thoughtful."

"Can I get you something to eat?"

"I wouldn't mind some of that mac and cheese Charlotte made."

"I'll pop some in the micro. Don't move a muscle."

"Don't worry."

I was just finishing off my second bowl when Cody came back with Zeke, who dragged Shakespeare off the couch by her collar and proceeded to chase her around the living room. Cody very nearly succeeded in not flinching when he saw me again—almost, but not quite. He got himself some food and a Guinness and sat on the floor with his back against the couch. The dogs stopped assaulting each other, sat down next to him, and waited for him to fork over the goods.

"You up to talking?" he asked.

"Sure."

"About Sissy Dillingham?"

"Um, I guess."

"Good. I want you to try to think hard. Can you remember anything else those two men said to you last night? Anything else relating to the Dillingham case?"

"Just what I told you. They said to stay off it."

"Then what we really need to know is why."

"I've been thinking about that. I mean, at first I assumed it was because whoever ran her over would probably rather not go to jail, right? But then I thought, if that was it, why would they pick on me? I'm not even covering it—not officially, anyway. Other than the story that ran the day after she got hit, everything's been under Mad's byline."

"But you've been working on it behind the scenes?"

"A little. Not much. I've kind of had my hands full with the Sinclair thing."

"So strictly speaking, if they wanted the *Monitor* off the hit-and-run story, Madison's the one they'd have to get to?"

"Good luck. He'd fight back."

"So are you saying you think they were trying to send a message to him through you?"

I shook my head. It hurt. "If they were, why wouldn't they just say so? No, what I've been thinking is that they weren't talking about the actual murder. They were talking about the Starlight. They had to be."

"But like you just said, if they meant that, why didn't they just say so?"

"Beats me. You know the criminal element better than I do. Look, remember what I told you about Sissy finding something at Historic Gabriel?"

"They were telling you not to go any further in trying to figure out what it was."

"Bingo. The question is, how did they know?"

The doorbell rang, and Cody got up to answer it. It was Mad, hair still dripping from his post-gym shower.

"Where's Emma?"

"She had to run up to the hospital," I said. "Where's O'Shaunessey?"

"Had to cover a hockey game at the last minute. Said he'd call tomorrow and see how you're doing. Where's the tequila?" I waved toward the kitchen. That hurt too. "You want a shot?"

"I don't think I'm up to it. You could get me a Diet Pepsi though. Put a little lemon in it?"

"Hey, what's the name of that purple dinosaur the kids go apeshit over? The one who sings that crappy song so you want to blow his head off with a shotgun?"

I stared at him. "Barney?"

"Yeah."

"Why?"

"You kind of look like him," he said, and disappeared into the kitchen.

Cody snickered before he could catch himself, then tried to look somber. Mad reemerged a minute later and the three of us lounged around the living room for a while before I remembered Cody and I had actually been talking about something vaguely important.

"So how did they know?" I said.

Mad looked clueless, so I filled him in.

"Damn good question," he said. "But hold on a second. You were always covering the Starlight mess. Maybe they just saw the paper, and figured . . ."

"That doesn't make any sense. There's been nothing in the paper about Sissy being on to something that might have saved the theater."

"Okay, so who knew what you were looking for?"

Then something else hit me. "Wait. What if it wasn't about the theater at all? What if they were talking about

Lindy Marsh asking me to look into Sissy's death? I mean, she could have told somebody about that, right?"

"It's possible, I suppose," Cody said. "How much digging have you done for her?"

"Well . . . none. I've been a little bit busy, you know. Plus, I haven't exactly been eager to start running around town asking who else was screwing her husband."

"So let's stick to the theater for the moment, okay? Who did you ask about what Mrs. Dillingham might have found out?"

"Let's see . . . Angela Giordano at the historical society. Roger Nash up at Benson. Mark Dillingham . . ."

Mad stopped sprinkling salt on his hand and looked at me. "You called Dillingham?"

"I figured it was worth a shot. He was married to her, after all. And Lindy Marsh, but she's been telling me all along that there's nothing there. Hmm . . . There were a bunch of people at S.O.S. . . . ."

"Wait. Let me get something to write this down," Cody said, and retrieved a notebook from his coat pocket. "Okay. Who at the Save Our Starlight group?"

I gulped. "Everybody."

"Everybody?"

"Just about. There was Madeline Hoover, of course, and Adele Giordano-Bronstein. Ivy Bator, Bunny Roberts, Charmaine Donaldson-Merke . . ."

Cody eyed me over his notebook. "Are you making this up?"

"Hey, there were three girls named Bunny in my class at boarding school. Keep writing. Lemme see . . . That woman who runs the Benson architecture library. What's her name . . . Pamela Mansfield. Also Robbie Renssellaer. And Joe Kingman, but he's not an S.O.S. person officially. How many is that?"

"Twelve."

"Wait, that can't be right. There's got to be more than that. I went down the S.O.S. membership list and called them all."

Cody didn't look pleased. "Didn't it occur to you that if this was really what got her killed, maybe it wasn't a good idea to be so obvious about it?"

"I wasn't *that* obvious. I just asked them if they knew what the press conference was supposed to be about."

"And did you get everybody?"

"All but one or two."

"Do you have the list here?"

"It's at the paper."

"We'll have to go and get it."

"Are you going to interrogate them or something?"

"That depends. Why?"

"Christ, Cody, don't you remember what those two assholes said? You can't go letting them know you're on to them. If me asking one of those people what Sissy was into got me roughed up, don't you think you might get . . ."

"Honey, Sissy Dillingham is dead. I'm a cop. People expect me to come nosing around asking questions."

"But what if . . ."

"Nothing's going to happen, I promise."

"Then why's that cop still outside my house?"

"Because he likes it there."

"This is depressingly familiar."

"It's just a short-term thing, I promise."

"How are you even justifying this, anyway? It's not like the G.P.D. can afford to bodyguard everybody who gets beat up . . ."

"It's not on the department. The guys are all doing it on their own time."

"Is this one of those thin blue line things?"

"I suppose it is."

"Oh."

"Hey, by the way, nice story in today's paper."

"What story was that?"

"The big one on Ashley Sinclair."

"Oh my God. I can't believe I forgot about it. Do you have the paper with you?"

He fetched it out of his car, and I spent the next fifteen minutes patting myself on the back. Emma showed up before Mad had a chance to strangle me, and the two of them went off to his place. They took the tequila with them.

Cody made me some tea, and since I'd been flat on my back for the past several hours I decided to sit up for a while. Shakespeare took this as her cue to occupy the empty part of the couch.

"Where's the third musketeer?" he asked as he dislodged the dog and sat down next to me.

"You mean Steve? Emma said he had a hot date. I guess he and the Lambda guy hit it off."

"So we've got the place all to ourselves?"

"Looks that way."

"Seems like we haven't seen each other all week."

"That's because we haven't."

"It's been kind of a crazy week for me."

"Listen . . . can I ask you something?"

"You want to know what's going on with Lucy."

"How did you know?"

"You have that look."

"What look?"

"The Lucy look. Like you're not sure if you want to put an ice pack on your head or commit murder."

"So what's going on?"

"Nothing new. She's just being awfully . . . persistent."

"Persistent how?"

"She just keeps calling. And coming by my house, and the station, and my mom's place . . ."

"Your mom's? You've got be kidding."

"It's strange. I've never seen her like this before."

"I thought you said she was always . . ."

"Yeah, but not like this. This is different. My gut says there's something she's not telling me."

"Like what?"

"I don't know. Maybe something happened back in Boston I haven't heard about. I put in a call to my old partner, but I haven't gotten a hold of him yet."

"What if she's telling the truth?"

"Huh?"

"Maybe she did just realize she made a huge mistake. Maybe she knows she really screwed up and now she's got to live with it. It's no fun to be in a hell of your own making, particularly if you're used to getting your own way."

"You know, I kind of feel sorry for her."

"Yeah, well, that makes one of us."

"I'm surprised she hasn't come sniffing around here."

"To do what?"

"To appeal to your sense of female decency, I don't know. It's right up her alley."

"Maybe she has. I haven't been home much, what with the Ashley story and everything. Emma did say we've gotten a lot of hang-ups, though."

"When?"

"I'm not sure. All week, I think."

"Might have been her. Then again, it might have been . . ."

I got his drift. "Somebody else."

He stared down at his beer. "It's a possibility."

"You really think they tried to call, but since I wasn't home they decided to beat the crap out of me instead?"

"That would depend."

"On what?"

"Look, it's probably not a good idea to speculate until we have some more information."

"Come on, speculate. Be my guest."

"Alex, I . . ."

"Don't even *think* about leaving me hanging like this. What were you about to say?"

"Well, this is just my instincts talking, okay? But what I was going to say is, phone threats are bush league. They're amateur hour. If somebody really wanted you off the story, somebody who knew what they were doing, they wouldn't bother with anonymous phone calls. They'd just . . ."

"Kill me?"

"Not necessarily. Murder is messy, and it pisses the cops off. Particularly when the victim is one of our own."

"So what are you saying?"

"I'm saying . . . Oh, Christ. I shouldn't even be saying anything. Can we just forget about it?"

"I'm assuming you know me better than that by now."

He put his cup down and took a deep breath. "Look, I may be way off base. But look at what happened to Cynthia Dillingham. Hit-and-run, out of nowhere, not a goddamn shred of evidence. No witnesses, no tire tracks, no nothing. Killed as she's crossing the street to get the mail, like she does the same time every day. What does that sound like to you?"

"Extraordinarily bad luck?"

"Alex . . ."

"A hit. A hit, okay? It sounds like a hit."

"Damn it, I knew I shouldn't have . . ."

"And then there's those two guys who grabbed me. Let's take a critical look at them, shall we? Ski masks, gloves, perfectly well equipped to trash my car. They come out of nowhere, beat the crap out of both of us, and they're out of there within five minutes. What does that sound like to you?"

"Alex, honey, try not to get so . . ."

"Those guys were professionals. That's what you're thinking, right? That we're not talking about some pissed-off amateur. This is their goddamn day job." I tried to get up, because I was feeling claustrophobic all of a sudden, but my side hurt so I sat back down. "You know what I was thinking when I woke up this morning? That I was pretty goddamn lucky they didn't do any major damage. No broken bones, no screwed-up internal organs, no sexual assault. But you know what I think now? I think they got the job done just exactly like they were supposed to. The damage is all . . . cosmetic. It's all fucking cosmetic. That was the point. Right?"

He waited until I calmed down a little, then put an arm around me. "I have a big mouth sometimes."

"I'd rather have you tell me the truth than not."

"I may be scaring you for no reason."

"Trust me," I said, "I'm plenty scared already."

25

YOU PROBABLY CAN'T CATCH AGORAPHOBIA LIKE YOU CAN catch the flu, but you can't prove it by me.

I didn't leave my house for four days after I was attacked, partly because I felt like I'd been hit by a truck, but mostly because I was scared out of my gourd. It wasn't rational, but all I could think of was what it'd been like to get grabbed from behind, to wonder if my number was up after living a grand total of twenty-seven years—in short, to know that my life was in the hands of two men in ski masks whose goal, as far I could tell, was to hurt me as much as possible.

I'd never really felt afraid in Gabriel before, not on a day-to-day basis anyway, and the sensation of being too terrified to leave my own home was not only infuriating but humiliating to boot. Cody kept a close watch on me—as close as he could while working on two murder investigations—and although his presence was comforting while it lasted, it would take all of five seconds after he left for me to devolve into a quivering mass of lime Jell-O. And this, remember, was with a uniformed cop named Bernie right outside my door, guarding my life for the bargain price of some coffee and all the banana muffins he could eat.

My low point, morale-wise, came on Tuesday, when a

bouquet of yellow roses was delivered to my door. The card, covered on both sides in tiny, precise letters, read as follows:

> *Dear Alex,*
> *I'm sorry to hear you're not feeling well right now. I hope you won't be sick for too much longer. I also hope that your time spent recuperating from your illness will allow you a chance for spiritual and mental reflection. Please dig down deep into your heart and think about what you would want if you were in my position. Wouldn't you think you'd deserve another chance at happiness with the man you love? Marriage is a holy sacrament, too precious to throw away lightly. I'm asking you as one woman to another to do what you can to help me put my family back together. Please remember that I was his wife long before you ever met him and that nobody likes a homewrecker.*
> *Yours very truly,*
> *Mrs. Lucy Cody*

On Wednesday afternoon, four days into my career as a closet case, the man in question came by with some food from Schultz's. It was a carbon copy of the lunch I'd brought him at the station that day, and I realized with a start that I couldn't picture myself having the *cojones* to walk from the deli to his office without an armed guard. This crap couldn't go on much longer.

When we were nearly done with the food—the abject terror not having done much to diminish my appetite, natch—his cell phone rang, and when he hung up he had a goofy grin on his face. "Why don't you go upstairs and get dressed?"

"I really don't feel well enough to . . ."

"You've been in those pajamas since Saturday night.

Like my mom would say, they could probably stand up by themselves by now. So be a good girl and go take a quick shower and get dressed."

"But I don't . . ."

"I've got a surprise for you. Should get here in about fifteen minutes, so get off your duff."

"Cody, I . . ."

"On your own or at gunpoint. It's up to you."

I did as I was told, and I had to admit that being clean and clothed did perk me up a little. I blew my hair dry, which I never do but which seemed a convenient way to delay the inevitable, and when I came downstairs Cody's smile was even wider and goofier than before.

"Ah," he said as he came over to kiss me on the cheek, "so there was a pretty girl under there after all."

"What are you up to?"

"Not just me. It was a team effort."

"Between you and who?"

"Me and your parents."

"My parents? *Please* don't tell me you told them about this. How could you go behind my back like that? You *fink* . . ."

"Don't be mad at me. I had to. I mean, I promised them I'd—"

"You *what?*"

The blush started at his hairline and migrated south. "When we were home for Christmas. They kind of cornered me, and . . . Well, after everything that's happened to you over the past couple of years, they're kind of worried about you."

"Worried how?"

"That you're . . . well, the word they used was 'reckless.'"

"And you agreed with them?"

"No, I didn't. In fact, for the record, I told them I thought you could take care of yourself. But they said . . . Look, I know this is going to sound all . . . what's that word you always use about them?"

"Patriarchal."

"Yeah. But come on, Alex. They're your parents. They worry about you. So they made me promise I'd, you know, look after you. Not that I didn't do a damn poor job of it this time . . . But they made me promise if anything ever happened, I'd keep them in the loop. What was I supposed to say? No?"

"You mean you said you'd spy on me for them?"

"Don't take it like that. It's only natural your parents would want to know if you were in trouble. If I were you, I'd stop pouting and appreciate it. I sure as hell wish my dad were still alive to worry about me."

That shut me up. "Okay, I'm sorry. I just wish you told me, that's all. Can you understand that?"

"I suppose so, yeah."

"Where was I during this whole conversation, anyway?"

"It was when you went over to see your old baby-sitter. You were barely even out the door and they sprang it on me. I got the feeling they'd been looking for an opening all weekend."

"So what did they say when you told them? About what happened to me last week, I mean."

"They were upset, obviously. Your mom said something about suing Albertini's, though I'm not sure she knows on what grounds yet."

"Speaking of which, did you find out anything about how . . ."

"Let's talk about that later. I said I had a surprise for you, remember?" He helped me on with my coat. "Now close your eyes."

"Close my . . ."

"Jeeze, Alex, I know felons more cooperative than you. Now will you just humor me for once in your life?"

I shut my eyes and clapped a hand over them, just to prove I was willing to play nice. He took my other elbow and guided me across the room; I heard him open the front door and felt a blast of cold air as he pushed me through it.

"Okay, open them."

I did.

"What the—"

"Do you like it?"

"Oh, my *God*. Are you seriously telling me this is *mine*?"

He pulled a piece of paper out of his pocket. "They faxed this to my office for you. Go ahead and read it."

" '*Notre chère Alexandra* . . .' Yikes. They must be pretty pissed at me. They never call me Alexandra unless I'm in big trouble."

"Just read it. In English, okay?"

" 'Our Dear Alexandra, if you insist on living in the fast lane, at least give your poor old parents the peace of mind of knowing you have an air bag. (Two, in fact.) When your Detective Cody arrests the miscreants who manhandled you, we hope to have the chance to thank them for getting rid of that rustbucket of yours before they go to the electric chair. Ha ha ha—just joking. We hope you enjoy your new wheels and before you start insisting on paying us back we'd like to remind you that you can't afford it and in any event we wouldn't let you. You may thank us by providing some nice Republican grandchildren before we're too old to enjoy them. Love, Mom and Dad.' "

"Well, what do you think?"

"It's the new Beetle."

"Yep."

"I've been *lusting* after the new Beetle."

"Who do you think picked it out?"

"You *didn't.*" I grabbed him and kissed him, which caused me a certain amount of pain but for once I didn't even care. Then I ditched him on the doorstep and fairly skipped to the curb. "Oh, my God, it's *gorgeous.*"

"You said you wanted red, right?"

"Ooh, ooh, ooh." I believe my glee actually made me incapable of forming words. "Ooh, ooh, ooh. *Wowie.*"

"You want to hear the specs? It's got manual transmission, obviously, because what self-respecting woman would drive an automatic, right? It's got a sun roof, air conditioning, cruise control, a CD player, plus a cassette player for those books on tape you're always listening to. The engine's in the front nowadays, so even though it's small there's actually a fair amount of cargo room. It's got a hatchback, and the backseats come way forward so it's not even that hard to get into. Oh, and there's a security system with panic button. Your dad reminded me about that three different times, by the way. You like?"

"Ooh, ooh . . . You even put a rose in the bud vase."

"Yeah, I did."

"You're *adorable.*"

"Me or the car?"

"Both of you."

"So you like my little surprise?"

"It's perfect."

"It's good to see you so happy."

I grabbed him and kissed him again. "Thank you. I totally love it."

"Hey, I just did the legwork. Your parents provided the financing."

"I can't believe it."

"So you want to take it for a spin?"

"Don't I have to, I don't know, get it registered or something?"

"All the paperwork's been covered. You still have to sign a couple of things, but I think you can live dangerously for ten minutes or so." He dropped the keys into my hand. "Go ahead, take her for a ride."

I gulped. "By myself?"

"It's just around downtown, honey. You'll be perfectly safe. It's broad daylight. I can even ask Bernie to follow you if you want."

"It'd be . . . it'd be a lot more fun if you'd come with me."

"Alex, I . . ."

I handed back the keys. "Besides, I still feel pretty out of it. I'm not even sure I can clutch right. How about if you take *me* for a spin?"

"Is that really what you want?" I nodded. "Okay, I have a couple of minutes before I have to be back at the house."

He opened the passenger door and helped me in. The car was all darkness and curves, snug and comfy like crawling back into the womb. Wowie. He put *Rubber Soul* into the CD player, and "Drive My Car" came blaring out of the speakers.

"It's the Beatles," he said. "Get it?"

"You're adorable."

"Feel free to keep saying that."

We drove around listening to the music for a while. Just as "Nowhere Man" was ending he turned into Lakeside Park, pulled into a spot facing the water, and cut the engine.

"Alex, are you sure you're okay? You don't seem like yourself."

"I don't?"

"You know you don't."

"I'll be okay."

"Listen, don't brush this off, but . . . Do you know what Post-Traumatic Stress Syndrome is?"

"Come on, you don't think I . . . I mean after all the crap I've been through, you don't think what happened could possibly . . ."

"Let's take a walk."

"Don't you have to get back to the station?"

"I'm willing to think of this as business."

He got out of the car, and when I didn't make a move to follow him he opened my door and pulled me up gently. We walked along the shore, deserted except for us and some scavenging seagulls.

"I know you're scared," he said, putting an arm around my shoulders. "You don't have to be ashamed of it. You also don't have to try and hide it from me."

"I don't know what you're . . ."

"Alex, I know you think you're tough, and you are. But you're forgetting what I've been doing for the past ten years. First I was in the Navy, and ever since then I've been a cop. I know what violence does to people, even people who feel like they should be damn glad just to be alive. *Especially* them."

"I don't understand."

"I'm sorry. I know I'm not explaining this right. What I'm trying to say is, you can't keep pretending you weren't affected by what you went through."

"I'm not pretending that."

"Yes, you are. Every time I see you, you twist yourself into a knot trying to show me how okay you are. But I can tell you're scared. And what's more, I can tell you're furious at yourself for *being* scared. All I'm trying to say is, I've seen guys three times your size drive themselves around the bend with that kind of thinking. Until you admit to yourself that you have a right to feel the way you feel, it's not going to go away."

"But . . ."

"It's been less than a week. Nobody expects you to be over this yet. Give yourself a break."

"Give myself a break? If I gave myself any more of a break, I'd be in pieces all over the floor. Christ, you practically had to pry me out of my house with a crowbar . . ."

"Shh . . . It's okay. Don't cry. Everything's going to be okay."

"How's it going to be okay? I've got to get back to work in a couple of days, and I'm too goddamn scared to go out and get the goddamn mail."

"It'll pass. I promise, it'll pass."

"God, I am so *sick* of having you see me like this."

That seemed to pull him up short. "Honey, you know I'm nuts about you. Why would you ever think you had to worry about how I see you?"

"I just don't want you to think I'm some . . . some hysterical, high-maintenance . . ."

"Ah."

I stared at him. "Ah?"

"You don't want me to think you're another Lucy."

"Oh, Jesus, I didn't say that."

"But that's what you're thinking, isn't it?"

"For Christ's sake, do you have to be so goddamn . . ."

"What?"

"Perceptive."

I'm not saying one five-minute pep talk cured me of the Assault Victim's Blues—possibly the only condition that doesn't have a support group in Gabriel, by the way—but it definitely helped. I was, at least, able to screw my courage to the sticking place and drive my brand-new, fire-engine-red roadster the mile and a half back to my house all by my little self. (Okay, Cody was in the passenger seat keeping an eye out for snipers.) We stopped by the newsroom on the way home, ostensibly so I could pick up some files but mostly so I could make everybody jealous at the sight of my new wheels. Then we went back to my place, where Cody got into his Camry—which was looking rather sad by comparison—and I settled on the couch for two more days of feeling sorry for myself.

Luckily, though, I was feeling brave enough to intersperse the self-pity with some actual work. The folders I'd brought back from the newsroom stacked up to more than two feet of paper, but with my attention diverted only by meals with Cody and the occasional viewing of *A&E Biography*, I was able to get through it all. There was the stuff I'd copied at Historic Gabriel, and the clip files from the morgue (including stories from the old *Gabriel Transcript*, the p.m. paper that the *Monitor* had consumed in the sixties), and some stuff from the New York papers that Intern Brad had copied from microfilm.

I'd seen some of it before, in the process of writing about the Starlight or Ashley Sinclair, but I'd never plowed all the way through. Now I was able to focus on it, without the pressure of deadlines or trying to find something specific to use in a story. When I was done, I had two notebooks' worth of scribblings and a head filled to bursting with names and dates and play titles.

I also had a sneaking suspicion.

It was Friday afternoon, four hours before Cody was supposed to pick me up for further psychotherapy, in the form of my first dinner out since The Incident. (And no, we were sure as hell *not* going to Albertini's.) I called the newsroom and caught Mad at his desk.

"Hey, can you come over to my house?"

"You mean now?"

"Yeah."

"What's up? Are you okay?"

"I'm fine. I've just been going through all these old clips and stuff, and I think maybe I found something."

"What?"

"It's nothing concrete, just a bunch of stuff that doesn't add up."

"Are you gonna tell me or aren't you?"

"Okay, I know this is going to sound obvious, so don't laugh, but I think it might be important. I've been going through this stuff for two days, and the more I read, the more convinced I am."

"Of what?"

"Of the fact that, regardless of whatever else went down back in 1926, Robbie Renssellaer is a big fat liar."

26

THAT'S IT? THAT SOME OLD GOAT PADDED HIS RÉSUMÉ?"

This from Mad, who was stretched out on my living-room couch. He hadn't moved much since he got there, only rousing himself to spear the occasional tidbit from the fruit salad he'd brought over from Schultz's. I'd asked him to bring me a Swiss cheese sandwich, but he'd refused to, quote, "aid and abet a cholesterol addict."

"Come on," I said, as he popped a strawberry into his mouth. "You're not paying attention. This Robbie thing is way more complicated than that."

"I don't see how."

"Okay, listen up this time, will you? Like I said, I've been going through all these old clips and my notes and stuff. And the more I've been reading, the more I think he's full of it. Like, take this award he won from the Upstate Theatre Critics Guild. Most Promising Juvenile. He won it in 1924."

"So what?"

"So according to his birth certificate, he was only five years old back then."

"And I say to you again, so the hell what?"

"I told you I pulled all these old theater files from the

Monitor and the *Transcript*. I found little write-ups on the other winners from the ten years before and afterward, and they were all around thirteen years old. The youngest one was ten."

"So Robbie was super-extra-special."

"Come on, Mad. Do you even remember how *young* five years old is?"

"Luckily, my childhood is but a blur."

"We're talking finger paints and Teletubbies. I just can't believe this guy was so all-fired talented at five that he beat out every other kid north of New York. Plus, according to what he told me, he didn't even start to get cast in community theater productions until he was six."

"So you think he lied about winning the award?"

"Nah, I saw the plaque myself. And besides, it was in the papers along with all the others. What I'm saying is, I think he was lying about his *age*."

"Didn't the clip say how old he was?"

"It was the only one where the age was missing. That kind of clued me in too."

"Hey, I thought you said you saw his birth certificate."

"Right, but what if it was a fake?"

"That's nuts."

"Is it? Remember, the kid's father was the mayor—and from what I've heard, he ran the city like some goddamn feudal lord. There wasn't a whole lot of municipal oversight back then, if you know what I mean."

"But what would be the point?"

"Think about it, Mad. What's the worst thing that can happen to a child actor?"

"He makes a movie with 'Fluffy' in the title?"

"He gets *older*. I'm betting that when they decided to try and make little Robbie a star, Daddy used his executive

powers to shave a few years off his age. He was a smallish
sort of kid, so he could get away with it."

"So?"

"So all along we've been assuming Robbie was seven
years old when Ashley Sinclair disappeared. But what if he
was more like . . . I don't know, ten or eleven?"

"Could he really pull it off?"

"Why not? Hollywood is all about illusion, right? If little
ten-year-old Robbie goes to an audition, and he looks
younger, and he acts younger, who's gonna know?"

"So what are you saying? You think Robbie was old
enough to, what? Kill Ashley himself?"

"I'm not necessarily saying *that*, just that maybe he was
actually old enough to know what was going on back
then."

"And that's why you're so pissed at him all of a sudden?"

"It's not just that. Listen to this. I've been slogging
through all these old play reviews, and there's kind of a
weird pattern forming. Most of Robbie's reviews are pretty
okay, right? But every once in a while there'll be a really
negative one. And guess what? The reviewer is never heard
from again."

"You mean like *dead*?"

"Oh, Christ, no. Not dead. What I mean is, as far as I
could tell, the person would never review another play
again, in either paper. Get it?"

"Apparently not."

"Somebody was putting the kibosh on panning him. It
happened four different times. I counted."

"You mean the M.E. or the publisher would can somebody just for saying Renssellaer blew the big one?"

"Could be. Could've been under pressure from the
mayor, or else maybe they'd get blacklisted by the theaters."

"Could they do that?"

"I don't know. Maybe not. But hey, the mall cinema would love to ban me, right? Maybe back then they could get away with it."

"So if it really was the papers doing it, why would there be any negative reviews at all?"

"I was wondering about that myself. But then I was thinking, why should the *Monitor* have been any more organized back then than it is now? You know how ridiculous it is to try and set any kind of policy about anything, with all the editors and reporters coming and going. Maybe every once and a while a nasty review would slip through the cracks, and Robbie's dad raised holy hell."

"How nasty are we talking about?"

"Let me see . . ." I shuffled through one of the folders. "Hmm . . . Here we go. This one by somebody named Victoria Monk. 'In the role of Medea's older son, young Robbie Renssellaer Jr. is, sadly, far more of a distraction than an asset. He seems to have difficulty concentrating on the task at hand, constantly breaking the fourth wall and drawing undue attention to himself. If only he would focus his considerable energy on his artistic endeavors, rather than clowning with the audience and trying to upstage his castmates, he might, at least, do no harm."

"Ouch. And I'm guessing Miss Monk never reviewed another show?"

"You guess right."

"What's 'breaking the fourth wall' mean, anyway?"

"Interacting with the audience."

"Huh?"

"When you're onstage, you've got the wall behind you and one on either side. That's three, right? The fourth wall is the invisible one between the actor and the audience."

"Thrilling. Okay, so Robbie was a lousy actor. I still don't see where you think that gets us. I mean, you already said you saw him on TV in that crappy movie with the little rat-dog . . ."

"*Fluffy, My Pal.*"

"Right. So what's the big deal?"

"Look, I do this critic thing myself, right? I can tell when somebody's being honest and when they're shining it on. And all I'm saying is, from reading all these reviews, I get the feeling that the people who said nice things about him were bending over backward to do it, and the ones who skewered him were shooting from the hip. Now, all along I've been assuming that Robbie was just this cute kid who—how did that reviewer put it?—Who did no harm. So on the strength of his looks and a little charm, he got cast in a bunch of movies, and when he wasn't cute anymore, he just kind of faded away. But now I think maybe it's more complicated than that."

"Complicated how?"

"I think he really sucked."

"So?"

"And if he was so incredibly untalented," I said, "how the hell did he get to be a movie star?"

I spent the next two days trying to get Robert Renssellaer to answer that very question. The good news was that this new obsession seemed to cure me of my inability to go outside all by my lonesome. The bad news was that, since my stories had helped transform him from Starlight benefactor to local ratfink, Renssellaer didn't plan on speaking to me for the rest his life. I tried calling, stopping by, leaving notes in his mailbox—no luck. Most of the time nobody answered, but finally the nurse came to the door and said he was, quote, "in seclusion."

"Why's he in seclusion?"

"Because he's in mourning."

"In mourning for whom?"

Then she slammed the door in my pretty little face.

At first I assumed his grief was for Sissy, one of the only people in town who treated him with the reverence he thought he deserved. Then I thought maybe it was for the Starlight, which he'd tried to save but whose demise his little charade had actually precipitated. In the end, though, I decided that if Robert Renssellaer were shedding tears for anyone, it was probably himself.

So what had really happened with him back in 1926? When I'd interviewed him in his funereal digs, he'd told me he got his big break during *The Quinn Affair*, when Austin Cusack was blown away by his performance and hooked him up with a Hollywood producer. That same story had appeared in a bunch of fan magazines during Robbie's fifteen minutes of movie fame. It made for good copy. But was it true?

It was hard to tell from the *Monitor* review of the show, which appeared to be yet another example of a critic just trying to say something nice about him. (In this case, the reviewer had rhapsodized about the fact that Robbie had pulled it off, considering he'd been a last-minute replacement for another boy who'd gotten sick.)

What if the story was as phony as his quarter-million-dollar pledge? Wouldn't that mean there'd been some sort of double-dealing back then, something even more serious than fudging his age and doping his reviews? Could Ashley have stumbled on to whatever scam Renssellaer Senior had been running? Robbie's movie career, while relatively short-lived, had earned him big bucks; as motives for murder go, it seemed good enough to me.

But with Renssellaer giving me the silent treatment, I couldn't see how I was going to find out anything else. Whether Robbie had been seven back then or a few years

older, he was still one of the only people around who still
had a pulse. Being a decade younger than everybody he'd
worked with made him, inconveniently, the only cast member who could possibly . . .

*Hold on. If Robbie had replaced somebody, maybe the
other kid is still alive and kicking.* What was his name
again? I made a mad dash for my stack of papers, and there
it was: Richie Edgar. I crossed my fingers and flipped
through the phone book. No Richard Edgar.

Rats.

Undeterred, I fired up my trusty Macintosh and did a
couple of Web searches for Richard Edgar. There were two
hundred and twelve of them.

Okay, if I were truly a hardworking human being I would
have picked up the phone and called each and every one.
But from where I was sitting, it seemed like an enormous
hassle—given the vagaries of phone tag and the fact that,
with my luck, the Richie Edgar I was looking for had probably been shot down over Dresden.

So how could I find out if he was still alive?

I decided to start on my home turf. I hopped in my extremely excellent new car and drove over to the newspaper.
It was a Sunday afternoon, so the only other cars in the parking lot belonged to the sports guys and Bill; Mad was Sunday reporter, and since he lives a beer can's throw from the
place, he doesn't inflict his rust-encrusted Volvo on the rest
of us. I figured I'd get the bad news out of the way first, so
I went down to the morgue to look through the bio files for
the dear departed. I finger-walked past "EDGERTON,
(RONALD)" and "EDGAR, (EMILY)" and . . . he wasn't
there. *Whew.* Of course, it could just be that he'd died and
the newspaper didn't know it—but at least he wasn't certifi-
ably deceased.

I went up the back stairs, avoiding the newsroom lest Bill

spot me and give me an assignment, which he has been known to do even if a girl isn't actually supposed to be working. Safely in the library, I shut the door and looked for Richard Edgar's bio file—and started jumping up and down when I found there actually was one. Unfortunately, though, it was pretty damn thin. There were exactly four stories inside: a profile from his days as a local child actor; a story about him being named Gabriel High Scholar-Athlete of the Year for 1932; a mention of him working with the Seabees in the Pacific Theater as part of a roundup of what local boys were doing in the war; and a story from the seventies about how he'd organized a reunion of guys who'd trained for World War II service at a now-defunct naval station at the opposite end of Mohawk Lake.

The last one described him as a civil engineer who lived in Atlanta. *Bingo.* I tried directory assistance, and sure enough there was a listing. I dialed, and got an answering machine. The woman sounded to be in her mid-thirties, and the message was of the happy-sitcom-family variety.

Hi, you've reached Rich, Donna, Billy, Susie, Buster and Princess. None of us can come to the phone right now, but we'd just be pleased as punch if you'd leave us a message at the tone. Goodbye and God bless!

I had a feeling I had the wrong Richard Edgar—unless, of course, he'd decided to start a second family at the ripe old age of eighty-something.

I grabbed the file and ventured into the newsroom. Mad was sitting at his terminal, scowling at the screen and sipping a Diet Pepsi that smelled suspiciously like the Citizen.

"Whatcha workin' on?"

"Don't ask."

"Listen, can you help me out with something?"

"I've kind of got a deadline here."

"It'll just take a second. How would you go about finding an engineer?"

"What kind of engineer?"

"Civil."

"You planning on building a bridge?"

"Don't be a smartass. I've been trying to get in touch with Renssellaer all weekend, and it's not happening. But I thought, what about that kid he replaced in *The Quinn Affair*? So I've been trying to track him down . . ."

"You mean he's still alive?"

"Maybe. I don't know for sure. At least, I don't know for sure that he's dead."

"But you know he was a civil engineer?"

"That's what it said in the bio file." I held out the clip. "This is from 1976. Guy organized a reunion at the old naval training station, patriotic bicentennial thing."

"This says he's from Atlanta. Why don't you just . . ."

"I tried calling information, but I'm pretty sure I got the wrong Richard Edgar."

"Hmm . . . Well, odds are the guy belonged to the A.S.C.E.—that's the professional society for civil engineers."

"Then let's call them."

"Probably not answering the phone on a Sunday."

"Oh. Right."

"Look, I'll see what I can do. Maybe somebody up at Benson has a membership list or something."

"My hero."

"Now go away and let me file this shit."

I started to leave, then stopped. "You know what drives me up the wall? I bet Gordon could find this guy's home number in two seconds flat—plus his wife's bra size and where he gets his hair cut."

"Christ, Bernier, what does Gordon have to do with anything?"

"Oh, I don't know. I've just had him on the brain lately."

"What the hell for?"

"No particular reason."

"Then if you're done free-associating," he said with a growl, "do me a favor and get lost."

27

But there *was* a particular reason, one that had been brewing in the nether-regions of my brain for several days now. So I retreated back to the library and called Gordon on his cell phone. He answered on the first ring—the first half a ring, actually.

"Meet me for coffee."

"Alex? Listen, I'm expecting a really important—"

"Meet me for coffee."

"What the hell are you up to now?"

"I have a proposition for you."

"What kind of proposition?"

"Meet me for coffee."

"I think you said that already."

"You gonna meet me or aren't you?"

"Give me a nibble."

"Don't be such a . . ."

"No nibble, no dice."

"Okay, be that way. Here's the deal. I've maybe got a story for you, and it's—"

"Why the hell would you give me a story?"

"Are you gonna listen? It'd be a story for me, a huge one

probably, but at the moment I don't give a fuck. I'm more interested in having you do me a favor."

"What kind of favor?"

"Meet me and find out."

"Argh. *Fine*. Where?"

"Café Whatever?"

"No way. That place gives me the creeps. Besides, I need sustenance. I'll see you at Schultz's in ten."

"Too small. Way too much potential for prying ears. How about the Chinese buffet place we used to go to?"

"Fine."

He hung up without resorting to undue politeness, and I drove the four miles to the restaurant, located on Gabriel's most All-American stretch of road: the chain-store ghetto. A couple of years ago the city made headlines for blackballing Wal-Mart when it tried to open a branch here—and a few people pointed out that the argument was rather idiotic, since nobody had been averse to every other pre-fab behemoth. On the way to the Chinese buffet I passed Kmart, Ames, Staples, Office Depot, Blockbuster, Target, a Sherwin-Williams, and two Rite Aids. Culinary options included Pizza Hut, Burger King, Subway, KFC, Dunkin' Donuts, Taco Bell, Red Lobster, Olive Garden, Ponderosa, T.G.I.Fridays, and the obligatory Golden Arches. Very un-Gabriel, I know, but they're there and sometimes I'm not even sorry.

I pulled into the parking lot just as Gordon was getting out of his van, a silvery blue monstrosity that looked like something you might want to hide in during a nuclear attack.

"What the hell do you call that thing?"

"A Volkswagen Vanagon."

"A what?"

"Could you not start?"

"I can't believe that *thing* is related to my car in any way."

"I got it for cheap, okay?"

"Where's the front end?"

"They didn't seem to feel the need to build one. But it's really roomy, see?"

"What does it get to the gallon?"

"Like . . . ten."

"How environmentally conscious."

"Shut up."

"Hey, you like my new wheels? Snazzy, isn't she?"

"Sweet of you to rub my nose in it. We gonna eat or what?"

We went into the restaurant, loaded up our plates with greasy comestibles, and repaired to a corner table.

"Okay," he said once he'd eaten two egg rolls, some lo mein, and a bowl of wonton soup, "what's your proposition? I'm all ears."

"Before I tell you, you have to promise me that this is just between the two of us for now. When the time is right you can take whatever you find out and run with it, but not 'til then."

"How long we talking about?"

"Not long. Maybe a week or two."

"You gotta be . . ."

"Look, it's really not going to matter, scoop-wise. Nobody else is on this, as far as I know."

"Then what do you need me for?"

"I'll get to that. But first I want you to promise you're not going to go blabbing to your editors until I say so."

"I assume otherwise it's no deal?"

"You assume correctly."

"Then fine."

"I've got your word on this?"

"Jesus, Alex, since when have you known me to screw over a source?"

"A source I wouldn't worry about. A friend I'm not so sure."

"Nice."

"Okay, here goes. You probably already heard I got roughed up a week ago."

"Yeah, I meant to send you some flowers or something—"

"Right. Anyway, did you catch the details?"

"Just what was in the paper. It wasn't much."

"Yeah, well, sometimes it pays to have friends in the press. They pretty much kept it to the bare minimum, cop-monitor stuff."

"So what's the scoop?"

"The day it happened, I got a phone message from somebody pretending to be a cop who worked with Cody. He told me to meet him—Cody, I mean—at Albertini's restaurant at eight. That's the place we ran into you on New Year's, remember?"

"Yeah. It wasn't half bad. Of course, there's this place in Little Italy . . ."

"When I got there, the restaurant was closed, and there was a sign that said they had a family emergency. When I went to get back in my car, these two guys grabbed me. Trashed me, trashed my car."

"Yeesh. You have any idea why?"

"Yeah. They threatened me, told me to stay off a story I've been working on. And no, I'm not going to tell you which one it was. So what I want to know is . . ."

"What you want to know is, how the hell did they know the restaurant would be closed down all of a sudden?"

"You scare me sometimes."

"Thanks."

"Now, Cody thinks these two guys might have been . . . That they weren't amateurs."

"You mean somebody put a *hit* out on you? Son of a bitch . . ."

"No, I don't think it was a hit, for Christ's sake. If it were, I wouldn't be sitting here right now eating vegetable moo shu. It was a warning. And what I want to know is, from who?"

"Hold on a second. Last time I checked, you were shacked up with a police detective. Why the hell don't you just ask him?"

"I *have* asked him. I've been asking him all week. Every time I do, he changes the subject or just shines me on."

"Relationship's doomed."

"Be nice. He's just trying to protect me. I got pretty freaked out about what happened, and I think he's worried that if he tells me what's up it's going to scare the shit out of me. He's probably got a point."

"So why do you want to know?"

"Come on, Gordon, it's me you're talking to. You know damn well I have to find out, whether I like the answer or not."

"And Cody doesn't get it?"

"I don't know. He usually does. This time is . . . I don't know, it's just different somehow."

"So where do I come in to all this?"

"You're the guy who can dig up any damn thing on anybody. You manage to find out shit that nobody else can, even personal financial shit, and on the record to boot."

"It's called investigative reporting."

"Thanks for pointing that out."

"Okay, let's get down and dirty." He pushed his plate aside and pulled out a notebook. "What time did you get that message from the pseudo cop?"

"My machine said twelve-sixteen."

"So if they had a plan, it had to be set by then. Hey, was the place open for lunch that day?"

"They don't serve lunch. It's dinner only, every night but Monday. The regular Friday hours are five-thirty to midnight."

"So the question is, how did they know at noon that the restaurant would be closed that night. Right?"

"Exactly."

"What kind of emergency was it, anyway?"

"That much, Cody did tell me. The owner's wife went into premature labor. Turned out to be a false alarm."

"And they closed the restaurant for that?"

"I guess he doesn't want it open if he's not there. At least that's what he said."

"Do you know what time this false labor thing went down?"

"Around ten in the morning."

"Okay, so what's your gut instinct about all this? You think maybe they closed the place on purpose?"

"Look, people have been joking about Albertini's for years. There's never very many customers, but the guys who run it never seem to care. They don't advertise, they don't take credit cards—it's just not your usual place, which is probably why I like it. But it's pretty obvious their books aren't kosher. How could they be?"

"And you want me to find out where the money's coming from."

"Bingo."

"Okay, so what's in it for me?"

"How about a story on various families of the Sicilian persuasion laundering their money upstate?"

"I hate to tell you this, but that's hardly news."

"It's hardly news in the abstract. But we're pretty damn

far from the city, Gordon. What if there's big money involved? You telling me this doesn't interest you just a little bit more than writing about overstuffed landfills in Oneonta?"

"I've got other stuff on my plate too, you know. I've got my own Sinclair profile thing to work on—nice job on yours, by the way. I'd really like to help you, but I don't see how this is going to get me—"

"Okay, fine. I had a feeling you were going to play hardball, so I saved myself a trump card."

"You're mixing your metaphors again."

"Remember how I said those two guys warned me off a story? Well that story was the Sissy Dillingham murder. That sexy enough for you?"

"Yowza." He sat there and digested it for a while. "Okay, so now I'm interested. If those guys were pros, and they're hooked up with Albertini's, and Albertini's is really washing cash for somebody, and all that has something to do with flattening Dillingham like a goddamn matzo over that crappy old theater . . ."

"Hey, I never said this had anything to do with the Starlight—"

He fixed me with his patented Gordon scowl. "And just exactly how stupid do you think I am?"

"Sorry."

"Now spill." Having zero choice in the matter, I told him the whole truth. "Man," he said, "it's too complicated even for me to sort out right now. But it's gotta help get my ass transferred back to the city—at least it's a start . . ."

"You know, Gordon, I hate to burst your bubble, but this isn't about you at the moment. I'm the one who got the crap beaten out of them, remember? And you promised you wouldn't blab this until I said so."

"Oh. Yeah. Absolutely."

"And listen, you've got to be sly about this. If I got beat up over writing about Sissy and the Starlight, you have to be really careful about how you . . ."

"Don't worry your little goyish head about it. I'm what they call 'street smart.' "

I was about to tell him that most boys in the 'hood don't wear ties with little pink flowers on them, but I figured such things were best left unsaid. "*Somebody* told those guys the coast would be clear so they could grab me. I want to know how the professional ass-kickers and the restaurant are connected, and how all that is connected to what happened to Sissy Dillingham."

"I have a feeling," said Gordon, with a rather nasty expression on his face, "that 'connected' is going to turn out to be the perfect word."

Sunday night I was home waiting for calls from the three men in my life—Cody, Mad, Gordon—when the doorbell rang. Unfortunately, I answered it.

"What do you want?" I said.

"I want you to stop seeing my husband," she said.

The conversation devolved from there.

I invited her in, because I had no desire to air my dirty knickers in front of the cop who was still squatting outside my front door. She went into the living room, fought a losing battle with the dog hair coating the couch, and perched on the edge of a cushion. I waited for her to say something but she just sat there, her big blue eyes drilling a hole in my forehead.

"Okay, Lucy," I said. "Let's get it over with. Just say whatever it is you've got to say."

"Aren't you even going to offer me something to drink?"

"Would you like something to drink?"

"Yes, please."

"We're, um, fresh out of white zinfandel."

"I'll take whatever you have. I don't want to be any trouble."

Yeah, right. I escaped into the kitchen, where I grabbed two half-empty bottles of wine (Steve's Chablis and my Shiraz) and two glasses. Predictably, she went straight for the white.

"All right. What is it you wanted to tell me?"

"I just wanted to talk, that's all."

"So talk."

"Alex, I . . . May I call you Alex?"

"Whatever." Clearly, everything my mom had taught me about civility had gone clear out of my brain.

"Alex, I just wanted to say that if . . . I mean, once Brian and I are back together, I plan to make him very happy."

"And just what do you expect me to say to that?"

"I suppose I just, well . . . I want your blessing."

"Are you completely out of your gourd?"

"I don't know what you mean."

"Listen, I don't know exactly what you're going through at the moment. Obviously, for some reason you got the idea in your head that you want Cody back, and frankly I don't blame you."

That perked her up. "See, I knew you'd under . . ."

"What I meant was, I don't blame you for wanting him back. I mean, he's a hell of a good guy."

"You couldn't be more right."

"What I don't understand is why."

"Why . . . what?"

"Why now? How come, after you cheated on him and did every damn thing you could to humiliate him by sleeping with half the cops in Boston, you suddenly decide to—"

"I did not sleep with half the . . . You couldn't possibly understand."

"For which I am eternally grateful. So why now?"

"I don't have to explain anything to you. You have no right to—"

"Hey, you came over to my house, remember? You obviously want to convince me to break it off with Cody. Right?"

"That's a . . . simplistic way of describing it."

"I'm a simple girl. So convince me."

She considered it for a minute, taking tiny sips of her wine. I poured myself a glass of Shiraz and took considerably more than a sip.

"I don't know if I can put it into words," she said finally. "It's just that I . . . I realized I still love him."

"And what is it you love about him, exactly?"

"What? Well . . . everything."

"Such as?"

"Well I married him, didn't I?"

"And?"

"Doesn't that say it all?"

"You know, for someone who busted into my house declaring her love for him, you're really not declaring it particularly well."

"It's impossible to say just why you love somebody. If you'd ever really felt like that, you'd understand."

"Are you serious?"

"You don't know what it's like. You've never been married, so you couldn't possibly understand. Brian and I just belong together, that's all."

She was really starting to piss me off. "You want to know why I'm so crazy about Cody? Okay, I'll educate you. I'm nuts about him because he's honest, and funny, and he doesn't play a bunch of bullshit games like ever other guy I've ever met. He's tough as hell without being macho, which as far as I can tell is a fucking miracle. He likes dogs, his and mine in particular, and he doesn't mind when they sleep on the bed. He likes my cooking, and he laughs at my jokes, and he gets along with my parents better than I do. He's damn good in bed, by the way, which I probably don't have to tell you. He's nice to my friends, even though they're not exactly his kind of people, and he's so loyal he'd take a bullet for you, which in my case he pretty much did. He wears boxer shorts. Oh, and he's a total hunk, even if you're not partial to redheads. The only thing I can find wrong with him is he doesn't speak a foreign language, but he's expressed an interest in having me teach him some French." I paused for another gulp of Shiraz. "Okay, now it's your turn."

She didn't take the bait, just sat there glowering at me. "You're not a very nice person," she said finally.

"Yeah, I know."

"You're really enjoying this, aren't you?"

"Not particularly."

"I'm not going to just disappear, you know. I have every intention of saving my marriage. There's nothing you can do to stop me."

"Oh come on, Lucy, give it a rest. You're making me embarrassed to be a girl."

"You think you're way above me, don't you? You *do*. You think you're superior because you're some hotshot reporter who sticks her nose in where it doesn't belong. You think you're such a big . . . such a big *hero* because you saved that girl's life last summer."

"What does that have to do with—"

"It wasn't really even you, you know. It was *Brian* who saved her. If it weren't for him you'd *both* be dead. He was the most famous detective in the whole country. He even got a medal for heroic service. I saw it on TV, and I read about it in all the papers . . ."

"You *what?*"

"I said I—" She cut herself off, and her complexion went from porcelain to ruby in a matter of seconds. "It's none of your business anyway."

I gaped at her from my perch in Emma's armchair, understanding whooshing at me like a knuckleball to home plate. "Oh, my God, Lucy. Do you have any idea how idiotic that is?"

"I don't know what you're talking about."

"This whole time, I've been trying to figure out what the hell would get you so riled up all of a sudden. But it's just the same old thing, isn't it?"

"I came here to talk, and you . . . Well, I've had just about enough." She stood up and headed for the door. I followed, and when she went for the doorknob I grabbed her by the arm, and not gently.

"You heard about what happened, and now you want him back. Catching a serial killer even trumps the deputy chief of the Boston P.D., doesn't it?"

"Let go. You're hurting me."

I did, and she immediately started rubbing her arm. She'd probably have a bruise in the morning—at least I hoped she would. "You know, Lucy, I think it's about time for you to go back to Boston."

"What you just did was *assault*. I could . . . I have half a mind to . . ."

"There's the phone," I said. "Why don't you call the cops?"

28

NIAGARA FALLS IS ONE OF THOSE PLACES YOU REALLY HAVE to see before you die. Never mind the wax museums and the heart-shaped hot tubs; the falls themselves are pretty damn spectacular, even surrounded by all that tacky crap. There's the big horseshoe on the Canadian side, the one that people persist in trying to go over in a barrel despite the fact that it's a remarkably stupid idea, and an enormous frothing whirlpool you ride over in a cable car. On the American side, there's also a little bridal veil you can walk under on a wooden staircase, if you plunk down your five bucks to take what they call the "Cave of the Winds" tour. My favorite thing is going on the Maid of the Mist boat, where you put on these flimsy blue rain ponchos and get so close to the enormous screaming falls you actually feel like you're going to capsize and drown in the company of a bunch of photo-snapping German tourists.

The last time I went there, though, I didn't get to see any of that stuff. What I did get to see was Richie Edgar.

Niagara Falls was where he lived, a fact that came courtesy of the American Society of Civil Engineers. I called him, and his granddaughter told me that although his hearing wasn't so great for the phone, he'd be happy to talk to me in person. So I drove the three hours, followed her directions, and there I was—in a tidy saltbox in a residential neighborhood a few miles from the falls, with a zoo's worth of windmill animals out front and what was probably a small fortune in vintage theater posters on the walls.

He was a nice old guy, deaf and wrinkly but damn sharp, and the first thing he wanted to know was why the hell a newspaper reporter from Gabriel was interested in anything he had to say. So I laid it out for him: how I'd been covering the Ashley Sinclair story, and since he'd been cast in *The Quinn Affair* I thought maybe he could fill me in on what had been going on at the Starlight back then. It didn't seem to put him in the jolliest of moods.

"Are you familiar with the expression," he said, "of 'the road not taken'?"

"Sure."

"Everyone has one. You're only, I'd guess, twenty-five years old, and no doubt you have your own. Acting was mine."

"Mine too, actually."

"You don't say? Well, it's a lot of people's, I expect."

"So why didn't you pursue it? As a career, I mean."

"My parents didn't approve. They were working-class folk, and they believed in the professions."

"But they let you act as a child, didn't they?"

"Then it was a hobby. That, they didn't mind."

"Do you remember much about rehearsing *The Quinn Affair*?"

"Much? I remember *everything*. It was the only time . . . I should say, it was the closest I ever got to the professional theater. It meant a great deal to me."

"Would you mind telling me about it?"

"What precisely do you want to know?"

"Well . . . everything, I guess."

"Are you familiar with the plot?"

"Come to think of it, no."

He got up, walked slowly but steadily over to the bookcase, pulled out a slim paperback, and handed it to me.

"That's my original script, from 1926."

"You've held on to it all these years?"

"Call it nostalgia, or perhaps just vanity. I've never been able to part with it." He grabbed the arm of the chair to support himself as he sat back down. "Now what was I saying? Oh, yes, the plot. The action takes place in a fashionable country house in the Catskills in the present day—meaning the twenties, of course, back when the Catskills were fashionable. It centers on a family called Drake. I suppose today they'd be described as 'dysfunctional.' You're familiar with the term?"

I nodded. The guy was nice, but he wasn't giving me credit for a whole lot of brainpower.

"The family consisted of a rather submissive mother and a dictatorial father, both in their fifties. And might I say, this seemed *exceedingly* old to me back then. Not anymore . . . Now where was I? Oh, yes. They have two daughters, Evelyn and Constance, and a son, let me think . . . Gerald. Evelyn is the older daughter, a widow with a young son named Jonah. Constance is a sweet young thing, very much under her parents' thumb. She's also under a great deal of pressure to please them. Her older sister made what you might call an unfortunate marriage, and it's up to her to marry well and restore some of the family's social position. Are you following this?"

"Um . . . absolutely."

"Now, the son believes that his parents are terrible prigs. That means 'uptight.' "

"Right."

"He brings a friend home from the city, a man named

Quinn who comes from a very humble background. His idea is to pass him off as a gentleman, just to prove that his parents' ideas about class and money are nothing more than social conceits."

"Sort of like *Pygmalion*?"

He looked at me like it just occurred to him I might have an I.Q. in the triple digits after all. "Yes, in a way, but much darker. Gerald's motives are by no means lighthearted. He doesn't just want to play a harmless joke on his family. He wants to . . . How to put it? To rub their noses in their own smallness. And Quinn is no helpless bumpkin, either. He's fully complicit in the scheme, and there's something . . . shall we say, utterly *dangerous* about him."

"Sounds interesting."

"That's just the beginning. At first, Gerald thinks he's in charge of the situation, but toward the end of Act Two it becomes obvious that Quinn has engineered the situation himself, convinced Gerald to bring him into the fold without him realizing it."

"So what happens?"

"Quinn insinuates himself into the good graces of everyone concerned. He becomes a son to the father, a father to the boy, a companion to the mother. He wins the hearts of both Evelyn and Constance, and sets one sister against the other in competition over him. How Winthrop—that's the playwright—how he does this, so rapidly and yet so deftly and believably, is nothing short of *genius*. And then, in the third act, Quinn gets his comeuppance. He comes undone—he actually falls in love with Constance, and he tells her the truth. He wants to marry her without false pretenses, but of course the father won't allow it, because he's really just a poor boy after all, you see? Constance agrees to run away with him, but when Evelyn finds out she's been made a fool of, she kills him."

"She *what*?"

"She takes her father's pistol, and she shoots him—right in front of her son Jonah. Her brother feels so guilty about the disaster he's caused, he takes the blame. In the end, he hangs for it."

"Yikes."

"I know it sounds melodramatic, but it's really quite powerful. You have to see it on the stage to understand."

"And Ashley Sinclair was cast as Constance?"

"That's right. Quinn himself was played by Brandon Bartlett, an immensely talented young actor. It was a shame what happened to him."

"And Priscilla Morton was originally supposed to play Evelyn?"

"Oh, goodness no. She was far too young for that. She was originally cast as the maid."

"The maid?"

"It's not as inconsequential a part as you might think. She's onstage a great deal, if only in the background, and she plays a rather pivotal role. She comes from the same economic class as Quinn, and she's the only one who sees him for what he is from the very beginning. She tries to warn the family, but no one will listen. Because she's just the maid, you understand?"

"And you were supposed to play Jonah."

"That's right." A scowl flitted across his face. "Quite a few boys auditioned for the role. I got it."

"And how old were you back then?"

"Thirteen."

"Really? I guess I assumed it was a much younger character. Robert Renssellaer said he was seven when he played it."

"Seven? You must be joking. He was only two years behind me in school."

I knew it. "I guess he's, um, fudging his age a little."

He made an ugly snorting sound. "Good God. At our age, what's the point?"

"Did he audition for the role when you did?"

"Yes. However, at the risk of sounding bitter . . . he didn't even make the callbacks."

"Then how did he get the part when you got sick?"

"*Sick.*" He savored the word, and not in a good way. "Sick is a damned good word for it."

"How do you mean?"

"Miss Bernier, my parents were working-class people. They weren't well off, and they certainly weren't sophisticated, but they never would have done anything consciously to hurt me. I want you to know that."

"I'm not sure I understand."

He took a deep breath. "It was a long time ago, and my parents are long gone, so there's no harm in telling you. But I want your word that you won't put it in the newspaper."

I put my pen down, the universal sign for *off the record.* "All right."

Another deep breath. "I was never sick. My parents . . . they were paid to take me out of town and say I'd fallen ill."

"Paid by whom?"

"By Robbie's father, of course. Who do you think?"

"Are you serious?"

"Why in heaven's name would I joke about this?"

"Sorry. I didn't mean it that way. What happened exactly?"

"My parents . . . they lived very much hand-to-mouth. There were five children, and when Mr. Renssellaer offered my father one hundred dollars simply to say I was unable to go onstage, he . . . Do you have any idea how much money that was back then?"

"Um . . . I assume it was a lot."

"For a workingman, it was a small fortune. So my father took it, and when I protested he said it was my duty to do it for the family, and that this acting business was just a waste of time anyway. He told me that when I was older, I'd understand. I can't say I ever have."

"But how did Robbie get the part? Didn't you have an understudy?"

He shook his head. "It was a relatively short run, so it wasn't considered necessary. And as for Robbie . . . He'd been hanging around the theater as always, watching rehearsals. The management let him, because his father was the mayor, and he could either make life very pleasant for the theater or very difficult."

"Was Robbie in on this?"

"I assume so, because the day I was taken away he went to Mr. Cusack and told him he'd spent so much time watching the rehearsals, he'd conveniently memorized my entire part. The producers thought it was a godsend."

"And was he any good?"

"I never saw him in the role. Frankly, I couldn't bear it."

"Listen, Mr. Edgar, this is probably going to sound nuts, but do you have any idea if Robbie and his father could have pulled off a similar scam to get him into the movies?"

"I have no idea, not that I'd put it past them." He closed his eyes for a minute, then opened them. "Is there anything else you need to know, Miss Bernier? Talking about all of this is making me awfully tired . . ."

"Could I have just a few more minutes of your time? I was wondering . . . have you been following the news coverage about Ashley Sinclair?"

That woke him up. "Religiously."

"And do you . . . do you have any sense of what might have happened to her? I mean, you were there. You're one of the few people left alive who actually were. If you're not too tired, would you mind telling me any impressions you might have had? I know it was a long time ago . . ."

"It doesn't matter. I remember those days better than I remember what I did this morning."

"And . . ."

"Oh . . . where to begin? There was so much going on, so many bright and interesting people, so much *glamour*. Not that I hated my engineering career, but . . . let's face it, it just wasn't the same. I often wonder, you know, what my life might have been, had I had the courage to . . . But that's enough of that, isn't it? You asked about the cast. I presume you'd like me to start with Miss Sinclair?"

"Please."

"She was . . . a rarity. She was kind, vivacious but still ladylike, extremely talented but never condescending. I suppose you could say . . . Well, I'm sure it wouldn't surprise you to hear that I had quite a crush on her. It was inevitable, I suppose. I was thirteen, she was six years older—enough of an age gap so that she thought of me as a boy, but I thought of her as . . . perfect. That's the word I always associated with her. Silly schoolboy stuff, no doubt, but probably understandable."

"Were the two of you close?"

"Oh, somewhat, but not as close as I would have liked. She was very kind about letting me puppy after her—I should say, she never made me feel that I was as much of a pest as I probably was. She took me to the movies once, just the two of us, to a matinee double feature. Two Adolphe Menjou pictures—*A Social Celebrity* and *The Ace of Cads*. It was a Tuesday, and it rained. Afterward she let me buy her an ice at the old Chantilly drugstore. She ordered lemon, because she liked things that were tart. It cost a nickel, and it came in a silver dish with a little spoon, the tiniest spoon you ever saw." He shook his head, like the memories rattling around in there were starting to hurt. "You see, I remember the past better than the present. I couldn't even tell you what I had for breakfast this morning."

"Do you know if Ashley was, um, seeing someone at the time?"

"Not that I noticed. And I *would* have noticed. I was very . . . finely attuned to her, you might say. But then again, I was only thirteen years old. I thought I was quite mature, of course, but I'm sure there was plenty going on over my head and underneath my feet."

"If you've read the news coverage, then you know that she was, um . . . expecting."

"I could scarcely believe it. I suppose this will sound terribly old fashioned to you, Miss Bernier, but back then good girls . . . *didn't.*" He was turning a little red about the gills, but he kept talking. "Although Miss Sinclair was an actress, and a very beautiful woman, I always thought of her as being so . . . pure. Granted, I was completely ignorant of such things, but I would have bet my life that she wasn't that sort of girl."

"But given that she . . . that she *was*, do you have any idea who might have . . ."

"Who could have been the father? I'm not sure I'm a very reliable source on that sort of thing. As I said, there was plenty going on over my head. For example, it wasn't a year later that Brandon Bartlett's wife divorced him and announced to the world that he was a"—he cleared his throat, like he was choking on the very syllables—"a . . . homosexual who . . . shall we say, who enjoyed the company of young boys."

"And you never got that vibe from him?"

"Heavens no. He was never anything but kind to me. He certainly never made any . . . advances. And believe me, I was interviewed by both the police and the actors union.

They were in the midst of conducting an investigation when he . . . took his own life. Such a tragedy . . ."

"Did you get the feeling that Ashley was involved with Austin Cusack?"

"That was what the gossip columns said, I know, but I can't say I ever saw any evidence of it. But you wouldn't have, you see. They were both consummate professionals. If they were conducting an affair, the theater wasn't the place for it. They both knew that."

"What about Priscilla Morton? What did you think of her?"

"I didn't get to know her very well, I'm afraid. She seemed pleasant enough, but unlike Miss Sinclair she didn't seem terribly interested in spending time with a thirteen-year-old boy. Her attention was aimed in another direction."

"Austin Cusack?"

"Now that, even *I* noticed. She hung on his every word, came to the theater even when she wasn't called. She obviously enjoyed his company."

"Did he mind?"

"Not that I noticed. Miss Morton was a strikingly beautiful woman, you know. More . . . exotic than Miss Sinclair, but some people would say she was equally attractive."

"Did Ashley mind her hanging around Cusack?"

"Again, not that I noticed. She and Miss Morton were great friends, rather like children themselves when they were together. They'd dress each other's hair, make themselves up to look like movie stars of the day. They also enjoyed playing cards and board games—Chinese checkers and Parcheesi in particular, as I recall—and sometimes Ashley would invite me to play too. Oh, and did I mention that she was quite an excellent cook? On a few occasions, she took over the boardinghouse kitchen and made an enormous meal for everyone—pot roast and mashed potatoes, green beans, applesauce, even a cherry pie." He smiled at the memory. "The whole atmosphere of the cast . . . It was very cordial."

"There was no tension?"

"Well, I wouldn't say *that*. There's always tension of one kind or another when you're putting up a show. If you've acted yourself, you know that very well. And this production . . . Everyone concerned knew it could be a phenomenal success, or in any event they *hoped* it would. It had the potential to be the next big thing on Broadway. All the stars were aligned in that direction—the director, the playwright, the actors, the subject matter. And sure enough, it was. It launched the careers of Mr. Cusack and Miss Morton, and bloody Robbie Renssellaer Junior. It would have done the same for Mr. Bartlett, if he hadn't been . . ."

"Outed."

"You asked about tension. If there was any beyond what you'd expect for a show of that caliber, I'd say it was between Mr. Bartlett and his wife. But of course, all that was explained when they divorced and she exposed him."

"They seemed unhappy to you?"

"I'd have to say yes, but not alarmingly so. After all, my parents weren't what you'd call paragons of domestic bliss. But Mrs. Bartlett—her first name was Winifred, and people called her Winnie—she was a rather dour sort, one of those people who always seems to have the weight of the world on her shoulders, and complains about it, but one senses she wouldn't have it any other way. Do you know the type?"

"I think so."

"She was what my mother would have called a 'sourpuss.' Quite a handy expression, isn't it? But given what she must have been coping with at home, it's hard to blame her, don't you think? Four children, and a husband who was . . . straying with other young men. And from what I gather, they'd been childhood sweethearts. Mr. Bartlett once mentioned to me that he'd known her since he was my age."

"Whatever happened to her?"

"I'm not quite certain. I seem to recall hearing she'd remarried, and her second husband died in the war. I rather hope it isn't true."

"How come?"

He gave me the look he'd been giving me before, the one that said he wasn't sure I had two brain cells to rub together. "Good God," he said, "how much can one woman possibly take?"

I thought about it for a while. "More than you'd think," I said finally. "Way, way more than you'd think."

29

I GOT HOME MONDAY NIGHT, NOT QUITE SURE WHAT I'D AC-
complished with my Niagara Falls road trip. Yes, I'd gotten iron-clad confirmation that Robbie Renssellaer was a
fourteen-karat weasel—but I'd pretty much figured that out
for myself. As for who killed Ashley Sinclair, I hadn't made
a whole lot of progress. All I knew for sure was that she was
friends with Priscilla Morton, who had the hot potatoes for
Austin Cusack—no big surprise since she'd wound up marrying him. And that Brandon Bartlett and his wife were
miserable together—again no big shocker since he'd turned
out to be a member of the man-boy love club. Also that
Ashley was a nice lady, and that if she and Cusack were
seeing each other, they were being discreet about it. Oh,
and one more amazing revelation: Winnie Bartlett was a big
sourpuss.

This was worth putting three hundred miles on my new
car?

As I got to the outskirts of Gabriel, I bypassed the cutoff
to my house and went straight to the Chinese buffet. Gordon
was waiting for me at a corner table, three dirty plates
stacked up and one half-full in front him.

"You're late."

"It looks like you've been keeping yourself entertained."

"Abject terror makes me hungry."

"I assume you're going to explain that remark."

"You're going to wish I didn't."

"Look, I'm starving. Let me just get some food and you can tell me the bad news, okay?"

"As you wish."

I did reconnaissance on the vegetarian options, and came back with a plate so overloaded the sweet-and-sour tofu was in danger of jumping ship. Gordon leaned back, rubbed his chopsticks together like he was sharpening knives, and watched me suck it all down.

"Aren't you supposed to be ladylike or something?"

"You should know me better than—"

"Don't talk with your mouth full."

I chewed and swallowed. "Fine. You do the talking."

"I thought I'd wait 'til you're done."

"What for?"

"As I recall, abject terror makes you sick to your stomach."

I put down my chopsticks. "What the hell is going on?"

"You don't want to know."

"Come on, Gordon, cut the crap."

"Okay, but don't say I didn't warn you."

"Duly noted. Now spill."

"Okay . . . You know how you told me to look into the whole Albertini's thing?"

"Yeah . . . ?"

"So I looked into it."

I waited for him to keep talking. He didn't. "Are you *try-ing* to be difficult?"

He sighed and pushed back his plate. "Okay, listen. I did some digging into their paperwork—health inspections, occupancy certificates, articles of incorporation, tax records, liquor license, that sort of thing."

"And . . . ?"

"The restaurant opened in 1923. It was owned by the same family for forty years or so. Those were the original Albertini's. So in 1966, the title was transferred to somebody named Dominic Castorano. Then six years later it was transferred again, to an Anthony Buccelli. He held on to it until the early eighties, when it was sold to something called the Wonderland Food Company."

"Doesn't sound too Italian."

"Oh, it's *very* Italian. More Italian than you want to know about."

"Which means what exactly?"

"Okay, here goes . . . I called a source at the Justice Department who knows about this shit. Apparently, the anti-racketeering guys at the FBI have Wonderland on a list of businesses suspected of having mob ties."

"Which is what people have been joking that Albertini's has all along. So what?"

"It's not the what that gets me. It's the *who*."

"So who?"

"You ever heard of Joey Buccelli?"

"No."

"He's a capo in the Vitalli family. Apparently, he's also Anthony Buccelli's uncle."

"So?"

"As in 'Joey the Screw.' "

"I think you better connect the dots for me."

"You remember about ten years ago, a whole shitload of those upper-tier mob guys went to jail? No? Well, they did, and they weren't too fucking happy about it. Joey the Screw was one of them. Apparently, this guy made his bones at nineteen, when he killed some rat with a screwdriver through the eyeball."

"Your command of the mob vernacular is truly astounding."

"Alex, this is some serious shit. Buccelli and those creeps he went to jail with—Knuckles Tucci, Salvatore Malfi, Jimmy Giordano—these are not nice people. A lot of the people who testified against them are no longer breathing."

"And you think one of these guys ordered a hit on the wife of the goddamn chairman of the goddamn Benson chemistry department?"

"How the hell do I know? All I'm saying is, these are not the kind of guys you want to fuck with."

"How do you know so much about this?"

"I'm from New York, you idiot. They teach the Five Families in nursery school down there, right after the Three Little Pigs."

"Christ, no *wonder*."

"No wonder what?"

"No wonder Cody's been so freaked out. He even wanted me to take one of his cop buddies to Niagara Falls with me, but I told him enough was enough."

"I'd take the National Guard if I were you."

"But wait a minute. If these guys are so nasty, how come they just roughed me up? How come they didn't . . . you know, kill me?"

"Like you said before, they were pros. They must have been following orders."

"Jesus *Christ*. Orders from whom?"

"Whoever's running things now that Jimmy Giordano's in prison. He was supposed to take over when old Vinnie Vitalli died, but supposedly now there's a turf war brewing over—"

"Wait. Did you just say *Giordano*?"

"Yeah. Jimmy Giordano. Like I said, he was one of the capos who went to jail back in—"

"Holy *shit*."

"What?"

"How common a name do you think that is?"

"What difference does it make?"

"I know somebody named Giordano. Two, in fact."

He looked in danger of having his four plates of food come back up on him. "Now I'm not sure *I* want to hear this."

"One of them's the head of the Gabriel historical society. She's—well, I doubt very much she's all mobbed up."

"How can you be so sure?"

"Well, she's an African-American lesbian who was adopted by the Giordanos when she was a baby, then got cut loose when she came out. She makes really good pizzelle, though."

"Oh."

"The other one is her younger sister, who's their natural kid. She used to be married to this big muckety-muck in materials science at Benson. But get this: she's also a member of Save Our Starlight."

"Oy vey."

"You said it. Hey, what about Kurtis Osmond? Did your pal at the Justice Department know anything about him?"

He shook his head. "Clean as a whistle, or at least he covers his tracks pretty damn well. I had somebody look him up on Westlaw, and he's been sued about a zillion times, but nothing that seemed to connect up with this."

"So what do we do now? About the Giordano connection, I mean."

"*Do*? Nothing. I wouldn't touch this with a—"

"Hold on. I thought you were this big brave investigative reporter. Since when do you go all chicken at the thought of—"

"Are you out of your tiny little mind? Alex, this is the Vitalli family we're talking about."

"So?"

"So picture every mean son of a bitch you've ever met, add them all and multiply them by a thousand. These are *not* the kind of people you want to piss off."

"Apparently, I already have. Remember?"

"Yeah, well, I haven't. I'd like to keep it that way."

"So you're just going to bail on me?"

"Better a live schmuck than a dead mensch."

"But what if there's a story here? A big one?"

"It's not going to do me any good if I'm sleeping with the goddamn fishes."

"Don't you think you're overreacting just a teensy bit?"

"Right. I covered one of these mob murders when I was on night cops. They found the guy in a Dumpster in Brooklyn with all his fingers cut off. Oh, and then he got burned alive."

I lost my grip on the teacup I was picking up, and the contents went sloshing all over the red tablecloth. "You really didn't have to tell me that."

"Look, I know you think I'm an asshole sometimes, but I really don't want anything to happen to you. You know that, don't you?"

"Yeah."

"So listen to me. These guys, they don't play nice. If they warned you to stay out of this, my advice is to stay the hell out of it. No story is worth getting dead over. You and Madison and I know that better than anybody."

"You want me to just leave it alone? How can I do that?"

"I don't know," he said. "But if I were you, I'd learn pretty damn quick."

There were two things waiting for me when I got home. One was an answering-machine message from Lindy Marsh. The other was a very pissed-off police detective.

"Where the hell have you been?" he said, greeting me at the door with a big scowl and exactly zero in the kiss department. "You said you'd be back no later than seven."

"I was. I got back to town around quarter of, then I went to dinner with Gordon at the Chinese buffet place. "

"You could at least have told me where you were going. I've spent the past two hours going out of my goddamn mind."

"Hey, since when do we punch a clock with each other?"

"Do you have any idea how worried I've been? God damn it, Alex, I thought you were—" He cut himself off and started pacing around my living room.

"Let me guess. Garroted by an enforcer for the Vitalli family?"

He froze in midpace. "How did you—"

"Jesus, Cody, I can't believe you didn't tell me."

"I didn't want to upset you."

"Well, congratulations. I'm upset anyway."

"How the hell did you find out?"

"For Christ's sake, Cody, I'm a *reporter*. I find shit out for a living, remember? I asked Gordon to do some digging, and he made the connection in like half a day. He's clever that way."

"And what did he tell you?"

"That Albertini's is probably washing cash for the Vitalli family. What do you think he told me?"

"And did he mention you better not fuck with these guys?"

"Since when do you swear so much?"

"Don't change the subject. Did he explain to you that these people don't screw around?"

"Yeah, he did. His advice was to stay the hell out of it."

"Remind me to thank him for that much, anyway."

"Are you investigating the Giordanos in Gabriel? Angela and Adele?"

"Yeah. So far we don't have . . . We don't have much."

He turned away, walked the three steps to the couch, and flopped down on it. He looked exhausted. I, on the other hand, had plenty of energy left for arguing, so I followed and sat on the coffee table next to his feet.

"How *could* you?"

"How could I what?"

"How could you keep me in the dark about something like this?"

"Come on, baby, don't be mad at me. I did what I thought was best under the—"

"Treating me like a goddamn *infant* was what you thought was best?"

"I told you, I didn't want to scare you. Come on, just calm down and sit with—"

"Don't you think I had a right to know what was going on? Like what sort of people I was dealing with?"

"Yes . . . I mean, no . . . I mean, I was going to tell you about it eventually."

"Oh, yeah? When the hell was that going to be exactly?"

He sat up and took one of my hands in his two big paws. I thought about snatching it back, but didn't. "I was going to tell you everything once we'd caught the bastards who beat you up. When the Dillingham case was closed, and there wouldn't be any threat hanging over you anymore. I was going to tell you then."

"Wonderful."

"Look, Alex, I can understand why you're angry. But don't—"

"You know, I knew you were being cagey about Albertini's, but I figured it was just because you were trying to keep me out of it."

"Which was right on. So why are you so upset about it now?"

I thought about it for a minute. "I don't know exactly, but . . . You should have told me. You just should have told me, that's all."

"Uncle."

"Huh?"

"Uncle. I give up. You're right. I should have told you."

"That was easy."

"A soldier knows when to retreat."

"But not surrender."

"God forbid. Which brings us to the part you're not going to like."

"Like I was liking the other part? Okay . . . what?"

"You know what. I want you to promise me you'll leave this be."

"Leave what be?"

"Do what they said. Keep out of the Dillingham case."

I yanked my hand away. "What?"

"I've been wanting to say that to you ever since I found out about the Vitalli connection, but I didn't know how to do it without letting you know about . . . Listen, just promise me, okay?"

"I'll be careful."

"Not good enough. Promise me."

"Okay, I promise." He looked relieved for about half a second. "Just as soon as I quit the force and start working for the I.R.S."

"What?"

"I'll stop doing my job just as soon as you stop doing yours."

"Do you have to be so . . ."

"We promised each other we wouldn't pull this crap, remember?"

"I know we did. But you have to believe me. This is different. Even your friend Gordon told you to drop it, and from what you've told me he's the most ambitious guy on the planet."

"Jesus Christ, this isn't about ambition. It's about . . . Oh, hell, I don't even know what's it's about."

"Your fundamental right to get yourself killed?"

"I have no goddamn intention of getting myself killed. I told you I'd be careful. That's the same thing you tell me when you go to work every day, isn't it?"

"It's not the same thing."

"Oh, yeah? How's that?"

"I'm trained to deal with this crap. You're not."

"I've done okay so far, haven't I?"

"Like when you got beat up and left half-naked in a parking lot?"

"That was a cheap shot."

He took a deep breath, tried to get a handle on himself. "I'm sorry."

"I damn well hope so."

"Why are you so goddamn determined to risk your neck?"

"I'm *not*. Really, it's not about that. It's just . . . I just have to *know*, that's all. That's all that this is about, I swear."

"You did your job, Alex. Now you've got to let the cops deal with it—specifically, me. All right?"

"But this whole thing is tied up with a story I've been covering for months. For all I know, those goddamn pieces

I wrote on the Starlight helped get Sissy Dillingham killed. This is as much my problem as it is yours."

"That's nuts."

"Maybe it is to you, but it's not to me. I just . . . I have to know what really happened. I feel like I . . . like in this weird way I kind of owe it to her to find out the truth. You can understand that, can't you?"

He'd calmed down a little, but he still looked very much like he wanted to strangle me. Finally, he just stared at the ground and said, "Unfortunately."

"Meaning you're going to lay off?"

"Meaning I obviously have no choice."

"I swear, I'll be careful. I won't do anything stupid."

"You'd better not."

"I promise."

"Good, because you know something? I'm in no mood to live without you."

I leaned over and kissed him, hard. "You know, that just may be the most romantic thing that anybody's ever said to me."

"What am I going to do with you?"

"For starters, you could thank me."

"Oh, yeah? For what?"

"Among other things," I said. "I do believe I may have managed to get rid of your ex-wife."

30

THE SENSORY LEVEL BETWEEN ME AND CODY BEING AS, SHALL we say, *heightened* as it was, I didn't actually get the message from Lindy Marsh until the next morning. When I finally heard it, I had a genuine guilt pang. Why, she asked, hadn't she heard from me? What had I found out about Sissy's death? Had I finally figured out how it was related to the extracurricular activities of her dear departed Barry?

The answer was . . . I had no idea. So, more than happy for something to take my mind off the *Godfather* saga for a little while, I decided to do what she asked—not that I had much idea of where to start. First, though, I had to placate Bill, who'd been stretched to the limit of his charity when he let me spend Monday in Niagara Falls on the grounds that it was "research."

Being therefore obligated to cover whatever stupid thing he wanted me to, I spent Tuesday morning at a City Hall recognition ceremony for a bunch of high school seniors who'd finished a six-month internship in local government. It was downright interminable, but sitting through it didn't turn out to be a total waste. Listening to Mayor Marty expound on the Marxist joys of work-study reminded me of a certain greasy-haired young lady I'd encountered in Barry Marsh's office. I decided to look her up.

I got Lillian to call the school district's work-study coordinator, who said that one Cassandra Jakelicz (pronounced YAH-kah-litch) was spending her afternoons shilling ice cream at a shop off the Green. Now *that* was my idea of on-the-job training.

I commuted the fifty paces from the newsroom to the store, and found my prey standing behind the counter drinking a soda out of a paper cup the size of a small garbage can. There were two other high school kids with her, cleaning the tables and making waffle cones and looking generally industrious. I went up to the register and she came over to meet me, wiping her hands on an apron with a picture of a grinning cow on it.

"What do *you* want?"

She clearly wasn't inquiring about my frozen dairy needs, so I decided not to mess around. "I want to talk to you."

"What for?"

"Do you remember me? We met the day that . . ."

"Course I remember you. I'm not stupid, ya know."

"I don't think you're stupid."

"*Yuh.*" It was the universal sound of teenage disbelief.

"If I thought you were stupid, I wouldn't bother to come over and talk to you, now would I?"

She chewed on that for a while. It seemed to pass muster. "Talk to me about what?"

"Is there someplace we can go? This isn't exactly for public consumption."

"I'm working. We gotta stay here."

"How about the table over in the corner?"

"Well . . . you gotta buy something first."

"Do you have any frozen yogurt?"

"Nope."

"Low-fat anything?"

"Nope."

"Anything remotely healthy?"

"Nope. But . . . we've got a bet going about who sells the first Piggy Trough. You could buy one of those."

"What in God's name is a Piggy Trough?"

"It's a new thing, got a scoop of every flavor. Twenty-four scoops."

"You gotta be kidding me."

"Do you want to talk to me or don't you?"

"Jesus, how much is it going to cost me?"

"Fifteen bucks. But it comes with a sparkler on top."

"Wonderful. If I buy this monstrosity, will you help me eat it?"

Finally, she looked like she was awake. "Sure. Okay."

"Then scoop away."

Five minutes later we were sitting at the corner table; between us was a dish of ice cream that could pass for a kiddie pool.

I've had worse assignments.

"So," I said through a mouthful of pecan praline, "how long did you work for Mr. Marsh?"

"I guess, like, four months. I started the beginning of last summer."

"And what did you think of him?"

"He was okay."

"Just okay?"

"Okay for an old guy."

"Was he nice to you? Did you feel like, you know, that he treated you with respect?"

"He was okay."

Oh, brother. "Did you like the job?"

She shrugged her bony little shoulders. "This one's better."

"How come?"

"My best friend Amelia works here too. Plus there's no boss."

"No boss?"

"The kids run the place. The Youth Bureau owns the franchise, see? We have all student managers and supervisors and everything."

"Sounds like fun."

"Yeah, there's a pretty long waiting list for it, juniors and seniors mostly, but they put me right in because . . . Well, after Mr. Marsh croaked, they said they felt sorry for me and I could choose anything I wanted and I'd get it."

"You're a sophomore, right?"

"Yeah." She paused to excavate an enormous spoonful of Rocky Road. "School sucks."

"Of course it does." Actually, I used to be the teacher's-pet type, but I decided it wouldn't ingratiate me with her. "Did you think Mr. Marsh wasn't a particularly good boss?"

"He was okay."

Jesus. If you put this girl in a blender with Robbie Renssellaer, you might have a normal interview. "Could you, you know, be a little more specific?"

"Aren't you going to eat any more ice cream?" I attacked the pistachio in the name of journalistic integrity. "Mr. Marsh . . . he liked to talk down to people all the time."

"He was pretty condescending, eh?"

"Huh?"

I decided to skip the vocabulary lesson. "You felt like he didn't treat you right?"

"He thought I was, like, a total zero. Like I . . . you know, like I wasn't there even though I was."

"So how come you stayed working for him?"

"My mom . . . she's always after me to join shit for my college applications. I used to, like, do drama, but I'm not into that anymore, 'cause it's all just a fucking popularity contest, you know? Anyway, the whole work-study thing kind of shuts her up."

I moved on to the black raspberry. The butterfat content was truly frightening. "So, Mr. Marsh treated you like the furniture. Is that pretty much how it was?"

She rolled her eyes at me. "Pretty much."

"So I bet you saw and heard a lot of stuff you wouldn't have otherwise, right?"

She froze, spoon in mouth. A wary look crept across her face, and she pulled the spoon out slowly. "Whaddaya mean?"

"Come on, Cassie . . ."

"Cassandra. I *hate* Cassie."

"Come on, Cassandra, we both know guys like Barry Marsh treat young women like they're subhuman." I hoped I was sending out vibes of feminist solidarity, Gen-X to Gen-Y. "Am I right?" She mumbled something I didn't catch. "Come on, am I right?"

"Yeah."

"So look, you don't owe him a damn thing. Why don't you tell me what you really thought of him?"

"Why are you so into this, anyway?"

Busted. "I'm . . . sort of looking into anybody who was connected to Save Our Starlight. Mr. Marsh was one of the heads of it."

That seemed to satisfy her. She slouched in the seat even more, and extended her spoon toward the vat of ice cream. "So what did I think of him? I thought he was a big shit, okay?"

"And why is that?"

" 'Cause he couldn't keep his dick in his pants."

"You don't say."

"The guy was a total horndog. Sometimes he didn't even bother to close the door to his office."

"You mean when he was in there having, um . . ."

"Nah, I don't mean he was throwing a hump, just talking on the phone. He'd make his dates with these chicks he was into, talk to them all sexy, like I couldn't even hear him. What a *prick*."

"Do you know who he was seeing?"

"Like, names? Nah. I tried to ignore that shit."

"Do you have any idea if any of these women might have been mad at him for dumping them?"

She digested the question along with some Death by Chocolate. "There were always ladies calling. Calling, calling, calling. I always thought, fuck, what's so hot about this asshole?"

"In the four months you were there, how many women would you say there were?"

"You mean that he was screwing, or just in general?"

"In general."

"Well, there was his wife. Now there's a bitch for you— always snooping through his stuff when he wasn't looking, screaming at him when he buys a doughnut instead of drinking the goddamn wheat-grass shit she makes for him. And that Mrs. Dillingham, the one who got pancaked a couple weeks ago. She used to hang around a lot talking about that old theater. Then there was some lady who called every fucking five minutes . . . Kitty or Pussy or something . . ."

"Bunny? Bunny Roberts?"

"Yeah, maybe."

"Do you think she and Barry were having an affair?"

"I dunno. She was always pissed about something, though. Half the time he'd have me tell her he wasn't there when he really was."

"Did he ever, you know, try to hit on you?"

"Me? You gotta be kidding."

"Why? You said he was a hound dog . . ."

"*Horn*dog."

". . . and according to his wife you fit his type."

Her face screwed up, like she'd just hit the lemon sorbet. "She said that about *me*?"

"No, she said he liked them skinny. You fit the bill."

"Yeah, well, if he dug me he sure never did anything about it. My stepdad woulda cut off his balls for him if he did."

"Listen, Cassandra, did you ever hear what he died of?"

"Heart attack."

"Yeah, but did you hear why?"

She gave me the same dunderhead look I'd gotten from Richard Edgar. "Because his heart didn't work right."

"Look, can you keep a secret?"

"Yeah, I guess."

"What would you think if I told you he died because he took Viagra when he wasn't supposed to?"

I'm not sure what reaction I was hoping for, but I definitely didn't get it. "He took what?"

"You've never heard of Viagra?" She shook her head. "Well, I guess there's no reason you should. It's a . . . it's an impotence medication." Another blank look. "For old guys who can't get it up."

"No *way*." She started laughing—so hard, in fact, that I was afraid some of the ice cream was going to come spurting out her nose. "You mean Marsh, he . . ." More rabid chuckling. "He gets all these women, and he can't even . . . What a *loser*."

I handed her a napkin. "I think it's more like a medical condition."

"What-*ever*."

"So let me ask you something else. Do you remember him getting a package in the mail a little while before he died? It would have been postmarked from Kentucky. Maybe a little box or a big padded envelope?"

"He got a lot of stuff," she said with a shrug. "Other arts places would send shit, and people who were looking for grants . . . Plus he'd get mail-order crap sometimes. Said he didn't want it sent to his house 'cause there was nobody to sign for it, but I always figured it was 'cause he didn't want his wife to see."

"Do you know if anybody else had access to his credit card?"

"How would I know? He sure as hell never trusted *me* with it or anything."

"Do you think . . . I know this is going to sound crazy, but did you get the idea that he had any enemies? Anybody who might want him dead?"

Her eyes widened, so I could see the white part above and below the iris. "No *way*. You think somebody, like . . . on purpose? That would be *so* cool . . ."

"I'm not saying that. I was just wondering if somebody might have wanted to."

"How about, you know, all the guys who were married to all the chicks he was fucking?"

"That's, er, one possibility."

"Who cares, anyway?" She tapped her spoon against the side of the bowl absentmindedly. "The man was, like, a waste of oxygen."

"Aren't you a little young to be this cynical?"

"I'm almost sixteen." *Tap tap tap.* "That's not so young anymore, ya know."

I didn't contradict her. "Try and think about the chronology for a minute. Who . . ."

"The what?"

"The order that things happened. Can you remember who he was seeing before Mrs. Dillingham?"

"He was seeing Mrs. Dillingham?"

"Do you think he wasn't?"

"I dunno. I told you, I tried not to pay attention to that shit."

"And you don't have any idea who else he might have been seeing? Besides Bunny Roberts, I mean?"

"Some lady in a stewardess uniform came by once looking for him, but he wasn't there. She was pretty pissed too. Oh, and a couple of times he had me send flowers for him over the Internet."

"Who did he send them to?"

She shrugged. "I don't remember."

"Did he not know how to do it himself? Use the computer, I mean?"

"Not at first, but he had me show him. He kind of got into it, Net surfing and all that. I kind of figured he was into porno."

"What made you think that?"

Again with the you're-a-twit expression. " 'Cause he was such a horndog."

"Oh. About the flowers—was he having you send them to people out of town?"

"Nah, in Gabriel."

"Then why do it on-line?"

"I dunno. Maybe so it would be anonym . . . So nobody would know who sent them."

I stared at her for a long time. "Can I ask you something else?" I said finally.

The wary look crossed her face and parked there. "I guess."

"Why do you pretend you're so goddamn dense when you're not?"

She started taking an intense interest in the cow-spotted tabletop. "I don't know what you're talking about."

"If you want to convince somebody you're a dolt," I said, "you might not want to use words like 'anonymous.' And I bet you know damn well what 'chronology' means too."

I walked out of the ice cream shop a few minutes later, Cassandra Jakelicz having rewarded my rapier insights by clamming up but good. My gut bulbous with too much dairy, I dragged myself up the newsroom stairs and collapsed into my swivel chair.

"Hey, Lillian," I said when I felt recovered enough to speak, "who do you know at the alternative high school?"

"Why, everyone."

"Anybody who'd give me the skinny on a really weird sophomore?"

"At the alternative high school, that describes precisely one-fourth of the student body."

"Great."

"What is it that you need?"

"I don't know. It's just a funny feeling I've got. I just talked to this girl, and even though she tries to act like she's got nothing going on upstairs, I kind of like her."

"And you're doing a story on her?"

"Not exactly. I just . . . I think she might be able to tell me way more than she's telling me. The first time I met her, I thought she was a real dolt, but now I'm not so sure. I think she notices a lot. I guess I want to figure out if I'm wasting my time."

"Hmm . . . I'd tell you to call Jessica Lindley, but I doubt she'd talk to you. It took me five years to get her to talk to me. But I could give her a call if you like. What's the girl's name?"

"Cassandra Jakelicz." I spelled it for her.

"And am I looking for anything in particular?"

"Nah, I just want to know what her deal is."

"Who is this young lady, anyway?"

"She was Barry Marsh's work-study secretary. She was in his office the day he died."

"Poor dear."

"That," I said, "is way more sympathy than she has for him."

31

I'VE BEEN ACCUSED OF A LOT OF THINGS, BUT KNOWING WHAT'S
good for me isn't one of them. As soon as my stomach had
calmed down enough for me to move, I went over to Historic Gabriel to talk to Angela Giordano. The place wasn't
even open to the public yet, but I kept knocking until she answered. She let me in, and in the name of social lubrication
I let her give me a cup of tea before I asked her if she was
related to a bunch of murdering criminals. She promptly
scalded herself with Celestial Seasonings Mint Magic,
which my keen journalistic sense took as a hint I was on to
something.

"So," she said once she'd run her hand under some cold
water, "the other shoe finally went *whack.*"

"I take it you were expecting it to."

"Sooner or later."

"You gonna tell me about it?"

"Let's take a walk."

She wrapped herself in a burgundy wool cape that made
her look like a jumbo version of Little Red Riding Hood,
and the two of us set out up the hill behind the historical society. Five minutes later it occurred to me that perhaps it
wasn't the wisest idea to take a walk in the woods with

somebody who wants to tell you about their connection to the Cosa Nostra, but by then it was too late to worry about it.

"Okay," she said once we'd disappeared into the trees. "How did you find out?"

"Find out what?"

"What do you think? That we were related to *those* Giordanos."

"I didn't. I mean, I was just asking."

"You mean you didn't know for sure?"

"Not 'til you admitted it."

She gave a sharp laugh that had exactly zero humor in it. "Fruits of a guilty conscience, I suppose."

"What could you possibly have to be guilty about?"

"Nothing, but . . . Even though I'm the last one to believe in the sins of the fathers, I still . . . I guess I'm downright *ashamed.*"

"Of having somebody make the connection between you and them?"

She nodded. "I'm almost glad though, you know. I've been worrying about it ever since I was a little girl, that someone would find out. It was one of the . . . When I got kicked out of the family, it was the great consolation prize."

"But how much of a secret can it be? I mean, Jimmy Giordano was all over the news when he went to jail, wasn't he?"

"That would be *Uncle* Jimmy to me."

"Yikes."

"You said it, sister."

"Didn't anybody ever ask about it before?"

"In this town? Are you insane? It would be *totally* un-P.C. to perpetuate ethnic stereotypes, now wouldn't it?" She was starting to sound a little manic. "Particularly to somebody like me? An adopted Italian-American Afro-American lesbian feminist? Isn't *that* a mouthful . . ."

"Then why is it so . . . awful for you to think about?"

"Look, my parents are from what you might call the ultra-liberal branch of the family. They adopted me, didn't they?"

"So they're not involved in the . . ."

"The family business? No."

"Then what's the big deal? I mean, what do you have to be ashamed of?"

"For Christ's sake, Alex, do I really have to spell it out for you? Those people are *killers*. They're the worst people you can possibly imagine—and forget all the talk about a code of honor, *omertà* and all that. These guys are sexist, racist, homophobic, patriarchal bastards on a *good* day. I could tell you stories . . ."

"That's okay. I think I get the picture."

"Oh, no you don't. I've never . . . I've never told anyone this. Not even Rachel. *Especially* not Rachel."

"What is it?"

"After I came out . . . I found out later that Uncle Jimmy offered to have me picked up and taken to one of those re-education places they had for troublesome adolescents back in the sixties and seventies. Girls in particular."

"A mental hospital?"

"A mental hospital."

"Jesus Christ."

"It gets better. After Rachel and I got together, he offered to . . . Well, by then he considered me a *vergogna*, an . . . embarrassment. Never mind that I was adopted, and black to boot. I still had his name, and apparently it drove him crazy. He asked my father if he wanted to have the two of us taken care of. 'Clean up your mess,' was the way he put it."

"You've gotta be kidding me."

"My dad didn't go for it. He didn't want anything to do

with me, but he didn't want me dead either. Nice of him, wasn't it?"

"That's . . . incredibly awful."

She blinked back tears, and seemed mad at herself for having to do it. "Ain't it though?"

"How did you find out about all this?"

"Adele told me. As evidence that our parents weren't such evil people after all. Can you believe it? 'Don't feel bad, Angie, Mom and Dad couldn't stand the sight of you, but at least they decided not to have you killed.' "

"Actually," I said before she could work herself up into any more of a frenzy, "Adele's really what I wanted to talk to you about."

"What about her?"

I didn't answer right away, mostly because I had no idea how to tell her. Suddenly, the muddy ground seemed absolutely *fascinating*.

"Come on, Alex, say what you've got to say. I can take it. I'm a Mafia princess, remember?"

"I'm glad you haven't lost your sense of humor."

"Just spit it out."

I took a deep breath. "Okay . . . Here goes. I think Adele may have had something to do with Sissy Dillingham's murder. Also with having me beaten up last week."

She stopped walking and faced me. "Are you serious?"

"I'm sorry, but yeah."

"What kind of proof do you have? You can't just go accusing her of something like that without . . ."

"Nothing direct. And believe me, I hope I'm wrong."

"Then what makes you think she's involved?"

"You know Albertini's restaurant?"

"Sure."

"According to somebody at the Justice Department, it's laundering money for the Vitalli family."

"You're kidding."

"You mean you didn't know?"

"How the hell would I?"

"Anyway, when I was attacked, it happened in Albertini's parking lot. The place was closed at the last minute, so it was totally empty, but whoever had me beaten up knew it was going to happen somehow. According to the cops, the guys who did it were probably professionals. And the one thing they told me was to stay off the Sissy Dillingham case, which is all mixed up with the Starlight."

"Which is all mixed up with my sister. Is that what you're trying to say?"

"I guess."

"Frankly, it sounds pretty weak to me."

"Maybe you're right. I hope to hell you are. It's just that . . . I'm sorry, Angela, but we started with the restaurant, and it led straight to Jimmy Giordano. Do you really think it could be a coincidence that Adele's his niece?"

"Wait a minute. This doesn't make any sense. Adele was working to *save* the theater, remember? What interest could she possibly have in . . . And Sissy Dillingham was her friend, for God's sake. My sister and I have our differences, but I can't believe she'd have anything to do with getting anyone killed."

"Maybe she got in over her head."

She opened her mouth to say something, then closed it. "That," she said finally, "I could believe."

"Meaning what?"

"Meaning she acts without thinking sometimes. Like . . . for a while her husband was worried she was a compulsive shopper. She used to buy all sorts of junk she didn't need and hoard it in a big walk-in closet in one of the guest rooms, with all the tags still on and everything. Artie told her she had to get counseling or he'd leave her. In the end he left her anyway, but the shopping was only one reason."

"What were the others?"

"She was insanely jealous of every woman he ever spoke to—constantly accused him of cheating on her. He finally decided if he was going to do the time he might as well do the crime."

"Who did he cheat with?"

"I have no idea. I'd assume it was the grad student he's seeing now."

"Is that why they finally broke up?"

"I'm not sure. Actually, from what I hear Adele thinks the whole thing was divine punishment."

"For what?"

"For marrying a divorced Christ-killer with a vasectomy."

"Ouch."

"Yeah. You know, one time when I ran into her a couple of years ago I tried to make a joke about how she married a nice Jewish boy and I married a nice Jewish girl, but she didn't go for it . . ." She shook her head. "Seems like she's hitting the Jesus stuff pretty hard nowadays, which would be fine if it were genuine."

"You don't think it is?"

"I think it's more like another addiction, or maybe just an escape. If she blames the divorce on God she doesn't have to take any of the responsibility, now does she?"

We were getting *way* off the subject. "Listen, Angela, do you know if Adele and your, um . . . Uncle Jimmy were close?"

"Never when we were growing up, not really. He always sent her presents—birthdays, first communion, that sort of thing. My parents could hardly throw them back in his face, but they also had no intention of letting us have anything more to do with that part of the family than we absolutely had to. After they died, though . . . It was a car accident—sudden, obviously—and the whole family turned out for the funeral. I stayed on the sidelines, not that I had any choice, but Adele was the center of attention. I don't know for sure, but I think she's been in touch with them ever since."

"So if she needed a . . . favor, she'd know who to call?"

"I still can't believe what I'm hearing."

"I know this is hard for you to take. But if Adele really is in this up to her neck, she's going to have to answer for it, and it'd better be before anybody else gets killed. Specifically . . . me."

I went back to the newsroom to bang out my piece on the work-study awards. Once it was filed with the usual Chester-mandated breakout boxes on each kid, I decided to distract myself by dealing with the festering mound of paperwork on my desk—stuff that should have been filed months ago. In the end, though, I wound up spending most of my time just staring at it, wishing the gears in my brain would spin faster. A *lot* faster.

What the hell was I supposed to do next? Talking to Angela was the closest to tempting the fates (not to mention the Vitallis) that yours truly had the *cojones* for. Confronting Adele seemed the very definition of suicidal, and I couldn't see how I could approach any of her S.O.S. cronies without it getting back to her—which also wasn't inclined to extend my life span.

Jesus Christ. I'm actually afraid of her.

I took the thought out for a test drive, and to my great displeasure found that it was true. I—the twenty-seven-year-old, weight-lifting, mountain-biking, cop-dating reporter—was scared stiff of a woman I'd actively pitied a couple of days before.

She'd been dumped by her husband after thirty years, her figure had gone all to hell, she had neither kids nor pets, and the closest thing she had to emotional fulfillment involved the baking of Starlight Theatre sugar cookies. Taken all together, it pretty much summed up my worst fears about what my life might be like twenty years from now.

Now, though, I didn't think of her as a sad sack so much as . . . well, a sad sack loaded with scorpions. It wasn't a pleasant image.

"Alex?" I must have jumped, because Lillian came over to give me a grandmotherly pat on the shoulder. "Are you all right?"

"Um, yeah, I was just thinking about something else."

"I didn't mean to scare you. I just wanted to tell you I'd heard back from Jessica Lindley at the high school."

"Really? What did she tell you?"

"Not very much, I'm afraid. It appears your Miss Jakelicz didn't make much of an impression."

"Can't say I'm surprised."

"All she told me was that the girl failed geometry, and that she'd been suspended twice last fall for cutting gym. Oh, and she did mention that she was active in drama her freshman year. She played Irina in their production of *The Three Sisters*. Apparently, the coach thought she had quite a lot of talent, but she didn't stay with it. That's about all she had to say. I'm sorry I couldn't find out anything more."

"That's okay. Thanks for trying."

I went back to shuffling through the papers on my desk, with even less enthusiasm than before. But what I was thinking about this time wasn't so much Adele Giordano-Bronstein as . . . acting.

Cassandra Jakelicz had told me she used to do drama, but I'd figured that meant she'd sung background to "I Feel Pretty" in the girls' chorus of *West Side Story*. But playing

Irina in *The Three Sisters*—that was something else entirely. The alternative high school has a top-notch drama department. If Cassandra had been cast as one of the leads in a Chekhov play as a freshman, it meant she had some acting chops.

Acting. There was too damn much of it going around, if you asked me; way too much drama, anyway.

There was the murder of Ashley Sinclair, a woman who'd lived her whole short life in the world of make-believe—as had everyone around her. Her best friend was an actress, who went on to become that even-more-fantastical of creatures, the movie star. Her presumed lover was a director, an expert in moving characters around a stage like pieces on a chessboard. And her leading man was a pretender two times over: not only onstage but in private, living a lie that would cost him both his career and his life.

Then there was Sissy Dillingham—who'd also died for love, in her own way. Whether it was for love of the lying Barry Marsh or the dying Starlight Theatre, I wasn't absolutely sure. But in the end, it didn't matter; she'd lost both of them anyway.

And there was Barry himself, the least sympathetic figure in the whole messy melodrama. He'd cheated on his wife a hundred times over, betrayed her even with her best friend, and he died after taking a drug designed to help old guys pretend they were nineteen again. And although his wife swore that his life and Sissy's death were intimately intertwined, the only thing I knew for sure was that his teenage secretary was a damn good actress.

Drama, pretense, lies—weren't they all just different riffs on the same thing? All that separates acting from lying is . . . what? Intent, for one thing. That, and the quality of the script—and the fact that your audience knows they're being had, is actually paying you for the privilege of being deceived.

Interesting.

Whatever these Deep Thoughts were worth, though, they were derailed by the telephone.

"Alex, I'm *so* glad I caught you."

"Who's calling?"

"It's Madeline Hoover," she said, sounding hurt that I hadn't recognized her voice. "Do you have time to talk?"

"Um . . . sure. What about?"

"It's about . . . She lowered her voice to a whisper. "It's about Adele Bronstein."

My feet slid off the stack of papers they'd been propped up on, and I sat up straight. "What about her?"

"I think she's . . . I think she might have been involved in Sissy's death."

Score. "Involved how?"

"I . . . I can't talk long. I'm up in the Arts Coalition office, and there are other people . . ."

"I'll meet you someplace."

"Could I come over to the newspaper?"

I looked around the newsroom. Over in one corner, the entire sports staff was screaming at a NASCAR race on ESPN; two feet away from me, Marshall was on the phone berating the head of the chamber of commerce for something or other. "This place is a zoo right now. Let's go someplace for coffee, okay?"

"Please, I have to do this off the record. I just ran across something that I . . . I can't believe."

"Why don't you go to the police?"

"I want to, but I . . . I *can't* be the one to tell tales about Adele. I just *can't*. I thought perhaps if I told you, then you could talk to your Detective Cody . . ."

There was something urgent in her voice, desperate and scared and sorry. "Madeline, are you okay?"

"I'll be fine. I just . . . I have to go."

"Where should I meet you?"

"Wherever you say."

"I'll pick you up at the west end of the Green in five minutes. We can go someplace out of the way. How does that sound?"

"That would be fine. Just please, don't tell anyone. I'm just so . . . *frightened.*"

"It'll be okay, I promise. The end of the Green in five, all right? I'll be in a red Beetle."

"All right."

I shoved a new notebook into my backpack and sprinted downstairs to the *Monitor*'s notoriously cramped parking lot. It took me most of the five minutes to wiggle my new car out of the space without scraping it, so it was a good thing I only had to drive half a block to pick her up.

She was standing near the curb, clutching her *All Things Considered* tote bag and looking panicky. She got in, slamming the passenger door a little too hard for my taste. She didn't say anything as we drove out of town, just rummaged through her bag for tissues and stared out at the window. There was traffic, so it took us ten minutes to get out of downtown and onto the sparsely traveled road that led to the diner I'd picked.

When we were a mile or so out of town, she turned in her seat and said something I totally wasn't expecting.

"You stupid, stupid girl," she said.

Then she pulled a gun on me.

32

W<small>HAT THE</small> *HELL* . . . ?"

"Just drive."

"I'm driving."

"Don't try anything smart."

"Madeline, what the hell is going on?"

"It didn't have to come to this, you know."

"Come to what?"

"I think you know the answer to that. Now just be quiet and drive until I tell you otherwise."

"Where are we going?"

"*Shut up.*"

I did what she said, because she was holding what appeared to be a very large firearm. The car was small, the seats packed close together—which meant the gun wasn't two feet from my head. I drove, brain cells colliding madly as I tried to figure out how I'd gotten myself into this and, more to the point, how the hell I was going to get myself out of it.

Mothers tell their daughters all sorts of ways to avoid just this kind of situation—at least my mother did, anyway. She saw a lot of nasty shit when she worked for the D.A.'s office in Boston right out of law school, and the day I got my learner's permit she sat me down and gave me a lecture entitled Roadway Psychos 101.

Always drive with your doors locked. Check the back seat before you get in the car, even if you're sure you locked up when you parked it. You could not possibly be stupid enough to pick up a hitchhiker, so I won't even bother with that one. Never give a ride to someone you don't know, even if he's a friend of a friend and he's a member of the goddamn Mormon Tabernacle Choir. If some man ever tries to force you into a car, don't go. No matter what. If he says he'll kill you unless you go with him, tell him to go ahead and kill you. At least you have a chance that he won't. Once you get into his car, you're as good as dead. Trust me. I've seen it happen a thousand times.

Her words were echoing in my head as I hugged the curves in my snazzy new car. Unfortunately, they did me no good at all—except to point out that at the moment, I was probably as good as dead. Lovely.

I thought about the cell phone in my backpack, tucked behind the driver's seat and as out of reach as if it were on fucking Neptune. Also inside it were my Spyderco knife, handy for slitting throats should the situation arise, and my enormous Maglite flashlight, which could split open a skull if it were wielded with sufficient vigor.

I had vigor to spare, but it didn't change the fact that every bit of my ersatz weaponry was well out of reach.

Son of a bitch.

We'd gone a good ten miles before Madeline spoke again.

"You just *had* to keep at it. You couldn't leave it alone, could you?"

I thought about pretending that I didn't know what she was talking about, but in the end I couldn't see the point.

"No," I said, trying to look at the road instead of the gun, "I guess I couldn't."

"Stupid."

"But how did you know that I was . . ."

"Not very smart to go running to Adele's big sister, now was it?"

"She *ratted* on me?"

"Not exactly. Apparently whatever you said to her got her worried that poor little Adele was into something she shouldn't. She went running over to express her sisterly concern, and of course Adele said she didn't know what she was talking about. Then she called to warn me you were . . . persisting. So I called you. I can be a very good actress when I need to be."

"You and everybody else in this goddamn town."

"What's that supposed to mean?"

"Nothing."

"Listen very carefully, Alex. This isn't nice, but you gave me no choice so I have to say it. You're going to die one way or the other. But *how* it happens is up to you. I can make it quick and painless, or I can shoot you in the stomach and leave you out in the woods somewhere. Tell me what I need to know, don't give me any trouble, and I promise I'll make it quick."

"Jesus Christ, Madeline. I've been wrong about people before, but you take the—"

"Save it. I want you to tell me everything you know about Sissy's death and the Starlight deal, and who else knows about it. *Now*."

This is absurd. Madeline Hoover's acting like an extra on the goddamn Sopranos. *Am I gonna wake up soon?*

"Look," I said, "can you please stop pointing that thing at me? I can't drive and . . . *think* with you pointing a gun at my head."

"Too bad."

"Please, Madeline, I'm not going to try any—"

"Shut up. Do you really think I'm that stupid?" Her voice was nasty now, and she'd tightened her grip on the gun. This was not my idea of progress. "Do you think I don't know what a *clever* thing you are? Even if everyone in the whole damn city tried to ignore it, they couldn't. You're too good at publicizing your pathetic little stabs at heroism, aren't you? Gabriel's own cute little crime-solving reporter. Do you have any idea how *sick* people are of you?"

I thought about telling her to go fuck herself. It wasn't likely to keep me breathing. "What did I ever do to piss you off so much?"

"I knew you were going to be trouble. But Adele said no, even *you* couldn't be that much of an idiot, not once we'd put the fear of God into you. I told her we should've had you taken care of once and for all, but she wouldn't hear of it— even told her people not to do you any serious harm. Can you believe it?"

"But . . . how the hell did you pull it off?"

"Adele called her people, they called the restaurant manager, and presto—he took his wife to the hospital. These people are *efficient,* let me tell you. And they know how to follow orders."

"Like the order to get rid of Sissy?"

"Even Adele knew we had no choice about that. Sissy didn't know when to drop it any more than you did. She had to dig-dig-dig until she found something to queer the deal."

"The deal to sell the Starlight to Kurtis Osmond?"

"That's right." She wiggled the gun at me playfully, like it was loaded with water instead of bullets. "Aren't you wondering why I'm telling you all this?"

"I assume it's because you enjoy gloating."

"Correct. And . . . ?"

"And you already decided to kill me, so what difference does it make?"

"Another razor-sharp insight from the girl reporter."

"Thanks. So I take it Osmond's in on this too?"

"Not really. He's just the front man, though he'll make a nice profit for himself. Adele and I have controlling interest, not that he knows it."

"But I don't get it. How could Osmond not know where the money was coming from?"

"Oh, lots of his investors have no desire to go public about their . . . relationship with him. You wouldn't believe the do-gooders in this town who pad their I.R.A.s with profits from his student slums. Sometimes even Osmond doesn't know who they are—it's all done through a bank in Rochester, and he doesn't give a damn as long as the checks clear. The money for the Starlight deal came from myself, Adele, and a few of her . . . shall we say, *family* members."

"Is anyone else from Save Our Starlight in on it?"

"Those imbeciles? You must be joking."

"But I don't get it. You've been doing the preservation thing for, like, twenty years. Why would you want to destroy the Starlight and put up some ugly . . ."

"For the money. Why do you think?"

"But how . . . I mean, you've been working for S.O.S. all along. You voted *against* the sale, for Christ's sake."

"Alex, in all my twenty years of preservation work, do you know how many buildings I actually managed to *preserve?* Seven. Out of God knows how many—maybe a hundred."

"So you mean you were . . ."

"Sick of losing. Sick of being the poor relation who watches the other side walk off with everything. I *knew* the Starlight was going to be demolished one way or the other. It was as inevitable as the goddamn sunrise. I knew I could

do my damnedest to save the building—I could lobby and
wheedle and beg and plead and it wouldn't make a damn bit
of difference. So that's what I did, the same as always. But
for once, I knew I wasn't going to be on the losing side."

"Jesus Christ. When Robbie Renssellaer showed up with
his money, you must have been scared shitless he'd ruin
everything."

She gave a creepy little chuckle. "You don't have any
idea how well we played you, do you?"

"What do you mean?"

"*I* was the one who got Sissy to bring in Renssellaer in
the first place. Then *I* was the one who made sure you got
on the scent about how he was really broke. Remember that
day we let you out of the Starlight? 'Oh, Alex, if only you
hadn't written that story . . .' " Her voice was high and shrill,
a parody of itself. "Sound familiar? See, Alex? We really
couldn't have done it without you."

"So you deliberately . . ."

"I knew Robbie's whole story, how he was practically
living on cat food, but he liked to pretend he was the king of
the world. It didn't take much to get him on board—within
fifteen minutes even *he* was convinced he could get the
money from those Hollywood bigwigs he's always bragging
about."

"But why drag him into it?"

"One thing I learned through all my years of that preservationist garbage was that it's all about expectations. Keep
them low, and your precious contributors think you've ac-
complished something no matter what kind of pathetic re-
sults you deliver. Raise them, and when they come crashing
down your whole project is history. So I made sure they got
raised by our friend Robbie. Then I made sure council found
out he couldn't deliver."

"But that day at Sissy's . . . Why the hell would Adele try to talk me into writing a story *supporting* the—"

"Because I knew damn well that nothing would make you give the other side plenty of press like trying to talk you into helping us. You're sadly predictable, you know. Now take a right."

I did what she told me, though going from a moderately traveled road to a totally deserted one seemed a very bad idea, survival-wise. I figure I might as well keep her talking, since she (hopefully) couldn't brag and shoot at the same time.

"I still don't understand why you had to kill Sissy."

"I asked you a question before and you never answered it, which isn't polite when the other party is holding a gun. How much do *you* know about it?"

"Just that she spent a few days at Historic Gabriel looking at old paperwork, and she finally found something. I have no idea what it was."

"Do you want to know?"

"Of course I do."

"It was a deed. One that transferred ownership of the theater from the man who owned it in the twenties and early thirties to someone else. It was never registered, but it was perfectly legal. It had been notarized and witnessed, then just put away."

"But why?"

"I have no idea. The fact is that it existed, and it meant that the title to the theater was in question. Theoretically, the real owner's heirs could register it, pay all the back taxes, and the theater would belong to them. But even if that didn't stand up in court, it could still have tied up the sale in lawsuits for years. You should have seen Sissy's face when she came running over to my house to tell me about it. She had no idea she was signing her own death warrant, as they say.

I made her promise not to tell anyone else, lest big bad Kurtis Osmond find out and do an end-run around us. I couldn't stop her from calling a press conference—but, alas, it was not to be."

"Where's the deed now?"

"Up in smoke, of course."

"Of course. You'd be way too smart to leave it lying around."

"Thank you. Now enough of the history lesson. Tell me who else knows what you know."

It was the question I'd been hoping she'd forget to ask. Fat chance.

What the hell was I supposed to do? Tell her that plenty of other people knew about it, in the hopes of convincing her she'd be killing me for nothing—but maybe putting Cody and Gordon and Mad in the line of fire? Or just . . . what? Suck it up and leave everyone else out of it?

And—this seemed the essential question—was one answer or the other really going to make any difference about whether she decided to blow my head off?

There was no way I could do the math on such short notice. I just gripped the steering wheel a little tighter and said, "I'm not going to tell you."

She touched the gun barrel to my temple. It was hard, and way colder than I would have thought. "Tell me, or I'll kill you."

"While I'm driving?"

"I said talk, or you're dead."

"You said you were going to kill me anyway. What difference does it make whether I talk or not?"

"My mistake. I meant to say, tell me or I'll kill you the hard way. Remember the hard way?"

"Yeah."

"So talk."

"No."

"*Talk.*"

"Tell me something, Madeline. Why the hell did you do it?"

"Who else knows? Your goddamn cop boyfriend?"

"Just answer me." I had no idea where I was going, except to distract her. "Tell me why you did it, and I'll tell you who else knows about it. I promise."

"Fine," she said after a minute of just staring at me. "I already told you. It was for the money."

"No it wasn't. Not just that, anyway."

That seemed to throw her for a loop. "I don't know what you mean."

"Yes you do. You're way too into this for it to be about something as cold-blooded as money."

"What?"

"You're enjoying yourself, aren't you? You're having the time of your fucking life . . ."

"So what if I am?" Her voice rose to something just south of a screech. "I'm entitled, aren't I?"

"Entitled to get your kicks over killing somebody? Are you nuts?"

"Don't even bother with the morality lesson. You have no idea what it's like to be . . ." Out of the corner of my eye, I caught the gun barrel shaking. I wasn't sure if it was a good thing or a very, very bad one.

"What it's like to be what?"

"Oh, but you'll find out eventually. Sooner than you think, believe me."

"Madeline . . ."

"*Wait.* No you *won't.*" She was starting to sound genuinely unhinged, and the look on her face was equal parts scary and pathetic. "You won't ever have to . . . You could thank me for that much, at least. Sparing you the humiliation . . ."

"What the hell are you talking about?"

That was when she snapped, but good. "There is *nothing* more invisible than a middle-aged woman, do you hear me? Nothing more unwanted, more—*useless*. Once you're not young anymore, and it's a battle not to put on ten pounds a year, and you know that no man is going to look at you twice ever again, if they ever did to begin with . . ." As far as I was concerned, she was starting to meet the official government standard for *stark raving lunatic*. "The world uses you up, grinds you down, spits you out. You walk down the street and people just look right through you . . ."

I had this cockeyed instinct to comfort her—until it struck me that calming her down was not in my best interest. If I was going to save my own skin, her hysteria was the only weapon I had against her .357 Magnum, or whatever the hell you called that cannon she was holding.

"Well of *course* they look right through you," I said in the bitchiest voice I could come up with. "I mean, why the hell would they want to look at you? You're a fucking *sow*."

Her next breath was a gasp, sharp and quick. "You *shut up*."

"No matter how much fucking money you have, it's not going to make any difference. You're just going to end up all by yourself, eating goddamn Häagen Dazs and watching TV alone all night . . ."

"*Shut up, shut up, shut up . . .*"

". . . staring at all these beautiful women on TV and knowing that no matter how stupid they are . . ."

"*Pull over.*"

". . . no matter how dense and dumb and idiotic, no guy in his right mind would ever even think about spending five minutes with you instead of them . . ."

Okay, so some if it was my own id talking—those three a.m. terrors that every woman has unless she happens to look like Julia Roberts and have the secret to eternal youth. But whatever it was coming from, it worked. Madeline was not only frothing mad, but crying to boot.

". . . and you know that no matter what you do, every day it's just going to get worse. You're just going to get older and uglier and . . ."

I figured it was now or never. I slammed on the brakes in midsentence, and both of us went careening toward the dashboard. I'd half expected the airbags to go off, but since we hadn't hit anything they decided to stay put. I grabbed for the gun but she held on, and suddenly there was an enormous *boom* and I felt something hot rip through my left shoulder and the window behind me exploded.

The boom and the pain and the explosion all happened at once, and when I looked up again Madeline still had the gun in her hand. She seemed a little dazed that she'd actually pulled the trigger, but she recovered quickly enough and brought it up to shoot me again. I made another desperate grab for it, and this time I managed to wrestle it down so it connected with the gearshift.

My shoulder should have been killing me, but I didn't even feel it. I just kept grabbing at the gun—trying to find the trigger, not knowing which way it was pointed—and she kept grabbing at it too, for all she was worth. It probably didn't go on for longer than five seconds, both of us belted into our seats and fighting for our lives in the leather-trimmed interior of a goddamn brand-new fire-engine-red VW bug. At some point I had this animalistic urge I couldn't possibly explain, and I just leaned over and sank my teeth into her upper arm—got a mouthful of wool coat and silk blouse and just kept biting until I finally tasted blood. She screamed like it really hurt—*good*—and she lost her grip on the gun for a second. I got hold of it but then she grabbed it too, and the next thing I knew it went *boom* all over again.

Madeline made a weird noise, halfway between a shriek and a groan, and I realized she'd lost her grip on the gun. I snatched it and pointed it at her, but by then I could tell she wasn't much of a threat.

In what you might call a bit of poetic justice, the bullet had hit her right in the gut. She was still alive; she was also in agony.

How it happens is up to you. I can make it quick and painless, or I can shoot you in the stomach and leave you out in the woods somewhere.

I admit it; I thought about it. Not for long, maybe just a second or two, but the idea of pushing her out of my passenger seat and driving away did indeed occur to me. I didn't do it, of course—partly out of a desire not to become that which I despise, but mostly because I wanted Madeline Hoover to live long enough to rat on everybody else.

So I tucked the gun between the driver's seat and the door, pulled out my cell phone, and drove to the emergency room. The wind whipped through the broken window, the speedometer hitting seventy-five as I passed across double-solid lines. And the whole way there I turned *Rubber Soul* up real loud, because although I didn't want Madeline Hoover to die, I had absolutely no interest in hearing her screaming for something to kill the pain.

There was a clutch of cops and medical types waiting outside the E.R entrance when I pulled in. Within seconds, guys in white coats had yanked the passenger door open, put Madeline onto a gurney, and wheeled her inside. I went to open the driver's door, and found my arm wasn't working so well anymore. One of the cops, a guy I'd never met, saw me and came over to open it, whereupon the enormous gun came tumbling out onto the pavement. He kicked it out of my reach, and seemed about to pull his service revolver on me when somebody else—it was Pete Donner, thank God— interceded and told them I was, quote, "one of the good guys."

This is not something a reporter expects to hear a cop say about her as long as she lives.

"Alex, my God, you're *shot*." Donner sounded just exactly as horrified as he'd been the last time he'd seen me in the E.R. He sprang up from where he'd been crouched by the driver's seat and yelled to one of the other uniforms to get a doctor on the double.

"It's okay," I mumbled, starting to get a little woozy. "It was a through-and-through . . . flesh wound . . ."

What I heard next was damn amusing, even through the descending haze. "Who is she?" the first cop asked. "Is she on the job?"

"Nah," Donner said. "She's Cody's girlfriend."

"Oh," I heard him reply before I went off to la-la land. *"Her."*

33

"WHAT THE HELL AM I GONNA DO WITH YOU?"

"Um . . . kiss it and make it better?"

"I'm not sure that works with gunshot wounds."

"You could give it a try."

I was sitting on an exam table in the bowels of the emergency room, shoulder bandaged up and arm in a sling. Cody was standing over me, the expression on his face a mixture of relief that I hadn't gotten myself killed and fury that I'd *nearly* gotten myself killed. That, and freckles.

"Did you talk to Madison?" he asked when he'd calmed down a little. "I thought I saw him on my way in."

"Yeah, he's gonna meet me at my house later to go over some stuff," I said, hoping the kiss-it-and-make-it-better part was going to start pretty soon. "Story's running on page one tomorrow."

"Of course it is."

"Don't worry, I won't let him print anything that'll mess up your case." I smacked my working hand to my forehead. "God, Bill'd *kill* me if he heard that . . ."

"I'm really sorry it took me so long to get here. I came as soon as I could."

"Where were you, anyway?"

"Interrogating Adele Giordano-Bronstein."

"But how . . ."

"Her sister Angela called me."

"What?"

"She didn't know what else to do. She said she knew Adele was into something even though she denied it, and she was terrified somebody else was going to get hurt. Said she talked it over with her girlfriend and they decided she had to say something. Finally gave me something halfway concrete to throw at Adele. I just wish to God she'd called me a couple of hours earlier."

"Is Adele talking?"

"Not yet. Hasn't lawyered up, though, which is damn odd. They're still working on her."

"Who's 'they'?"

"F.B.I."

"No shit."

"They've been . . . Well, they've been on this for a while. Sorry I couldn't tell you before."

"Can you tell me now?"

"It's no big secret anymore. Everybody's sniffing around—NYPD, State Police, feds, U.S. Attorney, the guys on the O.C. task force over at the Justice Department. It's a regular lawmen's clambake over there."

"You're kidding me."

"Nope. I doubt I'm getting anywhere near Adele Bronstein after this morning, jurisdictional turf wars being what they are. Anyway, they can have her."

"You mean it?"

He shrugged. "She can help them put a lot of bad guys away, now that they've got the leverage to flip her."

"You think she will?"

"Flip? Eventually, yeah."

"Good."

"How's your shoulder feel."

"Not too bad. I guess it just grazed me—at least that's what the doctor said. Grazed me pretty damn hard, though. I'd hate to find out what it feels like to really get *shot*. And speaking of which . . . what's going on with Madeline Hoover?"

"She's still in surgery. Docs say her chances are maybe fifty-fifty."

"Oh."

"Are you okay? Donner told me what happened out there."

"I guess. I mean, I'm plenty shaken up, but it's nothing compared to what Madeline wanted to . . ." I definitely didn't want to think about it. "I was just remembering something I said to her in the car—that I've been wrong about people before, but never like this. I still kind of can't believe it."

"Never like what?"

"Never, well . . . about a woman. It's hard to explain. It's just that . . . I thought I knew her, what sort of person she was, and I was just absolutely *wrong*. It makes you wonder, you know—like, who else in your life is a big fake?"

I was starting to get all teary, and Cody tossed the exam room for a Kleenex. Then he finally leaned down and kissed me, which was damn nice. And since my life is all about bad timing, the nurse picked that particular moment to come in and give me a tetanus shot.

They didn't keep me overnight this time, which was one hell of a relief. They just sent me home with a prescription for some heavy-duty antibiotics, a bagful of clean bandages, and orders to have my shoulder checked in a few days. Cody drove me home and tucked me into bed, then went back to work with the promise that he'd look in on me before I went to sleep. I tried to talk him into spending the night—not out of lust, for which I was in no shape whatsoever, but because I just wanted him there—but he said I needed to get some rest without having him bump my shoulder or wake me up with his beeper.

Naturally, I couldn't get to sleep—just lay flat on my back, trying to remember not to roll over and hurt myself, running the whole day over in my head.

I can be a very good actress when I need to be, Madeline had said. She was right. Oh *boy* was she right.

And who else, I wondered again, was playing the same game? Who was getting their jollies pretending to be something they weren't?

The whole cast of *The Quinn Affair* had done it, of course, if only onstage. But what about offstage? Robbie Renssellaer pretended he didn't know he was going to inherit his part; Brandon Bartlett pretended he was straight. That much I knew for sure. Could either one of them have killed Ashley because she found out the truth about them? Robbie—even if he was eleven instead of seven—seemed like a stretch. But what about his father, a guy powerful enough to have his dirty work done for him?

And what about the things I *didn't* know for sure? Priscilla Morton may have pretended to be Ashley's friend. Austin Cusack may have pretended to be in love with her, when it was really Priscilla he wanted all along. The fans who wrote and sent flowers and camped outside the stage door may have pretended to be harmless, when one of them was anything but.

And then there was the cast of characters in the present day. The late unlamented Barry Marsh, who pretended to be an upstanding citizen when he was an adulterer who made Bill Clinton look like a goddamn seminarian. And Sissy, who pretended to care about Lindy while she went behind her back and screwed her husband. And skinny little Cassandra Jakelicz—enough of an actress not only to do Chekhov at fourteen, but hide behind the mask of the adolescent dimwit when, I was pretty damn sure, she saw just about everything.

Leverage.

That was what Cody said the cops had over Adele—the power to make her talk when she didn't want to. I wonder, I thought as I finally drifted off to sleep. *I wonder if maybe I can figure out some of my own.*

I was lying in bed the next morning, debating whether I could possibly have any sick days left, when the phone rang. It was Gordon, asking if he could come over.

I thought about hanging up on him, and didn't. He showed up half an hour later, bearing (I'm not kidding) a dozen pink roses, a box of Russell Stover's Pecan Delights, the new Aimee Mann album, and the most obsequious apology I've ever heard. It went on for quite some time, and when he finished he sat on the couch, fiddled with his Liberty of London tie, and looked very much like he wanted to slit his wrists.

"I can't believe I could be such a cowardly sack of shit," he said for the umpteenth time. "Son of a bitch, Alex. When I heard what happened to you I just about . . . What kind of guy lets you twist in the wind like that? Not to mention, what kind of fucking reporter bails on a story? I'm a *worm* . . ."

"I told you to stop worrying about it."

"Yeah, well, you may not have heard this, but we Hebrew types are very good at the guilt thing."

"You see today's paper?"

"Yeah."

"Then you know how badly we scooped your ass. At the

moment, it's consolation enough. That, and the fact that I'm not dead."

"I'm really glad you're not dead."

"You know, that's just about the sweetest thing you've ever said to me."

"Don't mention it."

"Hey, how about if you start atoning for your sins by making me breakfast? I've only got one good arm, and I can't go anyplace cause my goddamn car is at the dealership getting a new window put in, not to mention about a gallon of blood taken *out* . . ."

He made what might best be described as a yucky sound. "I'd love to start atoning, but I can't cook."

"You mean you can't fry an egg?"

"I mean I can't cook at *all*. I'm the crown prince of take-out, remember?"

"Oh, right . . . Well, I'm starving." I got up off the couch, but gingerly. "Come on into the kitchen. You can at least be my left arm, okay?"

He followed me in, and between the two of us we managed to make some fried-egg sandwiches, which was the easiest thing I could think of. We sat at the kitchen table eating and drinking coffee, and when we were done Gordon pushed back his chair and took a deep breath.

"Here goes nothing. Er . . . there's another reason I came over here."

"Like begging for forgiveness wasn't enough?"

"Yeah, well, I'm also going to put my money where my mouth is."

"Meaning what?"

"Meaning, what's the last thing you'd expect a cutthroat bastard like myself to do?"

"Join Greenpeace?"

"Come on, you know what I mean. I've got something for you. Information."

"What kind of information?"

"About the Ashley Sinclair thing. It may not be much, but . . . Well, I kind of think it is."

"Gordon, I'm *shocked*."

"Hey, don't sound so sarcastic, or I'm liable to lose my nerve. This spirit-of-generosity crap doesn't come easy."

"Sorry. I'm all ears."

"Okay . . . We've both been digging into the story, right? So you've probably heard about the same characters I have—Ashley, the director, Priscilla Morton, Brandon Bartlett, those people. Right?"

"Yeah."

"So you've probably interviewed the same sources as me—the guy at N.Y.U., and Roger what's-his-name up at Benson, and the niece in New Jersey."

"Yeah."

"You ever talk to the guy who runs the Benson Cinema Archive?"

"Benji Moskowitz? Sure. He showed us a copy of *Heavens to Betsy*."

"Yeah, he showed it to me too. But did you get a chance to talk to him?"

"Not really. We were in a big rush. What's your point?"

"I spent a couple of hours with the guy. Did you know he's also working on his PhD?"

"So what?"

"It's in gay studies."

"Gay, lesbian, bisexual, and transgender studies, actually. That's what the department's called."

"Thrilling. Now ask me what his dissertation is on."

"What's his dissertation on?"

"Well he's a cinema freak, right? So his topic sort of

overlaps the two. It's kind of a *Celluloid Closet* thing, except about the stage—a look at how gays were treated in the theater during the first half of the century. Now, apparently Brandon Bartlett was this huge icon for closeted men . . ."

"Even though he was a pedophile? You can't be serious."

"According to Moskowitz, nobody back then really believed that stuff. The conventional wisdom was that it was typical anti-gay propaganda—if you're gay you must want to bugger little boys, right?—or else it was just something his wife made up when she found out he was cheating on her with other men. Besides, there was never any evidence, not a single kid."

"Oh."

"In other words, Bartlett was one of the first big martyrs of the gay-rights movement—sort of the 1920s version of Matthew Shepard, except he killed *himself.*"

"So what's Benji's thesis?"

"His thesis," said Gordon, "is that he wasn't gay."

"Are you serious?"

"Yep."

"What's his proof?"

"I didn't get into the nitty-gritty with him, but I guess the short version is that they couldn't find one guy he'd ever actually slept with. Then there was the fact that every gay actor he'd ever worked with said the same thing, which is that they never thought he swung that particular way. Plus he dated plenty of girls in high school, not that other gay guys don't before they come out . . ."

"Since when are you so in touch with the alternative lifestyle thing?"

"Look, I'm just quoting Moskowitz, okay? The bottom line is that as far as anybody knows, Bartlett never acted anything but straight."

"So why the hell does Benji think he killed himself?"

"Because he was *branded* gay, and back then that was enough to ruin his career, not to mention the rest of his life. Plus the whole thing about messing with kids . . . it was obvious he was never going to be able to see his children again, for one thing, and apparently he was pretty damn attached to the little ankle-biters."

"Hey, did his kids ever have anything to say about it once they got older?"

"Far as I could find, not a word. They were pretty young when he died, though."

"So wait a minute. Why do we think his wife would have said he was gay if he wasn't?"

He gave me his version of a Mona Lisa smile. "Think about it."

"Well . . . for one thing, she must have hated his guts."

"And why would your average woman start hating her husband's guts?"

Lindy Marsh's face popped into my head. She looked the way she had across the lunch table that day, exhausted and sad and . . . furious. "Because he was cheating on her."

"Give the girl a Kewpie doll."

"And Benji Moskowitz told you all this?"

He shook his head. "Just the part about Bartlett probably being straight after all. The rest is my instincts talking."

"You know, Richie Edgar told me Bartlett and his wife weren't getting along, but he figured it was because of him being gay."

"Who's Richie Edgar?"

"The guy Robbie Renssellaer replaced in *The Quinn Affair*. I tracked him down a couple days ago."

"Nice work."

"Thanks. Are you thinking this means what I think it means?"

"Yeah."

"Bartlett was cheating on his wife with somebody. Ashley was having an affair with somebody. What are the odds we're not talking about the same tryst?"

"Keep talking."

"The two of them had been working together in Cusack's theater company for over a year. What was it called . . . ? The Genesius Players. Bartlett's wife was a real pill, at least according to Richie Edgar. He meets Ashley. She's young, and beautiful, and the two of them fall for each other ass over teakettle . . ."

"Give it to me, baby."

"They start having an affair. She gets pregnant. Something's got to give, right? Maybe she wants Bartlett to leave his wife. Maybe he wants her to get rid of it and she won't. Maybe he asks for a divorce and the wife turns him down flat. Either way somebody's pissed off."

"And *somebody*'s pissed off enough to kill her, either by accident or on purpose. Q.E.D. God, I *love* this job."

"But who? The husband or the wife?"

"I haven't figured out that part yet."

"Tell me again why you're letting me in on all this?"

"You're not just in. It's all yours."

"What?"

"It's my gift to you. Do with it what you will."

"You mean you're not going to run with it?"

"Nope. Think of it as my penance."

"Why, Gordon," I said. "How very Catholic of you."

It took a week for me to get my car back, and another couple of days after that before the sling came off so I could actually drive it. After several miserable workdays spent typing with one hand, the sensation of having ten fingers

with which to grind out my deathless prose was totally deli-
cious.

Mobile once again, I tried to make myself look pre-
sentable, tucked a manila envelope into my backpack, and
went where I'd been meaning to go for a week and a half:
the Transylvanian digs of Robbie Renssellaer.

He answered the door himself, looking old and weak and
not the least bit like a movie star. I'd expected him to turn
me away—I hadn't even tried to make an appointment,
since I didn't want to get a definitive *stay away or I'll call
the cops*—so imagine my surprise when he invited me in.
And imagine my further stupefication when he led me into
his overblown living room and said this:

"I was hoping you'd come."

"You were? Why?"

"I wanted to tell you something. Off the record, of
course."

I dropped my backpack next to my chair, thinking maybe
I wasn't going to have to use my little surprise to strong-arm
him after all. "All right. What is it?"

"I've read in the papers, about what Mrs. Bronstein and
Miss Hoover . . . about their scheme. I wanted to say that I
was . . . very glad you didn't get hurt."

"Well, um . . . thank you." He looked shy and small in the
enormous wingback chair, and for a millisecond I got a
glimpse of the little boy I'd once seen on late-night TV.
"Was that all?"

"No." He just sat there for a minute, contemplating the
tips of his faded velvet slippers. "There was something else
as well."

More slipper-staring. Finally I couldn't take it anymore.
"There was?"

"Yes. You see, when I read about Mrs. Bronstein and
Miss Hoover, I understood that . . . that they had intended all

along to make me their straw man, someone that you build up simply so you can tear him down. And I just wanted you to know that . . . I had no idea."

"I know you didn't, Mr. Renssellaer. It's okay. Nobody thinks you had anything to do with it."

"But that's just *it*." He was starting to get agitated. "No one thinks I had anything . . . at all."

"I'm not sure I understand what you mean."

"Everyone believes that I was nothing more than a patsy. It isn't true. I *could* have gotten the money. I *could* have."

I was on the point of saying something vaguely patronizing, but something in his voice stopped me short. *He really meant it.* "How?"

"How . . . ?"

"How could you have gotten the money? No offense, but you obviously don't have much in the way of liquid assets at the moment."

"You don't understand. There are people in Hollywood, very important people, who . . ."

Here we go again.

"I'm sorry, Mr. Renssellaer. I really don't mean to be rude. But Madeline Hoover . . . when she was, um, explaining to me what happened, she said she was positive you didn't really have any connections in Hollywood anymore."

"That's because she didn't have any idea . . . She didn't know what . . . what I knew."

"And what was that?"

"I'll tell you, but once I do I want you to promise you'll do a favor for me."

"What kind of favor?"

"I'll get to that later. Will you promise?"

"I promise I'll consider it, whatever it is."

He seemed about to get petulant, but he backed off. "I

suppose that will have to do. Now, remember, none of this is for publication. Do I have your word on that?"

"Yes."

"Good."

"Now what was it you knew that nobody else did?"

"The fact," he said, "that Austin Cusack murdered Ashley Sinclair."

34

You have to understand what the theater company was like. The Genesius Players were like a family—not that I was a part of it, not really, but you have no idea how much I . . . longed to be. I sat in that theater every afternoon after school, watched every rehearsal I could. And I wanted so very much to be one of them, to be *accepted.* But I knew I never could. I didn't have . . . I didn't have the talent, you see. You're probably quite surprised to hear me say that. But believe me, Miss Bernier, no one has a better idea of my shortcomings than I do. I understand exactly how I achieved what I achieved. I'm not proud of it, but I took the opportunities that were presented to me, and after all these years I see no point in reproaching myself for it. Do you?"

"I'm not sure what you're talking about."

"Ah. Yes, well, that part's not important. I was telling you about the Genesius Players. They really were like a family, with all of a family's ups and downs and intensity of feeling. Ashley and Priscilla were like sisters; Austin and Brandon were like brothers. In a way it was only natural that they would . . . pair off. Unfortunately, Brandon had a wife. She didn't take kindly to the idea."

"You can hardly blame her."

"Of course not. But in the context of the company, it all made sense. I'm not sure I can explain it to you properly, describe it well enough to make you understand. Here were four attractive, immensely talented people working together night and day on the most important project of their lives. They'd rehearse, argue, rehearse some more, storm away, make up, then have scrambled eggs and bathtub gin at one in the morning.

"In this context, Mrs. Bartlett was an outsider. There's no other way to put it. And Ashley was . . . well, she was something very special. And even though she knew it was wrong, she couldn't help herself. She fell in love with Brandon, and he with her. He was a married man, and quite a devout Catholic. He never would have asked his wife for a divorce, not in a million years. But he pursued Ashley just the same, and the guilt of it nearly tore him apart."

"Look, Mr. Renssellaer, I've got to ask. If you were just a kid and not really part of the family, like you said, how could you possibly know so much about this?"

"I'm afraid I told you a little fib the first time we talked. I wasn't actually seven years old when I played Jonah. I was . . . eleven. I was small, though, and I could pass for much younger, and . . . *Ah.* I can see by your face that you already knew."

"Lucky guess."

His gaze returned to his slippers, and this time there was a tight, unpleasant little smile on his face. "What you don't know is that I was not only eleven years old, but what you might call a . . . snoop. I liked to hear things, listen to the grown-ups when they didn't know I was there. It was a form of . . . amusement to me."

"You mean you liked to eavesdrop."

"That's a nasty word, and I don't think we need use it.

Suffice it to say I was a rather small boy, and I could fit into spaces where no one else could. There were quite a number of places in the Starlight Theatre where such a boy could position himself to . . . soak up the scene, if you will."

"So you heard them talking about their problems, the romance between Ashley and Bartlett, that sort of thing. Right?"

"I didn't just hear. I also . . . saw."

"Saw what?"

"You'll think me some sort of Peeping Tom, and that isn't the case. But a number of times—not on purpose, you understand—a number of times I did see Ashley and Brandon . . . *in flagrante delicto*, as they say."

"You watched them have *sex*?"

"Must you use that sort of language?"

"Um . . . sorry. So where would you watch them, er, disporting themselves?"

"Her dressing room. There was . . . a rather large cabinet in one corner. It could accommodate me nicely."

Oh, yeah, you're nobody's idea of a Peeping Tom. "So you'd hide in there and wait for something interesting to happen."

"Precisely." He looked at me like I was a kindred spirit. *Yuck.* "Usually it would just be Ashley talking to Priscilla about the play, or their lives, that sort of thing. And I don't want you to get the wrong idea, Miss Bernier. I would *never* try to watch them disrobe, not intentionally . . ."

"Oh, of course not."

"Occasionally Brandon would come in, and they'd talk, or . . . do something else."

"Tell me about the day she died."

"Actually, it started the day before. She and Brandon had a terrible fight about . . . the baby. I had no idea she was carrying a child, you see. No one did. She hadn't even told Priscilla—in any event *I* never heard her say anything about it. I'd never even heard her talk to Brandon about it, but obviously he already knew. I could tell from what they were saying."

"And what were they saying?"

"Ashley wanted him to leave his wife and marry her. He wouldn't hear of it, of course. He wanted her to go away for a few months and then give the baby up for adoption, but she wouldn't hear of *that*. She said it was her child and she had no intention of giving it up to strangers, even though she knew having a baby out of wedlock would ruin her career. He said that a divorce would ruin *his* career, and that he would never be in a state of grace with the church, and she said why he hadn't thought about *that* when he was sinning with her all along. It was very ugly.

"In the end he stormed out and she just stayed there and cried for hours. It was awful. You can't imagine how bad I felt. I wanted to . . . to put my arms around her, to comfort her, but all I could do was stay inside the cupboard until she finally went home."

He sounded so miserable I actually got halfway to pitying him, which was a lot further than I thought. "What happened the next day?"

"I'd just joined the cast after poor Richie fell ill, and my father arranged for me to be excused from school to rehearse. But there was something . . . off. Even I could sense it. Ashley could barely stand the sight of Brandon, and his nerves were stretched to the breaking point. Neither one of them was concentrating on the show. Austin was disgusted with the both of them, and he called it off around seven o'clock, which was unusual considering how close we were to opening night.

"Then he and Brandon went into the lounge to have a

smoke, and they had a terrible row. You could hear it all the way downstairs in the dressing rooms—not the words, just the sounds of their voices. No one was particularly disturbed by it, though. Austin had a rather legendary Irish temper, you see, and there was always a big blowup at some point during a production. You might say it was part of his creative process. So even though the two of them were shouting at the top of their lungs, no one thought much of it.

"Eventually it blew over and most everyone dispersed for dinner, with orders to come back at eight-thirty for a final costume fitting. But I . . . I didn't go. I wanted to know what they'd been fighting about, you see, and whether it had anything to do with the argument Ashley and Brandon had had the night before. So I snuck back into her dressing room, hoping they might come in and talk about it. And she did come in. She sat at her dressing table and tore a sheet of newspaper into little bits while she waited. It was obvious to me that she expected Brandon. But when someone knocked on the door, it wasn't him."

"It was Austin Cusack."

He nodded. "He was in what I can only describe as a *towering* rage. I'd never seen anyone that angry before, not even my father. He said she was acting like a child, and she was going to ruin not only her career but Brandon's, and she was putting the entire production at risk. He couldn't believe she'd known she was pregnant and had accepted the part of Constance anyway. She had to know the play might very well go to Broadway, and where would that leave him? He'd have a leading lady who was visibly pregnant without the benefit of marriage. He said she was setting him up for disaster, and she was ruining his best friend's life in the bargain."

"How did Ashley take it?"

"She was quite shaken, as you can no doubt understand. Austin's temper was a force to be reckoned with. She was quite . . . overcome. She was crying and pleading with him not to be angry with her, that she hadn't meant to hurt the show, that she loved Brandon and she knew they could work it out somehow. I think she was on the point of saying she'd go away quietly, as Brandon had asked. I could tell she would have promised him anything, just to make him leave her alone. But then he made a mistake."

"What kind of mistake?"

"He tried to give her the name of a doctor he knew of in New York, one who performed . . . certain medical procedures for society women. He even offered to give her the money. She didn't take it well. She actually got furious at him, screaming at *him* about 'what kind of woman do you think I am, that I'd kill my own child just for the sake of your precious play?' She was completely out of control, and so was he. It got physical. She slapped him across the face, and he grabbed her by the arms and shook her. She kicked him in the . . . you know, and it knocked the wind out of him. He doubled over, and she tried to run past him but he grabbed her by the arm and she screamed . . ."

"Why didn't you do something, for Christ's sake?"

"What was I supposed to do? I was just a little boy, and I was . . . paralyzed. Don't you think I wish I'd done something?"

I wasn't sure he wanted to hear the answer. "What happened next?"

"It all happened so quickly. He got hold of her, and she tried to scratch his face, but he caught her wrists and stopped her. She struggled, and I remember she kept screaming 'you bastard' at him over and over. He was shouting at her to be quiet, that someone was going to hear her. She picked up a bottle from the makeup table and threw it at him, and it hit him on the temple and shattered all over the floor. That was when he . . . he picked up the saint."

"The what?"

"Saint Genesius. It was a statue, for good luck . . ."

"The patron saint of actors. Son of a bitch."

"Austin had a set of them made—there was always one in every dressing room whenever they were performing. It was only about a foot tall but it was heavy, made of bronze, and he hit her with it. I think . . . I hope . . . that he just wanted her to be quiet. But he hit her too hard. And as soon as it happened he seemed to snap out of it, come back to his senses. He tried to shake her awake but it was no use. She just lay there, blood all over the floor. It was clear she was dead. Even I could tell that. He looked . . . absolutely stricken. He kept trying to wake her up, saying, 'Ashley, oh, my God, I'm sorry . . .' "

Renssellaer's version of Cusack's voice trailed off, loaded with grief and panic. Maybe he wasn't such a lousy actor after all.

"What happened after that?"

"I watched him look around the room. He seemed absolutely desperate. I could see exactly what was running through his mind. *What do I do now*? Then he noticed the stack of bricks in the corner. They were enlarging the dressing rooms, you see, and there were construction materials everywhere. Austin had actually complained about it to the management. But now he looked at those bricks like they were his salvation. He left the room for about ten minutes. He must have been dismantling the part of the wall they'd put up that day, where the mortar was still fresh.

"I wanted so badly to leave, but I didn't dare. Austin might return at any second. And Ashley . . . her body was right in front of the cabinet, and I couldn't have opened it without . . . disturbing her, and . . . stepping in the blood. I wasn't two feet from her face, and from the crack between the doors I had no choice but to look right into her eyes. They were lifeless, empty, but they were still . . . beautiful.

"Finally Austin came back. He wrapped her head in a sweater and carried her away. He was lucky, in one respect. The theater was empty, which it rarely was. He was gone a long time, and when he came back he had a mop and bucket and he cleaned up the floor. He had to go out two or three times for fresh water, because it would turn bright red so quickly . . ."

"Wait a minute. They didn't find any sweater in the wall with her."

"He said . . . I found out later that he burned it in the furnace."

"Then why not just burn the body?"

"He was afraid it wouldn't burn entirely. They'd had problems with the furnace—it was another thing he'd complained to the management about, that the theater was too cold. But the owner was always having money problems, and he couldn't afford to fix it and finish the dressing rooms at the same time. He gambled, you see, and he would borrow right and left, and then he'd have a successful show and he'd pay it back . . .

"But I'm getting off the subject. Austin . . . he was afraid the furnace wouldn't work right—something would go wrong and they'd find her. But it wasn't just that. It was also out of . . . respect for her."

"*What?*"

"It was the same reason he hadn't just thrown the bloody sweater into the wall with her, you see. He wanted her to have as much of a . . . proper grave as he possibly could."

"How nice of him."

"There's no need for sarcasm, Miss Bernier. You have to understand that Austin Cusack wasn't a bad man. He was under so much pressure about the play, and he cared about Brandon so much, and he truly felt Ashley had betrayed him. He wasn't a criminal. He just . . . snapped."

"Yeah. I think these days they call that manslaughter."

"You don't understand. Artistic people are *different.* Those who are capable of acts of great creativity and inspiration can't be expected to . . ."

"Control themselves enough not to kill their friends when they get pissed off? You've got to be kidding me."

"I don't condone what Austin did. I'm simply saying I understand. When you've lived a bit longer, Miss Bernier, you'll see that things aren't so black and white as you might think."

"Moral relativism."

"What?"

"Never mind."

"So now you know what happened. The entire scene didn't take longer than forty-five minutes, from the time Austin walked into the dressing room until he'd cleaned everything up. The rest of the cast returned after dinner, and Ashley simply wasn't there. Austin told them he'd excused her because she was tired, and that he'd decided everyone should go home and rest up for the next day's rehearsal. No one ever saw or heard from her again. Now you know why."

"But what about the . . ." I cut myself off, since I wasn't sure even I wanted to know the answer to this one. But then—surprise, surprise—curiosity got the better of me. "What about . . . the smell?"

"The . . . Ah. You mean the body."

"Wouldn't someone have noticed the . . . odor?"

"I'm not entirely sure."

"Huh?"

"The wall was fairly solid, so perhaps not. And there were . . . there were always rats, you see. It was yet another problem with the building. The owner tried to trap them, to poison them, but they never went away. And sometimes they'd die, and if they weren't found, the smell would . . ." He was starting to look vaguely nauseous. "After Ashley, I wondered . . . Whenever that same smell . . . I wondered whether it was . . ."

"Her." I had a sudden urge to punch the old guy right in the nose. "Jesus Christ. Why the hell didn't you tell anybody?"

His eyes went back to the slippers and parked there. "I was . . . afraid."

"Of what? Of Cusack?"

"Well . . . yes. You just heard what he was capable of."

"But wait a minute. You said he wasn't a bad guy, that he just snapped. Did you really think he'd kill you for ratting on him? And . . . hold on. You also said you knew why Cusak didn't throw her body into the furnace. How the hell would you know that if he didn't tell you?"

"I . . . I think we've talked about this enough. These aren't pleasant memories for me, and I'm getting rather tired . . ."

"Oh my *God*. You blackmailed him, didn't you?"

"I don't know what you—"

"That's how you got your movie contract. You told Cusack that if he didn't help you out, you'd turn him in. Didn't you?"

"I don't have to sit here and listen to such—"

"Didn't you?"

"I think I'd like you to leave now."

"I'm not going anywhere."

"You're not a very polite young lady."

"Did Brandon know what really happened to her?"

"I don't . . ."

"Come on, you know I'm not going to leave until you tell me."

He seemed about to keep arguing, then just packed it in. "Honestly, I don't know for sure. But . . . I believe that he did. I don't know that the words were ever spoken between him and Austin, and he did go on to play his part in *The Quinn Affair* opposite Priscilla. But it was obvious that their friendship was over. And from the way Brandon looked at him, I thought he knew, deep down. He started drinking more, as did Austin. Cirrhosis eventually killed him, you know, and I've always believed the alcoholism began then and there.

"As for Brandon . . . Shortly after the play closed his wife exposed him. I knew he wasn't a homosexual, of course. I knew very well she was lying, but he never said a word in his own defense. It was as though he thought it was his fate, that he was getting what he deserved. I've always believed the guilt got the better of him after Ashley disappeared, and he finally confessed the truth about the two of them. Winnie had suspected the affair, but she didn't know for sure. She certainly didn't know about the baby."

"You overheard them saying all this?"

He shook his head, a sour look on his face. "I never did that again. These are just my own suspicions about what happened with Brandon, why Winnie did what she did, and why he took his own life."

"Because he was branded gay."

"No. I've always believed it was because of Ashley, of what he knew Austin had done to her. I don't think he could go on living . . . knowing he was the cause."

"But there's something I still don't understand. What

does this have to do with getting the money to save the Starlight?"

"Ah . . . You see, Austin and Priscilla had three children. All of them went into the business, and they're quite wealthy. None of them would want the truth about their father to come out. It would be more than worth a few hundred thousand dollars to keep it quiet, to protect his good name—tax-deductible dollars, at that."

"So you were up to your old tricks again. You were going to blackmail them."

"I see you're determined to make me feel small. But it would behoove you to remember that it was for a good cause."

I figured I'd pushed him far enough. "All right. You said you wanted to ask me a favor. What is it?"

"It's . . . I want to write my memoirs. I believe there would be a . . . market for a book on what really happened to Ashley Sinclair. Don't you think so?"

"What does that have to do with me?"

"I want you to be my collaborator. My ghostwriter, if you will."

"What? Why me?"

"You already know a great deal about the history, and I need to do it quickly. I don't have the luxury of time, and I need . . . I'm in need of some financial assistance at the moment."

"I'm sorry, but I think I'm going to have to pass."

"But you promised . . ."

"I said I'd consider it. I just don't think it's the kind of project I'd be suited to."

"Why ever not?"

"I don't do fiction."

"But this would be . . ."

"Are you really planning on telling the actual truth about yourself, warts and all?"

"I have nothing to hide."

"I've got two words for you. Richie Edgar."

"You mean the poor boy who . . ."

"Who your father paid off so you could get your big break."

"I don't know what you're . . ."

"He's still alive. I talked to him, a couple of weeks ago."

His wrinkly eyes widened. "Ah, well . . . Yes . . . Perhaps you're right. Perhaps you're not the proper . . . The appropriate person to . . . to take on a project of this magnitude."

Then it finally seemed like the right time to do what I'd come there for in the first place.

"I've got something else for you, though," I said. "Something that might make you more money than a book deal." I pulled the manila envelope out of my backpack and handed it to him. "Actually, you have Sissy Dillingham to thank for it."

"Sissy . . . ?"

"The paper you're holding cost her her life, so I'd be damn grateful if I were you."

He squinted at it. "I don't understand. What is this?"

"It's a photocopy of an old deed Sissy found at the historical society, buried in a huge crate of documents from the mayor's office nobody'd touched in years. The original's gone for good, unfortunately, but . . . Well, I just couldn't believe she'd get her hands on something that important and not make a copy. Turns out she made four, and squirreled them away so well even the cops didn't find them until they knew what they were looking for. This one was in a safe deposit box nobody knew she had."

"But what does it mean?"

"I'm not sure it would stand up in court, but that doesn't

necessarily matter. With this copy, and the statement Madeline Hoover made before she died, and my testimony, it should be enough for a halfway-decent lawyer to squeeze some money out of Kurtis Osmond. It'll be worth it to avoid having his new building tied up in litigation for the next five years."

"You mean . . . ?"

"Apparently, at one point the owner owed your father money, and he transferred the title to him," I said. "Which means that, officially or unofficially, for most of its existence the Starlight Theatre belonged to you."

35

THE MURDER OF ASHLEY SINCLAIR REMAINS UNSOLVED, BUT it won't be that way forever. Once Renssellaer got his big fat check from Kurtis Osmond, he was so sloppy-grateful he made me a deal: when he drops dead, the interview goes back on the record.

I doubt that'll be anytime soon, since he's one of those crusty old coots who tend to outlive everybody. I'm also not sure that Gordon's good intentions will last indefinitely, so maybe he'll go after the Brandon-was-straight angle himself one of these days. Or who knows—maybe by the time Robbie exits the Earth I'll have made it to the *Times* myself, and Gordon and I can do it on a joint byline.

You might think that not being able to publish what I know about Ashley would drive me nuts. You'd be right.

You might also think that leaving Barry Marsh's death a karmic matter—rather than a criminal one—would drive me nuts as well. And on that point, you'd be wrong.

In case you're curious, here's how it went down.

The morning after Cody and I had a post-Sissy, post-Ashley celebration dinner at this new Indian place off the Green—Albertini's assets having been frozen like a cocktail shrimp for the time being—I paid a call on Lindy Marsh. I hadn't actually seen her since the whole Madeline/Adele fiasco went public, so how she was coping with the fact that Sissy's death had zip to do with her husband was very much an open question.

Answer: She wasn't taking it well.

When I got there she was still in her lavender silk peignoir, which looked expensive but had a red-wine stain down the front. She also smelled like smoke, which totally threw me considering the whole ballet thing. Sure enough, when she invited me into the kitchen there was a pack of Benson & Hedges Deluxe Ultra-Light Menthol 100s on the table. Even when I smoked, I didn't smoke that crap.

"May I get you some coffee?"

"Sure, if it's no trouble." I sat down at the table and pushed the overflowing crystal ashtray as far away as possible.

"It's no trouble," she said. "I was just about to make some for myself." She scooped some grounds into a French press and filled it with water from the kettle. "Is there something specific you wanted to talk about?"

"I mostly just came to see how you were doing."

"How kind. I was rather afraid you'd come here to say 'I told you so.'"

"Why would I do that?"

"Because you were right. Sissy's death was entirely unrelated to Barry. And I'm nothing but a stupid woman who . . ."

"Don't beat yourself up over it. It's totally understandable you'd want there to be something . . . more going on."

"But there wasn't, and that makes me a fool."

"You're not . . ."

"You know what always hurt me most of all? That none of the women ever *meant* anything to Barry. He'd risk our marriage, and humiliate me, just for his own amusement. Do you have any idea how hard that is to accept?"

"Maybe it was sort of an addiction. Maybe he couldn't help himself, you know?"

"Oh, who knows . . . I just wanted so much for it to *matter.*"

"I understand."

"Actually, Alex, I hope you never do."

"Listen, there's something I've wanted to ask you for a long time, but I was caught up in so much else and I didn't really know how. Did you know he was taking Viagra?"

She shook her head. "It was hardly something he'd discuss with me."

"Why not?"

"Intimacy . . . hadn't been part of our marriage for quite some time."

"Did you know he had, er, issues in that area?"

"I'd be the last person he'd tell, believe me."

"Were you surprised he took it?"

"No. Wait, let me rephrase that. I wasn't surprised to hear he would have sought . . . medical help if he needed it. I was surprised he would have taken it knowing the risks."

"Why is that?"

"Barry was a risk-taker in one area and one alone, which was his pursuit of women. Risking his life simply wasn't his style."

"But what if he needed to take the drug to continue his . . . extracurricular pursuits?"

"I assume that's why he did it." She went back over to the counter, pushed the plunger on the coffeepot, and filled two mugs. "Do you take milk or sugar?"

"Just a little milk would be fine." I waited until she sat back down. "Listen, Lindy, can I ask you something else?"

"Of course."

"Do you think there's any chance that he might not have taken the Viagra on purpose?"

She stared at me through the steam rising from her coffee cup. "What do you mean?"

"You thought some woman might have killed Sissy out of jealousy. What if someone killed Barry for the same reason?"

"That's . . . impossible. It's unthinkable."

"Why? If he really went through as many women as you say, he must have pissed off a lot of people."

"But no one who ever cared for Barry could possibly . . . No one who ever loved him could want him dead."

"Hell hath no fury, remember?"

"But he bought the Viagra *himself.* The police told me he ordered it over the Internet."

"Maybe he had second thoughts."

She shook her head. "You didn't know Barry. He never had a second thought in his life. Once he made up his mind to do something, he did it."

"Then maybe . . ."

"No, it had to be an accident. He took it when he shouldn't have, and . . . Please, Alex. I want you to promise me you won't pursue this. I won't hear of it, you understand? *Do you understand?*"

She reached for her cigarettes, fumbled trying to get one out of the pack, finally got it lit. The smoke wafted across the table, and I waved it away. Amazing how disgusting the things smell when you're not the one smoking them.

"If you're sure he would've taken it if he ordered it, then either he took it on purpose, or . . ."

"I really must insist that you . . ."

". . . or he wasn't the one who ordered it."

"What . . . what are you saying?"

Something Cassandra Jakelicz told me came flashing back, like a movie clip on Bravo.

There was his wife . . . Now there's a bitch for you . . . Always snooping through his stuff when he wasn't looking . . .

"He ordered it on his credit card," I said. "Who else could possibly have had access to it?"

"Stop it."

"Who else besides . . . you."

"Get out."

"You couldn't take his cheating anymore, could you? You know, I can't say I blame you."

"I don't know what you're talking about. That's obscene. *Now get out of my house.*"

I did, because I couldn't think of anything else to do. I mean, I didn't have any proof. I had plenty of motive, but zero evidence—and no witnesses, except for a certain fifteen-year-old girl who liked to pretend she was a whole lot dumber than she was.

I went straight from Lindy Marsh's house to the ice cream store. She wasn't there, but there was yet another skinny teenage girl at the counter.

"Hi, I'm looking for Cassandra Jakelicz."

"She's off today. Went to hang out by the lake."

"The lake? It's freezing out. Are you sure?"

"*Duh*, I'm, like, her best *friend*."

"You must be"—I grappled for the name—"Amelia. Right?"

"Right-o."

"You think I could find her at the lake right now?"

"Yuh. She likes to hang out at the pavilion where the old movie studio was. You know the one?"

"Sure. Thanks."

"Who are you, anyway?"

"I'm a reporter for the *Monitor*."

"Hey, whatcha wanna talk to her about?"

"Just some stuff about her old boss."

"Her old . . ."

"The one who died. Barry Marsh."

Whoever Amelia was, she was no Cassandra. At the very mention of his name she seized up like the proverbial deer in headlights. Her braces-clad mouth fell open, her face went white, and her eyes very nearly popped out of her head.

Oh my God.

I had a feeling I owed Lindy Marsh an apology.

I drove to the lake with my head all agog, and found Cassandra exactly where Amelia said she'd be. She was bundled up in a winter jacket and watch cap, sitting on the edge of the raised pavilion with her feet dangling over the edge. She heard me coming, looked up, then looked back down again.

I climbed the steps and sat down next to her. "Hi."

She seemed to debate whether saying hello was on her list of things to do today. Finally, she said *hi* back.

She still didn't look at me. We both sat there for a while, staring out at the water, not saying anything. The silence stretched on so long even she couldn't stand it anymore.

"What do you want, anyway?"

"I'm . . . writing a screenplay," I said. "I thought maybe you could help me."

She turned to face me, an actual flicker of interest in her eyes. "You serious?"

"It's a really good story. Do you want to hear how it starts?"

She thought about it for another long minute. Finally she just said, "All right."

"Okay . . . Here's how it goes. There's this teenage girl. She's pretty smart, but for some reason it suits her not to let anybody else know it. She's gonna be damn beautiful someday, but she's still young and gangly and she hasn't figured it out yet."

"What are you . . ."

"This is purely fictional, you understand. I'm speaking theoretically. I bet I don't have to explain what the word means, do I?"

"Go . . . go on."

"This girl goes to work for an older man, and he turns out to be one creepy son of a bitch. He thinks he's God's gift to women, treats them like they're toys put on the planet for him to play with. When he gets tired of one, he just moves on to the next. Are you following me so far?"

"I . . . Yes."

"He does all this right in front of the girl, like she's not even there. Maybe he even hits on her, too." I glanced over at her. She didn't stop staring at the lake, but she didn't contradict me either. "Maybe this girl actually gets involved with this older man . . ."

"She *doesn't.*"

"Okay, she doesn't. She can't stand him. She wants to quit, but for some reason she doesn't."

"Maybe . . . her mom won't let her. Maybe she says she has to stick it out."

"That's right, because her mom doesn't know what's really going on, does she? She doesn't know what the man is like. So the girl . . . she's very smart, remember? She finds out that he wants a certain medication, but his doctor won't give it to him. Somehow, the girl figures out why, what it might do to him if he took it. Do you have any idea how that might be?"

"Maybe . . . It could be he talks to the doctor on the phone with the door open."

"Of course, because he treats the girl like she isn't even there. Like . . ."

"Like she's too dumb to know what's going on two feet in front of her face."

"Right. So now the girl knows that if he takes this particular medication, it'll probably kill him, see? So she talks it over with her best friend, and the two of them . . ."

"Leave her friend out of it. The friend doesn't need to be . . . It's not important for the story."

"Fine. We'll leave her out of it. So she gets a hold of his credit card, and she orders it over the Internet. When it arrives, she grabs it before he can even see it, because she's the one who opens the mail, right? It's perfect. So she puts it into his food, or maybe his coffee. And that's that."

She turned to me with a pitying look. "That would never work."

"Why not?"

"Because what if the police dusted the bottle for fingerprints? His wouldn't be on it."

"Ah. That's a good point. But she's smart, remember? Maybe once he's keeled over she puts it into his hand. Do you think she'd do that?"

She turned to face the lake again, looking out at a point where the water met the gunmetal-gray sky. "She . . . she might. If she'd thought it all through before she did it . . . she might."

"Oh, she'd think it through. I'm willing to bet on it."

"It's not much of a story, though." The down jacket was way too big for her, a hand-me-down probably, and her shrug was almost imperceptible. "It's not very interesting."

"You're right. It's only got four out of the five Ws."

"The what?"

"It's got the who, the what, the where, and the when. But what it's missing is the *why*."

"Why what?"

"Why she'd do such a thing."

"It's your story. Why do you think she'd do it?"

"You know, I've been working on that one. My guess is, she'd do it because she thinks this guy is a menace. Sort of like a . . . predator. She thinks it's her duty to take him off the map."

"You make her sound like some kind of superhero," she said, swinging her legs back and forth against the pavilion. The cold was starting to get to me, but she didn't seem to feel it. "Like Wonder Woman or something."

"Maybe she thinks what she did is heroic."

The silence took over again, the only sound coming from the seagulls and her combat boots banging against the wall. It was so long until she spoke again that the noise actually made me jump.

Or maybe it was something in her voice.

"What if she . . . she didn't do it for that kind of reason at all? Or what if it was more complicated than that? Maybe there was more than one reason. There could be, you know."

"Complex motivations are fine. They make for good drama."

"I know."

"All right. What do you think her motives might have been?"

"Maybe she did want to stop this man from hurting other people. But maybe she also . . . maybe she wondered . . . what it would feel like."

"What what would feel like?"

"What it would feel like to . . . kill somebody."

Jesus Christ.

"Would she . . . Do you think she'd really wonder that?"

"Maybe she watched the news and saw all these boys shooting up schools, asshole boys killing kids who never did anything bad to them, and she thought . . . you *dolts*." She'd barely even raised her voice, but the intensity of it was downright scary. "Why would you kill good people? And why do something so stupid, run around with guns, and in the end you either die or you go to jail? Then who wins? Not *you*."

"Yeah, I've kind of wondered that myself."

"But what if she thought there was a way she could find out what it felt like without hurting anybody? Anybody who didn't *deserve* it, anyway . . . What if she thought she could pull it off without anybody even knowing it ever happened? Wouldn't *that* be a way to get one over on the whole fucking world?"

I wasn't sure whether to answer her or just jump off the pavilion and run for my life. "I don't know," I said finally. "It might be pretty damn unsatisfying."

"How do you mean?"

"Would she really be happy doing this incredibly clever thing and then having nobody even know about it?"

"That would depend."

"On what?"

"On what kind of person she was."

"Well . . . what do you think?"

She shrugged again. "I don't know. It's your character."

"Well . . . I'm still trying to figure her out. That's why I was hoping you could help me. You know what kids are like these days a lot better than I do."

"You can't generalize. Not everybody's the same."

"That's true."

"Maybe this girl is different from everybody else. Maybe she doesn't feel like she's . . . part of the world."

"Why would she feel that way?"

"I don't know. Maybe she just always has, ever since she was a little girl. Maybe she always knew she didn't belong."

"And once she's done it, once she's gotten rid of this evil guy . . . how does she feel then?"

She was quiet for another minor eternity. "Maybe . . . she doesn't feel so good. Maybe it didn't feel the way she expected."

"How did it feel, then?"

"Maybe it felt . . . empty."

"Empty how?"

"Maybe she didn't feel anything. Maybe there was no thrill, no rush, just *nothing*. And maybe that . . . Maybe that was the worst thing of all. Maybe it really scared her. Maybe it scared her a *lot*."

"And do you think that this girl . . . Do you think she'd ever be tempted to do that kind of thing again, just to see if she'd feel something this time?"

She stared out at the water some more, then looked down at her kicking feet and shook her head, hard. "No."

"How can you be so sure?"

"She just never would, that's all. She'd probably . . ."

"What?"

"She'd probably think about what she did some more, and maybe . . . it would start to get to her. Maybe she couldn't eat, could hardly sleep at night, started fucking up in school even more than before. Maybe she'd wish and wish and wish that she could take it back, just to make this empty feeling go away, but she *couldn't*. No matter what she did, she could never . . . never make it go away."

"It's a sad story."

"For him, or for her?"

"I'd have to say . . . both."

"Can I . . . ask *you* something?"

"All right."

"How does it end?"

"What do you mean?"

"The girl . . . what happens to her? Does she go to jail?"

"Do you think she should?"

"I guess . . . if she got caught, she'd have to be punished. Wouldn't she?"

"There are lots of different kinds of punishment, you know."

"Like what?"

"Like she could go to jail, or the kid's version of it anyway, and when she came out she'd probably be way worse than she was before. She'd probably be stone cold."

"Do you think she'd deserve it?"

"Yeah, I do. But it probably wouldn't happen."

"Why not?"

"There wouldn't be any real evidence, would there? Maybe they could try to get her friend to testify against her, but what else is there to corroborate it? She committed the perfect crime."

"So you think she'd . . . she'd get away with it?"

"Like I said, there are lots of different kinds of punishment."

"What do you mean?"

"Even if this girl . . . even if she decides to live a good life, to go on the straight and narrow once and for all, she's always going to be looking over her shoulder, isn't she? I mean, there's no statute of limitations on murder. Even if it's totally unlikely she'll ever get caught, she'll always wonder."

"Yeah."

"And like you said, if she really does have a conscience, she'll always wish she could go back and undo it, just to make that empty feeling go away. But she never can, can she? She'd always be wishing she could get someplace else, do something else, *be* something else. She'd wish for it with all her might, but because of what she did she could never get there. She'd be stuck there, with herself, for good."

"You know, I . . . I did a play about that once. Not really the same thing, but . . . kind of about that, in a way."

"I know. I've been thinking about that, actually."

She was quiet again, for even longer than before, looking out at the ugly gray sky.

"To Moscow," she said. "To Moscow."

Epilogue

I NEVER TOLD ANYONE ABOUT CASSANDRA JAKELICZ—NOT
Mad, not Gordon, and sure as hell not Cody. You probably
think that's obscene, and in a way it is; nobody likes the idea
of a murderer going unpunished, or of a death going un-
avenged.

Austin Cusack was never punished either, though, and
for some reason that bothers me a whole lot more. Because,
well . . . Maybe on some level I really do believe that after a
lifetime of lying and cheating and making his wife miserable, Barry Marsh really did get what he deserved, karmi-
cally speaking. Ashley Sinclair, on the other hand, most
certainly did not. She was young, innocent, sweet, talented.
If she'd lived, she would have made a lot of people happy—
particularly people like me, who like to sit in darkened theaters and escape their real lives for a couple of hours.

Her only crime was falling in love with a man she should
have left alone. That, and trusting yet another man—one
who decided in a fit of rage that his life was a hell of a lot
more important than hers.

When it came to Cassandra, though, all I can say is . . . I
just couldn't see the point. Even if the cops could ever prove
it, which I doubted very much they could, what would get-

ting locked up in some godforsaken place do to her? In the greater scheme of things—okay, I was probably practicing some moral relativism of my own here—wasn't it better if she *didn't* go away and learn how to be a real criminal? And what was the use in making Lindy Marsh face the fact that her husband had been murdered, when she was unhappy enough already?

Maybe this makes me an accessory after the fact. I sure hope not.

I have a very big mouth most of the time, and it took all my powers of self-control not to tell Cody—particularly the first time I saw him after Cassandra and I had our little script conference.

He came over to my house for dinner, along with Mad, Gordon, Steve, Doug (as in Mr. Lambda cocktail party), Emma, and a vet student she'd brought along in an attempt to play yenta. Once Gordon had driven the girl home (a clever tactic on Emma's part) and the other four had gone bar-hopping, Cody and I sprawled on the living-room couch with the various dogs.

At one point, post-groping but pre-anything-else, he reached into his back pocket and pulled out an envelope. All I saw was the Boston postmark.

"Want to see what I got in the mail?"

Jesus Christ. The goddamn-Boston-goddamn-P.D. wants him back. I knew it was going to happen sooner or later, and after the goddamn Adele Bronstein thing I bet they're just falling all over themselves to drag him back to . . .

"It's from Lucy."

I fell back onto the cushions. "Oh *good*."

"Good?"

"Um, what does she have to say?"

"It's . . . well, it's what you might call a Dear John letter."

"You're kidding me."

"Nope."
I snatched it out of his hand.

"'Dear Brian, I'm sorry, but although I had high hopes that we might be able to save our marriage, I see now that it will never happen. Being in New York with those people has changed you too much, and you're no longer the man I fell in love with. I'm sorry if this causes you pain but I have to be honest about my feelings. I would appreciate it if you didn't try to contact me anymore, as I feel it is important to make a clean break. Sincerely yours, Lucy.'"

"Nice, huh?"
"Classic."
"Hey, who did you think it was from?"
"Oh . . . nobody in particular. You want another beer?"
"I'd just as soon have you not move."
"Hmm . . . Good answer."
"How's your shoulder feeling?"
"Totally fine."
"You know, Alex . . . Do you realize that I'm the cop, not to mention the guy who was in the goddamn SEALs, and *you're* the one with the hole in your shoulder?"
"What are you, jealous 'cause I got shot and you didn't?"
"Hell no. I just think it's ironic is all."
"Yeah, well, I'm gonna have the scar like forever."
"It's kind of . . . Well, honestly, it's kind of sexy."
"Are you nuts?"
"Tough-girl thing drives me wild. So sue me."
"You're one weird fellow, Detective Cody."
"Yeah. I can't imagine what we might have in common."
"Hey, I forgot to ask you—what's up with Adele Bronstein?"

"Feds've got her. Word is she asked for witness protection."

"From her own family?"

"They don't take kindly to having one of their own testify against them. Doesn't make for much of a life expectancy."

"Does she have enough on the Vitallis to get herself in the program?"

"Looks like it."

"Yikes. I hope she likes Arizona."

"Arizona?"

"Isn't that where they send everybody?"

"I think they try to be a little trickier than that."

"Do you think she's going to have to do some time first?"

He shook his head. "I wish. Her lawyer got her a sweet deal, all things considered. She's definitely been made out to be the second banana in all this."

"Don't you think she was?"

"Yeah, I do. I mean, Madeline Hoover was pretty happy to take credit for being the brains behind the whole thing, once she knew Adele'd flipped on her."

"But you don't think that makes Adele any less guilty?"

"Not one damn bit."

"Yeah, well, don't forget that if Madeline'd had her way, I wouldn't have just gotten roughed up. She wanted me dead. Adele was the one who held out for cosmetic damage."

"Nice of her."

"Hey, it's better than the alternative."

"What do you make of Madeline, anyway, now that the whole thing's over?"

I tightened my grip around his middle. "Man, I don't even like to think about it. But since you asked . . ."

"Never mind."

"Nah, it's okay. I guess, well, if I were going to get all psychobabbly about it, I'd say her career was totally frustrating and sad and apparently so was her personal life. I think it made her pissed off at the whole world. Maybe she was a nice normal human being at the beginning and by the end she was still pretending to be but on the inside she was all twisted and mean."

"Sounds logical."

"Or maybe she was just fucking greedy."

He laughed, deep and long. It was one of my favorite things about him. "Listen, I gotta know . . . How the hell did you get rid of her?"

"Madeline?"

"Lucy, you dope."

"Suffice it to say I had an opportunity to put her in touch with her true motives."

"Which were?"

"The same as always."

"Meaning?"

"Meaning she likes to see cops with their clothes off," I said. "And at the moment, I totally agree with her."